The PAINTED GIRLS

ALSO BY CATHY MARIE BUCHANAN

The Day the Falls Stood Still

PAINTED
GIRLS

CATHY MARIE BUCHANAN

RIVERHEAD BOOKS

a member of Penguin Group (USA) Inc.

NEW YORK

2013

RIVERHEAD BOOKS
Published by the Penguin Group
Penguin Group (USA) Inc., 375 Hudson Street, New York, New York
10014, USA • Penguin Group (Canada), 90 Eglinton Avenue East, Suite
700, Toronto, Ontario M4P 2Y3, Canada (a division of Pearson Penguin
Canada Inc.) • Penguin Books Ltd, 80 Strand, London WC2R 0RL,
England • Penguin Ireland, 25 St Stephen's Green, Dublin 2, Ireland
(a division of Penguin Books Ltd) • Penguin Group (Australia),
707 Collins Street, Melbourne, Victoria 3008, Australia
(a division of Pearson Australia Group Pty Ltd) • Penguin Books India
Pvt Ltd, 11 Community Centre, Panchsheel Park, New Delhi–110 017,
India • Penguin Group (NZ), 67 Apollo Drive, Rosedale, Auckland
0632, New Zealand (a division of Pearson New Zealand Ltd) •
Penguin Books (South Africa), Rosebank Office Park, 181 Jan Smuts
Avenue, Parktown North 2193, South Africa • Penguin China, B7
Jiaming Center, 27 East Third Ring Road North, Chaoyang District,
Beijing 100020, China

Penguin Books Ltd, Registered Offices:
80 Strand, London WC2R 0RL, England

Text by Edgar Degas from *Huit Sonnets d'Edgar Degas* courtesy
Wittenborn Art Books, San Francisco, www.art-books.com.

Library of Congress Cataloging-in-Publication Data

Buchanan, Cathy Marie.
The painted girls / Cathy Marie Buchanan.
p.   cm.
ISBN 978-1-59448-624-1
1. Sisters—France—Fiction.   2. Teenage girls—Fiction.
3. Ballet dancers—Fiction.   4. Artists' models—Fiction.
5. Paris (France)—History—1870–1940—Fiction.
6. Historical fiction.   I. Title.
PR9199.4.B825P35   2013   2012038433
813'.6—dc23

Printed in the United States of America
1   3   5   7   9   10   8   6   4   2

Book design by Marysarah Quinn

For Larry, always

To view the Edgar Degas artworks

referenced in this book, visit

www.CathyMarieBuchanan.com/art.

1878

No social being is less protected than
the young Parisian girl—by laws,
regulations, and social customs.

—*Le Figaro*, 1880

❧ Marie ❧

Monsieur LeBlanc leans against the doorframe, his arms folded over a belly grown round on pork crackling. A button is missing from his waistcoat, pulled too tight for the threads to bear. Maman wrings her hands—laundress's hands, marked by chapped skin, raw knuckles. "But, Monsieur LeBlanc," she says, "we just put my dead husband in the ground."

"It's been two weeks, Madame van Goethem. You said you needed two weeks." No sooner had Papa taken his last breath upon this earth than, same as now, Monsieur LeBlanc stood in the doorway of our lodging room demanding the three months' rent Papa had fallen behind in paying since getting sick.

Maman drops to her knees, grasps the hem of Monsieur LeBlanc's greatcoat. "You cannot turn us out. My daughters, all three good girls, you would put them on the street?"

"Take pity," I say, joining Maman at his feet.

"Yes, pity," says Charlotte, my younger sister, and I wince. She plays her part too well for a child not yet eight.

Only Antoinette, the oldest of the three of us, remains silent, defiant, chin held high. But then she is never afraid.

Charlotte grasps one of Monsieur LeBlanc's hands in both her own, kisses it, rests her cheek against its back. He sighs heavily, and it seems tiny Charlotte—adored by the pork butcher, the watchmaker, the crockery dealer—has saved us from the street.

Seeing his face shift to soft, Maman says, "Take my ring," and slips her wedding band from her finger. She presses it to her lips before placing it in Monsieur LeBlanc's waiting hand. Then with great drama her palms fly to the spot on her chest just over her heart. Not wanting him to see in my eyes what I know about Maman's feelings for Papa, I turn my face away. Whenever Papa mentioned he was a tailor, apprenticed to a master as a boy, Maman always said, "The only tailoring you ever done is stitching the overalls the men at the porcelain factory wear."

Monsieur LeBlanc closes his fingers around the ring. "Two weeks more," he says. "You'll pay up then." Or a cart will haul off the sideboard handed down to Papa before he died, the table and three rickety chairs the lodger before us left behind, the mattresses stuffed with wool, each handful worth five sous to a pawnbroker. Our lodging room will be empty, only four walls, grimy and soot laden, deprived of a lick of whitewash. And there will be a new lock on the door and the concierge, old Madame Legat, fingering the key in her pocket, her gaze sorrowful on the curve of Charlotte's pretty cheek. Of the three of us, only Antoinette is old enough to remember nights in a dingy stairwell, days on the boulevard Haussmann, palms held out, empty, the rustle of the silk skirts passing by. She told me once how it was that other time, when Papa sold his sewing machine to pay for a tiny white gown with crocheted lace, a small white coffin with a painting of two cherubs blowing horns, a priest to say the Mass.

I am the namesake of a small dead child, Marie, or Marie the First as I usually think of her. Before her second birthday, she was rigid in her cradle, eyes fixed on what she could not see, and then I came—a gift, Maman said—to take her place.

. . .

"God bless," Charlotte calls out to Monsieur LeBlanc's retreating back.

Maman pushes herself up like an old woman, staggering under the heft of widowhood, daughters, monies owed, an empty larder. She reaches into her apron pocket, tilts a small bottle of green liquid to her lips, wipes her mouth with the back of her hand.

"We owe for the week's milk, and there's enough for that?" Antoinette says, chin jutting.

"Haven't seen a sou from you in a month. Still a walker-on at the Opéra, at seventeen years old. You got no idea about work." Antoinette pulls her lips tight, looks down her nose at Maman, who does not let up. "A measly two francs they pay you for loitering on the stage," she says, "and only if whatever costume the wardrobe mistress pressed happens to fit. Too high and mighty for the washhouse. Nothing good will come of you, I can see that."

"Like mother, like daughter, no?" Antoinette says, holding a pretend bottle to her lips.

Maman lifts the absinthe the smallest bit more but only twists the cork back into place. "You'll take your sisters to the dance school at the Opéra in the morning," Maman says to Antoinette; and light comes into Charlotte's face. Three times a week she says how the Paris Opéra is the greatest opera house in all the world.

Sometimes Antoinette shows Charlotte and me the steps she learned at the Opéra dance school, back in the days before she was told not to come back, and we stand with our heels together, our feet turned out, bending our knees.

"Knees over your toes," Antoinette would say. "That's it. A plié."

"What else?" Usually Charlotte asked, but sometimes it was me. The evenings were long and dull, and in the wintertime a few pliés in a bit of candlelight took away the shivering before curling up on our mattress for the night.

Antoinette taught us battements tendus, ronds de jambe, grands battements, on and on. She would stoop to adjust the ankle of Charlotte's outstretched foot. "Such feet," she would say. "Feet of a dancer, pet."

Almost always it was Charlotte she bothered to correct. Maman liked to say how it was time I earned my keep, how even the girls in the Opéra dance school were handed seventy francs each month, but already Papa had slapped his hand down on the table. "Enough," he said. "Marie is to stay put, in Sister Evangeline's classroom, where she belongs." Later, alone, he whispered into my ear that I was clever, my mind meant for studying, that Sister Evangeline had bothered to wait for him outside the porcelain factory and tell him it was so. Still I joined in, and even if Antoinette said my back was supple and my hips were loose, even if I sometimes found myself dancing my own made-up dance when the music of the fiddler down below came up through the planks of the floor, we both knew Papa's word would hold. Her eyes were on tiny Charlotte, extending a leg behind her in an arabesque and then lifting it high above the floor, all the while Antoinette making adjustments and calling out, "Arms soft. Knee straight. Neck long. That's it. You got a neck like Taglioni, pet."

On Antoinette's name day when she was eight, Papa brought out from inside the sleeve of his coat a figurine of Marie Taglioni, hovering barefoot, wings spread, only the toes of one foot upon the earth. Nearly fifty years ago she claimed a place for herself in the heart of every Parisian by dancing *La Sylphide*, and still her legend lived on. Antoinette kissed the tiny face of the figurine a dozen times and put it high up on the mantelshelf to be adored. Anyone looking there would have seen it, a tiny sylph, beside Maman's old clock. But then Antoinette failed the examination that would have promoted her from the second set of the quadrille to the first and was dismissed from the Paris Opéra Ballet for arguing with Monsieur Pluque, the director of dance. "That mouth of yours," Maman said.

"I only said to him I could make more fouettés en tournant than

Martine, that my footwork was superior to that of Carole." I could picture Antoinette standing there, arms crossed, insolence on her face. "I'm ugly and skinny, that's what he says back to me."

The figurine was gone from the mantelshelf the next day, maybe to the pawnbroker, maybe smashed upon the cobblestones.

With the news that Maman is sending us to the dance school, Charlotte threads her fingers together, knuckles whitening as she works to hide her joy. I keep my face still, my dismay to myself. The petits rats—the scrawny, hopeful girls, vying for the quickest feet, the lightest leap, the prettiest arms—are babies, like Charlotte, some as young as six. It puts my nerves jumping, the idea of me—a thirteen-year-old—lost among them at the barre, rats who earn their name by scurrying along the Opéra corridors, hungry and dirty and sniffing out crumbs of charity.

Antoinette lays a stilling hand on Charlotte's arm, catches my eye, makes a tiny nod telling me to wait, that she is not done with Maman. "Old Pluque won't take Marie."

"That's for him to decide," Maman says.

"She's too old."

"She'll catch up. Tell him she's clever." Her voice is harsh, edged in scorn. She knows the pride I felt that Sister Evangeline bothered to wait for Papa outside the gates of the factory.

"I won't take her."

Maman draws herself up to her greatest height, a full three inches shorter than Antoinette. She leans in, her face close. "You'll do as you're told."

I spend my mornings sitting at a little desk reciting from the catechism the Act of Contrition or reading from a little book the story of Joan of Arc or writing out from memory the Ten Commandments or copying from the blackboard the column of figures I was told to add. Sometimes I look up and catch the corners of Sister Evangeline's lips lifting to a smile, and I feel the warm glow of a flaring lamp. Even so, ever since Papa got sick, I have wondered about the usefulness of all the hours, the greediness in staying put in the classroom instead of earning a wage. Sister Evangeline says she is nowhere close to finished with my religious education, that she does not like me reaching for the hinge of my desk, the key inside my pocket, the bits of iron I know to bring good luck, when I am called upon to recite. She says I do not know a single hymn. How could I, when I have no skirt decent enough to get myself let into Mass at église de la Sainte-Trinité? She spent long hours preparing me for my first Communion, but between wearing a gown borrowed from an altar boy instead of one of the lacy ones all the other girls wore and figuring out the wafer we were told was Christ's true flesh was nothing more than plain bread, I cannot claim to have felt the Real Presence of Him at my side. Even so I do know by heart the Creed and Our Father and Hail Mary and Glory Be. And as for the rest of what I am meant to learn in school, already I can work out what a cabbage and two onions cost faster than the fruiterer. I know to count the change I get, how to figure out if it is right. I can write whatever I want and read anything I care to in the newspapers. If I asked Sister Evangeline the point of more schooling, if I asked whether all the arithmetic in the world could save a girl like me, I know the answer I would get. There is no changing that I am a girl without a father, with a mother always fingering the bottle in the pocket of her skirt, a girl with a face no shopkeeper would want greeting his customers at the till, a girl living on the highest floor of a rue de Douai lodging house with a spiral staircase too narrow to climb without my skirt brushing the walls and a courtyard too cramped to get a crumb of sunshine, a girl set loose on the lower slopes on Montmartre, a stew of bourgeois and poor, laborers and craftsmen, artists and models, a district famous for cabarets and dance halls and coquettes humble enough to lift their skirts for a crust of bread, a cup of broth for the babies wailing at home. Sister Evangeline's answer? "Well," she would say, lines forming on her smooth brow, an untruth creeping to her lips, "one just never knows."

A black look comes over Maman, same as yesterday when she yelled and Antoinette spit, landing a gob on Maman's shoe, and she hit Antoinette and then hit her again when she only laughed. Maman is puffy faced and stout, with hands brawny as a man's, and Antoinette, narrow hipped and bony, with fingers spindly as twigs. Still she widens the gap between her feet, readying herself for blows.

Is it impossible that I should take to dancing, that one day I will appear upon the Opéra stage? Maybe the dance mistress will be happy with a girl old enough to wipe her own nose, plait her own hair. If she is cruel, if the little girls jeer that I cannot make a straight line of demi-tours, Sister Evangeline always says I work as hard as a mule, also that I have a head for picking up what is new. There is the seventy francs to think of, too. I could go to a textile factory and make half the amount, or the washhouse and maybe come close to matching it, but working twelve hours a day, six days a week and only if the overseer saw his way to pretending I was already fourteen.

Tomorrow could be the day Monsieur Pluque's wife feeds him his favorite breakfast and ties his cravat with a little more care, the day he climbs the stairs at the Opéra with an extra dose of warmth. Belly full of brioche, might he put my name on the dance school register, hauling me up from the gutter, giving me a sliver of a chance?

"I'll go," I say, fingernails digging into my palms.

The cords of Antoinette's neck grow slack. Maman drops onto the hard seat of a chair.

LE FIGARO

23 MAY 1878

CRIMINAL MAN

Italian criminologist Cesare Lombroso has found a high incidence of certain anatomical features in his study of criminal man. Facial characteristics commonly occurring among the criminals studied include a forward thrust of the lower face; broad cheekbones; a low forehead; and dark, abundant hair. With each of these characteristics appearing in prehistoric man or apes, Lombroso postulates that the most heinous of today's criminals are throwbacks to an earlier, more savage version of man. He points out that the reappearance of disease or characteristics down the ancestral line is well documented among scientists. Studies by esteemed French anthropologists support his conclusions.

Dr. Arthur Bordier measured the skulls of thirty-six murderers on loan from the museum at Caen and found that the skulls closely resembled those of primitive man in two key measurements. The foreheads of the murderers were small. It was the result he expected, given the association of the frontal lobes of the brain with intelligence. The rears of the skulls—housing the lobes associated with action—were oversize. Bordier concludes that a brain more inclined to action than thought is something a modern criminal has in common with a primitive savage. The findings are supported by the work of Dr. Louis Delasiauve, who measured the heads of two hundred inmates at La Roquette prison and found similar cranial evidence of evil moral tendencies in nearly half the criminals studied.

It seems French anthropologists and Lombroso are in agreement. The typical criminal is savagely ugly: *monstrum in fronte, monstrum in animo*.

~ Antoinette ~

The gloomy morning creeps through the one window of our lodging room, dimly lighting the mattresses in the corner. On the one where I slept, still Marie is curled around Charlotte. The other is empty. Maman is already off to the day of heaped linens awaiting at the washhouse. I tickle the cheek of Marie, and she swats at my hand. "Get up, you lazy lout of a girl," I say. "Maman—wonders never cease—left us a full loaf, and I got boiled eggs."

Marie opens an eye, just one. "You don't?"

I take two warm eggs out of my pocket, put them in her face. She touches one and flops onto her back. The head of that girl is still cobwebby, far from remembering the promise of yesterday—the razor eye of old Pluque at the dance school inspecting her bag of bones before the morning is done.

Charlotte pulls the shabby linens up over her ears, indignant, like an empress with ladies-in-waiting who are blighting her day. I yank at the linens, and she says, "Go away. Go away, or else."

"Or else what?" I say. "Or else you won't eat your egg, your bread? You'll go to the Opéra, belly howling? Is that it, pet?"

"I remember now," Marie says.

Quick as lightning, Charlotte is upon her knees. "What time is it?"

"Loads of time," I say.

"My stockings? You mended them? You said you would."

By the time I finished with the stockings, the streets were quiet. The fruit peddlers and operagoers, the workmen—staggering and reeking with their arms around each other's necks—were snoring in their beds. Candle snuffed, I sat there in the blackness, fearing for Marie. Should I grind a bit of soot into the slippers she was to wear, rip the skirt, forget about fetching hard-boiled eggs come the light of day so she went to the Opéra unsteady and weak? Each was something I could undertake and maybe raise the scorn of old Pluque. But then the next minute, my mind flipped back to thinking how a smear of greasepaint might hide her sallow skin. Back and forth I went. How to diminish. How to boost up. All I knew for sure was even if old Pluque saw his way to giving her a chance, even if she clawed her way up from the dance school to the corps de ballet, she was too skinny, too vulgar in her looks, too much like me to ever move up from the second set of the quadrille, the bottom of the scale. She would be stuck, a measly eighty-five francs a month, another two for every evening she danced. It was not enough, not without an abonné paying the rent. And abonnés, those wealthy men ogling every night from the orchestra stalls, where they have it arranged their wives are not allowed to sit, desired girls higher up the pay scale, girls with the dainty chin and rosebud lips of Charlotte, the ones other men dreamt of luring into their beds. Even if half those men could not tell an attitude from an arabesque, they wanted girls it stirred their cockles to watch. The right girl was worth the rent, the meals out, the flowers, the hairdressing bills. And if she was of the highest rank—an étoile—then he'd better be rich. He would have a carriage to pay for and fancy gowns, even a lady's maid.

Marie and Charlotte eat their eggs: Marie slowly, sucking each crumb of yolk from her fingertips, Charlotte like it is a race, like I will deliver her an egg tomorrow morning and another the morning after that.

I hold out my two old practice skirts, and Charlotte snatches for the not so shabby one, but I flip it high over my head, out of reach. "Such a grabby girl," I say. "Marie gets this one." A ratty skirt won't stop old Pluque from seeing the Taglioni neck of Charlotte, the high arch of her instep, her angel face. He will be drooling, dreaming up all those abonnés one day tossing bouquets to her feet.

I nudge the rattier skirt toward her. She stands still as stone, arms crossed. I let that skirt fall to the grime at our feet, the floor Maman don't bother to scrub, and Charlotte snatches it up.

"Word of truth, pet, the eyes of old Pluque are going to be glued to your dancer's feet, your Taglioni neck. He's going to piss himself, old Pluque, when he sees the swan that just glided into the Opéra."

I pull two silk roses—pinched from a café up in the place Pigalle—from my pocket, both exactly right for tucking into a chignon. From my other pocket, I take out a tiny lacquer pot, greasepaint filched from the loge assigned to the walkers-on at the Opéra. The pout disappears from the lips of Charlotte, and I knock the brush against the edge of the sideboard, calling over slouching Marie.

I brush out her hair for a full twenty minutes, saying a hundred times, "Such hair. Magnificent hair," before I set to work, scooping up a mane so thick that when it is done in a single plait my fingers cannot reach around the girth. That hair—dark in color and glossy as a mole in the sun—is the single gift God thought to give to Marie. With its thickness, there is no need for a postiche, those bits of netting ballet girls stuff full of shed hair and tuck into their chignons, making them twice their natural size. I twist the thick rope of Marie's hair, coil it around and around, shush her gripes about the poking as I pin it into place. When I finish, I step back and see how Marie would be improved with that paltry brow of hers covered up. "Plenty of the ballet girls got bangs," I say, opening up a drawer of the sideboard, pulling out the scissors that so far have been spared the window of the pawnbroker. Charlotte looks up from bending over the leg she is stretching to loosen, propped atop the back of a chair. "Your head is too full of curls, pet."

I turn back to Marie. "You're sure?" she says and grips her bottom lip between her teeth.

I put myself between her and the sideboard, snipping strands of hair pulled loose from the coil, daubing greasepaint, rubbing it in, always keeping her cut off from the looking glass hanging beyond my back.

"All this fuss and I haven't got a chance," she says.

"You complaining about my hairdressing?" I tuck a flower behind her ear instead of hiding it at the back of her head and step away, giving her a clear view of the looking glass, the butterfly just hatched.

She sees it and her smile opens up. But then it is those teeth of hers, twisting sideways, jostling for a crumb of space. Should I say about keeping her mouth closed up in front of old Pluque? No need, not with her lips snapping shut, her face switching back to grim.

"Pretty as a peach."

"Such a lying tongue," she says.

"Christ, Marie."

"Monstrum in fronte, monstrum in animo."

She reads the newspapers she plucks from the gutters. She goes to the school of those nuns, wanders lost Saturday mornings when the classroom is shut. She knows things, says things, thinks things better left in a closed-up drawer. "What, Marie? What?"

"Monstrous in face, monstrous in spirit."

"Gibberish for the piss pot," I say. "Insulting, too, with everyone saying how much we are alike."

But she goes on about throwbacks and savages and says she's got the look of an ape, a criminal. Can I see it in her low forehead, her wide cheeks, the jaw pushed forward in her face?

～ Marie ～

I stand before Monsieur Pluque, waiting for him to look. My arms are en repos, my feet in first position, not that he can see them with his great desk in the way. Shoulders down, I say inside my head. Neck long. Hands and elbows soft. Be still. No fidgeting and don't bother about Charlotte, posing front and center in the better practice skirt, snatched from the satchel the minute Antoinette was gone from sight.

The office is vast, twice the size of our lodging room, but plain, except for the desk, which is carved with serpents and creatures with shifty eyes and bared fangs. It gives me the same feeling I had approaching the Opéra's back gate, looking at the decorations there—mostly garlands and flowers and scrolls—but the fence posts appeared no different from upended swords; and beyond, the Opéra's façade was full of winged creatures, laughing masks. High up over the rear entrance a blank-eyed head loomed. Already I was trembling when Antoinette said how everyone but the operagoers uses the back gate, entering the Opéra through the doors beyond the courtyard of administration. We would not walk around to the front, to the hundredfold more adornments, the gawking eyes, the gaping mouths. I could have kissed her at the news.

Inside the Opéra I looked around at the plaster walls, the plain wood floors, nothing close to as tatty as our lodging room; but when the Opéra opened three years ago, the newspapers were full of accounts of marble and mosaics and gilt, bronze almost-naked women twisting around each other and holding up the candelabra lighting the stairs. "It's not so grand," I said.

"It's the other side—the public side—that's magnificent," Antoinette said. "That side isn't for you and me."

A woman with a nose like a sharp beak approached, limping up to us from behind. In a voice flat as slate, she said, "Mademoiselle van Goethem, you know to check in with me."

"Ah, Madame Gagnon, concierge of all the Opéra." Antoinette's face flickered to a smile. "Now, how's that old knee of yours holding up?"

"Same old slippery tongue as always."

"You prefer being introduced as concierge of the rear entrance?"

"I prefer a girl who says the truth."

Antoinette smirked, lifted her chin to Charlotte and me. "Old Pluque is waiting for us upstairs." And for a tiny moment I wondered if he really was.

"Your names don't appear in the register." Madame Gagnon put herself between the three of us and the stairs farther down the corridor.

"You know, same as I do, old Pluque never bothers with the register." Antoinette shifted her weight over to one leg. "Go on up, pet, and get old Pluque. Tell him Madame Gagnon said to get himself downstairs."

Without the smallest gap, Charlotte ducked around Madame Gagnon and set off in the direction of the stairs, and I felt a tiny pang that Antoinette knew to pick Charlotte instead of me.

"Won't be a minute," Charlotte called out.

"Go on up," Madame Gagnon said through teeth clamped shut, and Antoinette pulled at my arm.

On our way to Monsieur Pluque's office we made a little detour, stopping at the small table in front of the stage-door keeper's loge. Charlotte and I both put our hands on the horseshoe waiting there, and Antoinette told us it was what every actor and singer and ballet girl and walker-on did. Her hand atop ours, she gave a little squeeze. "Nothing to be afraid of now, Marie."

While we waited outside Monsieur Pluque's office, I gripped my hands together to keep from picking at the patch of skin scraped close to raw on my thumb. Eventually a gentleman appeared in the doorway, and I clutched tighter, fearing it was time. He took a moment in the corridor, slipping off strange spectacles—round in shape but with lenses tinted blue. But he was not Monsieur Pluque. No. He tipped his hat to Antoinette and said, "Mademoiselle van Goethem," and then he went off down the corridor. His frock coat was a good one, but the wool of his waistcoat was more than a little limp and his beard, a mix of chestnut and grey, was not properly trimmed. With Antoinette always saying you can tell by a gentleman's shoes if he is rich, I leaned out from the wall. His were freshly varnished but the toes bent up, like he had been wearing them a hundred years.

Before he was even out of earshot, Charlotte said, "An abonné?"

"Monsieur Degas, an artist," Antoinette said. "He's at the Opéra day and night, all the time sketching away. Ballet girls most of the time. He painted Eugénie Fiocre once."

"An étoile," Charlotte said. "She married a marquis." It was a story all Paris knew, one that kept the charwomen and sewing maids and wool carders sending their daughters to the dance school. The laundresses, too.

"His pictures must be pretty," I said.

Antoinette shrugged. "Ballet girls fixing their stockings or scratching their backs."

But who would put such things upon their walls? Antoinette made a habit of saying anything—to keep Maman from scolding, Charlotte from griping, me from knowing what she thought I could not bear or because lying was a habit she did not care to break.

. . .

Monsieur Pluque finally looks up from his desk, and then down again quick, and I can tell he wants to laugh—maybe at my skirt; maybe at my arms, still held en repos; maybe at Charlotte, bowing in a curtsey so low her fingertips reach the floor. But he does not. No, he strokes his mustache, covering up his mouth. "All right, Mademoiselles Marie and Charlotte," he says, getting up and pointing at the floor in front of his desk. "Over here."

Then he spends a long time just looking, eyes wandering face to feet. He probably knows all about Cesare Lombroso, about murderers and whores and crooks of every sort being born that way, about the signs they carry in their faces that tell the world. Will he ask me to leave now, to wait for Charlotte in the corridor? I pull in my chin, thinking to shrink my jaw, but what if it makes my neck appear short? Just stop, I tell myself. He makes a circle in the air with his finger, and we turn. "On your bellies," he says after a long while.

I get onto my belly and wonder at the nerve of Charlotte, who says, "Monsieur Pluque, I know all the barre exercises, the center ones, too. I can copy anything Antoinette shows me. I really can. I can do a line of demi-tours that is very straight. I can show you." She gets herself ready, one foot out in front, arms croisé. Should I do the same?

"On your belly, Mademoiselle Charlotte."

No, I should not. His voice is like a wintry gust.

"Now, plié," he says. "No, no, no, Mademoiselle Marie. Keep your rump from popping up." Then his hand is upon my backside, pushing it down flat, and my bent knees splay out to the sides. "Loose hips."

I know from Antoinette it is something a dancer needs, hips loose enough to let the fronts of the thighs roll out to the sides when she leaps or stands still, even lifts up a leg. With him unable to glimpse my twisted teeth, I allow myself a smile.

Then he tells us to straighten our knees and raise our shoulders and ribs, arching our backs. Crouching beside me, he pushes my forehead with the heel of his hand. "More," he says. "More arch."

It makes me wince, the way he barks.

"Antoinette has you practicing back bends?"

"No, Monsieur."

"It's unusual," he says, "such suppleness in a girl your age."

He tells us to stand and we do, Charlotte more slowly and making a pretty flourish with her arms.

"Now for your feet," he says, moving to a spot just in front of Charlotte. He claps his hands twice. Somehow she knows he is asking for a foot, and she moves her arms à la seconde and makes a grand battement that ends with her ankle in his waiting palm. She stretches that ankle straight, arches her entire foot, not just her toes, but he says nothing about her dancer's feet.

I copy the way she got her foot into his hand, but I make a mess of it, and he has to scoot out of the way, that or get himself kicked. I gasp, just a little, and he chuckles, like it does not matter in the least, and then he acts no different about my feet than Charlotte's. He calls for a violinist and while we wait, he goes back to looking at the papers on his desk and my mind drifts to wondering whether his telling Antoinette she was ugly and skinny is even true.

An old man with a white mustache and a violin comes into the office and makes a little bow. "Something in four-four, a little mournful," Monsieur Pluque says, coming around to the front of his desk again. The old man lifts up his bow, sets it down on the strings and then there is music filling up the air.

"Dance, when you are ready," Monsieur Pluque says.

I stand still as death, feet in first position, arms en repos, my mind flitting, crisscrossing to such an extent that I cannot make sense of what we have been asked to do. I feel my skin bristle, nerves aflame.

And then Charlotte whips around, not teetering a bit, in a straight line of demi-tours, and Monsieur Pluque claps his hands together, loud, just once, and the music halts. "No. No. No. Enough," he says, again a loud bark. "I asked for demi-tours? No. I am not interested in what steps you think you know." He clears his throat. "Shut your eyes. Listen to the music. Then tell me what the music says." The music starts up again.

I shut my eyes. I wait, listening hard to the music reaching underneath my skin. But I do not know what to do. I listen more, harder, and I cannot think of anything except that the music sounds like a leaf drifting down from a tree. And then it comes to me, sudden, like a clap of thunder one minute and teeming rain the next: I am supposed to be that drifting leaf. I start slowly, just my head, side to side, and listen for slapped together hands stopping the violin. I add my arms, little sways back and forth. The music grows and so do my swaying arms. And I let myself drift, feel myself lifting up, then floating, then tugged by the spinning wind, then drifting some more. I keep it up, until the music slows down and then stops, and I am a leaf quiet on the ground. I open my eyes. "Exactly," Monsieur Pluque says, but I do not know if he is talking to me or Charlotte.

With the two us wedged into the single chair in front of his desk, he opens up a tall book of pages thick from handling. He asks for our full names, our street and the number of our lodging house, our mother's name and occupation and then our father's, and I should be speaking up, saying Papa is dead, but I do not and eventually Monsieur Pluque remembers what he already knows and says, "Oh, yes. Never mind."

"That book of yours, it's where you write out the names of the petits rats?" Charlotte asks.

He leans back, his mouth puckered to a tight ring, and tilts his chair onto two legs. "Mademoiselle Charlotte, you remind me remarkably of Antoinette, with her tendency to say whatever she pleases and never wanting to wait," he says, and I know we are meant to remember Antoinette losing her spot with the Opéra ballet. He flips his chair forward so it is back on all four legs. "Mademoiselles Marie and Charlotte, tomorrow morning, then. Nine o'clock. Madame Gagnon, downstairs, will have your names in the register. Follow one of the petits rats up to Madame Théodore's practice room. Come early. You won't find it on your own."

With the way I swallow a smile, there has to be the ugliest of grimaces upon my face. And Charlotte, gripping the arm of the chair, looks to be holding herself firm against some force wanting her to leap up. "Dismissed," he says.

We are quiet in the corridor, quiet while we jump up and down squeezing each other tight, quiet while we change out of the practice skirts. We stay quiet on the stairs, also passing Madame Gagnon's loge. Even with the rear entrance doors only a step or two away, I whisper when I say, "But where is Antoinette?" She is not on the bench, waiting, like we arranged, and I cannot think of a time when Antoinette said to meet at such and such a spot and was not there.

Charlotte peers into the sunshine of the courtyard beyond the doors. "She'll be out by the gate." Same as for me, the possibility of Antoinette forgetting us does not exist.

We pass through the doors and then we gallop and leap and knock shoulders as we run across the courtyard bursting with our news. But out by the gate, still there is no Antoinette. Still she is not there.

❧ Antoinette ❧

That old Pluque, such a louse, with the way he said my name, not a minute ago, when I was upstairs telling him I brought Marie and Charlotte to audition for the school. "Antoinette van Goethem," he said, so full of scorn, like I picked his pocket a dozen times, and right in front of Marie and Charlotte. Not that either took notice—not with Marie blanched whiter than the pearly teeth of Charlotte and Charlotte curtseying like she was bowing down to a herd of abonnés, applauding on their feet. Old Pluque, he won't like it, not a bit, such airs as she puts on.

When the girls were in the toilet, changing into practice skirts—the loge of the petits rats was a hundred flights of stairs away—I said how it is with Papa dead and Maman turned to absinthe and me left in charge of two girls who don't have the smallest clue about fending for themselves. I let him know I knew all about the abonnés, how there are some who don't give a lick whether a girl is twelve or sixteen, and in a final bit of petitioning on behalf of Marie, that no way was Charlotte wandering the corridors of the Opéra without her sister close at hand. "You turn an eye the other way," I said. "I know enough to know I can't count on you."

And old Pluque, he had the nerve to say, "Those sisters of yours, they'd be better off looking after themselves." But I did not blurt out about staying up half the night mending stockings and washing practice skirts and worrying myself to death. I did not say about pinching eggs on account of those two girls or fussing with their hair. No, I thought about Marie and Charlotte and clamped my lips tight.

I spend a minute in the darkened stairwell, waiting for the hotness of my cheeks to fade. Sure as sure Madame Gagnon is going to step into my path, and I will not give her the happiness of seeing my face red.

Passing by her loge, I peek past the door, and there she is, loathing in her slanty eyes that old Pluque is truthfully upstairs considering Marie and Charlotte. "Old Pluque said to thank you for not delaying the girls," I say. "And don't you worry none. I let him know you are good and miffed about the way he don't bother with the register."

"Never did you know when to keep that trap of yours shut."

I lift my skirt and make a little curtsey. "Well, then," I say, "off to see what Monsieur Leroy's got for me."

Monsieur Leroy hires the walkers-on at the Opéra, signing us up for a week's work at a time, and scowling Madame Gagnon—she knows she don't have a chance of poisoning him against me. Forever he is walking clear around the office of the chief of singing, all so he don't have to pass by her loge, not when she is always lecturing about the register he don't often bother to update.

I join the line outside his office and lean up against the wall, thinking it miserly that the Opéra don't splurge on a couple of benches for the walkers-on, especially when the dressing rooms of the étoiles are all done up with draped silk and tassels and chaises longues an empress would see fit to use. I never been inside one. But I expect what I hear is true. Always, even when the evening's entertainment is an opera, an abonné gets his moment of leering at the ballet girls upon the stage, at least the fifteen minutes of a ballet divertissement stuck between the acts; and if he wants

more, just a stairwell away is the Foyer de la Danse. It is where the abonnés linger during intermission and before the curtains open up, always
without their wives, all barred from going inside. Around them the most
beloved of the ballet girls limber up, wearing close to nothing, an ankle
upon the barre positioned at the eye level of the abonnés gulping champagne upon the banquettes. Those nearby dressing rooms of the étoiles,
they have to be grand. No one would want the richest of the abonnés, the
ones venturing up to the rooms as invited guests, complaining about the
shabbiness of the decor.

The lineup is not much, not yet, and I hate to talk low about my fellow
walkers-on, even if my words are true, but plenty of them are dawdling
on their lumpy mattresses, heads splitting and mouths pasty dry from
drinking up the two francs Monsieur Leroy handed over after the curtain
dropped last night. I reach second in line, so very close to sitting down
across from Monsieur Leroy, when a boy I put at eighteen gets up from the
spot. He is passing through the office doorway when he winks a saucy
wink. Boys don't wink usually, not at me, and I look over my shoulder, but
there is only a child with a scabbed nose and then after him, an old lady
missing both her eyeteeth. With the winker already stepping into the
corridor, I miss the chance to look to my feet, smiling the smallest little
smile, just enough so that saucy winker can guess about me being pleased.
He was not much to look at, no, not with that scrub-brushy hair of his
creeping low on his forehead and his black eyes sinking too deep beneath
the weighty ridge of his brow and his jaw looking like the sort on those
dogs it is best to steer away from in the streets. Still, I like a boy who
winks.

I make up my mind then and there to wink back next time, but then I
start to wonder about missing my only chance. I ditch the lineup, figuring
that boy cannot have got much past the back gate of the Opéra. But outside there is no sign of him. "Dunce," I say. Now it is back to waiting all
over again in that miserable line of Monsieur Leroy, but as I turn back to

the Opéra, there is the winking boy, leaning up against the wall, his foot propped behind him and a home-rolled smoke hanging from his lips.

He winks, and I wink back.

He pulls on his smoke. "I like a girl who winks," he says.

Looking to the scuffed toes of my boots, I say, "You a walker-on?"

"Just for a bit of fun. You?"

"I appear on the stage pretty regular, most nights, some afternoons, too, if they are figuring out about the blocking and need someone for holding a spot. You get anything today?"

"Old Leroy says I got to pay a fine before I get anything more," he says. "Three minutes late and he tells me I owe half an evening's wage."

I don't say about the fines being nothing new, just shift my weight onto my back leg, thinking to chat for a bit.

"Those ballet girls and singers, always on the stage, they aren't paying fines."

"You're wrong about that," I say. Almost always when I tell about being a ballet girl, back before, a boy leans in close. "Was once a ballet girl myself."

His eyes wander over me, head to toe and then back up again. "A coryphée?"

I nod, finishing with my chin jutting a little high. It is the posture I take when I lie, particularly with Maman, and most often my lofty chin is enough to shut her up. I never did pass the examination elevating me from the second quadrille to the first, never mind the ones coming after that; but the winker, he don't know one rank from the next and no need to start explaining about the lowest rung—second quadrille—and the rungs that come after that—first quadrille, coryphée, sujet, première danseuse, étoile.

He takes another pull and tilts his head back, his chin ending up just a little higher than my own. "Prove it," he says.

Arms croisé, I plié in fourth position, and then, rising onto the toes of my left foot, I bring the toes of my right to my knee and whirl around fast, whipping that lifted leg out to the side and then pulling the toes back to the knee. I make the turn again and again—eight very nice fouettés en tournant, even with my skirt getting in the way. I stop steadily, and feeling foolish now that I showed off the only step that ever got me a nod from old Pluque, I make a lowly curtsey, worthy of a walker-on.

He breathes out a whistle, long and low. "Got time for a glass?" he says.

Marie and Charlotte are meeting me at the bench just inside the doors when they are done, and I've got to see Monsieur Leroy, and there is the broom of Madame Legat to borrow, the clipped locks of Marie's hair to be swept up. Also there is Charlotte, who is going be leaping with excitement and expecting kisses and Marie filled up with trepidation no matter what the morning held.

"Can't," I say to the winker. "Waiting for my sisters." Smoke drifting up from his parted lips, I jerk my thumb in the direction of the rear entrance. "They are seeing about spots in the dance school."

"Not you?"

"Done with all that."

The weighty ridge of his brow lifts up.

I hold my back good and straight. "Not pretty enough."

"You got pretty eyes," he says. "Like chocolate pools." The winker leans in, putting his face close enough that I smell his smoky breath. "I like how straight you stand up, too."

"No slouching. Not in the ballet." I tilt my chin toward the couple of practice rooms tucked up under the rafters of the Opéra roof.

"Come for a glass," he says. "A glass and a few laughs."

"Maybe a drop of cassis, so long as it's somewhere close."

"I'm Émile." He squashes the butt of his smoke on the Opéra wall, leaving a sooty streak. "Émile Abadie."

"Antoinette van Goethem," I say, and he takes my hand from hanging at my side and puts a kiss just beneath the wrist.

"I know a place."

We walk side by side, passing two cafés, both with maître d's out front, wearing aprons stiff with starch. We come to a corner and instead of saying "We turn here," he puts his fingers on my back, steering me off the main boulevard, and then he leaves them there, hovering light and then a little heavier when I don't do anything to dodge those hot fingertips.

The tavern we enter is musty smelling and dimly lit with yellowed tiles covering the walls. I like it right away, reminding me as it does of a place Papa used to take me for a five-sou meal up in the place Pigalle. We slide in, along one of the straight-backed benches lining the walls, so that we are sitting side by side behind a long table that could stand the touch of a rag.

For me he orders cassis and water and for himself, a glass of red wine. The drinks come fast, and I gulp mine down, thinking a bit of bolstering can do no harm. "Smoke?" he says, nudging a home-roll across the tabletop.

"Don't smoke."

He lights up, makes a little smirk on seeing my glass close to drained and says, "I'll be getting you something a little stronger next time around."

"A glass of red," I say, "since you're such a bossy boy."

I ask where he lives, and he says he used to stay at his mother's place, the place where he spent most of his years, in the faubourgs, east side. He is moving around just now, splitting his time between one friend and the next. "You know how it is, wherever I find an empty corner." I keep my eyebrows from creeping up that he don't have so much as a mattress and yet is gulping red wine.

By the time he gets around to asking about my family, my third glass is ordered and drained, and I feel a growing warmth toward a boy so accustomed to enjoying himself. He makes a habit of nodding when I talk, and he keeps his eyes from straying, even when a pair of giggling girls comes into the tavern, and I have this feeling, like there is not a single place he would rather be than beside me on the bench. I tell him about Marie and her nose always stuck in a newspaper and Charlotte and her dancer's feet and Maman and her swelling sadness. I say about Papa being a fine tailor and coughing until he could not go to the porcelain factory to stitch the overalls no more and taking his last breath with his three girls all cuddled around and then Maman blubbering for us to get him onto the floor before the mattress got spoiled. Émile says about his own father, how he was gone even before Émile was born. He says it is something I should think about when I feel down about Papa. And it is true, I remember him bouncing me on his knee and plucking a button from behind my ear and singing good and loud and twirling around each of his girls and then Maman when we heard the fiddle music through the planks of our floor. Émile got none of that, only a string of no-goods who came and went as they pleased. One of them pawned his slingshot. Another busted his clavicle. He undoes two of his shirt buttons and pulls the collar wide, showing me the lump left behind. I put two fingers on the lump, the black hairs creeping high on his brawny chest. He buttons up his shirt, shrugs in a way that says it don't matter in the least and orders another round.

We drink up, and there is no denying my drunkenness, not when he says about his mother siding with the brute and throwing Émile's belongings out into the street, and I lay my hand upon his arm. "Another?" he says, and I want to say yes, but already he spent a lot and I don't have so much as a single sou. I wave away the question and take the smallest mouthful of red wine. I keep talking, spacing out my sips, dreading the bottom of the glass and leaving that musty tavern where the bristle hairs of his forearm are tickling the skin of my own.

I tell about Monsieur LeBlanc standing in our doorway, his belly bursting from beneath his waistcoat, about him demanding three months' rent, and maybe it lets Émile in on me being without a single sou, or maybe it is just that he is dreading the bottom of the glass, too. Either way, he says, "Come on, Antoinette, let me buy you another glass. We're having such a lovely time."

He orders another round, also mussels in parsley sauce and a plate of radishes, and I know the moment when I could've got myself back to the Opéra in time for Marie and Charlotte is long past. He puts the mussels into my mouth with his fingers and bites into radishes and slides the leftover half onto my tongue. We stay late into the afternoon, laughing and licking wine from our lips, his hand on my thigh, back and forth, moving ever higher and me not minding in the least.

Only a woman sitting slumped across the tavern stays as long as we do, always gazing down, just past the glass of cassis she cannot muster the will to take. It breaks my heart, the loneliness in the face of that woman, the fellow sitting beside her, reading the newspaper and dozing off without so much as a moment's notice given over to her, and here is what I imagine brought her to this place. She spent the evening before at the Élysée Montmartre, watching all those ladies with black stockings and ruffled petticoats kicking up their legs but mostly lifting a glass and mingling and flirting and seeking out a way not to be so lonesome no more. After the dance hall, it was off to the Rat-Mort for her and more laughing and carrying on and maybe a bowl of soup before putting down her head in a tiny room off the likes of the rue Bréda or the rue de Douai. Half past eleven in the morning, she got herself up and tied the soiled petticoat from the night before around her waist. She put on that drab cloak, not bothering about the wrinkles or even half the ties, and slunk her way to the tavern, counting on a glass of cassis to take the sting out of another day. But now, sitting here, she finds herself not wishing in the least to start the rigmarole all over again.

I whisper some of this to Émile, letting his scrub-brushy hair tickle my nose, letting my bottom lip dampen the lobe of his ear. He shuts his eyes, tilts his head back, leaning it against the yellowed tiles. "Let's go, Antoinette. Let's get out of here."

He steers me out of the tavern, hanging on to my arm, me stumbling and bumping the table of that lonely lady as we go. She looks up from her knocked-over glass, and I see her hopeful, her sagging cheeks lifting to round. But we don't strike up a conversation. No, Émile only reaches into his pocket and, into the pooled cassis, he puts two francs, enough that he don't owe her a moment of his day.

Then we are behind the tavern, in the shadows there. I have my back against the wall, and the hand of Émile is on my neck, tender, but then he is pressing up against me, and he is not so gentle no more. Against my hip, I feel what I done to him, the hardness there, and I open my mouth to his rooting tongue. My head swirling, his hands pawing at the drawstring of my blouse, yanking at the neckline, I think about this being what a lip— my lip—on the lobe of an ear brings.

My first time it was a boy, a walker-on at the Opéra. He said to follow him, and I trailed behind, through the labyrinth of passageways beneath the Opéra. Why not? His face was pretty, except for the pockmarked skin, and it was not a bit usual for a boy to pay attention to me. He kissed me and stroked me and got down to doing what it was he brought me to the passageways to do. But back upstairs, that boy, he did not have the decency to call me by my name. No, he just looked the other way, and I guessed it was seeing me so up close or maybe the way I held myself so rigid beneath his pumping body that pushed him into ignoring me.

Émile is like a madman, sucking, mauling, pressing in, and none of it feels very nice, not like the slow moving hands of the boy at the Opéra. I think about calling him off. And then my heart pounds, just a little, because I doubt him listening even if I do. He hikes up my skirt and hauls down my drawers, and I wonder about this moment being the cost of wine and mussels in parsley sauce and bristle hairs tickling my arm. His fingers grope and poke and prod a tender place, and I call out, "You're hurting me," and when it don't alter anything at all, I put my hands upon his shoulders and one foot upon his thigh and give a mighty shove. He staggers back, his dark eyes upon me, my half nakedness. I pull my blouse up over my shoulders with trembling hands. I remember my ugliness and turn away.

"Antoinette," he says. "You make me crazy, is all."

"I want to go home."

"I'll walk you."

"I want to go by myself." Hauling up my drawers, holding my blouse in place, I set out.

Close to where the alleyway meets the street, he catches up. "Antoinette," he says, grabbing my arm, letting go when I jerk it away. With him staying put, I know he don't have the intention of keeping me prisoner, and I stop.

"Give it to that landlord of yours," he says, holding out a fistful of coins, plenty of them silver, a couple of them gold.

"A soldiers' mattress. That's what you think?" I sound like Charlotte, sniveling over the smallest slight.

"It's what I got left."

"Don't want it."

He nudges those coins toward me. With my own belly full and those of abandoned Marie and Charlotte empty, empty like my evenings next week now that it is too late for Monsieur Leroy, I turn my back in a pitiful show of pride.

But Émile is not bothered. No. He drops the coins at my feet. "For LeBlanc," he says. "You're not fit for the streets. Don't want you on the streets."

He leaves me in the alley, pulling up the neckline of my blouse, picking up coins.

Almost eighty francs, enough to keep the fists of Monsieur LeBlanc from pounding at the door, enough for pork crackling and full bellies, enough to make spinning a tale about vanishing from the Opéra as easy as swallowing soup.

~ Marie ~

It is an ugly picture, Maman seated on a chair, her head dropped back, her lips gaping, a bit of scum clinging to the corner of her mouth. I lean in close, smell her hot breath. Absinthe. Yes, always absinthe—the bite, the whiff of anise. And why not? Why not wash away the troubles of a widow with three girls to raise? I say it to Antoinette, so full of scorn to find Maman still here when the washhouse opened an hour ago. Antoinette grasps Maman's shoulder, gives her a rough shake.

"Leave her. Leave her be."

"The washhouse won't be keeping her, skipping days, soused half the time, sure as sure pulling off buttons and scorching everything in sight."

"She'll go later."

"We need water," she says, picking up the zinc bucket, pausing to look at me, hard. "Don't give her none of what you got left. She don't mind asking, and she finished a bottle last night." Already I put into Antoinette's hand the wages I collected at the Opéra yesterday, all but the ten francs she told me to put aside for a new practice skirt or sash or a pair of stockings without holes. She has taken over from Maman the paying of the rent owed to Monsieur LeBlanc. She stands, feet apart, arguing over every sou.

She pulls her shawl down from the peg. Then she is out the door, and I listen to her footsteps, quick on the stairs.

She could speak properly if she cared to. I know, because sometimes she mocks me, mimicking my correct speech, never once mistaking a "she doesn't" for a "she don't," a "have" for a "got." And once when we were walking in the boulevard Haussmann, a young man with a silk cravat bowed to Antoinette and handed her a bouquet of flowers, pale pink with tiny bell-shaped heads bobbing in the breeze. She spoke with him a good few minutes, perfect French, before she noticed the pack of boys watching and snickering across the boulevard. She lifted her chin then and threw the flowers in his face. After that she was off, down the pavement, and when I finally caught up, she looked to be fighting tears. "How I wanted those flowers," she said. "Should've kept those hateful flowers."

𝒶 little gurgling noise rises up from Maman's throat, and her head flops forward hard enough that the snap of it causes her to wake up. She blinks a couple of times, her chin pulled in tight to her chest, shying away from the daylight creeping into the room. Her wandering gaze comes upon me, putting a wrapped-up wedge of hard cheese into my satchel for my midday meal. "Marie," she says, her face changing from vague and doughy to rosy and warm. She has correctly remembered yesterday was the last Friday of the month.

I clutch the ten francs in my pocket. I am soft, and she knows.

"How about a meat pie for your supper, or a roasted chicken might be nice?" she says, pulling herself up onto unsteady feet.

"You're late for the washhouse."

"A touch of the colic this morning."

"Maybe fried potatoes," I say, thinking of the half dozen on the larder shelf.

Swaying, reaching for the table brazenly, like there is no shame in needing it, she says, "Roasted chicken was always your favorite."

I would rather a roasted chicken, a bit of mopped-up gravy, but I know where she is headed. "You know the expense of meat, Marie," she will say. "It's more than I got to spare." Or it could be even worse. The last time she went without a bottle too long, she turned weepy and made a claim to have loved Papa with all her heart, a heart he cleaved in two. "Those trollops," she said. "All those trollops up in the place Pigalle, he preferred them to what he got at home for free."

From my pocket I count out enough that she will not have to choose between a roasted chicken and a bottle of absinthe, and hold it out to her. Antoinette will shake her head that yet again I succumbed to Maman's tricks. But Maman looks at me with bewilderment on her face and then closes my fingers over the coins. "Already you're giving up most of what you earn," she says. "I got a few sous stashed away."

"Oh."

"You got an angel in your heart, Marie." She puts her hands on my shoulders and then hauls me into her arms, which are stronger and softer and warmer than Antoinette would guess. "It's that poor dead sister of yours, my dearest dear."

What I know about angels, all clearly put down in Sister Evangeline's catechism, is that they are numberless and good and happy and endowed with tremendous gifts, that they love us and protect us in body and soul. But some of those angels sin. They are drawn down by infernal ropes to the lower reaches of hell. And those wicked angels, they come back, laying snares, awaiting a moment of hatred or envy or despair, a chance to plunge a girl into the torment of eternal flame.

I wonder, sometimes, if Maman is right that Marie the First lives in my heart. I was trembling in Monsieur Pluque's office. He had said to dance, and I could not think and then suddenly, like a clap of thunder, I knew to be a drifting leaf. Was it Marie the First putting such an idea in my head, an idea I never before thought? Was the idea of becoming a leaf one of her tremendous gifts? Other times, though, I switch over to thinking Marie the First clings with blistering fingers to that descending infernal rope. If she is a good angel and in my heart, like Maman says, she watched Papa cough until it kept him from the porcelain factory and Maman grow weary when there was no bread and then Papa take his last breath. Why did she not send one of her tremendous gifts? And where is she now that Monsieur LeBlanc pounds at the door? I am not so sure I want the angel of my tiny, dead sister dwelling in my heart.

"Tonight, roasted chicken in your belly," Maman says, loosening her arms, stepping back from me. "And always, an angel in your heart."

The practice room is large and square with a barre affixed to the wall. The floor is slanted, they say, to get us ready for the stage, an explanation that curls my fingers into tight fists. There is an earthen stove in the corner; chairs—one for the dance mistress, another for the violinist accompanying us; and benches along one wall for the knitting, reading, snoozing mothers too watchful to set their darlings loose in the Opéra. Maman does not come, but Antoinette climbs the hundred flights of stairs just to stick her head around the door and give a little wave before rushing off to see Monsieur Leroy.

For a month I have been moved up to Madame Dominique's class and girls my own age. By a stroke of luck she had come to Madame Théodore's class to speak to the violinist, but she lingered, her watchfulness causing even the wickedest of the petits rats to keep her toes away from the backside of the girl next in line at the barre. When it was time for limbering—bending forward and arching backward and laying a chest flat on the floor with legs spread out wide to the sides—Madame Dominique's eyes stayed put on me. Then she walked over and gave me the same exercises Monsieur Pluque had back in the spring, and I felt so full of hope but afraid, too, because hope is something that usually gets snatched away. A week later just as Madame Théodore was about to begin class, Madame Dominique showed up and said I should go to her practice room the next morning, that from then on it would be her calling out the steps and correcting me. I could have split in two with joy at the thought of what I was leaving behind—the squealing and wriggling amid the glissades and entrechats, the hair pulling and scuffles amid the grands jetés and pirouettes, the squabbles over the watering can, just whose turn it was to dampen the floorboards. But that was not all. There would be no more Charlotte whispering corrections to me at the barre and butting ahead of me in line and sniveling that so-and-so called her Madame Fine Airs. And one last sweetener, my first week up with the older girls, Madame Dominique took us into the theater to watch a dress rehearsal of the ballet divertissement slotted into act four of Monsieur Gounod's new opera, *Polyeucte*.

You could have knocked me over upon seeing the stage—a columned temple; a scarlet, tasseled canopy; statues in marble, bronze and gold; a gilded chariot drawn by four stallions; magistrates, nobles and Roman soldiers, nine hundred costumes all told. Most stunning of all, though, was Rosita Mauri, brought from Barcelona by way of La Scala in Milan, to dance as Venus in the divertissement. Madame Dominique told us she was less refined, less classically correct than the French étoiles, but that no one matched her in strength, in swiftness crossing the stage, in quickness of footwork. I never saw such batterie, Rosita Mauri's legs beating, her feet quivering midair. I never saw such pirouettes, sharp, brisk, never once dropping from the tips of her toes. The mouths of the corps de ballet hung open. Eyes glinted bitterness. I wanted to dance as Rosita Mauri did—like a man in fierceness and strength, like a woman in lightness and grace. Afterward, she made a low curtsey, and when she looked up, her face was aglow with joy. It was a pleasure I knew, something I had touched once or twice in the practice room, the pleasure of having become music, the pleasure of being filled up head to toe.

· · ·

$\mathcal{G}$ am figuring out the rules of my new class, how a girl called Blanche always gets the first spot at the barre and the front row once we move to the center of the room for the second part of class, the way Madame Dominique picks her to show the proper positioning of the knee in an attitude, the ankles in a cabriole. I see the other girls whispering and Blanche off by herself, stretching with her leg upon the barre if we are awaiting our turn to show a string of grands jetés, or practicing coupés if it is a chain of piqué pirouettes. At the end of class Blanche packs up her bag and is fast as a rabbit on the stairs. It is better than stalling, hoping that just once one of the laughing, arm-linking girls will say, "You'll walk home with us today, no?" The girls were nicer to me in the beginning, gathering around and asking where I lived and did I think Marie Sanlaville was furious that Rosita Mauri was picked to dance as Venus in *Polyeucte*. I said she probably did not mind, at least not so much when the newspapers started calling Gounod's score unbearable in its monotony. I felt a little proud of my quick thinking, how each of the gathered girls, after the question, knew I could read. Then, after a week, Madame Dominique shifted me to the second spot at the barre, and at first I was sure I was moved only because always I was botching exercises and Madame Dominique wanted me standing behind Blanche, who never did. But the girls turned sour, and soon enough it was not just Blanche off by herself, making her muscles long, her coupés sharp.

With me up front Madame Dominique is always lifting my drooping elbow, tapping my rising-up shoulders, catching my leg high in a grand battement and further arching my foot. It did not take long to figure out that the days she lavished attention on me were days when I found myself taking the stairs alone after class. I started keeping a tally of her attentions, no different from the rest of the whispering girls, and maybe the tallying was something better not begun because now I cannot stop.

Today, like every day at the barre, I watch Blanche with the eyes of a hawk, noticing the tiny flourish of her hand as she opens her arm, her neck always long, even when arching back. I copy everything I can, trying to remember exactly when we are turned around, repeating the exercises with the left leg, and she is gone from my view. For battements frappés I hold my arm à la seconde, repeating the exercise already completed on the right, doing my best to recall the snap of Blanche's foot striking the floor, and nearly jump out of my skin when I hear her whispering to my back, "Arm bas, Marie." I lower my arm quickly, before Madame Dominique sees my mistake. But why is Blanche coming to my aid? Then, a little later, when I make the mistake of lifting my toes from the floor in ronds de jambe, from behind she whispers, "À terre. Ronds de jambe à terre." I take a chance and speak low my thanks. As always, she keeps her face forward, her chin level, her neck long, her arms soft, her footwork neat and fast. But afterward, as we turn back to facing the front, she smiles.

When I came in last night, Antoinette kissed my cheeks and said she was going out to the pork butcher to buy us some chops and then on to the sweet seller for red caramel pipes. Maybe because she was growing warm flitting around the room wrapped up in her shawl, there was a glow upon her cheeks, like the sun was shining in our lodging room.

Charlotte let go of clutching the sideboard where she was swinging her leg in a stream of battements en balançoire and gave her full attention to Antoinette. "Really?"

"We're celebrating," Antoinette said.

"Celebrating what?"

"Got myself steady work." Her eyes lit up. "I'll be appearing in a play over at the Ambigu."

The play was called *L'Assommoir*, and she was to be one of several dozen laundresses, appearing in a washhouse tableau. The work sounded not much different from what she already occupied herself with at the Opéra, except at a theater not nearly so grand and in a play anyone who ever opened a newspaper would know was based on a low-minded book. More surprising still, she was acting as a laundress, the very work she would have no part of in her real life. Even so, all evening she brimmed with pleasure, lost in her head—humming, laughing at nothing, even pecking Maman on the cheek when she came in from the washhouse.

It is what I am pondering at the barre as I make a relevé, an easy step where the heels are drawn up from the floor. But then Madame Dominique thwacks her cane against the barre, a fingerbreadth from my hand. "Second position, Marie," she says, letting out a great sigh, and the spot that sometimes aches between my shoulder blades glints red.

For the rest of the barre I cast gleeful Antoinette out of my head. Twice I see the mix of surprise and pleasure that sometimes comes to Madame Dominique's eyes; and once, when I stay balanced in an arabesque even as I lift my hand to just hovering over the barre, she nods, the tiniest of nods.

Monsieur Degas sits in his usual spot, going back and forth between scribbling in his notebook and leaning back in his chair, gawking like his own mother never did tell him it was rude. His eyes are piercing and quizzical, maybe a little lonely, tired, with pouches underneath. I cannot say about his mouth, hidden as it is by his muddle of a beard, but with the way he thinks nothing of staring, it would not surprise me in the least to hear snappish words fall from his lips. It is a little creepy the way he watches, looking underneath my skin, the way he does not have the decency to look away when I happen upon his gaze. Today I have felt it plenty, boring through me, hot on my flesh.

When Madame Dominique calls us to the center, Monsieur Degas picks up his chair and sets it down again at a spot where he has a clear view of me in the second row just behind Blanche. So blatant, his shifting spots. So bold, like scrutinizing a skinny, bare-armed petit rat is the most natural thing in the world. The other day I worked up the nerve to speak to

Lucille, a lazy girl with a tipped-up nose, who does not care enough about dancing to be mean. "He's harmless," she said. "Give him a smile. There are sugarplums in those sagging pockets of his."

Another girl—Josephine—not so well liked by the others with her different-colored sash for every day of the week and slippers that have not been darned a hundred times and mother always watching, always fussing with her darling's hair and sitting up taller when it is her turn to cross the floor in a chain of piqué pirouettes, said, "Maman saw a gendarme going into his building in the rue Fontaine. She stopped him. He said people were complaining. Too many comings and goings, too many little girls visiting Monsieur Degas. And now Maman says I'm not to speak to him."

Josephine's arms are soft and round, no jutting elbows, no spiny knobs atop her shoulders, and I thought of how a sugarplum would mean nothing to her, and I remembered Antoinette, too, how she nagged that I was getting too skinny and me snapping back there was nothing in the larder except the skins of an old onion and a pair of empty shelves.

With Madame Dominique done working us for the day, my legs are close to collapsing. We were made to stay late on account of half the class landing heavy-footed. "More like ogres than sylphs," she said. She looked sternly at Lucille and Nelly when she announced the extra hour, this after correcting Lucille three times and Nelly four and each of Linette and Josephine and Alice just once. Blame could not be put on Blanche, not with Madame Dominique praising her saut de chat and calling the rest of us to the front of the practice room to marvel at the precision of her footwork, the toe exactly meeting the knee midair, her chin a little lifted, her face proud, bearing the snootiness of a cat, and probably it was not the fault of Chantal or Margot, who both got tiny nods, or Perot or Aimée, who each earned a touch on the shoulder as Madame Dominique walked the length of the barre during ronds de jambe. For me, there was the thwack of her

cane and then the tiny nod as I held my arabesque, and afterward in center, there was the smallest smile, so slight it might have been a twitch. Next
class I will draw her gaze, hold it still. Next class I will give to Madame
Dominique a saut de chat rivaling that of Blanche.

I take pitiful care undressing, loosening my sash, folding it into quarters, rolling it into a coil, like it is spun from pure gold instead of worn-out
silk. Antoinette says it is six francs for a new one, six francs none of us
have. I tuck my rotting skirt into my satchel like a doting mother laying
down a sleeping child. All the heeding means I am last to leave, last to
begin the descent from the practice room, starving and aching tired.

Six days a week I creep along the staircases and corridors, passing
rehearsal halls and the courts of the decorators and the loges of the chorus,
the coryphées. My ears fill up, empty, fill again—the whining strains of
violins, the jerked quiet trill of a diva, the rampaging shriek of a maestro,
the foul mouth of an étoile. Most often I like making the descent, touching
the walls, considering that I am part of it all, this Opéra, so thick and
sturdy and permanent, this place of trickery, this place of limbering and
sweating, leaping and turning, cramming every bit of learning into my
bones, getting ready for the examination where any one of us in Madame
Dominique's class can be elevated to the quadrille and the Opéra stage.
Today though I suck my bottom lip, wondering. Into which half of the
class do I fall? Pitiful, heavy-footed ogre? Lighter-than-air sylph?

I loop around the first landing of the staircase and see Monsieur Degas
at the foot of the next flight, sitting on a little bench. For a moment my
breath is gone and I remember Antoinette telling me not to loiter and
all the mothers with their watchful eyes. The trick will be not to stop, to
take the steps three at a time. I have done it before, soaring down the
flights, when I was bursting with the news of being put up with Madame
Dominique.

The scuffing of my flying feet draws Monsieur Degas's weary eyes,
and as I round the landing with the bench, he calls out, "Mademoiselle van

Goethem," and I do not like it that he knows my family name when Madame Dominique always calls me Mademoiselle Marie. "Please stop!"

He stays put, his backside planted on the bench, and unaccustomed to defying gentlemen, I come to a halt halfway down the flight of stairs, a decent head start.

He gets to his feet, and with me sidling two steps lower, he plops himself right back on the bench. His hands, palms facing down, make a tiny shuddering movement, a gesture meant to still.

"I'm called Monsieur Degas," he says, putting his hands in his lap. "I'm a painter."

"I know," I say. "Ballet girls scratching their backs."

Even with his bushy beard, I can tell by his eyes, he is swallowing so as not to laugh. "Will you take my card?" he says, pulling one from the pocket of his rumpled waistcoat. "I'd like you to model. My address is there. I pay six francs for four hours."

"Perot won't do it?" I say, thinking of her small, white teeth in a perfect row.

"Perot?" His brow wrinkles up.

"Josephine is pretty, but her mother says she isn't to speak to you."

His eyes flicker closed, then open again, wearier. "Your face is interesting," he says. "And your back. Your shoulder blades are like sprouting wings."

"I'm skinny."

He pushes aside my skinniness with a wave of his hand, and I wonder about a sash the color of a robin's egg. He leans forward, holding out a card. "You'll take it?"

I climb three steps, pass my hand between the spindles guarding me from him and take the card. He is in the rue Fontaine, number nineteen, as close as the pork butcher and the fruiterer.

"You can read?" he says.

"Of course." I say it haughtily.

"Come after your Thursday class, one o'clock."

"I'll see if Papa allows it." And then, imagining the most brutish fathers are the ones who lift barrels all day long, I add, "Once he gets home from the coopery." Immediately I suck in my bottom lip, clamp down with my teeth. Have I learned nothing about lying from Antoinette?

Monsieur Degas's weary eyes tighten a notch. He knows I do not have a father, except one buried in the ground.

LE FIGARO

19 NOVEMBER 1878

ÉMILE ZOLA AND L'ASSOMMOIR

In spite of the fact that we are fed up with *L'Assommoir*, the novel that Émile Zola dipped his quill into the chamber pot to write, we are forced to talk about it, since everyone talks about it, since it is a topic of conversation from the tavern to the salon.

Zola claims serious scientific aims in writing the story. He calls it a naturalist novel, literature of our scientific age, a novel of observation, a work of truth, the first novel of the common people that does not lie about their authentic smell. He has conducted an experiment, he insists, by placing into a certain milieu a young laundress of a certain temperament. From there, the story advances according to the rules of science rather than his own fanciful whims. It turns out the way it must, given the twin forces of heredity and environment, their authority in determining the young laundress's fate.

L'Assommoir has been attacked with unparalleled brutality, accused of every crime—with good reason. Zola has taken an unworthy corner of life, catalogued every detail of it, placed a woman of poor character there. The kindest comment I can offer on the result: It is tedious as rain. The harshest: It is pornography. There is far too much brute fact in *L'Assommoir*—pages describing sexual and digestive functions, pages devoted to vulgar language, pages detailing brutality and drunkenness. We should sooner introduce smallpox into our homes than permit this unclean volume to come into contact with our pure-minded maidens and innocent youth.

Antoinette

I was looking for Émile Abadie since the springtime when the trees were all loaded with blossoms and new grass was underfoot and there was rain enough to make me want to cry every day that passed without seeing that scrub-brushy hair of his, those stout fingers that put the plumpest of the mussels into my mouth. The scorching pavements and bleaching sun of summertime were come and gone; and the trees were stripped bare, waiting for the mantle of winter to set in, when finally I set eyes upon that boy.

Earlier I was at the Opéra where I bothered to climb the million stairs and poke my head into the practice room of Madame Dominique. There was Marie, looking like one of the graces, even in that greying skirt. The way she was holding her neck long and floating her arms from one position to the next and arching her back better than any of those other girls, it made me ashamed that I ever held a speck of doubt. It put a lump in my throat, thinking of her someday upon the stage and elevated beyond the second set of the quadrille. For a tiny moment, I wished I was not so quick to snap at old Pluque, but then I remembered doing a thousand retirés, all for the sole purpose of learning the exact position of the toe against the opposite leg, and that bit of longing was gone quicker than a swatted fly. I went next to the practice room of Madame Théodore and held open the door but only a little bit. Charlotte was getting flayed for replacing a changement—the simple jump Madame Théodore asked for—with a trickier jump called an entrechat. I would have to say to Charlotte again about doing what she is told, about showing off, about her talent shining through without embellishments, without an entrechat stealing the place of a changement. Then it was off to see Monsieur Leroy and getting myself signed up for another month's worth of afternoons blocking, another week's worth of evenings holding my head bowed and gliding silently across the stage, pretending to be a nun in the opera *Robert le Diable*.

Afterward I headed to the Ambigu Theater, where the word was a group of gentlemen were putting on a play about the common people and wanting actors from the working class for all but the starring roles. They claimed such hiring would guarantee a production steeped in truth, but with the way they were touting the authentic actors, promising them to be of the like theatergoers had never before seen, I did not doubt the idea was hatched more as a stunt to draw attention than a wish to show the common people as they truly are. Either way, with one of my eyeteeth turning brown and my skirts so threadbare that I wear two at a time, I figured I was common enough to get myself a part.

The Ambigu was a half-hour walk past the Opéra, going east, first along the rue Poissonnière and then the boulevard Saint-Martin, but I deviated a block or two from that straight line. Arriving at the tavern where I drank cassis and red wine, those happy hours with Émile, I opened the door, peering into the gloom, waiting for my eyes to adjust. But just like always there was no Émile slouching on a high-backed bench.

It was back to the rue Poissonnière and feeling the weight of the day, the harshness of the wind. And like so many times before, I began recounting that months-ago afternoon—the way he said my eyes were like chocolate pools, the way he said "We're having such a lovely time," the way he was desiring me, the way I shoved him off.

When I got to the theater, my eyes wandered over the four stories, taking in the arched windows, the double columns, the statuary, nothing as grand as the Opéra. I was loitering, putting off going inside and finding whoever was in charge and proving myself to be of the like theatergoers had never before seen, when a wagon pulled up. My eyes went from face to face, taking in the sagging cheeks, the stringy hair, the home-rolled smokes, the black gaps where there used to be teeth. Authentic actors, sure as sure, rounded up in the faubourgs and brought to the Ambigu. I was about to dodge and find the lineup sure to soon grow long, but before I turned, my gawking gaze lit upon scrub-brushy hair creeping low on a forehead, black eyes sinking beneath the ridge of a brow. I was on the edge of calling out his name, but already Émile Abadie was leaping over the side of the wagon and loping over to me.

"Antoinette van Goethem," he said. "Been looking all over Paris for you."

With the jolt of it, I slipped to my saucy self. "Guess you didn't think to look at the Opéra."

"Can't."

"Why not?"

"On account of you," he said.

I crossed my arms.

"I went three times," he said. "That goat they got guarding the rear entrance, she wouldn't say where you live."

"Madame Gagnon," I say, my voice flat.

"Paid her ten francs to say you lived in the rue Saint-Séverin, and I waited there, watching steady for two days, before I knew it was a lie. I went back to the Opéra after that and she starts screaming, and the sergeant comes running from his post and she says I put my hand on her neck, and that sergeant, he says he'll be watching, that if he catches sight of me, I'll be getting a pair of shackles and La Roquette."

"Not worth a few days at La Roquette?" I said.

He lit a home roll and poked the butt end toward me.

"Still don't smoke," I said, holding my face from showing disappointment that lingering on every detail of our afternoon was not a habit for him. "And what are you doing here, Émile Abadie? Can it be an entire wagonload of riffraff is getting parts in the play?"

"They say they want the production truthful." He jutted his chin toward three gentlemen in good silk hats, all huddling over an open book just outside the entrance to the Ambigu. "Better me playing a low-ranking drudge than some actor with filed fingernails."

"I come to see about a part myself."

Then he was tugging me by the arm and hauling me over to those three men and saying, "That's the one in charge of casting, wearing the gloves. Don't say nothing about the Opéra though. They want us amateurs."

With not one of those three important gentlemen lifting his eyes from the book, Émile cleared his throat. "Monsieur Martin," he said and dipped his chin to him. "This is Antoinette van Goethem. She is wanting a part in the play."

With those other two now looking me up and down, Monsieur Martin said, "Mademoiselle van Goethem, allow me to introduce Monsieur Zola and Monsieur Busnach."

There was nothing snobbish-looking about the one called Zola. No, his face was large and fleshy and would not be out of place amid those making up the wagonload. His eyes were kind, and he dipped his chin. The one called Busnach, without the smallest pause, said, "She's perfect. Face of a laundress," meaning my looks were well suited to working half-undressed in steamy heat and entering bachelors' quarters to gather up what is soiled and scrubbing back to brightness the filthiest of underclothes. I lifted my chin, set my jaw, and old Busnach, he glanced away.

I saw the harsh look Monsieur Zola threw him, and after that the rolled eyes old Busnach gave him in response. Then Monsieur Martin got down to the business of laying out the wages and the schedule, which conflicted in every way with all I'd agreed to with Monsieur Leroy not an hour earlier. Monsieur Busnach saw the fidgeting of a girl trying to decide and said, "Tell me, Mademoiselle van Goethem, are we wasting our time?"

I stood silent, parting my lips to give them the idea that any second I would speak. Émile leaned close, said, "A bit of fun," into my ear, and I said, "Nothing wasted," to those three gentlemen. "You'll be happy to hear, I make a habit of being on time."

It is how I got to be a laundress in a play called *L'Assommoir*. Marie says the story is from a book Monsieur Zola wrote and got herself in a tizzy when I said about meeting him and then a further tizzy when I said I never heard of his book.

"Antoinette," she said, hands on her hips, chest all puffed up, "they wouldn't know how to fill up the newspapers without *L'Assommoir*."

I gave that girl a fierce look, one to warn her off gloating when, all those years she was busy with Sister Evangeline, I was off earning a wage.

"It's about a laundress called Gervaise, over in the Goutte-d'Or," she said.

I knew the neighborhood, not fifteen minutes away, a place where the lodging houses were at least as shabby as our own. I looked at Marie, about to say maybe I was appearing in a play about our own lives, but already her nerves were twitching. She shifted a hand to atop her belly, settling the flip-flopping beneath.

On my way to the Ambigu there is a bit a snow drifting down, melting to nothing on the pavements. I hold out my tongue, tilt my head back, catch a few flakes and laugh. I've got myself a sweetheart waiting at the Ambigu. We'd been rehearsing close to a month and still I was not entirely sure, but then a week ago, with a bunch of us authentic actors idling out front of the theater, having a few laughs after finishing up, I knew. Émile was there beside me and then his arm was around my neck and his wrist resting on my shoulder. With that arm of his staying put, I leaned into him a tiny bit and he shifted his weight in such a way that it was not possible to be closer than we were. I looked up at him after that, and he gave me a little wink, and anyone who saw would have been thinking, Émile Abadie is sweet on that Antoinette. His arm upon me, he was telling all the world.

There'd been a bit of groping and kissing before, even his hand beneath my blouse, nothing more, not until that day he put his arm around my neck in front of anyone who cared to look. An hour earlier we were sitting a ways off from the others in the dingy house seats of the Ambigu. He took my hand and put it on his trousers, the hard ridge beneath the buttons of his fly. A girl knows what to do, and I did it but only over his trousers and only a single stroke before I took my hand away. "Don't know about that, Émile."

"But you're my sweetheart."

I made my lips pouty, gave a tiny shrug, letting him know it was not near enough apparent to me.

Émile is out front of the Ambigu, waving me over and smoking with Pierre Gille, a boy I don't much like. He is always creeping up on the laundresses, putting his hands where they don't belong. His trap is filthy, a jolt, considering his delicate lips, his pale eyes and blond locks, the pretty dimple in his chin. Like Émile and the rest from the wagon, he is acting the role of a boozing laborer, but with those angel looks of his, I don't see how he got himself the part.

Émile puts icy fingers on my throat and looking proud like a rooster, says, "You going to warm me up, Mademoiselle Antoinette?"

"I got no use for chilly fingertips." I bat at his hand, give a pouty smile. Pierre Gille is standing there, smoking, seeing how it is with Émile and me. It won't make a difference though, won't put an end to the hushed, lowly words of Pierre Gille. "Your fig still throbbing, Antoinette? That slit of yours aching for meat?"

Émile drops the butt of his smoke, grinds it into the ground. He holds his arm out in such a way that I know it is for me to take and be promenaded like a lady in the Champs-Élysées. I link my arm with his, and a few steps away I say, "Those snowflakes falling down are a pretty sight."

"I watched you catching them on your tongue," he says. "Prettiest thing I seen all week."

Those sweet words hanging there, I go quiet, shy. I want to say something back, and last night I was lying awake, wanting to clobber snoring Maman and thinking up some sweet words for Émile. I came up with "I like that scrub-brushy hair of yours, tickling at my nose," but it was not good enough, not when the other day he pulled back from kissing my shoulders, lapping at my neck and put those stout fingers of his on that sunken spot between the ends of my collarbones. "This little hollow," he said, "tenderest place in all the world."

I halt a little, still hanging on to his arm, and look up into those two black eyes. "You're the prettiest thing in all my life."

"Pretty?"

"Sure."

"I got the face of an ape," he says, and it reminds me of all the nonsense talk of Marie. It makes me ache, such thinking, same ache as when I saw the rims of Charlotte's eyes shining wet over losing her silk rose, same as when I came upon Marie, bawling into her mattress over whether Madame Dominique was lumping her in with the ogres of the classroom instead of the sylphs.

"I wouldn't change a single thing," I say, putting my hand upon his stubbly cheek.

Inside the Ambigu the authentic actors lounge in the house seats, chatting, snoozing, doling out the cards for a game of bezique. It is what we been told to do until the play moves to the tableau preceding the one where we are onstage. Then it is off to the green room and keeping our mouths shut until the stage manager shoos us to the wings. The washhouse tableau, the one where I appear, comes second, but afterward, even with most of the other laundresses calling out their good-byes, today, like every day, I stay put in the theater. Émile goes on in the third tableau and again in the seventh, and with more than an hour in between, I wait and then the two of us slink away to our own little spot at the back of the house.

Émile says all the rules are meant to keep us from roaming and pulling the wool padding out of chairs and tugging lamps off walls and collecting what we can to pawn. He is always explaining what I can see just fine on my own. "Opening up your eyes," he says, and I keep my face looking interested. I nod. Why not, when it gives him pleasure, a feeling of such cleverness about the world? Lately those two sentinels they've got keeping watch been loosening up, and for two days now, Émile's been whispering in my ear about knowing a place, a storeroom with a lonely old chaise. "Such a lovely time," he says.

When he is done with the third tableau, he finds me lounging in the back of the house. Soon as he is seated, his hand is upon my thigh. "You'll come to the Brasserie des Martyrs tonight? A dozen of the boys are planning on a few laughs."

"Can't," I say, knowing the promises I made Marie and Charlotte, also that all evening Émile and Pierre Gille are going to be clapping each other on the back. "I got slippers to darn for Marie, and I told Charlotte I'd show her about making a postiche for her hair."

"Coddling them isn't helpful, Antoinette. They're better off learning to fend for themselves."

I shrug, and he strokes my thigh, and I feel a yearning and shut my eyes. "That lonely old chaise," he says. "I want to see you lying back on that lonely old chaise."

"Don't know."

His hand pats my thigh, leaves it for his own, and I feel a longing for that hand back upon my thigh, also patience wearing thin.

"And if someone comes upon us?" I say. Marie is always reading aloud from the newspapers, the gossip about the ballet girls and their love affairs or the bits and pieces about *L'Assommoir*. They are covering the finest of points—how Mademoiselle Hélène Petit is studying for her role of Gervaise in a real washhouse; how loads of theaters, thinking they were too decent, said no to running the play; how every costume and every set is exactly like Monsieur Zola described in his book. And all the fuss makes me think, indecent or not, *L'Assommoir* is going to be playing at the Ambigu for a very long time. It holds me back from the chaise, knowing I have more than nothing to lose if I get myself sacked. I have sisters counting on me at home.

Émile pulls a key out of his pocket, touches the pointy end to that sunken place at the base of my neck where a hundred of his kisses been put. "I'll be locking the door," he says.

"Where'd you get it?"

"Took it out of the lock. It was just waiting there for me."

I peek from under my eyelashes into his eyes and give a sugary smile. There is not much I would like more, and I want him to know, want him gripped by the idea of me lying back on that lonely old chaise.

"Not a soul's been in there for a hundred years," he says. "It's all cobwebby and full of dust."

"Tomorrow," I say. Another day of dreaming for him. And, for me, I've got to wash, to mend my drawers. Maybe it is even a chance to pinch something with lace from the basket of Maman. A bit of luck and she will come in from the washhouse carting linens for delivery.

❧ Marie ❧

I sit at our little table, wishing for Antoinette to come waltzing through the door, brightening up the room with her dancing eyes and bits of barley sugar popped into our mouths or stories of the authentic actors at the Ambigu, dead drunk and falling off the stage or pissing in the wings. Something is aflame inside the girl, glowing like she is. Just yesterday, as Charlotte and I grew fed up with waiting and sat down without her to a late supper of hard bread and broth, she poked her head around the door. "Going ahead without me?" she said, holding up a sack. "I should eat all these custard tarts from the pastry cook by myself?"

While I wait, Maman huddles on a mattress, sewing the torn neckline of her best dress, not bothering about me. "Bastard," she says. "Pawing and tearing like I got me a sewing maid at home." When she showed up in the torn dress a few nights ago, bellowing loud enough that she woke up even Charlotte, Antoinette said, "Don't know why you expect any different, slumped in a café, drooling absinthe." Maman stabs her needle now, catching her finger. Her work shoved aside, she collapses onto the muddled dress.

I stare down at Monsieur Degas's card, flat on the table in front of me, looking like a ticket to cross the river Styx. The nail of my forefinger tugs at the frayed skin alongside the nail of my thumb, and I lick away blood. Antoinette is overdue by an hour, which is getting to be usual for her, and tomorrow is the day Monsieur Degas expects me after class. I can wait no longer to seek a bit of advice and crouch beside Maman on the mattress, arms cradling my knees. "There is a painter," I say. "Madame Dominique lets him watch our class."

Maman looks up at me with woolly eyes.

"He said my face is interesting."

"You got the mark of my dearest." She rolls onto her back.

"He wants me to model," I say, cutting her off from starting in on my dear, dead sister. "Josephine's mother says to stay away from him."

With a clumsy flick of her wrist, she brushes the warning of Josephine's mother from the air. "Tell him you aren't undressing until he's got the fire good and stoked."

My surprise would not have been more if she spit up a hundred-franc gold coin. "Naked?"

Her chin dips a little, and she hiccups. "Good and stoked."

I picture myself shivering, Monsieur Degas's burning eyes roving over bare, gooseflesh skin. I lean my face in close to Maman's, wanting her to see me—a fearful girl, sucking on her lip. And I could swat her for the smug smirk on her face, her pride in such a useful bit of advice doled out.

"What's he paying?" she says.

I give her the coldest of glares; and, dull as a bag of hammers, she lifts up her eyebrows, waiting. "Six francs for four hours," I say.

She pats my thigh, like I am a dog done performing a fine trick. "You stick to the modeling," she says. "Nothing else."

A harsh wind licks at our tatty shutters, fills up the room. I leave Maman to wrapping herself in bedclothes and go back to waiting at the table for Antoinette. I know what is keeping her—the boy she brought around the other day. I did not like the look of him, all swarthy and shifty eyed. How had such a lowly creature brought merriment to Antoinette?

What was the lure that kept her staying out with him instead of coming home to supper with Charlotte and me?

At first he kept his hands in his pockets and acted like meeting Charlotte and me was nothing at all. Antoinette told him our names, and he gave each of us a piece of barley sugar, twisted, exactly like the ones she had given us the last couple of weeks, and I realized she had pocketed them from those he handed over to her. It was how I knew he was her sweetheart, that and the way he started poking her in the ribs, causing her to laugh and swat at his hands and act like she never before had so much fun. I watched his fingers trace the neckline of her blouse, and then Antoinette not minding in the least how he pulled her up against him, a hand groping her backside. No, she threw her head back and laughed again. She puckered up her mouth and kissed the air, and he drew her closer and kissed her on the mouth. It was like we were not even there, and I knew he saw us only as a bother, the little sisters Antoinette went home to at the end of the day. He ignored Maman, too, which did not seem right, even if she hardly looked up from the linens she was sorting for delivery.

I perk up at the noise of Antoinette on the stairs. She is hurrying because she is late; and in the scuttle of her feet I hear sisters to look after, a mother getting in the way, a sweetheart promising her a few laughs if only she was not always rushing off to the rue de Douai. I meet her at the door, and, seeing me there, lip between my teeth, she says, "What is it, Marie? You aren't looking well."

"Nothing," I say, wishing I had stayed waiting at the table. "I only wanted to see who was chasing you."

She closes the door. Puts her hands on her hips.

My stomach rumbles and, wanting to keep the complaint from her ears, I take a step back, but too late. Already she is sliding fingers along the ridge of her brow, the way she tends to with a headache coming on. "I got nothing more than a piece of barley sugar," she says, holding out a honey-yellow twist that surely came from Émile Abadie's pocket, and I think how Monsieur Degas's six francs would buy crackling for a week.

I take the twist, bite it in half, holding the sheared end out to her.

"Save it for Charlotte," she says. "I saw her on the pavement, running up and down with a hoop and a stick and two dogs nipping at her heels. The pork butcher and the fruiterer were slapping at their thighs and calling out 'Charlotte, you're faster than a fox' and 'Keep it up and those two dogs are dropping down dead.' "

When she mimics the pork butcher, she puffs herself up, making her cheeks round, her belly full enough that she has to prop it up from beneath. For the fruiterer she is nervous and twitching, eyes darting like there is a flock of howling specters flitting around the room. And with her aping so exactly right, I forget about Monsieur Degas, until she says, "Now tell me why you're in the doorway, all nervous like a hen?"

"Monsieur Degas wants me to model tomorrow."

She waits, ducking her head a little, like I should tell the rest.

"Maybe naked." I say it lightly, like I am not fearful of Monsieur Degas's burning eyes on my bare skin, but she appears no more concerned than Maman.

"You agreed to a price up front?"

"Six francs for four hours."

"More than fair." She nods.

"Maman said to stick to the modeling. Nothing else."

"That woman don't got the sense of a flea." She huffs like a blustering horse, turns her attention back to me. "Flesh don't mean nothing to him. Already he's seen a hundred naked girls."

But she does not roll her eyes and say Maman spoke drivel fit for the gutter like the rest of her slop, and it keeps me from curling up in words meant as balm. I let out a tiny sigh.

She goes back to stroking her brow, stopping only when she looks up and says, "I'll go with you tomorrow, just this one time."

"But he expects me early, at one o'clock."

"You'll go to the Ambigu after the Opéra and tell Monsieur Busnach I got a fever, a sickness running through the rue de Douai. Tell him no one's been struck down more than a day so he will not think of giving away my part."

"I don't know." I picture a man in a frock coat turning as I clear my throat, looking down his nose as I stutter through what I had practiced a hundred times, and I feel what some call butterflies but is really more like a hive of buzzing bees.

"Makes perfect sense," she says. "I get docked three francs. You make six with a chance of Monsieur Degas asking you back."

"What if he wants more than modeling?" I blurt it out, knowing I have two seconds before Antoinette turns away, tired to death of indulging a girl of thirteen.

"Then I'll snap his arm in two." With that she is off, opening the drawers of the sideboard, looking for a bit of cloth not too badly soiled, or a cup not too badly chipped, something to pawn, something worth the price of a small loaf.

The next afternoon I am marched down the rue de Douai and around the corner into the rue Fontaine. I was taking my time in our own stairwell, stopping to adjust the laces of my boots, when Antoinette tugged my arm and set me tripping and stumbling and working to free myself. "Enough with the dawdling," she said.

Charlotte is with us, too, looking miserable at being dragged along. When we get to the heavy doors of Monsieur Degas's building, Antoinette says, "Such sulking, Marie. Eugénie Fiocre herself wasn't too high and mighty to pose for Monsieur Degas," and Charlotte lets out a huff.

"Such nonsense," Antoinette says, scowling at the ridiculousness of one sister aching that she is not the girl upon whom Monsieur Degas's burning gaze fell and the other panic-struck that she is.

Inside Antoinette claps the knocker on a door with a small plaque: *Edgar Degas, Painter.* A stout woman with a broad, honest face and the apron of a housekeeper peeks around the door, and taking in the three of us—with our three shawls to take away and fetch and three sets of tracks to sweep up—makes a little tut. "Marie?" she says. "One of you lot is Marie?"

I poke up my hand, gingerly as a lamb, and she puts out an arm, awaiting the heap of shawls. "Over there," she says, pointing toward Monsieur Degas, looking off into nothingness with his chin held up by his palm. But the fierceness of his pondering keeps my feet glued to the floor, standing ever so still, and it is no different for Antoinette and Charlotte.

It is my first time inside a painter's workshop, and what hits me right away is the strong smell of turpentine and the clutter covering every speck of level surface, every crumb of open wall. The room is vast with sheets of sunlight coming through bare windows and a plain, sturdy table and long bench, both buried under a jumble of brushes and sponges and candlesticks and crockery and saucers of paint and bowls of water and ends of charcoal and boxes of pastels. There are a half dozen rickety chairs—two propping up canvases; another hung with a paint-smeared smock; another holding a rosewood box spilling over with tubes of color; another, with a splintered leg, toppled over on its side; the last, standing empty. The walls are painted with grey distemper and hung floor to ceiling with pictures, so many that if I was called away now I would not be able to describe a single one. There are more, leaning up against the walls, one edge on the floor, turned so the back of the canvas faces into the room.

"Don't blame me," the housekeeper says. "He doesn't want me touching a thing, and I'm not to sweep up, not with the possibility of dust settling in fresh paint."

She goes over to the table, heaps our shawls onto the single empty chair, and stands there, hands on her hips, eyes roving over the mess until they come upon a palette and two brushes. Holding them up, she says, "I'll clean these, no?" and Monsieur Degas leaves whatever thoughts he was thinking up and nods.

Eyes settling upon the three of us standing there, he lets out a great sigh, wishing we were not spoiling the tranquility of his afternoon. "Your back," he says to me. "I'll start with your back." He points to a screen in the corner of the room. "You can undress there."

Standing light-headed behind the screen, fingers fumbling with the drawstring of my blouse, I hear Monsieur Degas hollering for the housekeeper—Sabine, he calls her—to tidy up a couple of chairs for the sisters I brought along. But the thought of stepping out from behind the screen, hands struggling to hide the two little mounds budding on my chest and the crop of black hair appearing between my legs, with my sisters watching—one wincing and the other with eyes wide—is not something I have the guts to do.

Holding my gaping blouse shut, my eyes sweep the corner of the room hidden behind the screen. I take in the washstand, the tiny iron bedstead, the rumpled sheets, the spirit lamp on the floor, the scrap of paper tucked beneath it with a drawing of a ballet girl sitting slumped on a bench. There is no more to the picture than a few lines of charcoal, a few dashes of pastel, but the exhaustion of the girl is there, in the ribs heaving with each breath, the late night and bellowing father of the evening before, also the long hours at the barre, striving to balance a second longer or land a little softer, the aching thighs rolling open even at rest. I step out from behind the flimsy screen. "You should go," I say to Antoinette, to Charlotte, holding her neck long, her arms en repos, waiting for Monsieur Degas to look up from the table, the rubble he is picking through.

Antoinette takes a long breath. "You're sure?"

"But we're here now," Charlotte says, her voice telling how close she is to stamping her feet, with Monsieur Degas not yet having noticed her grace and Antoinette already standing up from her chair to leave.

So as not to change my mind, I undress in a hurry, eyes glued to the exhausted girl, to the thinness of her limbs, to the softness of the pastel highlighting the ridge of her collarbone. I inch out from behind the screen, clutching at my nakedness.

～ Antoinette ～

In the lobby of the Ambigu, I blink away the sunshiny day outside and see old Busnach striding over all high and mighty to scold me about missing yesterday. I feel the urge to sneer, but thinking better than to fuel his flame, I wrap my shawl tightly, warming myself against the sickness lingering from yesterday. It don't come naturally, swallowing sneers and holding my tongue, but I've got to. Along with a regular wage, the Ambigu means afternoons in the company of Émile. I let my breath out slow, but old Busnach only nods his head and thanks me for sending my sister with the news that I was not well. "The rest don't bother," he says.

Today we are rehearsing like it is the real opening night, with costumes and the stage all set up like a washhouse for the second tableau. There are tubs and hot water and steam rising up and dirty linen and clotheslines that work and my own arms plunged up to the elbows in suds, and I cannot help but think of the money spent making something those theatergoers could find in pretty much any shabby street.

L'Assommoir is mostly about the pitiful life of a laundress called Gervaise, and the tableau with me onstage covers the part where she finds her lover, Lantier, is gone off and then fights with Virginie, who lured him away. When we were first rehearsing the brawl, Busnach wanted Virginie down on the floor, soaking wet and drawers ripped open, and Gervaise paddling her bare rump with one of those beaters for thrashing linens clean. It is what Monsieur Zola wrote, or so says Busnach, and he is always going on about *L'Assommoir* being a naturalist play and needing to be exactly true to life, just like the book. Always, he is reading out such and such a page and being a stickler about every last thing, drivel like the first bucket of water wetting only the shoes of Virginie. I was wanting to tell him I been to the washhouse a hundred times and never once did see a woman getting spanked with a paddle on her bare rump. But there won't be a paddled bare rump, not with the censor bureau breathing down the neck of Busnach. Even so, with the dousing and the name calling and the blow that brings blood to the ear of Virginie, the theatergoers are going to be applauding on their feet. Already opening night is sold out, and not a speck of doubt, half those tickets were bought on account of all the fuss over the washhouse tableau.

We are starting at the top of the tableau, with the authentic actresses scrubbing away and the three real actresses—the ones with speaking parts—calling back and forth, waiting for the entrance of Gervaise. But Monsieur Busnach is not happy. No, he is shaking his head and clapping his hands sharp. "We need another line up front. You ladies," he says, and I know he is addressing the authentic actresses because he calls the real actresses by name. "You ladies, tell me something you might hear at the washhouse."

I poke up my hand after a while, when none of the others do. Never have I been one for licking boots, but old Busnach is not so bad and Émile is watching and a little idea flew into my mind and already I know the smile it will put on his face. "Mademoiselle?" Busnach says.

I fish in my tub, look up crossly, and then in a good, strong voice say, "What's become of my bit of soap? Somebody's been and filched my soap again."

There is giggling from the authentic actresses, all of them knowing the way soap gets lost in sudsy water, the way it melts, the way it is easier to tell your mother it was pinched than that you were careless again.

"Perfect," Busnach says. "From the top."

He points a finger, and I say my bit, and he is grinning like he never does.

After that we make it through the rest of the tableau without the barking of Busnach, and it just about slays me, looking morose and bored and tired while wringing linen and wiping my brow and pushing up the soggy sleeves of my blouse. Busnach liked my bit about the soap enough to put it in his play, and now I have myself a speaking part.

I glance up at Émile from time to time, sitting in the third row, his feet propped on the seat in front of him, a home roll dangling from his lips. He don't wink or nod, like he usually does. He does nothing to show a bit of pride. Maybe in the storeroom, between those tableaux when he is required on the stage, atop the chaise that is not a bit lonely, not no more.

The first time he took me there, I could see the trouble he went to, shifting crates, wiping away dust, leaving a scarlet hair ribbon on the chaise, all so I would feel like a queen. There was none of the yanking and mauling, like behind the tavern that time. No. He lifted me up and set me on the chaise. And then, kneeling beside, he put the heels of his hands under my chin and spread his fingers on my cheeks. "Just looking into those chocolate pools of yours," he said. I kept my eyes locked onto his, feeling no need to glance away. He put his lips on the sunken place between my collarbones. He touched the drawstring of my blouse and said, "Can I?" and I said, "You can," just like we were countess and count. Blouse fallen from my shoulders, I watched his eyes grow large, taking in the paleness of my breasts, the rosiness of my nipples. His mouth tender upon my gooseflesh skin, his hands gentle upon my midriff, I closed my eyes, feeling like the most adored creature in all the world.

There was a tiny bit of clumsiness, both of us fumbling with the fancy clasps of a garter filched from the basket of Maman. The rest of the time we were there, in the storeroom, kissing and stroking and cleaving, until my back arched up from the chaise and I was shuddering, with him collapsed upon me and shuddering right back.

I suppose he knew I was no virgin, but I wanted to say how my first time was nothing, not compared to the lovemaking upon the chaise. I looked into his eyes, knowing he would see the glossiness of my own, and when he did not smirk, I said, "It felt like getting adored."

"Well, Mademoiselle Antoinette, I intend to keep up the adoring every single day."

And now, every day, just like he said, I find myself laying back on that old chaise, and that bit of time in the storeroom, while tableaux four, five and six are taking place, is the sweetest hour of my day, the bit I put my mind on when the morning is cold and I don't want to get up from the nest of my mattress, the bit I recount as I shut my eyes for the night.

It is on my mind even now, in the loge of the actresses, as I wiggle out of my washhouse costume. Any delay and it means being stuck waiting for the wardrobe mistress to come back from the room of costumes, her arms freed up for another load of aprons and skirts.

Marie's been poking fun, laughing and saying I've got a sweetheart, that she never knew me to take such care with my hair, with my toilet. Well, she was until I told Émile to come up the stairs to our lodging room and show himself to Marie and Charlotte. The second he was gone, Marie leaned her back up against the door and said, "There goes a beast," and then she started in about him disrespecting Maman, not shutting her trap until I said in my harshest voice, "Not a single word more."

"Bluebeard," Charlotte whispered.

"What?"

"Oh, nothing. Like you said, not a single word more."

"It's a story I told her," Marie said, "about an ugly king with a blue beard. He made a habit of hanging his slaughtered wives from hooks on the wall."

"I can tell you the end," Charlotte said.

I shoved a chair from my path, and she took a step away slow, but I could tell her legs were ready to spring. How was it those two girls could not see what was before their own eyes, how Émile made me step light and breathe deep? The feeling was like the one that comes on the first day of spring—with the sunshine and warm breezes and the whole world waking up—except that the day kept coming again and again.

The next morning Marie was up even before the tiniest fragment of light was reaching between the slats of the shutters. I dozed on the mattress, listening to the sounds of the rue de Douai stirring awake—the clatter of hooves; the rattle of cartwheels on cobblestones; the morning greetings of the baker, the fruiterer, the pork butcher.

Sprawled on her back, Maman was snoring, her breath catching, resulting in great snorts. Despairing about her ever shutting up and bracing myself against the coldness of the room, I heard Marie come back in, taking care to shut the door behind her without a sound. She stood there, blinking away, getting accustomed to the grey light, and then on seeing me awake, startling and jerking a small package wrapped in brown paper behind her back. "Our morning meal?" I said, knowing it was no baguette she was hiding there.

"What?"

"Behind your back."

"Shush. You'll wake up Charlotte." She sucked on her lip a second. "I've been over to the rue Laval to see Madame Lambert."

According to Madame Legat, downstairs, it was a tincture of Madame Lambert saved Lucy Roux from birthing a child. "Marie," I said, "the odds are far against it, in case you never heard." But inside, I was remembering my nervousness a week ago, those long days of stewing until my courses finally came. I even made a bargain, one I was dim enough not to keep. Let the bleeding start and I would say to Émile about pulling out in time.

"It's vinegar," she said, tossing the package to me. "Soak a bit of cotton and put the wad up inside before you let that boy have his fun."

I imagined her blushing and chewing her lip and hardly able to explain to Madame Lambert what it was she came to get. "I know it wasn't easy, going to Madame Lambert." Color crept onto her cheeks, and she said she was getting water and, in a flash, was out the door and upon the stairs.

When I next went to the storeroom with Émile, I said about those bits of cotton and the vinegar and asked him not to look. "Don't mind in the least," he said, turning his back. "I got to salt away a few sous before we set up house." Oh, I was grinning, even as I fumbled, drawers around my knees. The future he saw for himself included me. He imagined us settled down, a lodging room of our own, and I was more than just another girl, a link added to the chain.

So now I have two tiny chores on those days I get myself adored, which is very nearly every single one. The rinsing out of those bits of cotton, I take care of at the pump, six doors down from our lodging house. For the laying out to dry, I spread the cotton flat upon the highest shelf of the larder. The second tiny chore is putting a little x in the calendar I snatched from the desk of Busnach. The old goat deserved it, the way he kept me waiting for near half an hour. He excused himself from the office, saying it would take but a minute to sort out why the payroll clerk could not find my name on his list. But I could hear him chuckling in the corridor with Monsieur Martin and not rushing in the least. He won't be missing that calendar. No. On his jumbled desk it was opened up to a page showing the fluttering leaves of autumn, when already the trees were stripped to bare.

The covers, front and back, are leather with gold lettering, and the pages inside, scalloped and painted up with snowflakes or strawberries or leaves turning yellow and red, depending on the month. Every page has a few words, too, fancy letters with curlicues becoming vines sprouting with leaves. Someday I might ask Marie what it all says, but for now I keep it in a hiding place, wedged into a gap between the chimneypiece and the wall, only getting it out late at night to make a little *x*, marking the day as a day I was adored.

Why do I bother keeping track? Maybe I only want to make use of the calendar, pretty as it is. Maybe it is my way of marking a day as momentous even if it looks like there are going be ten momentous dates for every one left blank. It makes me happy, putting down an *x*, counting them up, seeing that there are now twenty-seven when yesterday there were only twenty-six.

Still basking in the rosy glow of getting myself a speaking part, I pull my washhouse costume over my head and tie the two ends of the drawstring at the neckline in a hasty knot. It is what we been told to do to keep the drawstrings from ending up on the floor. "Always rushing," says Colette, another of the authentic laundresses, one I have no fondness for, not with the flesh always spilling from her neckline, not with the way she is always brushing up against the authentic laborers, even Busnach, in the corridor when there is no need. Just the other day, she puffed up her chest and gave herself a little stroke. "Like peaches," she said to Pierre Gille. "Sweet on the tongue."

"I like to watch the play," I say, and it is true. After the washhouse tableau comes the descent of the laborers tableau, with a river of workmen coming into the city from the heights of Montmartre and Saint-Ouen. It is where Émile—a mason—first appears, crossing the stage in white canvas trousers with a trowel and a half loaf tucked under his arm. With the reddish glow of the gas lamps lighting up shops that match those of the rue des Poissonniers, it is easy to be tricked into thinking it is early morning in the Goutte-d'Or. If I don't dawdle—never mind sluttish Colette—with a bit of luck, I will catch the part where Émile halts mid-stage and blows a bit a warmth into his hands.

After that the tableau grows syrupy as caramel, with a roofer called Coupeau shunning the workmen stopping in at L'Assommoir for drink and half the time losing their reason in the bottom of a glass and not bothering to head back out to the forges and mills. He halts Gervaise on the pavement and declares his true love and hears her pretty little speech about the life she wants for herself. "My ideal, you know, would be to work quietly, to be sure of always having some bread, a clean room, a bed, a table and two chairs," she says. "That is all I should like, and life would be happy." Syrupy talk, but I admit to a lump in my throat and I saw tears in the eyes of some of the other girls. I imagine it is a dream we all dreamt, and with Coupeau proposing marriage and promising Gervaise she is going to get her wish and her saying yes, it don't seem impossible she is lifting herself from the gutters of the Goutte-d'Or. It is the place in the story brimming with hope.

Colette huffs, a sneering sort of huff. "You like to watch Émile Abadie."

"So."

She shrugs, pulls her washhouse blouse up over her head, exposing me to the full glory of her swelling breasts. "A brute."

I shrug back.

"Don't you think?" she says, and I imagine her lip split open, a look of shock upon her face.

"I don't. Not in the least."

Her mouth twists a little sideways and her pretty teeth grip her fleshy bottom lip in a look of concern. "He isn't respectful."

I give my washhouse dress a good snap, narrowly missing her chin, and toss it onto the pile collecting on the outstretched arms of the wardrobe mistresses. "He don't care for flesh shoved in his face is all," I say, before leaving Colette with her skirt pooled at her feet.

Like always, after finishing his tableau, Émile comes out to the house seats, still wearing the trousers of a mason. But he don't sit down beside me and start with the teasing, the little kisses snuck onto my neck. Today from the aisle at the end of the row, he jerks his head, telling me to come. And then he don't have the decency to wait up for me. No, I scamper behind, calling out when we are two flights of stairs from the others. But still, he don't wait.

"Well," I say, catching up to him at the door of the storeroom, only because he is taking a moment to twist the key in the lock. "You like that bit about the soap?" But he don't laugh or say I ought to be asking Busnach for credit in the program or a private loge. No, he glances up from the lock, wearing a hard face.

I sit on the chaise, rather than laying back. He steps toward me, and I look away from his cold eyes, and next thing his hands are upon me, yanking at my arm until I am twisted around and hunched over the chaise with my backside facing him.

It is all over in a minute—my skirt lifted, my drawers yanked down, his hardness thrusting inside me from behind, then him buttoning up his fly.

It takes but a second to coax my drawers and skirt back into place, a further second to get myself seated on the chaise. The quiet between us blaring loud, I sit there, knowing I have every right to stand and boot him in the shins, to spit in his face. "What was that?" I finally say.

He runs his fingers through his scrub-brushy hair. "I got needs, Antoinette. I was looking high and low for you yesterday and you were nowhere to be seen. Didn't get a wink of sleep last night," he says.

I draw myself up to my full height, put my face close to his. "Don't you ever try nothing like that again." Or, what? It will be the end of me? I will scold him, again, and lift up my skirt the very next day? "Isn't right, Émile. Not in the least."

"You can't stand me up," he says, unable to lift his gaze from the dusty floor. "Can't bear it, Antoinette." He peeks out from under his brow. "Where were you, Antoinette?" He reaches toward my cheek, all hesitant, and I do not pull away,

"Spewing into a bucket dawn until dusk," I say, holding my voice meek. We are made up now, and I will not tell about escorting Marie to a modeling job, not with his badgering about me coddling her and Charlotte. Keeping them babies, he says, when the only thing for the poorest girls of Paris is to grow up faster than fast. Another time I might have said the truth. I might have said how those girls don't have much of a mother at home, how I want to be, for just a little longer, the shield that keeps them from the harshness of the world. But right now I don't have the strength of even a tin plate.

1879

~ Marie ~

Turns out, Monsieur Degas is not so bad, maybe a little peculiar, but he would not hurt a flea. Oh, he is grumpy, more so with Sabine than anyone else. He hollers when he cannot find a brush, when he cannot find a clean rag, and then hollers again when he finds his pastels all lined up, back in their box with all the crumbling ends gone.

Today he is happy. I know it the minute I walk into his workshop and see three of his canvases turned around instead of facing the wall. It means that at this moment he is thinking less harshly of his work, also that I have something new to look at while posing hour upon hour.

After half a year of my modeling maybe twice in a month, he has grown obsessed, and now I must come every day. Always he wants me standing upon one of the dozen platforms spread around the workshop. He needs to observe me from above and below, he says. It began on a scorching Tuesday, when I arrived to find him staring for a good quarter hour at a pastel of me holding a fan.

For that drawing he had wanted me posed in fourth position, my right foot ahead of my left and the toes of both feet pointed out to the sides. That part was nothing, easy, with my hips naturally loose and getting more so with all the exercises for training the legs to roll outward in the hip sockets. The hard part was the way he had one of my hands holding up a fan and the other reached around the back of my head like I was massaging my neck. It was the kind of picture he liked to make—a ballet girl hot and tired in the practice room and taking a second to fan herself while awaiting her turn. At first I had to work up a look of exhaustion, but with Monsieur Degas caught up in his sketching and being extra miserly with the breaks, I held the pose for most of three hours and soon my neck genuinely ached and my shoulders truthfully slumped. The more tired I became, the merrier he grew. I slouched a little more. "Yes. Yes," he said. "Yes. That's it."

On that scorching Tuesday, he just kept pondering the picture, the thumb of his one hand tucked up under his chin and his forefinger curled against his mouth. His eyes were narrowed, and he looked to me like a man on the verge of thinking up his greatest thought. I stood there, dying of thirst and telling myself not to move, not to draw his attention away from that picture, not until Sabine was back from fetching a glass of water.

After I had drunk my fill, he cleared his throat and said, "All right. Mademoiselle van Goethem," which was his way of saying I would be posing naked, that I was to go behind the screen and get myself undressed. If we were starting with me in practice clothes, he would say, "In your skirt, then, Mademoiselle van Goethem," and I appreciated the tiny kindness of him not barking out how I should strip bare.

He began a set of drawings—simple drawings, lines of charcoal with a touch of white pastel—with my finger resting on my chin; with my arms spread wide and holding my skirt; with a hand upon the fallen strap of my bodice, as if pulling it up. Sometimes he wanted my hair off my neck, up in a chignon. Sometimes he liked it hanging down my back in a braid or even loose, collected over a shoulder. As often as not, I was naked. The part that never changed was always he wanted my feet in fourth position, and

I began to wonder if that was the great idea he was thinking up while he stared at that picture of me with the fan: that I would stand in fourth position and he would draw me a hundred times.

Afterward, I would look and see spindly arms upon the page, jutting hips, a chest hardly different from a boy's. I would peer deeper, trying to see what Monsieur Degas did. And maybe I looked too hard, because in the scribbled black lines, I saw a girl vulgar in her face. I saw not a chance of grace upon the stage.

Today he wants me naked in the same old fourth position but with my hands clasped behind my back and elbows held straight. It is the way he wanted my arms yesterday and the day before that, and I am beginning to think the position is just as cast in stone as that of my legs. "Chin higher," he says. "Ah, yes!"

He moves to his easel, picks up his charcoal and my skin prickles under his hot gaze. Then I spend an hour getting rebuked for my chin dropping, my back swaying, my elbows relaxing, even the teeniest little bit. Today he makes a habit of moving his easel over a few steps and drawing me from that angle and then moving it over again, always telling me to stay absolutely still, which twice makes my nose twitch at the thought of a sneeze coming on. "If you've got to blow your nose..." His voice is threaded through with annoyance. He sweeps an arm toward my satchel, leaning up against the screen, as if I am free to fetch the handkerchief he knows is not inside. When I dare to lick my lips, he hurls a stick of charcoal at my feet, which will later make him yell, accusing Sabine of hiding the charcoal he cannot find. He keeps up with the sighing and moaning and grumbling, but the periods of quiet in between grow.

I dream of sausage rolls for supper and think how Blanche, who has begun walking home with me after class, pretended not to care in the least when I told her how I am wanted at the workshop every day. It makes her jealous, me being singled out, even if it is only Monsieur Degas, when she is used to Madame Dominique always choosing her. I shift my mind to one of the paintings turned around from facing the wall. There is a mass of ballet girls in the back corner, adjusting skirts and stockings and staring down at their feet. At the front are more ballet girls, three, one fiddling with the bow of her sash; two sitting down, with their skirts arranged behind them so as not to crush the tarlatan. I know a ballet girl modeled for each of the figures in the painting, because once Monsieur Degas explained how the drawing of me with the fan was a study for a larger work. The girl reaching around to her sash, with the tipped up nose, might be Lucille, which I am sorry to say would mean Monsieur Degas is not too particular about the girls he picks for modeling. Every day she is scolded for her lazy, shuffling feet. "You are French," Madame Dominique says, stamping her cane. "Our style is refined." About the other girls, I cannot say. There are close to a hundred in the dance school and more than that in the corps de ballet.

In the painting, the girl sitting on a bench draws the eye. Her shawl is blaring red, and you can see misery welling up. She is off by herself for one thing, and she is hunched over, maybe even wiping away a tear. Maybe she cannot keep up with the class. Maybe her sister came in late the night before, when already the grey light of morning was slipping through the shutter slats. Maybe she heard her laughing in the stairwell, saying to a boy that, yes, on Sunday afternoon, those few free hours allowed the working girls of Paris, she would go to the Rat-Mort when that woeful girl wanted her sister to spend the time with her. Maybe she woke up to the noise of her mother vomiting up absinthe. Her feet are cut off, which is a habit of Monsieur Degas, something a little planning could fix. And he always leaves swaths of blank floor instead of filling a picture up. Like as not, it is the reason his pictures do not get exhibited with the finest of the artwork at the Salon. It does not help, either, that he makes us ballet girls look common, with our yawning mouths and knobby knees and skinny arms, even though it is what we mostly are.

If I was not afraid of losing out on six francs, if I had a bit of nerve, I would tell him I want to look pretty instead of worn out. I want to be dancing instead of resting my aching bones. I want to be on the stage, like a real ballet girl, instead of in the practice room, even if it is not yet true. Does he not know people want something nice to hang upon their walls?

He calls out for his midday meal, and I expect like every other day Sabine will bring a dish of boiled macaroni and a veal cutlet, and I will wrap myself in my shawl and sit myself down with one of the old newspapers he puts behind the screen for me ever since I worked up the nerve to ask.

Once I am covered up, I say, "That girl in the front, the one in the red shawl, she looks beaten down, like she isn't at all ready to face the class about to start."

He nods.

"Maybe her papa died."

He looks at me then, for a long time, with the softest eyes, and when Sabine finally appears, pushing open the workshop door with the fullness of a hip, he says to me, "You're fond of veal?"

A warmth swells for Monsieur Degas, who snaps and yells but has the soul of a lamb underneath, who is sorry he hurled the charcoal. "I'm hungry enough to eat my own lips." And then he smiles from behind his bushy beard.

I sit at the table, upon a long bench, and carve up what has to be the largest piece of meat ever set before me, and savor every bite, except that I see Monsieur Degas glancing up from the morning's drawings spread before him and holding back from hurrying me along. But then, by a stroke of luck, Sabine comes back into the workshop and using her sternest voice announces a Monsieur Lefebvre is here, that she will show him in.

Monsieur Degas lets out a mighty sigh. "I don't take callers while I'm working."

"He came from Monsieur Durand-Ruel's gallery," she says, hands firm upon her hips. "He is wearing a fine coat. Cashmere. Legion of Honor rosette in his buttonhole, too." And plate of veal before me, I make a little wish for her to hold firm to her ground so I will have a chance to finish up the meal.

Monsieur Lefebvre's fine coat does not hide the boniness of the man underneath. It hangs from his shoulders no different from the way it would fall from a length of doweling. His silk hat shifted to his hands, he makes a little bow. Strands of silver hair fall forward, loose of the heavy pomade meant to keep it in place. He is in the middle of shaking Monsieur Degas's hand and saying how he admires the pastels, the oils, most particularly the ones of the ballet girls, when his gaze falls upon me, my mouth full of veal. "Mademoiselle van Goethem from Madame Dominique's class," he says, and I dip my head, keep my eyes on the floor. Why does he know my name?

"I take an interest in the petits rats," he says to me and then to Monsieur Degas, "I find myself glimpsing beyond the jutting collarbones and red hands of their awkward age. Nothing pleases me more than smoothing the passage from the school to the quadrille and on through the ranks of the ballet."

"Ah," says Monsieur Degas. "When I found her in Madame Dominique's practice room, I thought her shoulder blades were like sprouting wings."

He clears the patch of table just beside me and moves a sheet of grey wove paper showing three views of me to the spot. In a few scribbles, I am drawn, once from the back, once from the side, once from the front, always naked, always standing with my feet in fourth position, my hands clasped behind my back. When Papa was alive, I made a habit of undressing behind the square of worn-out linen strung across the corner of our lodging room. And in the last year, with him gone and the square of linen thought to be more useful upon the mattresses and me almost fourteen and the mounds of my chest swelling, I turn my back to Antoinette and Charlotte and Maman, dreading one of them caring to joke.

The drawing I mind most is the one from the front. It is not so much the smudge of grey where my legs meet or the line of charcoal turning, tracing the budding mounds of my chest. It is not so much my nakedness. I hardly mind posing undressed, not for Monsieur Degas, not anymore, and thinking back to the way I quaked the first time, it makes me wonder what a girl can get used to, how the second time is easier than the first and the third time easier still. What I mind is my lifted chin. My comfort with the upward tilt is that of a girl posing in the quiet of a workshop, posing naked, yes, but before a man who has seen her nakedness thirty times before. It shames me, Monsieur Lefebvre looking down at the drawing, never guessing how I cringe even when Sabine comes into the workshop. That face looks to be the face of a girl wearing a proper blouse and a skirt reaching to the floor.

Monsieur Lefebvre's gaze lingers on the wove paper, lingers long. Eventually he removes his gloves and reaches a long finger toward the drawings. It quivers, hovering over the spine of the one showing me from the rear, then lands, tracing the curve of the charcoal line from between my shoulder blades until it is lost in the fleshiness of the rump. His pink tongue licks the corner of his mouth, and sitting there, upon the bench before the table, my spine arches away, the tiniest amount. "Ah yes, sprouting wings," he says.

His attention moves from the drawing to me, and I study the veal cutlet on my plate. And then the two of them talk like I am not even there: The way my elbows and knees are too large for such slender limbs. The protuberance of the muscle running from my hip to my knee. The paltriness of my brow. If I was brave like Antoinette, I would make some crack about did they notice the way I had a pair of ears. But me, I wait, holding myself straight because slouching is worse than spitting according to Madame Dominique.

"Let's see those wings, Mademoiselle van Goethem," says Monsieur Degas. "Show us that graceful, childish back."

Does he mean for me to bare my flesh to Monsieur Lefebvre? Does he mean for me to drop the shawl from my shoulders right here, when always in his workshop I undressed behind the screen? I look up, and he turns his palms to the ceiling with impatience upon his face. Six francs for four hours. The pay is good and the four hours not yet up.

My back facing the pair of them, I let my shawl slip from my shoulders, but I hold it pressed tight against my chest in front. There is the sound of breathing and then a finger, this time, on my own flesh-and-blood spine and me, in an instant, much faster than a thought, flinching away from it. Someone lurches closer, a rushed, abrupt step, and I know that finger has been jerked farther away from my back.

"Come," says Monsieur Degas. "I'll show you a finished piece."

They turn, and I pull up my shawl, wrapping it tight. So quick, I had flinched. Quicker than a thought. Like Marie the First knew, before anyone, about the reaching-out finger—Monsieur Lefebvre's, I am almost sure.

He stays another half hour, looking at pictures, writing a little in his small leather book. But the mood in the workshop has shifted to jittery, and it is nothing more than good manners keeping him there. Twice, Monsieur Degas shows a painting and then changes his mind, turning it around so that the two of them are left looking at the empty side of a canvas stretched over a frame. "Not finished," he says. The second time Monsieur Lefebvre reaches to restore a flipped-over canvas, Monsieur Degas barks, "No. Just leave it," and then, more gently, "It requires more work."

After that the workshop grows quiet, with the two of them speaking few words, their voices snappish when they do, their arms folded over their ribs. Before leaving, Monsieur Lefebvre comes over to the table and, even if he is older than my own father, bothers to say good-bye. I scramble to my feet. He makes a tiny bow, and I catch his scent of a room closed up too long. "Until next time," he says.

Until next time? What does he mean? That he expects to come upon me at the Opéra when never before have I laid eyes on the man? That he will seek me out? No. He only wanted to appear noble, to let me think for a minute the great divide between the two of us did not exist, like there was the possibility of friendship between a man wearing the Legion of Honor rosette and a girl with a protuberance of the muscle running the length of her thigh.

"Such an unpleasant man," says Monsieur Degas once Sabine has closed the door behind Monsieur Lefebvre's back.

She scowls, says, "You aren't polite."

Monsieur Degas points a finger in my direction and waves it to the spot in front of his easel, whisking me back to work.

Antoinette

It being a Monday, the Ambigu is closed, and Émile's been saying for a week about the fun we are going to have at the Brasserie des Martyrs, with a dozen of us authentic actors meeting there at nine o'clock. Already I polished up my boots and gave myself a good lathering in our tiny tub and took from the satchel of Marie those silk flowers I pinched, back when she was first meeting old Pluque, and yesterday I pleaded with Maman to take my best skirt to the washhouse and launder it with the care she does the best of silks. And I have a new blouse, filched from her delivery basket, wrapped in a sheet of brown paper, stashed on the highest-up shelf of the larder where no one would go searching, expecting to find a crust of bread.

Soon as I turn onto the rue des Martyrs, I make out Émile, leaning up against the wall of the brasserie, having a smoke and laughing with Colette. She puts her hand upon his chest, only for a second, before trailing it across the fleshy plumpness on her own. I hold my breath that Émile don't reach out. But no, he only pulls on his smoke, and a lungful of air rushes from my nose.

With me nearly upon them, Émile steps out from the wall. Hand upon my cheek, he says, "Well, look at you," and I feel a smugness rising that Colette heard his words. She leans in, makes a show of kissing me, like we are long-lost friends. Tilting her head toward the door, she says, "Suppose the others are inside." Then, leaving, she gives a little wink. "Come on in when you start missing me."

"Don't like that girl," I say to Émile.

He puffs out a ring of smoke, and then he is leaning in and nuzzling at my neck and saying, "Aren't you smelling extra sweet."

Inside the gas lamps are flaring, but with so much smoke the room is cast grey. All the divans are velvet with carved legs, and the oak of the long tables and benches is gleaming away. And never before did I see anything like the jumble of the prints and looking glasses, the statues holding up the doorway lintels, the gilt moldings covering up every speck of wall. It makes my head swim, so much to see, all at once, plus it smells a mishmash of tobacco and beer, kitchen grease and onions, damp mop and boots.

We pick our way over to the table crowded with a dozen boys I know from the Ambigu. Colette is wedged between Paul Kirail, his trimmed hair stiff with pomade, and Michel Knobloch, his dim face dull as gutter water. Five times that boy stood in the prisoners' box of the court. Five times he's been sent off to prison, convicted of some petty crime— vagrancy, assault, theft. To hear him tell it is to wonder if he don't know the difference between a verdict of guilty and President Grévy himself threading the red ribbon of the Legion of Honor through the buttonhole of his lapel. No matter the look of boredom upon the faces all around, he blathers on, recounting the cherries he stole, the trail of pits the gendarmes followed to the alleyway where he was gorging himself behind a cart. Émile saying, "You're thick as two planks," don't stop him. No, he carries on, about those cherries not being ripe and his belly seizing after getting locked up in a cell. Pierre Gille is there, too, wearing a cravat and a silk waistcoat over a pressed white shirt. "You're looking a dandy," Émile says.

Pierre Gille lifts his eyes from his glass of beer. "Can't say the same for you. Not in the least."

Émile juts his chin. "That shirt of yours still hot from the irons?"

Pierre Gille smirks, looks me in the face. "I see you brought your mattress."

Émile puffs a breath out through his nose. "I see you are all alone."

Pierre Gille picks up his glass, swallows the last of his beer. "Not for long."

"Another?" It is the way it is with the two of them, all insults and drinks bought.

"Course."

"And the rest of you?" Émile says.

With that, seven of the boys are lifting up their glasses, draining them dry while the offer lasts.

Émile and I settle onto the bench, filling the gap beside Michel Knobloch that those arriving earlier were wise enough to leave. None of us have seen Paul Kirail in months, locked up as he was for pickpocketing a gentleman who bothered to chase him down the Champs-Élysées for a measly five francs. He takes the smallest of sips, wipes a speck of the froth from his mustache, with a handkerchief, no less. "I'm reformed," he says when Émile mentions about him finishing up his time. "Prison is no place I ever want to see again."

Peering over the lip of his sweating glass of beer, Pierre Gille says, "Too many fellows want you as a wife?"

The others laugh, and Paul Kirail starts picking at the cuffs of his shirt. "I enlisted," he says. "Be living the life of a soldier at the garrison over in Saint-Malo soon enough."

"Saint-Malo?" Michel Knobloch says. "I believe Papa was in his youth one of those thieving pirates of Saint-Malo—a corsair."

Émile sets down his glass, pulls his fingers tight into his fists and says, "That, Knobloch, I doubt very much."

"You calling me a liar?" It is what everyone's been calling him for a hundred years. That boy, he don't have sense enough to make up a lie a single soul would mistake as true.

"You lie like you breathe." Émile returns his attention to his beer.

"It's nothing new," says Pierre Gille.

The eyes of Michel Knobloch gallop from face to face. Some turn away, sheepish. Others stare back with chins bobbing up and down.

After a long gap, Pierre Gille swirls his beer, says, "The king of France protected those corsairs. He kept them from being hanged, so long as they sent a portion of their haul his way."

"Imagine that," Émile says. "Plundering and no chance of waking up a guest of La Roquette."

"No chance of trading the stink of Paris for the salty breezes of New Caledonia," Pierre Gille says.

I know where the talk is going—to the luck of all those convicts transported to New Caledonia, a far-off island colony of France, to carry out the hard labor of cutting down forests, building roads and harvesting sugarcane. More than once I heard Émile discussing the life there with Pierre Gille, who claims to know all about it from the cousin of a friend. An inmate keeps his head down and mouth shut for two years, or so says Pierre Gille, and next thing he knows, he is doing the light work of sewing prison garments or cooking up the sizable portions of meat the prisoners get served three times a week. He said, too, about the labor there being paid with a cut of the wages held back until an inmate gets himself released. Then he is handed over the nest egg, large enough to buy a patch of land for planting and harvesting himself. The government, he said, wanted only to establish a foothold in the land.

Pierre Gille lights himself a smoke and, speaking loud enough for all the table to hear, says, "The cousin of my friend got the guards there liking him well enough that he ended up as gardener to the warden. When his time was done, that warden, he gave him his own patch of land. He got to use his prison wages for a pair a mules and a cart." He swallows a mouthful of beer. "And the guards, none of them are above selling on the outside what the inmates arrange to steal. That cousin of my friend, before he was a gardener, he was a cook. He made himself a fortune pilfering the rum the inmates get four times a week. The bookkeeper was happy enough to take his cut and cover the whole business up."

"The guards are merciless with thumbscrews and whips. That's what I heard," Paul Kirail says. "They punish the inmates by sticking them in a pit without a speck of light."

Pierre Gille blows a puff of smoke into the face of Paul Kirail. "You only got to stay on the good side of the guards."

Émile opens up his mouth and, with him always backing up Pierre Gille, it is no surprise when he says, "Serving time in New Caledonia is nothing more than an apprenticeship for settling the land." I hate when he talks such gibberish, like leaving me behind while he went off to some place neither of us could point to on a map would not bother him in the least. I know it is not true. But still.

Pierre Gille tilts his glass to that of Émile, and then the two of them clink rims. Michel Knobloch lifts his beer, reaching to join the toast. "Better than being shut up alone to pace the narrow limits of a cell," he says. "A fellow likes companionship."

Pierre Gille scowls. "About the corsairs," he says, ducking his glass away from that of Michel Knobloch, "they disappeared from France more than sixty years ago, well before your papa was even wiping his own ass."

Then all the boys, like wolves, are laughing, reaching, clinking beers, choosing the pack over the runt. Michel Knobloch looks caught between fleeing the brasserie and forcing a crack of laughter to his throat. Émile snuffs out the stub of his smoke, plucks that of Michel Knobloch from between his fingers and then Émile moves that smoke to his own lips. It gives Michel Knobloch the jolt he needs to push himself up from the bench, fists clenched at his sides. I put a hand upon the tensing thigh of Émile, and then—stroke of luck—the tavern keeper climbs to standing upon a chair, cups his hand around his mouth and calls out, "My lords, this is the moment when people who have been well brought up call for more drink."

Michel Knobloch turns away from the table, stomps off toward the door, and Émile says, "Well, then," and raises up his hand, beckoning the tavern maid.

A dozen glasses of beer he orders. And then he hands over a five-franc note, waves away the change. Always, when we are in the cafés, he is pushing away my few coins and saying, "You got rent to pay." Mostly it works to remind me that he don't. No, he's been lodging amid artificial flowers in the storage shed belonging to the father of Pierre Gille, and even so, he don't appear to be putting anything aside for setting up house, like he said. I say nothing, not with those boys from the Ambigu gathered all around, just feel a hotness creeping into my cheeks. The tavern maid makes a show of blowing him a kiss, but she don't get so much as a dipped chin back. Pierre Gille rolls his eyes and calls out after her, "I got a squeeze for that lovely rump of yours even if my friend here don't."

"You're a pig," I say.

"Weren't you saying you wanted to suck on a bit of pork crackling the other day?"

"Must've been old Paul here," I say, even if it is not right, picking the boy least inclined to answer back.

Pierre Gille looks down that pretty nose of his a good while. Then he shrugs and says, "I see the beer is making you brave, Mademoiselle Antoinette."

After another glass of beer for me and two more for each of the others, I stop thinking about what cutting thing I should've said back, and I feel a growing warmth, like a circle of light shining upon these friends of mine and Émile. The boys start forgetting themselves, turning right around in their chairs and leering at the few girls in the brasserie. Colette is giddy, making a fuss over the silk waistcoat of Pierre Gille, going on to Paul Kirail about how plenty of women like their men in uniform, even bothering to admire my hair, which I have arranged in a puffed-up chignon with a black ribbon running around the edge and the silk flowers of Marie tucked in at the back.

Émile is laughing, making a habit of touching my hand, clinking glasses, and we are having such a lovely time. But then Émile orders another round of twelve, when between the two of us, we drunk no more than seven glasses of beer. "Émile," I say, quiet. "It isn't your turn." Always he is spending instead of saving up.

"Isn't your business." He reaches into his pocket and pulls out another five-franc note.

The tavern maid brings the beers. The beers are drunk up, and then Émile is calling the tavern maid over and ordering cassis all around. I swallow the cassis, twist sideways on the bench, away from Émile, who is slapping the table at the hilarity of every other word that comes out of the mouth of Pierre Gille and calling out for the tavern maid yet again.

Colette gets up from our table, makes her way across the room to a lively party of slumming gentlemen, judging by their polished shoes. The rue des Martyrs is one of those places that has people calling Paris the city of love, and the ladies sharing the table of those men—flesh escaping their necklines, lace of their underclothes in plain view—don't come as a surprise. But I gape at Colette, so chummy with all those boulevard tarts, so cool when a gentleman twice her age puts his hand upon the stocking her skirt is arranged to show off. Of course they are slinking off together before I even get used to the idea of her being a coquette.

At first I ignore the hand of Émile, beneath the table, secretly upon my thigh. But it starts creeping higher, and I bat it away.

"What?" he says.

"How much you got saved up, Émile?" I blurt it out.

He looks at me, blank.

"Not a sou. Isn't that right, Émile? Not a single sou. You going to offer me a home holed up with you and Pierre Gille in a storage shed? Is that it, Émile?"

Pierre Gille, he puts down his glass with enough of a thud to draw the attention of the boys from the Ambigu, even those already entirely soused. "Already harping, is she?"

"Certainly is," Émile says.

I grab at my shawl, feel the wetness of the corner left dangling in the swill of the floor, and get up from the bench, bothering to brush my breast against his arm as I turn away.

But outside Émile is not upon my heels. Of course not, not with all those boys gawking inside. It takes less than a count of three to remember about all those plates of mussels with parsley sauce I took from him, those glasses of cassis, those bits of barley sugar. Never once did I say no. The sniffles come, then the swallowing, the hot tears.

When I look up, Colette is not a stone's throw away with her back up against the wall of the brasserie and her arms around the neck of her gentleman. With me sniffing, both their faces turn to gawk. "Antoinette?" Colette says.

How I wish for a handkerchief. With a handkerchief I could blow my nose. And why don't I have a single one when they are there for the taking, by the handful, in the delivery basket of Maman? Then Colette is close, her gentleman calling out for her to come back. She gives me a handkerchief, and I see the *C* embroidered into the corner, proof of a girl making plenty more than the Ambigu pays.

"Colette!" her gentleman calls out, sounding like he is scolding a dog.

"One minute," she calls back.

"Thank you," I say.

"Boys can be a lot of trouble."

"It's nothing."

"Colette!"

"Open up your eyes and you'll see I need a minute with my friend." He stands stock-still a second, like he cannot quite believe such a girl speaking so harshly to him. Then he is gone, wandering into the blackness beyond the halo of a gas lamp.

"Go," I say.

She shakes her head. "Prefer a gentleman not too cheap to stand me a glass of champagne."

"I like your handkerchief." I rub my thumb over the tiny *C*.

"Keep it," she says. "Come back inside. Meet my friends."

But sitting among the boulevard tarts, the drawstring of my blouse undone, forgot, my head thrown back, my skirt hiked, and the gentlemen agog, awaiting pleasure, don't appeal to me, least of all now. No, I want a quiet life, like the one Gervaise dreamt up, a bed to sleep in, food to eat. And going back inside would mean Émile taking more jeering from Pierre Gille, and already I feel sorry about the harping, the carrying on, bringing him shame. "Émile wouldn't like it," I say. "And besides, I got friends to meet at the Rat-Mort." In truth I am going home to cuddle up with Marie and Charlotte. What I want most is to feel the breath of Marie on the back of my neck, to feel her stir, to hear her whisper, "You're home, Antoinette." I am not going to ask her about what I done—the harping, the stomping off. She would take my side, but I have this idea she would do so too quick, too hopeful that I came to my senses about that riffraff called Émile Abadie.

"That boy isn't deserving," Colette says.

It would be a waste of my own breath, explaining about being adored, about his fingers tender on that little hollow between my collarbones, about his hand finding its way to my own, atop the table inside the brasserie. But those words of hers, hanging there like lead in the air, my mind falls upon that first time in the alleyway and then lands with a thud upon that other time, when I chased him through the Ambigu only to be twisted around until I was hunched over the chaise.

I rattle my head. Away. I need away from chirping Colette.

Marie

At the Ambigu I part the dusty velvet draperies hanging in the entrance-way to the fourth-floor balcony, the lowly benches tucked up under the eaves. Right away an ancient concierge is upon me, tugging my shawl from my shoulders, and then pointing to an empty bench. It gives me a little jolt, such quickness, considering the veins like blue cord riddling her hands.

Last night Antoinette came in at what has become her usual late hour, and I woke up to her crouching over me and quietly calling out, "Marie? Marie, you awake?" This, when she knew I would be slaving at the barre in the morning, same as always, nine o'clock.

I let out a sleepy moan. "What is it, Antoinette? All of Paris burning down?"

"I got you a ticket for tomorrow night."

I sat up. Like the rest of the laundresses, she was promised a single ticket but only once they could no longer fill up the seats with paying customers. "You'll be shutting down soon?" It meant the three francs she was paid for each performance would come to an end.

She shrugged, looking a little cross. "Maman's been pleading for the ticket."

"I want it." I reached out from my nest of ragged linens and touched her knee. "I do."

"Can't complain," she said. "We been running close to a full year now."

Even in the dim light, I saw lips pulled thin, strained, and I knew she felt the looming hardship of her employment at the Ambigu coming to an end. "You'll get something else," I said, knowing it was true. She was quick-witted and venturesome and always she looked after Charlotte and me.

By the time I get myself slid over to the center of the bench, the concierge is back, with a little stool she tucks under my feet. She nudges a program toward me, and I say, "I've got one," and pull from my pocket the program Antoinette gave me at home. The concierge looks a little vexed, even more so when she holds out her hand and says, "For the service," and after a few seconds of nothing, I remove my feet from her little stool and push it back to her with the side of my foot.

The people coming to the fourth balcony are not so different from me, with their sagging cheeks and twisted teeth. "For the service," says the old concierge, causing pockets to be turned inside out, sous to be dropped upon the papery skin of her reaching hand. Just once a footstool was handed back, by a lady, who came in wearing, same as me, two shawls instead of a mantle against the cold.

With the orchestra stalls way down below, where the ladies have furs and the gentlemen pomaded hair and the concierges dresses trimmed with lace, and the benches way up here, and in between, the second and third balconies crowded with shopkeepers and tutors and clerks, it appears all of Paris has come out to get a look at *L'Assommoir*. Antoinette said she would not ruin the surprise by telling how the play turns out. So what I know is Gervaise is a laundress, poor and marked by a limp and left to fend for herself by a scoundrel called Lantier until a roofer called Coupeau shows up.

I lean a little closer to the stage, wondering if the heavy curtain did not just budge, like someone had begun leaning his weight into the controlling crank.

Finally the curtains part, and the applause starts up, even before Gervaise turns to the audience from the window, where she was watching for Lantier, who does not come back. And it starts up again, when Coupeau sticks his head around the doorframe and asks Gervaise if he can come in. The three cane-bottom chairs around a little table, the iron bedstead, the bureau with a missing drawer and the mantelshelf holding pawn tickets and zinc candlesticks, I read all of it is exactly as Monsieur Zola wrote in his book. It comes to me, sitting there, that I could be looking down upon our very own lodging room, except that Maman and Papa's bedstead went to the pawnbroker even before Papa took his last breath and Antoinette has too much sense to leave the pawn tickets for Maman to find. And there is Papa's sideboard, too, with all six drawers in place.

I just about fall off the bench when the curtain opens up on the second tableau and Antoinette, fishing in a tub with real steam rising up and collecting on her dewy brow, says, "What's become of my soap? Somebody's been and filched my soap again!" Everybody laughs. Everybody except me. I sit there, marveling that she managed to keep the surprise of getting a speaking part to herself. "My sister," I say to the lady beside me on the bench and point out over the balcony.

"The one who said about the soap?"

I nod, and then the woman is leaning over and whispering into the ear of the man with a waxed mustache next in line.

Antoinette mops her brow, beats her linen, shakes the suds from her hands, exactly like she is in the washhouse in the rue de Douai. I sit on the edge of my seat waiting and waiting for another word from her but it does not come and soon enough the curtain closes up on the washhouse looking so very familiar to me.

Émile Abadie crosses the stage in tableau three, amid a swarm of workingmen. Instead of walking with a bit of purpose like Coupeau, Émile saunters, stopping to blow warmth into his hands. In the next tableau Gervaise and Coupeau work day and night, finally saving up enough to get Gervaise a little washhouse of her very own, and I keep thinking back to sauntering Émile Abadie, a loafer, tethering Antoinette to a larder with empty shelves.

Monsieur Zola calls his book an experiment, and the newspapers like to say how he claims to have taken a particular woman and dropped her into a particular setting and then let the story unfold the only way it could, given Gervaise's temperament and the neighborhood of the Goutte-d'Or, what Monsieur Zola calls the milieu. The story unfolding before my eyes, it has to be a tale about working hard and getting what you want most—a little washhouse, an examination passed and a chance upon the stage—even if you are living on the lower slopes of Montmartre, in such a place as the Goutte-d'Or or the rue de Douai.

But then in tableau five, Coupeau falls while working on a roof and in tableau six he is drinking in the taverns and in tableau seven Gervaise loses her washhouse and her taste for work and finds one for drink. In tableau eight the baker is refusing her any more bread and the landlord is demanding the money he is owed and in the last, tableau nine, she is wretched. "There are some women who are very glad when they are taken off. Oh, yes! I am very glad," she says upon her deathbed, which is not a bed at all but the gutter of the boulevard de Rochechouart, not ten minutes from our lodging house.

Monsieur Zola's tale is not about getting a washhouse or a chance upon the stage. It is about being born downtrodden and staying that way. Hard work makes no difference, he is saying. My lot, the lots of those around me, were cast the moment we were born into the gutter to parents who never managed to step outside the gutter themselves.

In the fourth balcony, same as the rest of the theater, people get to their feet, stamping and hollering, hands cupping their mouths or beating together overhead. Not me though, I sit, quiet and still, and wonder about the people around me, the woman with the footstool taken from her feet. Did they not see? Did she not see?

I stay put on the bench, the pads of my fingers rubbing my measly brow. Even when the balcony is empty of all but me and the old concierge, holding her back as she stoops to pick up ticket stubs and greasy wrappings from the floor, I have not cleared my head of Gervaise. I see her huddling to keep out the coldness of a winter's night, also bits of paper fluttering down from behind the proscenium arch, landing like merciless angels upon her back.

Antoinette stayed behind with Émile Abadie, so I am alone when I open the door of our lodging room. The stifling heat comes as a shock after the bitterness of the night outside, after months of shivering, even under the bedclothes, and wrapping myself around one of my sisters to share our warmth. I take in Charlotte sleeping soundly on our mattress, the warmest of our blankets in a kicked-off heap at her feet. Maman is slumped over on the table, her arm serving as pillow to her head. In the corner the fireplace is ablaze, casting the room in a pretty glow, in warmth. Stepping into the room, I see the black hole of a missing drawer, like a gaping mouth in Papa's sideboard.

I drop onto a chair. A life, unfolding the only way it can, or so Monsieur Zola said. "Well, never mind about him." I whisper it to myself twice, the second time a little bit louder than the first. I push myself to standing up. I make my shoulders straight.

I have Madame Dominique's class in the morning. I have my chance.

1880

Antoinette

The widow Joubert is dead, bludgeoned to death with a hammer, according to the baker and the pork butcher and Marie, who should know, with that nose of hers always stuck in the newspapers she brings home from the workshop of Monsieur Degas. It is not right to speak badly of the dead, but old widow Joubert, she made a habit of snooty looks. High and mighty, she was, with that newspaper shop of hers, always putting on airs and chatting up the gentlemen buying their evening papers, always scowling when I was close, not even bothering to make a secret of watching me. What would I want with a lifted newspaper? Sure *L'Illustration* has got pictures, but when you cannot sort out the words underneath, those pictures don't hardly make sense. Still, I lingered near, if only to make her batty. But smashed ribs and a broken-open skull, teeth shattered to smithereens? No one is deserving of that. And so I stand huddling with the crowd gathered at the place where the rue de Douai, the rue Fontaine and the rue Mansart all meet up, at the spot where the shop of the widow Joubert is still shuttered closed.

By the time the mortuary carriage heads up the rue Fontaine, the pavements are lined three deep. It is not possible to see the casket, covered up as it is with bouquets and wreaths, one bearing the inscription *To Our*

Mother. It must be her two sons driving the carriage and their two wives, leading the women's procession trailing behind. At the spot just opposite the shop, one of those women lays a hand upon her heart and, weakness coming to her knees, staggers forward a few steps. As the crowd gasps, the other woman goes to her aid and the procession stops. The widow is to be buried in the cemetery up in Saint-Ouen, and when the staggering woman waves the brothers onward, they have the good sense to know she is not going to make it and escort her to the seat between them on the carriage bench.

The sun is dull and grey in a sodden sky, and I wrap my shawl a little tighter against the dampness of a spring not yet properly come. With winter lingering and the contribution of Maman little other than the reek of her hot breath, I don't know just where the wood to heat our lodging room is coming from, unless, of course, she takes it upon herself to burn up more of the sideboard drawers. *L'Assommoir* shut down the end of last week and Monsieur Leroy at the Opéra says there are not enough roles even for the walkers-on who did not abandon him for more than a year. Marie and Charlotte are getting paid seventy francs by the Opéra each month, and even if Marie is not visiting the workshop of Monsieur Degas so regular anymore, she's got herself a new job, at the bakery across the street, kneading the dough for eighty baguettes every morning between the hours of half past four and eight o'clock. It was a surprise, the boldness of Marie in looking for work, but the bakery taking her on was not. Forever the baker's son—Alphonse—went to smoke on the stoop of the shop at the exact time she passed by on her way home from the Opéra. More than once I watched that boy part his lips, working up his nerve, but Marie kept her eyes steadfast on the door of our lodging house instead of giving him a tiny look, the little nudge he needed to call out "good day." New job or not, that girl is turned stingier than a wolf and, every chance she can, bothers to tell about the slaving. "Tires me out," she says. "My legs are fine for dancing, though. But, oh, my arms ache."

The hardship of it—working alongside a nicely stoked oven, surrounded by the stink of fresh-baked bread. I said as much yesterday, and that girl, she turned her attention from rolling her knuckles over the knotted-up muscle of her calf, and said, "You aren't home enough to see my weariness. Always off with that boy, out half the night in the brasseries when you haven't yet found work."

"At least I don't got my own private stash hidden away." It was true. All of the three francs I was paid each performance at the Ambigu was long ago spent on rent and milk and eggs and the bit of pork put onto the table from time to time.

"I match what you used to contribute, and there's the baguette I leave every day."

"You keep an entire baguette for yourself." It shut her up, me knowing about her pay at the bakery including two baguettes, not just the single one put on the table for me and Charlotte to divide into three before Maman gobbled more than her share. Maman told me about being shamed near to death when she went to the baker on behalf of Marie, demanding a second baguette, only to find out Marie was already, every morning, leaving with two.

Her bottom lip disappeared into her mouth. "I'll put both on the table for dividing up tomorrow," she said. "I really will."

By nightfall I was feeling remorse and snuggled close to her on our mattress. Maman was God knows where and Charlotte was on the other side of Marie, breathing the slow breaths of sleep, likely dreaming up herself curtseying low upon the stage with a heap of hurled roses at her feet.

"About *L'Assommoir*," Marie said. More than two months come and gone since she was in attendance at the Ambigu, but still, like a half dozen times before, she was fixed on going over the play. "If Coupeau hadn't fallen and turned to drink, then Gervaise would've got her dream."

"Don't know about that. She showed a talent for picking the wrong sort of men. First Lantier, then Coupeau."

"So you're agreeing with Monsieur Zola?" Her back grew rigid against my breast. "About Gervaise's life turning out the only way it could?"

"It's a story." I said what I should've been saying from the start. "Nothing more." I put my fingers into her thick locks, gave a little rub. "The rue de Douai isn't quite so grubby as the Goutte-d'Or. You aren't Gervaise."

"I'm not pretty like her."

"You got twice the brains. I don't hear no one else thinking things through the way you do." I did not say about the colossal waste of time all her fussing amounted to, how it never accomplished a single thing except a thumb picked raw and a mind fully awake in the middle of the night, not to a girl sounding so sorrowful as she.

"You're not going to poke fun?"

"Not tonight."

She threaded her fingers between mine, and we lay still a long while, and I knew she was feeling my warmth, same way I was feeling hers. "All that money you're bringing in," I said, "where's the rest of it?"

"Don't want to end up like Gervaise," she said. "I really don't. I need meat on my bones, or I can forget making the quadrille. I can't be kneading bread and dancing and modeling and just allowing the troughs between my ribs to grow and grow."

"Maman? You're still giving money to Maman?"

She sucked in a deep breath, let it out slow. "I bought a practice skirt, at the pawnbroker. Got it for ten francs, and it's good as new."

"It don't add up, Marie."

"Josephine—the one with a different-colored sash for every day—her mother made arrangements for private lessons with Madame Théodore." She stopped and even in the darkness of the room I knew her to be sucking her lip. "I did the same for myself, twice a week. I'm behind, Antoinette. I got started late. And the examinations for promotion to the quadrille are only three months away."

That will of hers, it knocked me over, especially coming from a girl so inclined to doubting herself. "You're like Baron Haussmann, flattening half a Paris once he got it in his head to widen the boulevards." The air was thick with the ambition of Marie, trying to raise herself up from the gutter to the stage. "Keep that second baguette," I said. "Keep it for yourself."

The night was a long one, full of tossing and turning and a dream of Marie growing larger and me shrinking to a speck, and I wondered if what I saw was the view from the heavens, Marie approaching, me falling away. What was it made that girl want so much? She craved the stage. But why? And was there something lacking in me that I was over it in a week when old Pluque kicked me out of the quadrille? Was she truly meant for dancing, while I was not? Yes, that was it. But was I intended for something else? Then my mind went to those fifty francs, tucked into a little drawstring pouch and hung from a nail behind the sideboard of Papa. Émile came with the pouch the morning after I left him at the brasserie. He stood in the doorway of our lodging room and said, "It's not much. But you put it someplace safe."

What I was thinking, lying there, feeling each breath Marie took, was that not a single sou in that pouch of savings was put there by me.

Today is Saturday, my sixth day as an apprentice laundress, and the overseer, Monsieur Guiot, tells me I can expect to be working late. Everyone wants their best starched and pressed for attending Mass. "How late?" I say.

"Until you ladies finish up."

Already Maman was gone, leaving the washhouse after making a little show of putting her hand on my arm and reminding me about the widow Joubert getting bludgeoned just around the corner and being careful on my way home.

There are four of us left, ironing, one using a headblock and a little iron rounded at both ends for the fussy work of the bonnets, two more working away at a huge pile of shirts and petticoats and camisoles and drawers, and me, doing the lowly work of stockings and pillowcases and handkerchiefs. Ironing is the easiest of the jobs I been rotated through this week, and I was surprised when, this morning, Monsieur Guiot said, "The ironing table for you, Mademoiselle Antoinette." But now I know it was only that the ironers finish up last on a Saturday night. I look to the pile of damp linens keeping me from Émile, that boy I was planning to meet in a quarter hour, that scrub-brushy head of hair I have not dragged my fingers through all this week of working from seven o'clock in the morning until seven o'clock in the evening. From the stove, I pick up a hot iron and, like I been taught, scrape it across a brick and wipe it clean on the rag tucked into the waistband of my skirt.

Monday it was twelve dragged-out hours I sat alongside Monsieur Guiot in the overseer's booth, unpacking bundles of stinking linens, and watching him mark the items in his book, and then me stitching to the inside of each the colored thread indicating just who the linen should go back to once it was clean. I pricked my finger three times, bled onto two shirts and one petticoat, causing a brute of a laundress called Paulette—her sideburns reached around to form a mat of black hair on the underside on her chin—to gripe about the extra bleaching and my sloppiness. Maman gave me a shock by bothering to call out from a nearby zinc tub, "Don't hear no one grumbling about the extra work of picking that shedding beard of yours off the linens."

And then Tuesday through Thursday I was put at the tub beside that of Maman, and she showed the patience of a clock as she explained about starting with the whites and spreading the linens over the washboard and soaping one side before turning them and soaping the next. The linen was then to be pounded with a beater, rinsed, soaped a second time, scrubbed with a brush, rinsed again and hung soaking wet over the trestles where it dripped onto the tile floor, just slanted enough to drain away the slop.

Friday I was at the trestles, dipping the whites into a small tub of bluing and cranking the handle of a wringing machine, causing the linens to pass between cast-iron cylinders and the skin of my palm to blister and tear away. Maman made a bandage from a worn-out duster and whispered into the ear of an old woman with a scar cutting across her lip. Soon enough, that old woman held up palms yellow with calluses and turned away to crank the wringing machine, and I went to hang the wrung-out clothes over the brass wires of the drying lines. I cannot say for sure what got into Maman, turning her all motherly, but I suppose she was happy enough to have me back earning a steady wage and maybe just a tiny bit prideful about a daughter catching on so quick. Whatever it was brought about the kindnesses all week, it kept me from hurling linens into the face of Monsieur Guiot and trooping out the door.

I spread a pillow slip, the last of the linens in my basket, over the thick padding of the ironing blanket, and seeing the number of shirts still awaiting an iron, I send up a little wish, asking for the other ironers to see that there is no sense in teaching me about shirts, not tonight. "I suppose it's about time to see Monsieur Guiot about my wages," I say to no one in particular but loud enough for all the women around the ironing table to hear. "And just in time for the last Mass, too."

The stoutest of the women looks up from her work and licks her fleshy lips. "Monsieur Guiot," she hollers, and he leans his head from the overseer's booth. "It isn't fair, not a bit, you assigning an apprentice to the ironing table on a Saturday. And now she's got the nerve to suggest leaving first when she is the very reason we are so late tonight."

"Mademoiselle Antoinette," he says, with a sternness that don't match the rest of his face, "all the ironers stay until the ironing is done." Then he steps down from his booth, out the front door, and starts unfolding the shutters, closing us and the steamy windows of the washhouse off from the rue de Douai.

The griping ironer sends a little huff my way and drops a dozen shirts into my basket. Even with the zinc tubs empty and the boiler simmering instead of bellowing out hot steam now that the stoker is gone home, the washhouse is sweltering, steamier than the thick soup of Paris in July. I feel the heat of the iron-warming stove on my back, the sweat trickling down, the clamminess mounting under my arms, my breasts, between my legs. I smell the dank odor of my sweat rising up. A week ago the warmth of the place was a relief after the chill of our lodging room. But just now, with soggy underclothes clinging to wet flesh and time parading forward, trampling to nothing those minutes I need to cross the street to our lodging house, fly up the stairs and put on a fresh blouse before going to Émile, the boiling air is a curse.

Before Monsieur Guiot is through with the shutters, the laundresses are freeing themselves of neckerchiefs, loosening their blouses, hitching up their skirts. He comes in, rubbing his hands together against the cold outside, and don't appear in the least baffled by the naked arms, the bare necks. No, he goes back to his overseer's booth without a single word, and I loosen the drawstring of my own blouse.

I spread a shirt over the ironing table, and when no one bothers with a word of instruction, I dip my fingers into the cornstarch and water and sprinkle it onto the linen like I saw the others do. I run the iron over the collar, make a fold across each of the tips, and press till the creases are sharp, till the little triangles of fabric stick out like wings. My collar looks no different from those of the others, and I move on, running the iron over the front of the shirt, up the placket, across the buttonholes, which is not any more difficult than breathing air. But then the tip of the iron nudges a bone button and that button lurches away from the shirt to the thick padding of the table, all without making a sound. I hold myself back from snatching, from calling attention to that sheared-off button, the hole the size of a pea left behind. I pass a hand over the shirt, float it across the table, gathering up the button along the way. Then, with that bit of bone safe inside the pocket of my skirt, I run my iron over the sleeves and back and fold the shirt into a perfect square, tucking the section of placket with the hole up underneath, out of sight.

I move on to a second shirt, starching and pressing and folding, setting it atop the one with the hole where the button used to be. By the time I add a third square of crisp, folded linen to my stack, I feel smug about matching the pace of the others, each a full-fledged laundress. Grabbing another shirt from the pile, I let out a haughty huff. I take my iron from the warming stove, scrape it across the brick, sprinkle starch and wonder about swapping the ruffled shirt now spread before me for a plainer one. But it is not possible, not without raising the ire of those sneering laundresses. I lower the iron atop the ruffles, know there is no chance for them to come out anything but a creased mess, which turns out to be exactly true. I sprinkle more starch, wonder about arranging the shirt so that only the ruffle is caught underneath the nose of my iron. It works, more or less, except for those stubborn creases set in the ruffle by my own hot iron. More starch, more heat. Put the weight of my body onto that iron. Hold still, giving those creases a chance to flatten out.

"Antoinette!" It is the bearded laundress hollering my name and then knocking into me and grabbing at my iron. She holds it over her head, wanting to clobber, and my arms fly up. "Monsieur Guiot. Monsieur Guiot," she calls out. "Such a stupid, stupid girl. She burned a fine shirt right through."

Then he is beside the ironing table, staring down at the burned ruffle, touching the charred edge. His fingers jump to the colored thread stitched into the collar. "Monsieur Berthier," he says. "His missus won't accept a mended shirt."

I look at my tatty boots, the leather soggy and marked from a week of standing in slop.

The bearded laundress snatches at my stack of shirts. "Let's just see," she says.

She snaps open the one on the top of the pile and then the next, and I see her face twitching anger. No creases. No scorch marks. Collar wings pressed to exactly the same size. But then she is lifting my first shirt, her stubby finger tapping the hole. "Where's the button?" she says.

"Don't know."

"Don't know?"

I shake my head, feel that pocketed button heavy upon my thigh.

Monsieur Guiot examines the buttons still on the shirt, looks me hard in the face. "It's a week's wages, Mademoiselle Antoinette, to repair the hole, to replace the missing button, the burned shirt."

"At least," the bearded woman says.

I keep my eyes on my boots, knowing a single glimpse of her gloating face is enough to set me off. It is not a bit usual, me keeping my trap shut, not with all those eyes watching. Just ask old Pluque. But no way am I getting unjustly sacked again, not without first collecting what I am properly owed. I nod my agreement to Monsieur Guiot and a feeling comes over me, almost prideful, like I won a spat. He dismisses me from the ironing table, tells me to wipe down the wringing machine while the others finish up. "Thank you for your kindness," I say, making a little bow.

With Monsieur Guiot back in his booth and those laundresses who did not bother explaining a single thing back to work, I sidle past the ironing table, giving the bearded hag a look fierce enough that her eyes dart away. I pick up a bucket, and on my way to the spigot, I pluck, from the linens awaiting delivery, three shirts and a camisole with openwork and ribbon and lace. Émile won't mind me being a little sour beneath all the trimming, the silk.

It is nothing to unload those pinched items from my bucket into the alleyway out back of the washhouse, not when the only spigot is on the far side of the boiler, not when that sweltering cauldron blocks old Guiot's view of the alleyway door. And if he guesses it was me took his linens and, Monday morning, sends me into the street, I could not care less. There will be the weight of coins in my pocket, coins put into my hands at the pawnbroker after passing the shirts across the countertop, more than enough to make up for those wages old Guiot is keeping from me. I turn my mind from Marie, the way her face lit up when I said about going to the washhouse with Maman, the way it would fall if I were to get myself sacked.

Late, I gallop the five blocks between the rue de Douai and the Brasserie des Martyrs where Émile is waiting for me. With the night so brisk and the lacy camisole like cold water on my skin, I see silk underclothes are not useful, not when it comes to warmth. Their worth don't go beyond rousing a boy, rousing Émile. Oh, how I miss the old chaise at the Ambigu, the comfort of a warm spot, the padding beneath my back, the hour between tableaux three and seven. Nowadays I see my share of alleyways and stairwells and once the toilet of a dance hall up near the place Pigalle. It is strange, the way it is easier to appreciate what you had once it is gone from your life. Émile says not to fuss, that soon enough he will show me the greenery, the waterfall of the Bois de Boulogne. It will be the soft grass of springtime tickling my naked flesh.

Before I reach the brasserie doors, I see his back, also those of Colette and Pierre Gille, heading away. "Émile," I call out, feeling the sting of him not waiting for me. He turns around, lopes back. Casting an arm around my neck, he pulls me in tight to his chest, and I feel the warmth of his mouth against my hair, smell the beer and tobacco on his breath. "You were leaving?" I say.

"Been waiting more than an hour." He staggers back a step, gives a tiny smirk at showing his drunkenness.

"The overseer kept me late."

"It's only a washhouse, Antoinette." What he means is that I should've plunked down my iron and marched on out the door. "He owed me a week's wages," I say. I don't explain about not collecting a single sou. No, instead, I tell about the bearded lady, hoping for a laugh, and when that don't work, I say, "Look here," and open up my shawl, showing off my bit of fancy lace.

He puts a hand upon my breast, groping, and then his mouth is upon my own. His breathing changes, growing ragged, and feeling the hold I have on that boy, the drudgery of the week falls away and I open up my lips.

"We aren't waiting." It is Pierre Gille hollering from down the street.

He grabs Colette by the arm, but she shakes him off and calls out, "You lovebirds coming?"

Then Émile is yanking my arm, and I wonder if he would not heel and roll over if it was what Pierre Gille said to do.

We set out for the Élysée Montmartre, a dance hall not too far from the place Pigalle. The three of them are knocking into one another and talking nonsense, and Colette is lifting up her skirt and doing a little jig for no reason except to taunt Pierre Gille, who I can see is turning sour. Cannot say I blame him, with those pretty calves of hers flashing before his eyes, those heaving breasts only sometimes missing his arm, and then those dainty hands shoving him away. She holds her shawl high up, over her head, and spinning wildly, she hollers up to the nighttime sky. "It isn't free, Pierre Gille. Not for the likes of you. Not for the likes of Pierre Gille."

"Shut your trap," he says.

She moves her pouty lips to a fingerbreadth from his own. "You want some, Pierre Gille," she says, her voice velvety like the blackness of a sweltering night.

He leans in, his lips parting. She slaps his face, and then she is off, running down the pavement, howling, doubling over at the joke of it.

We catch up outside the shuttered-up stall of a fishmonger, where she is muttering to a scrawny, sniffing dog with a tawny belly and a grey snout. "Sit," she says and that old dog moves to his haunches, his ears lying back against the black fur encircling his face and reaching down his back almost like a hooded cape. He lifts one skinny paw up in front, awaiting a little pat. Colette stoops, taking up that skinny paw. With her other hand she rakes the fur of his back, and that dog, he arches his neck, half shuts his eyes, like the attention of that girl is the greatest pleasure in all the world.

Then it is the boot of Pierre Gille smashing into the arching neck of that dog. There is a single yelp, paws skittering backward, and a dog lying still on the pavement with his neck twisted in an unnatural way and blood running from his mouth.

In a flicker, Colette is standing straight, screaming, "Scum. Blackguard. Son of a whore." Her fists fly, striking the chest of Pierre Gille, his face, until he gives her the shove that sends her toppling to her rump.

"Murderer." I lunge, spit the word in the face of Pierre Gille.

He slaps me then, hard, my head jerking sideways, the skin of my cheek numb and then aflame, prickling with heat. I look to Émile, fearful of blows, smashed bones between boys with the hotness and bluster of liquor in their blood. But Émile, he don't move, not a speck, no charging, no fist thrust in defense of a stinging cheek. And my racing heart, it don't settle, not a bit. No, the slow, steady breath of Émile, it lights my fear like a bellows does a flame. Those whispered words—my most precious, my dearest sweetheart, my best darling—are none of them true? I slap Pierre Gille, wait for him to return the blow, for the salty taste of a split lip when it comes. I strike, again, because Pierre Gille is going to hit back and Émile is going to stir. He will pick me over Pierre Gille.

Then Émile is upon me, holding my flailing arms tight to my sides, saying, "Christ, Antoinette, stop with the show." Pierre Gille smirks, fishes in his pocket for matches and a home roll, and I send the heel of my boot, hard, into the shin of Émile. He drops his arms from holding me, and Colette whimpers, her face in the coat of the dog.

Pierre Gille lights up, leans his back against a shutter of the fish-monger, his foot propped beneath him like he is lapping up the sunshine of a summer's day. He takes a puff, holds out the smoke to Émile, and I remember a story Marie told me, one she knew from Sister Evangeline about a dove returning to an ark with an olive branch gripped in its beak. When Noah saw that olive branch, he took it as an offering from God, a sign of disappearing waters, a promise of peace. I told Marie I would be hurling that old olive branch back in God's face. Imagine, drowning the whole world, all except a lone family and the pigs and goats lucky enough to find themselves upon that boat.

Émile takes the smoke offered by Pierre Gille, moves it to his lips.

"Let's go," says Pierre Gille. "Had about enough of this pair of whores."

Émile takes a single step away from me, from Colette, the dead dog. Then he takes another and another, keeping pace with Pierre Gille as they shrink to nothing in the street.

LE FIGARO

26 MARCH 1880

CONCERNING THE NEW PAINTING EXHIBITED AT THE GALLERY OF DURAND-RUEL

BY EDMOND DURANTY

From the trunk of the old tree of art a new branch emerges, an art that is wholly modern. The new painters on display at the gallery of Paul Durand-Ruel—Edgar Degas, Édouard Manet, Pierre-Auguste Renoir—have forsaken the tradition of painting scenes from history. Instead they seek to capture moments of everyday life in our modern age.

Along with fresh subject matter, there is a new focus on truthfulness. The new painters have said farewell to the body treated like a vase, with an eye for the pretty curve. They seek to know and to embrace the character of a subject, to portray it faultlessly. A back makes known temperament, age and social position. A hand reveals the magistrate or the merchant. A face's features tell us with certainty that a man is dry, orderly and meticulous, rather than the epitome of carelessness and disorder. As the new painter strives to reveal character, the neutral or vague background disappears. The trappings that surround a subject indicate his wealth, class and profession. A figure sits at the piano, irons at a worktable, dodges a carriage while crossing the street or waits in the wings for the moment to enter the stage. The new painter's pencil is infused with the essence of life, and his artworks capture the true story of a heart and a body.

Let us hope the slender limbs of this new branch of art thicken, that tender leaves multiply to a lush canopy.

～ Marie ～

Today it feels like the connection between my brain and my feet was cleaved with an ax. Antoinette did not come home Saturday night, and of course I worried and dreamt up the worst. A second woman, a tavern owner, was murdered, stabbed to death, a week ago. Antoinette knew all about it, and even if she ordered me and Charlotte to be off the streets by ten o'clock, it did not keep her from stumbling home in the black of night. I lay there amid a tangle of linens, filled up with fear about Antoinette being bludgeoned with a hammer or pierced full of holes. This, after a day of kneading bread and my regular class at the Opéra and my private one with Madame Théodore, then laundered linens to deliver late in the evening, some as far away as the third arrondissement, when Maman's carrying on and knocking into furniture made it clear she could not do it herself.

Nothing was improved by the light of day. Charlotte was feverish and crying for Antoinette, who showed up at midday, looking greener than pea soup and with her lips still carrying the stain of tint. I could not bring myself to ask, could not bear the answer I feared—that the lure of staying out with Émile Abadie was greater than the lure of coming home to Charlotte and me. I thought of the hundred ways Antoinette looked after us, how she mended our stockings and brought us eggs and arranged our hair and rouged our cheeks and managed to get us past Madame Legat at the Opéra door, all in the hours before she showed us to Monsieur Pluque. She accompanied me to Monsieur Degas's workshop that time I was afraid and made sure I was not late. She said a hundred reassuring things—*L'Assommoir* was nothing more than a story, my forehead was no different from that of anyone else, no chance would I not be elevated to the quadrille. She climbed the stairs to the practice room and saw the unsteadiness of my fouettés en tournant and afterward taught me the trick of picturing a taut string pulling me up taller from the crown of my head. She paid the rent owed to Monsieur LeBlanc, put meat in our bellies, knew what to pawn when they went empty too long. And I felt ashamed that I did nothing nice in return and made a promise to myself that I would, soon. Most of all, though, I was scared. Staying out overnight was more evidence we were losing Antoinette.

The next night was no better. For endless hours I held a cloth to Charlotte's brow, until she finally said, "I'm hungrier than a goat," and gobbled up the pork cutlet somehow produced by Antoinette. Charlotte drifted off after that, without a word of thanks, and it made me think again about how ungrateful I was myself. By then midnight was come and gone, and I worried I would slumber too deeply and not wake up in time for my eighty loaves. I looked into blackness, and wondered about Antoinette and the pork cutlet and where she had spent the night, and waited for the clickety-click of cartwheels on cobblestones that would tell me it was time to get up.

So far I have managed to muddle my way through the barre and three adagios without drawing attention to my faltering, my heavy legs, my absence of heart. I was first in the practice room this morning, which is not often the case, not with the bakery. Sometimes I stayed a few minutes extra because the macaroons were not yet cool and the baker's son, Alphonse, wanted my opinion on the cocoa or pistachios he had added to the egg whites. Were the macaroons too bitter now? Too dry? Would I like a second? He wanted me to be sure. I did my best to answer honestly—he had been so gentle and patient in teaching me about the baguettes. But always, I knew the barre awaited, that Madame Dominique closed the door on any girl arriving late.

All alone, I lifted the watering can and sprinkled the floorboards closest to the barre and then, like always, I placed my feet in fifth position and began to limber up by bending forward from the waist, my free arm moving from à la seconde to sweep the floor and then overhead as I lifted myself through standing tall to arching backward. But as I returned to standing straight, the scene before me turned grey at the edges and then the grey swelled inward till there was but a pinprick of brightness left. I was wondering about the clamminess of my forehead and the way the roots of my hair seemed to stand on end, when my knees gave way.

It was the other girls, noisy on the stairs outside the practice room door, who snapped me back awake. I picked myself up off the floor and found myself a place at the back of the barre and then in the last row once we moved to center. They were not my usual spots, but Madame Dominique said not a word.

As she calls out the first of the day's allegro combinations, my tired brain flits to a chance meeting in the rue Blanche the other day. On my way home from the Opéra, I felt a hand upon my shoulder and turned to see none other than Monsieur Degas. "Mademoiselle van Goethem," he said, "a word with you." But he did not ask me to go to his workshop the following day or the next week. No, he just stood there, not at all himself, rolling one hand over the other like he was washing up. "Monsieur Lefebvre came back," he finally said. "He wanted a picture of you."

There were a hundred pictures, some left on the floor for Sabine to sweep up, most only a few charcoal lines. Only once had I seen myself in a larger artwork, the kind of painting an abonné such as Monsieur Lefebvre might want to hang upon a wall. It was an oil of a dancing lesson—ballet girls stretching at the barre, others resting upon a bench, and in the middle, me, skinny and exhausted, cooling myself off. I remembered posing for the work, the toil of holding up the fan.

Monsieur Degas looked grave, and I touched my fingertips to the stone wall of the apothecary where we stood. "The oil of the dancing lesson?" I said.

"No." His eyes fell. "A charcoal drawing, three views of you posing for the statuette."

"A statuette?"

"Yes, yes," he said, batting the air clear of my words. "You know the drawing?"

"A statuette of me?"

He nodded, curt. "For the fifth exposition of the independent artists next month."

My hands gripped together, and I pulled them tight against my heart. Monsieur Degas—the painter of dancers, the painter of Eugénie Fiocre— he was making a statuette of me.

"It was the one he took his glove off to touch," he said, looking hard into my eyes, wanting to know that I understood. "He put his finger upon your spine."

Of course I remembered flinching from the touch, but that was a hundred years ago, nothing in the face of this news about a statuette, a statuette of me. "Oh, Monsieur Degas," I said, shrugging away the worries collecting on his face. "I'm as happy as a finch." I was more than a figure in a painting of a dozen girls. I was a ballet girl singled out, singled out for chiseling from marble, for casting in bronze.

His shoulders rose and fell heavily, as a great sigh escaped his nose and mouth. His eyes fluttered shut, settled closed. His fingers, brought to the bridge of his nose, parted, traveling the width of his brow. "I told him he couldn't have it," he said, his voice trailing off.

We lingered there in the rue Blanche, his gaze upon me still. Was I to feel grateful? Relieved? I did not. Whatever shame, whatever fear had come with baring my flesh and then the finger of Monsieur Lefebvre tracing my spine was gone, chased off by my swelling pride. Monsieur Degas shrugged away the worry of me, lifting a shoulder up only the smallest bit, but I saw it all the same.

Now I feel panic rising—I cannot remember the steps of the allegro combination that Madame Dominique only just finished calling out. She goes off to the corner to discuss the music with the violinist for our class. The rest of us are meant to be marking the combination, preparing for the moment when he lifts his violin from his knees to beneath his chin. Blanche's feet are still, but, as is the habit of most ballet girls, she is using her hands to mimic her feet while she works out the glissades, the jetés, the entrechats. I move closer, close enough that she cannot pretend I am not there, but still, without glancing up, she goes about the business of marking the steps. "Blanche," I whisper.

She shows me the annoyance upon her face, moves a shushing finger quick to her lips.

"Please," I say.

"Sissonne de côté, entrechat quatre, glissade, two brisés, jeté, assemblé, changement." She turns, giving me a view of her back, and goes back to marking the steps.

But it is not enough. No starting position. No direction for the glissade, the brisés, the assemblé. No mention of which foot to land in front. She knows it yet turns away. Yesterday the combination was tricky, with six girls botching it, including Blanche. And then it was my turn. I linked the steps perfectly and landed the final jeté in a steady attitude, and Madame Dominique burst into applause.

I am not nipping at Blanche's heels in the practice room. No, she is still the better dancer, but I have moved up from class dunce. With Blanche's gliding, leaping hands blocked by her scrawny back, I know it is not just me who has noticed the gap between the two of us narrowing. When I told her about the statuette, all she said was that Monsieur Degas looked like a lunatic with his blue spectacles and his great bushy beard, which made me sorry I had not kept my excitement to myself. And Saturday the two of us set out after class to the rue Laffitte, where Josephine said she had seen a picture of me in the Durand-Ruel gallery. We were barely under way, just out front of the Opéra, when we put our noses up to the window of the Adolphe Goupil gallery, something I had never done before. The ceiling was tall with large panes of glass lit up by the sky and a single crystal chandelier. The draperies framing the window were velvet, held open with gold, tasseled cords. The sofas, all scrolled wood and tufted brocade, were clustered together in the center of the room and turned outward so that they faced the walls, which were covered with pictures from the wainscot on up to the ceiling. I looked from one to the next, searching, and there was not a single one with cutoff feet or great expanses of empty floor, and definitely no laundresses bent under the weight of heavy loads or stooped over a hot iron, all of which were usual in Monsieur Degas's workshop.

Blanche pointed. "That one with Eve taking the apple, it couldn't look more real."

"Monsieur Degas's pictures are different," I said.

By the time we reached the rue Lafitte, I thought it was a mistake to have asked her to come. The street was full of galleries but none near as grand as that of Adolphe Goupil. When we came to number sixteen, I saw the building was stone and the window a good size and polished clean. Still, Blanche said, "It doesn't hold a candle to Goupil's."

"Let's go." We could not see any picture of me through the window and Blanche was in no mood to say anything nice, even if Monsieur Degas drew my legs with two feet attached.

"We're here to look at your picture," she said, opening up the door.

The place was empty, and there were lamps with garish reflectors shining light upon walls that were not nearly so tall, not nearly so crowded with pictures as Goupil's. A gentleman wearing a waistcoat and a watch chain was soon upon Blanche and me, looking us up and down. He had little curls over his ears where his hair was turning grey, and his brow was wrinkled at the surprise of finding two skinny girls with worn-out boots in his gallery, but his cheeks were round with a smile and he would not snap at us to get out.

"We came to see the picture of her," Blanche said, jutting a thumb. "Monsieur Degas made it."

"Ah. The pastel," he said. He made a little cough into his fist. "Follow me."

And there I was, on the far wall, in pastel and black chalk—two legs, two feet, two arms—reading the newspaper beside the stove in Monsieur Degas's workshop. I wore my practice skirt and the blue sash I bought with my bakery money and you could make out the braid running atop my head that it had taken me a good half hour to get right. There were bracelets upon my forearms, which was strange when I did not own a single one. The picture hung upon the wall beside another of Monsieur Degas's, the one of the dance lesson with the brokenhearted girl and her blaring red shawl.

Reading the newspaper was how I passed the time while waiting for Monsieur Degas to mix his pigments with oil or find a pastel of a particular shade of blue. Not a week ago I was doing just that and letting the warmth of his stove seep into my tired bones, when he called out, "Don't move, Mademoiselle van Goethem. Don't move the breadth of a hair."

Of course, with him hollering, I looked up.

"Eyes down, reading the newspaper again."

I put my attention back on a story about the murdered tavern owner, how her watch was stolen, how any Parisian coming upon the watch was to contact the inspector in charge of the case. The posing went on and on, with the intervals between Monsieur Degas hurling a crumpled sketch upon the floor growing longer, which usually meant he would not be stomping off, cutting short the four hours and paying me the full six francs anyway. I did not dare turn the page, and so, by the time Monsieur Degas stepped back from his easel, I knew all about the heart-shaped opening over the face of the missing watch.

The gentleman held a hand out to the picture. "*Dancer Resting*," he said. I felt my shoulders straighten, seeing myself there upon the gallery wall in the prettiest of frames and looking more like a real ballet girl than a starving waif from the rue de Douai.

"Doesn't look done," Blanche said. I could see what she meant, especially after gazing into the Adolphe Goupil gallery and seeing the paintings there, so polished, almost like tinted photographs.

"The new painters, like Monsieur Degas, are not so concerned with finish," he said. "Their aim is only to re-create exactly the sensation of what is seen, to capture life."

"Oh," I said.

I did not understand and it must have shown, because he went on: "Degas's pictures, every one, tell the story of a heart and a body." He folded his arms and focused his eyes upon the picture of me. "It's easy to see you're a dancer. There's the erectness of your back, the outward rotation of your legs, the practice costume. Your hair is put up. You're skinny; a hard worker, one who doesn't always get enough to eat." He paused, glancing my way, maybe to see if calling me skinny was hurtful, but said so gently, it was not. "Your skirt is neat, new. I see ambition in that. And you can read. In a moment of quiet, you turn to the newspaper. It says a lot, the way a girl chooses to rest." He gave me a kindly smile. "Well? Has Monsieur Degas succeeded?"

"He drew bracelets upon my arms. There isn't money for that." I shrugged, then smiled, thinking of myself passing the examination and joining the quadrille. My pay would increase—fifteen extra francs a month, plus a bonus of two francs for every evening I spent upon the stage.

"Dancers are always collecting trinkets from their admirers," he said. I felt a creeping bit of pleasure that maybe Monsieur Degas and this gentleman believed that one day someone would think enough of my dancing to put bracelets upon my arms. But the idea made me jumpy, too.

Sometimes the girls talked about admirers—or protectors, as they were usually called—gossip they collected in the Opéra corridors or at home from older sisters and cousins and neighbors holding spots in the corps de ballet. Always I stayed quiet, gripping my ribs, the hair upon my arms standing straight up. They were the finest of men, Perot claimed, wishing only to make a ballet girl's life easier so she could keep her mind on her work. They were ambitious, Lucille said, wanting nothing of a girl except her name linked with his and envy stirred up among the rest of the abonnés. Blanche and Ila and Louise held that they were gentlemen, tired of their wives and looking for a bit of pleasure. But Josephine shook her head, and speaking in a low voice, her eyes always on the lookout for Madame Dominique, told how abonnés dreamt up the unnatural and forced it upon a girl. Fingers creeping where they did not belong. Girls pushed to their knees. Licking. Orgies. I sucked my lip and willed Josephine to stop but never once pulled away from the mass of huddled girls.

I glanced from the picture of me to the one of the girl in the blaring red shawl, and I remembered, back in Monsieur Degas's workshop, how the picture made me dream up her life and try to guess what had put the weariness on her face. "New painting?" I said.

He nodded, and I nodded back.

"I don't see why he's drawing Marie," Blanche said, her face in a pout. "He'd be better off drawing an étoile." She did not like the prophesy of the bracelets. She did not like me singled out. Yes, I was her friend, but it did not change that there were only so many spots in the second quadrille, that the two of us were vying for the rank.

"The first of his ballet paintings was of Eugénie Fiocre, starring in *La Source*," the gentleman said, and the pout on Blanche's face grew.

Madame Dominique calls out, "Josephine, Marie, Perot," and the three of us move to center and stand in fifth position. The violinist shifts his bow to hovering over the strings. I manage the sissonne, the entrechat, the glissade before Madame Dominique's sharp clap stills the room, quiets the violin. "Glissade dessous, Marie," she says, meaning that my front foot is to finish behind.

Again the music starts up, again the sharp clap. "It's two brisés, Marie."

After my third blunder, her voice is curt. "You may sit down, Marie."

I move to the bench and huddle there like the brokenhearted girl in the blaring red shawl. With one arm wrapping my waist and the other propped upon my thigh, I wonder if it was being told to sit down that had that other girl wiping her eye upon the bench.

Always at the close of class, the girls together glide through a révérence, each of us bowing low to show our respect to Madame Dominique, who keeps behind any girl failing to lower her eyes and then raise them to meet her own. "A tradition from the days of courtly dance," she says. "Sacred. Inviolable." I join the girls in center as is expected and make a révérence with every speck of grace I can muster, bowing extra low to show humility. I say a little prayer, too, for Antoinette, vague hopes that she does not make a habit of staying out through the night, that she does not end up pierced full of holes. Each of us in the class holds still in the ending position of the révérence, arms à la seconde, a foot stretched in a tendu to the front, until Madame Dominique gives a tiny nod and says, "Dismissed." Then there is the clamor of girls laughing and chatting and scuttling down the stairs to the petits rats' loge.

The loge is three times longer than it is wide, with a strip of low cabinets in the center, running from end to end. Each of us has our own spot— two feet of countertop holding a looking glass and a gas lamp, the cupboard underneath, a stool we seldom have the time to use. The din picks up as we put on boots and toss practice skirts into satchels and mothers holler from the doorway for their daughters to hurry up, to wrap their shawls a little tighter, to be gentle with the tarlatan skirts. "Fifteen francs for a new one," says a mother. "It'll be the washhouse for you before I get another skirt."

I am rolling my sash into a neat coil, when I see Madame Dominique's black skirt before me. I lift my eyes and stop myself from sucking on my lip. "See me before you leave," she says.

Wanting the other girls, especially Blanche, cleared out before I get the scolding I am due, I take my time wrapping my slippers with their ribbons, folding my tarlatan skirt. Humble works best with Madame Dominique, and I try to push my mind from Blanche's meanness, but I am stuck—a peddler with his cart too loaded up to pull—thinking how I will work harder, how one day I will be at the front of the barre and demonstrating exercises while Blanche is made to watch. But in truth there is little chance of me catching up when almost always she is first in the practice room, when never does she waste a minute pampering tired legs, easing the soreness from her back. She means to dance upon the Opéra stage. She means to have roses flung to her feet, bracelets upon her arms. Once when I said the thing I wanted most was to pass the examination elevating me to the quadrille, she said, "The quadrille is only the beginning for me." I nodded, because I knew it was true. She has no father, never has, only a brother gone to Saint-Malo years before, a sailor on the high seas. Her mother went from brothel to brothel in the afternoons, arranging the coquettes' hair. Afterward she washed dishes from early evening and right on through the night in the kitchen at Le Meurice. Mornings she bawled and told Blanche she would not last another week, that the Opéra was their only hope. She was too careful with her wages to spend them on absinthe; and it gave Blanche, who already had a two-year head start at the Opéra, the added advantage of not kneading the dough for eighty loaves before class every day.

When all the girls, all except Blanche, are cleared out—galloping the stairs and smirking about me staying behind—she comes over to me. I watch her lick her lips, wring the skirt clutched in her hands. "Monsieur Degas was right," she says, "putting those bracelets upon your arms. You'll be elevated to the quadrille. You'll be admired."

I pull my satchel tight against my belly, tug at the frayed skin of my thumb.

"I should have helped. It was mean not to help," she says and sinks down to a crouch. She leans her head against the stool where I sit. "I've got to grow another three inches, or I have no hope of being an étoile." Then she tells how her mother measures her height twice a month and is undertaking to lengthen Blanche's spine. She is made to lie on her back, her toes wedged under the larder's apron, while her mother curls her fingers around the base of Blanche's skull and pulls. "It doesn't work. What I need is meat. I haven't grown a speck in four months."

Before I manage a word, she is up and through the doorway leading to the corridor. And I wish I was quicker. It was true: Not a soul among the étoiles or even the premières danseuses was as small as Blanche. But still, I should have said how everyone knew her talent, how she outshone every other petit rat.

Madame Dominique comes into the loge and settles her backside upon a low cabinet in front of my stool. "You have a new skirt, no?" she says.

I nod.

"Extra lessons with Madame Théodore?"

"Twice a week," I say.

"The abonnés, they want their protégés upon the stage, and yet they keep a girl out half the night." She shifts her body sideways so that she is looking me fully in the face.

I make the smallest shrug, not a bit sure.

"You know the examinations are not far off, and still you come to class exhausted."

"I made the mistake of going to bed too late."

Her lips pull tight. "The shadows under your eyes are nothing new."

She taps the coral ring she wears on her pinky against the cabinet, waiting, and I scrape the frayed skin of my thumb, hidden, behind the shield of my other hand.

"I could speak to him?" she says. "To your protector? He must be made to understand the rigor of the examinations." She touches my hand, stilling the picking going on underneath. "You must arrive rested for class. You need an allowance for meat. A new skirt isn't enough."

It comes to me that she thinks I have a protector, that he bought my skirt. "I work at a bakery."

A line appears between her eyebrows.

"I'm only kneading dough, saving my legs," I say. "I go in the morning, first thing."

"Before class?" A palm moves to her cheek, holding up her heavy head.

"Half past four. I'm finished by eight o'clock."

"Oh, Marie. Every morning?"

I nod. "I'm modeling, not as much as I was."

"I see." Her hands drop. "It's noble. But, oh, Marie. It's impossible. Already you're wearing yourself out."

I was told to sit out class, would not have got the combination right even if she gave me a fourth chance.

"There are other ways." She says it quietly, eyes upon the floor.

"A protector?"

"I thought you'd taken one on. I saw your new things. Madame Théodore said about the classes."

"You'll help me? I don't know the abonnés."

"No," she says, too fast. A decision already made, before, on behalf of some other girl. "I won't."

Her eye twitches then, something I have never seen, not with her steady gaze. And it makes me wonder if in that twitch there was not a flickering bit of shame at failing a girl, a girl she is charged with pushing along from petit rat in her practice room to ballet girl upon the Opéra stage.

~ Antoinette ~

Colette insists upon gathering up the dead dog with its twisted neck and blood-leaking mouth. She is carrying on, blubbering and sniffling, not bothering to wipe the snot from her face. Part of me is all for joining in, bawling and pounding my fists upon the ground, but how would it all end? There is no mother coming with a soothing teat, no sweetheart with embracing arms. Colette and me, we are on our own and all the blubbering in the world won't change a single thing. She spreads her shawl over the ground and shifts the dog's hindquarters onto the wool. "You got to leave it," I say.

She slides one hand beneath its muzzle, the other beneath its breast. Taking great care with the neck, she spares that broken mutt the cold stone of the pavement. "Well, help me," she says.

Marie is waiting for me, I know, dipping only her toe into sleep. Always she stirs awake the second I settle under the covers and then, with my heat beside her, sighs and drifts into proper sleep for the first time of the night. I know the look of peacefulness come to a slumbering girl, also the dusky hollows brought on by losing rest. But Colette is watching me with the naked eyes of an urchin new to the streets.

Together we lift, begin walking, each of us holding a gathered edge of the shawl and in between, the weight of a dead dog swaying in time with our steps. It appears Colette knows where we are headed, and I put one foot ahead of the other, following. My heart is cleaved that Émile should take a smoke from a boy who slapped my face, crushed that he walked away. Already I know I want his hot breath upon my skin again, his stroking fingers upon my flesh. If he don't come begging to me, I am going begging to him, and I don't see any point in pretending something different for an evening or a day. Maybe it was something he understood even as he put that offered smoke to his lips. Maybe it was not so much choosing Pierre Gille ahead of me, not if already Émile knew it would not change a single thing between him and me.

As we turn the corner Colette says we are going to the house of Madame Brossard on the lower slopes of Montmartre and continues at an even pace. I know the parents of Colette are dead, that her family name is not Brossard but Dupree. She was chummy with the boulevard tarts at the brasserie, also a gentleman twice her age. She owns four dresses, all of them silk, none of them worn out, and tonight, upon her neck, she wears the fanciest of watches. It hangs there, winking, catching the flickering light of the lamps, drawing the eye. But to her it is only a trinket, something to toss in a drawer. She is not the smallest bit modest, the smallest bit shy about her heaving breasts, her pretty calves, her plump lips. Not an hour ago she was lifting up her skirt and taunting Pierre Gille and calling out for the world to hear, "It isn't free." All of it says there is only one possibility: The house of Madame Brossard is a brothel, a shuttered house of Paris. Still it takes a further block of trudging before I say, "Just who is Madame Brossard?"

"She is the madam of the house where I live, and, yes, I work as a coquette, since it's what you really want to know."

We turn into an alleyway running alongside a grey house, two stories in height with piano music and chatter spilling into the night from the tavern on the ground floor. The alleyway is dark except for the light cast by a lantern hanging in a cage above the nook of a door. "We leave the dog here," Colette says, lowering her end of our bundle beside the stone stoop, reaching for a brass door handle. "We'll get soup, maybe even a bath for you, depending on Madame Brossard's spirits."

The wooden steps leading to the first floor are swept free of grit and brightly lit by three gas lamps, each with its shade polished clean. The walls of the staircase are thick, easily swallowing up the din of the tavern down below. From the alcove at the top, I glimpse velvet draperies and two girls in silk, each sitting sideways upon a brocade sofa, her chin propped up by an arm resting upon the thick cushions of the back, and giving her full attention to the gentleman lounging in between. Colette, who appears to be no second-rate whore, takes me by the arm, hauling me down a dimly lit corridor to a large kitchen with a roaring hearth.

"My God, Colette," says a jowly woman with a wineglass in one hand and a polishing cloth in the other. "Is that blood on your skirt?"

"There is a dead dog beside the door in the alleyway, a dead dog wrapped in my woolen shawl." Colette begins to sniffle, explaining between sobs about a boy kicking the dog, kicking it with all his might, snapping its pretty neck. Her shoulders heave, and Madame Brossard escorts her by the arm to a large oaken table, nudges her into a chair. She turns to me and says, "Won't you have a seat, Mademoiselle . . ."

"Van Goethem," I say, taking up the chair beside Colette. "Antoinette."

She lays a hand upon my shoulder by way of greeting, and with her so near, her nose twitches at the stink of me after a week in the washhouse and an evening hauling a dead dog.

"The dog's got to be buried," Colette says.

"You'll eat, the both of you, and we'll get you cleaned up."

She picks up a tiny bell, muffling it sharply after the second ring, and I wonder if it means the house has more than a single maid, that each has her own call. She moves to the hearth, returns with a steaming pot and two bowls and begins ladling a thick soup of onion and beef into each. A maid, no older than Marie, comes into the kitchen wearing a starched apron, and Madame Brossard gives instructions about drawing a bath and a set of clean underclothes for me and telling Maurice, who I guess is a barman in the tavern down below, there is a grave to be dug in the courtyard. "Shall I send for the hairdresser?" she says to Colette.

"I could use a little spoiling just now."

Near starved, I lap up the soup, more rich in meat than that served in the cafés. When there is not but a single shell of onion left upon my spoon, Colette glances over her shoulder to the doorway where Madame Brossard disappeared and switches her close-to-full bowl for my empty one. Sitting there, at the oaken table of Madame Brossard with its eight chairs gathered around, I picture the girls of the house assembled, playing a game of bezique, laughing, licking the grease of a roasted duck from their lips. For a moment, I let myself imagine staying on, with Madame Brossard providing the soup, ordering the baths, calling the hairdresser. But that dreamed-up life, it don't include Marie and Charlotte. It don't include Émile, and I want the three of them more than I want coddling and thick soup and a madam bearing the burden of deciding every detail of my day. "Madame Brossard is being generous?" I say.

"Pauline, another of the girls, failed the medical exam. Her card wasn't stamped."

"I got a job, working as a laundress in the rue de Douai."

"It's a good house, Madame Brossard's."

"No offense, Colette, but whoring isn't the trade for me."

"Still. Might as well get yourself a bath." In the fireplace a cauldron hangs from a hook. Orange tongues of flame lick its sides, and curls of steam feather out from above the rim. The tub waiting beside the hearth is more than double in size the one we have at home, and it has a high, sloping back just meant for lolling.

Not fifteen minutes later I lean back in the tub and know I have failed

Marie. But maybe Émile is right about coddling being hurtful, about Marie needing to toughen up, about Charlotte never figuring out the world don't spin solely for her. I close my eyes, and after a while there comes the gentle pull of hair being combed and combed again and finally curled with hot tongs by a hairdresser accustomed to his customers sighing in a tub.

"Enjoying yourself there, Antoinette," Madame Brossard says, skirt swishing by.

I smile, arch my back, like a cat getting scratched beneath the chin.

"Colette tells me you were a ballet girl with the Opéra?"

"A long time ago."

Once my hair is set and my skin wiped dry, she laces me into a corset—my first since the Opéra stage—tight enough that even the very little I have is heaved up, and then buttons me into a fine dress of mauve silk. She pours a glass of red wine, hands it to me saying, "On the house." She dusts my nose with rice powder and brushes my lips with tinted pomade and walks me over to a round looking glass hanging from a chain over a buffet. At my neckline white flesh mounds above mauve silk. That pretty dress is smooth upon my ribs and tapers to my clinched-to-narrow waist. My hair gleams from the combing, my lips from the tinted pomade. My skin is soft, like velvet, from the powdering. And all I want is Émile, for him to see me looking maybe not so pretty as Colette but the prettiest I ever been. "Well?" says Madame Brossard.

"You're wasting your time on me," I say, but she only shrugs, like a licked-clean bowl of soup, a cauldron drained of water, a hairdressing bill, a swallowed glass of red wine are nothing at all.

In the alcove just outside the salon, Colette says, "See if you can't enjoy yourself tonight. Madame Brossard will be watching and you'll tire of scrubbing linens soon enough," but my mind is on tomorrow being Sunday, my day of freedom from the washhouse. I will search for Émile, starting at the storage shed of the father of Pierre Gille, then calling in at the Brasserie des Martyrs, those other taverns preferred by him. Colette clasps her hands together and tucks them up under her chin, like she is making a tiny prayer, and then, she is off, smiling, kissing the cheeks of all but one of the six men in the salon, and after that approaching the neglected gentleman and putting her hand upon his chest, "Now, you're new at this house, no?"

"Monsieur Arnaud," he says, and she takes his glass, which is only half drained.

"You need more wine, Monsieur Arnaud. At this house, we are all for having a jolly time."

She strokes the lapel of another gentleman, one thinking he is at the Opéra, judging by his walking stick and white gloves. "I see you're keeping the tailor busy, Monsieur Barbeau," she says. "That cut suits a man who keeps his back so good and straight." Then she is across the room, ruffling the locks of a gentleman, who might as well be an owl with his small, sharp nose and eyebrows, like tufts of fur sticking out from his brow. "Such a fine crop of hair," she says.

I stand in the alcove, swallowing red wine, glad to be feeling the nerve that comes with a drained glass before the eyes of those six gentlemen wander off from following Colette, slinking about the salon, a regular minx. And then Madame Brossard is there, tilting a bottle. Again, I swallow, finding the bottom of the glass a second time and with it, enough boldness that when I see a gentleman, hardly old enough to have sat beneath a straight razor, look me up and down, I let my lips grow pouty and give him the sauciest of smiles. Émile, he don't appreciate me like he should.

That boy, he lifts up his wine a bit and his eyebrows, too; and, with nothing more behind me than an oaken door, I know his raised glass is for me, my mauve dress, my powdered nose. He is like a cherub, except stretched tall: lips like a woman's, a cleft in his chin, skin like milk, flaxen curls—a pretty boy like Pierre Gille. I lift my again-filled-up glass, and at the thought of Émile watching from the corner of the room, I run my fingers along my neckline of mauve cord.

Colette's got her arm linked around that of Monsieur Arnaud, and she is strolling him around the room, saying, "Now this is Monsieur Picot, a timber merchant," and about the cherub, "This is Monsieur Simard, who is apprenticing to be a banker like his papa," and about two men side by side on the sofa, their foreheads close, "This is Monsieur Mignot and Monsieur Fortin, who own a fish-packing house in Le Havre and have been like brothers to each other ever since meeting in the lycée there." The almost brothers stand up, shake the hand of Monsieur Arnaud; and, glimpsing their trousers and mustaches, I want to blurt out about them sharing a tailor and a barber, too. The cherub glances my way and swallows another mouthful of wine.

"We are all friends here, Monsieur Arnaud," Colette says and, even without the bobbing chins of the gentlemen, I know it is true, that these gentlemen, with their joking and knee slapping and foreheads leaning in, don't come to the house of Madame Brossard only for the company of Colette.

She moves on to the girls. "This is Adèle from the Loire. We call her Petite. This is Odette, a bona fide Parisian. And Constance, all the way from the Pyrenees." Petite is fair and small and plump enough that her arms are like dough, poked by a finger at the spot where the elbows should be. Odette looks like a ballet girl with her long neck and sloping shoulders and pretty waist. And Constance is tall and dark as a Spaniard. It puts me to thinking that variety was on the mind of Madame Brossard when she brought each of the girls into the house and, then, to wondering if Pauline with her unstamped card was not skinny like me with a crop of dark hair. Only Colette is a great beauty, but I can see all the girls are cheerful, laughing and petting, bounding to their feet the instant a gentleman finds his glass half empty.

"And this here is Antoinette," says Colette, steering Monsieur Arnaud to me. "We met at the Ambigu. A bit of fun the two of us had there, as walkers-on in *L'Assommoir*. Antoinette was clever enough to get herself a speaking part."

The gentlemen turn in my direction and the cherub says, "Well, Mademoiselle Antoinette, why not share your talent with us."

All those fine men are looking, none turning away, wandering off down the pavement with a smoke hanging from their lips. I set my glass upon a half column holding a potted fern, and even half soused, I know enough to keep the thickness of the wine from my tongue. "Now gentlemen." I say it quiet and those men lean in, hold their eyes steady, same as for Hélène Petit at the Ambigu. "You must imagine me as a laundress, bare arms dripping with suds, a bit of collected steam rolling down my neck. It is sweltering hot in the washhouse." I brush imagined sweat from my forehead with the back of my hand, open up my shut eyes to ten pairs staring back, the lips of the cherub parting. "Peek through the shutters of a washhouse closed up to the street for the day, and I promise, you will not find a single laundress with her blouse laced up tight." The cherub licks his lips. Colette laughs. And I loosen the cord at the neckline of my mauve silk.

The timber merchant claps. The cherub slaps his thigh. Colette puts a hand over her heart. I feel a warmth, like soup in an empty belly, and I hold up a palm. "But, gentlemen, back to the washhouse of *L'Assommoir*."

I fish in my imagined tub, just like upon the stage of the Ambigu, and look up, away from the tub, and bring anger to my face. "What's become of my bit of soap?" I say. "Somebody's been and filched my soap again."

Everybody is laughing, clapping, lifting glasses. The cherub says, "I remember you. I remember that line."

"Me, too," says one of the gentlemen owning the fish-packing house in Le Havre.

"As do I," says his almost brother.

My eyes float from face to face, each friendly, rosy with warmth, and it don't feel all that different from being adored. Then Colette is beside me, arm linked around my own. "Our Antoinette has danced upon the Opéra stage."

The knuckle of one hand presses against the cherub's lips. Getting to his feet, he calls out. "Encore."

"Yes," says Colette, dropping my arm and beginning to clap.

These gentlemen, each picked the lower slopes of Montmartre over a dull reception, a respectable dinner. Starving for a lark is what they are, and the same can be said for those showing up in the orchestra stalls or the Foyer de la Danse of the Opéra without their wives. It puts a little gloating in my heart, being the choice of these gentlemen when Émile and Pierre Gille and the rest of those boys don't bother with a bit of regard. I wonder about a string of fouettés en tournant. Those few words about the soap are nothing compared to the spectacle of a ballet girl lifting a leg and whipping around fast.

I let my gaze linger upon the cherub's gawking eyes and lift my arms to croisé, getting myself ready to turn. But the salon shifts, the corner where the timber merchant sits between Petite and Odette dipping up and the corner where Madame Brossard stands, looking on, dipping down. I lift my glass from the half column, toasting the room instead. "Another time, gentlemen," I say. "Another time."

The cherub waves me over, and I scour my mind for his name. He pats the sofa beside him, and I sit down clumsily, with a bit of wine slopping over the rim of my glass but only onto my hand.

"You belong upon the stage," he says.

"Don't know about that." I lick up the wine from the patch of skin at the crook of my thumb, and the cherub don't look away. No, his pretty face is transfixed.

He reaches for a lock of my hair, curled and arranged around my face. I shift my head, jostling that curl from his fingertips, and he snatches his hand away, a scolded child. He fiddles with the rim of his glass, and with him turning shy instead of bitter, when we are sitting upon a sofa in a place such as this, I give him a little wink. "Just got those curls," I say. "Don't often get curls."

"Suits you," he says. "More wine?"

I hold out my glass, bothering to wonder if Madame Brossard minds me swallowing wine that was not offered by her. He pours half his wine into mine, and both of us put those glasses to our lips, peering at each other over the rims.

"Such eyes," he says. All those ladies turning and looking out over their fans on the grand staircase at the Opéra, their beauty is nothing more than curling tongs and rice powder and a dozen sewing maids put to work on a single dress. I put my attention on the mouth of the cherub, which is pink and full and soft instead of thick and chapped and holding a smoke handed over by Pierre Gille. "Pretty lips," I say. "Cherub lips."

We talk about *L'Assommoir* and the opera stage, about me appearing in *Coppélia* and *La Sylphide* and *Sylvia* even if the first two were before my time. He remembers me, he says—a sylph with wings upon my back. He is certain. He really is. He fills up my glass and we toast the Opéra and the house of Madame Brossard and the bank where he don't much like sitting behind a great desk, and we keep up the toasting until our glasses are drained and filled up again and then we toast some more—the Empress Eugénie and Napoleon III hiding out in England since the Prussians ran them out of France, then Jules Grévy, who the cherub says is a better billiards player than president. When I say, "To the Republic," and lift up my glass, he fills it up with wine but don't take a swallow himself.

Colette and Monsieur Arnaud are gone from the salon, and Petite is combing her fingers through the hair of the timber merchant, her dress gaping open, baring her pink nipples. Constance is dealing out cards to the almost brothers and Odette.

The cherub touches the curl closest to my ear. "No squashing," he says, and I laugh and feel fingers, not so calloused as those of Émile, upon my cheek. I shut my eyes, breathe in the scent of him, which is cloves and soap instead of tobacco and skin gone unwashed too long, and feel those fingers upon my throat and then upon the neckline of my dress and then upon the silk over my breasts. There is a stirring, low, an ache, and then the mouth of the cherub upon my own. I let it fall open a little, tasting the sweetness of him. He pulls back a little and whispers into my ear, "I'll speak to Madame Brossard."

I could pretend, I tell myself, it is the old chaise underneath my back. It is something half the sewing maids and flower sellers and charwomen of Paris undertake from time to time—an easy cup of chocolate, a glass of champagne, a pair of gloves, the landlord held off another day. But before that boy gets up from the sofa, he strokes the hollow between the two ends of my collarbones, that special place of Émile, and I open up my eyes and know I will not follow him to wherever it is that Colette and Monsieur Arnaud disappeared to from the salon. A hotness gathers behind my eyes, a bulge swells in my throat, and I don't dare blink. I look away from the cherub, count the gas lamps in the shifting room. Five. Or is it six. The potted ferns. Four.

"Another time," he says. He is but a boy, unsure.

I stand, feel my head swirl. I turn back to that boy and totter, stepping on the hem of my skirt. "I never been so soused," I say, "and I don't recall your name."

"Jean Luc. Jean Luc Simard."

And then Madame Brossard is there, calling Odette over to tell Monsieur Simard about the peddler who was selling flowers cut from the cemetery not a stone's throw away. Madame Brossard takes me by the elbow, steers me from the salon, calling out over her shoulder, "Just imagine it, Monsieur Simard."

A cemetery is a fine place for plucking flowers. Tomorrow I will gather up fistful upon fistful to lay around the hem of my spread skirt as I wait for Émile outside the storage shed of the father of Pierre Gille.

~ Marie ~

Between the rue de Douai and the rue des Pyramides, Charlotte and I count twenty-six posters announcing the fifth exposition of the independent artists. Monsieur Degas is listed third, with fourteen others, including two I know from the newspapers—Pissarro and Gauguin. I have made a habit of counting the posters, and once when I walked farther than the half hour of today, I counted forty-three. All of Paris knows.

"Another one," I say.

"Twenty-seven," Charlotte says.

"Makes me nervous, so many people seeing the statuette."

The exposition opened last Thursday, April 1, and the three days of waiting for today to come were the longest of my life. There was no earlier chance, not with Madame Dominique's classes and Madame Théodore's private lessons and the kneading of the baguettes. Friday evening I very nearly broke my own rule of being curled upon my mattress by eight o'clock and headed out. But how could I after pleading with Maman and Antoinette to tiptoe, to shut their squawking mouths? "I need to sleep," I said, hollering and blubbering and rubbing my eyes. "Madame Dominique told me I need to get more sleep."

The examinations were nine weeks off, and Madame Dominique was back to doling out tiny nods. Blanche had stayed nice and said my fouettés en tournant were better than hers and showed me a combination the minute I was stuck. Once when the day was hot and we were sitting in a patch of sunshine with our backs resting up against the Opéra wall, she put her face in her hands. "Maman can't go on, working every minute of every day."

I tilted my head onto her shoulder.

"Five months now I haven't grown."

"I've got the face of an ape. It will go against me in the exam."

She shrugged, huffed a little laugh because what else could she do?

"A monkey and a shrimp upon the stage," I said.

"If there's a bit of fairness in the world."

She was right about elevation to the quadrille for both of us being fair, and probably Madame Dominique would agree. Always she was saying, "A little more sweat, if you please," but never was the girl scolded for laziness, me or Blanche. She still easily held the first spot at the barre, but I had nipped at the heels of others in the class, sometimes hard enough that a girl fell back to nipping at my own. I worried, sometimes, that still my jetés lacked height, that Josephine's back was growing suppler than my own, that only I noticed the strength of my fouettés en tournant. But a ribbon came off my slipper the other day, and I knew what it meant when both Linette and Alice made up excuses for not lending me a bit of thread. Blanche and I and a handful of others were pulling away from girls like Linette and Alice, girls still botching combinations, still dropping to their heels instead of holding steady on their toes in an arabesque. The quadrille—the chance to be a real ballet girl with white on my arms and a costume of fine silk, to appear as a sylph and be adored—was growing more and more possible with each day. And when I thought of the music of an entire orchestra reaching inside me, filling me up, instead of a single violin, I felt myself grow lighter on my feet.

Even so the patch on my thumb was picked to a pulp. I cut my fingernails short and warned myself not to count my chickens before they hatched. But still my mind wandered, thinking and rethinking, fearful of the thing I was sweating and slaving in the practice room to get. From the bakery came the baguettes we ate in the morning, the wages I handed over for rent and wood and milk, those I kept for practice clothes, for pork cutlet and veal stew—those extra portions of meat I allowed myself—always a nervous eye on the door of a café up in the place Pigalle, always fearful of Antoinette coming upon me there. If I was elevated to the quadrille, I would be dancing upon the stage some evenings; and it would mean getting back to our lodging room after midnight, far too late to be waking up early and kneading baguettes. The girls in the corps de ballet were supposed to rise late, get to the Opéra in time for class in the afternoon and be prepared to stay all hours, rehearsing or dancing upon the stage. But the ballet girls that slept until noon had fathers buying their meat, fathers or abonnés.

Twice after class, when Blanche and I were crossing the courtyard of administration to the Opéra's back gate, I saw Monsieur Lefebvre. The first time, he was talking to another gentleman beside a carriage, a fine one with a pair of plumed horses, glass windows and a gilt *L* upon the door. The bench for the driver was padded and there was a seat for the groom at the back, when most would have expected him to stand on the footboard at the side. I told myself to call out but knew I did not have the nerve. Then Monsieur Lefebvre bent forward from the waist and tipped his hat.

I smiled, just a little, and said, "Hello" and then after a tiny pause, "Monsieur Lefebvre," so that he would know I remembered his name.

After we had crossed to the far side of the street from where the carriage was parked, Blanche said, "You know him?"

"He came into Monsieur Degas's workshop."

"Such a carriage." She craned her neck to get a second look, and I was thankful that, with the carriage in the way, Monsieur Lefebvre could not see her gawking.

A week later he was there again, and he called Blanche and me over to his carriage and ushered us inside. Was Madame Dominique working us sufficiently hard in preparation for the upcoming examinations? he wanted to know. His pink tongue flicked against the corner of his mouth. Was the date set? He would like to attend and would inquire about obtaining a pass. We must conserve our energy, he said, and then he asked Blanche if she lived up near me and insisted on taking us as far as the sweet-seller shop in the rue Fontaine. He told us Madame Lefebvre adored its red caramel pipes.

When we pulled up outside the sweet seller's, he said we should wait in the carriage, that hardworking ballet girls, such as ourselves, would benefit from a sweet. He came back with bits of almond paste and sugarplums and red caramel pipes. We stuffed our mouths, Blanche more so than I, because my teeth were ugly enough without red smears, and Monsieur Lefebvre's questions never let up. What was I paid by the Opéra? He knew about my extra lessons with Madame Théodore and wanted to know what they cost. Was it true my father was dead? My mother a laundress? My sister, too? He did not take a single sweet for himself, which explained how a man rich enough for a carriage with glass windows and creaseless, polished shoes had cheeks as hollow as a black night. Blanche stayed mostly quiet, but she did blurt out that no one could match me when it came to fouettés en tournant, that he would be watching me in the quadrille come next fall. "Yes, such turns!" he said, and it made me think those two times Madame Dominique gave us our class upon the stage in preparation for the examination, he was watching from the blackness of the house. "I'll put in a good word, make sure Monsieur Pluque and Monsieur Mérante, too, know the attention she deserves." Monsieur Mérante was the Opéra's ballet master, and passing on the red caramel was not a mistake.

"And Blanche," I said, "she's got arms like the wings of a dove. Madame Dominique told her that."

"Uncommon grace." He looked over to Blanche, and I felt a tiny pang that he watched her, same as he watched me.

After his carriage went around the corner, with me and Blanche left on the pavement outside the sweet seller's, she grabbed my elbows with both her hands. "A carriage with velvet seats, silk draperies!" she said. "And he knows both our talents. He said I've got uncommon grace."

I did not know whether I wanted Monsieur Lefebvre's attention or even if sugarplums bought from a sweet seller meant anything at all, but I was sure Blanche had only met him on account of me. It was bold, her saying how he admired her grace, and it made me feel like there was something she could snatch away from me. My face must have fallen, and it must have made her think twice about whether I would ever again open up my mouth about her dove arms to Monsieur Lefebvre, because the next thing she said was, "I was only thinking he might mention me to Monsieur Mérante, too." She linked her arm around mine. "It'd be nothing for him to give you what the bakery does." She yanked me down the pavement, galloping and hopping and twice twirling me around.

In the rue des Pyramides I count three more posters, and it tips Charlotte over to sour. "Antoinette said he only paints ballet girls scratching their backs," she says. When I first told Charlotte about the statuette, she put her full weight over to one hip and stuck out her chin. "A statuette? Like Marie Taglioni? But you've still got to pass the examination for the second quadrille." Antoinette rolled her eyes and said, "Such a dunce, Charlotte. He don't see Marie as no ordinary girl," and I felt a growing warmth in my chest. But then yesterday Antoinette came in from the washhouse in the evening, looking all bashful with her hands behind her back. "I can't go to the exposition with you tomorrow," she said, and my heart grew tight. She held out a coiled ribbon. "A little starch and a hot iron and your old ribbon is good as new." The wrinkles were flattened, the tatty edges trimmed. I touched the ribbon, newly crisp and smooth.

"You're off with that boy somewhere," I said.

"He's got a name, Marie."

"I'll take Charlotte. Charlotte will want to go."

"Let me plait your hair in the morning," she said and made a meek smile, but I only shrugged.

Oh, but never mind Charlotte. Never mind Antoinette. My feet are light upon the pavement, and the breath of springtime is rolling across the land, calling up tender blades of grass, coaxing canopies of green from the hard kernels of their winter beds. There is happiness in sniffing air full with cherry blossoms; but more than that, I have this feeling, like I sit before a cake, watering at the mouth while the baker adds a glaze, a drizzle of chocolate, a decoration of candied fruit. First there was a single poster—bold red letters against a background of green. Then there was the knowledge they were everywhere—walls, doors, bridges, gates— that a hundred buckets of paste were emptied to put the posters up. There was the location, too, announced underneath the artists' listed names: 10, rue des Pyramides. I did not know the street and asked Antoinette. "Right bank," she said. "Connects up with the Pont Royal." The rue des Pyramides was five minutes from the lapping, twinkling Seine, closer still to the flower beds and reflecting pools of the Jardin des Tuileries, practically on top of the Louvre, the fortress that houses the greatest artworks in all of France. The rue des Pyramides, it brought to mind a stone monument, standing until the end of time.

Since Monsieur Degas told me about the statuette, he has not called me to his workshop, and so I have only my own mind to dream up how it will look. I thought about the figurine of Marie Taglioni, the one Papa gave to Antoinette. It was cast in terra-cotta, painted with airy white, the softest of pinks, then hardened up in a kiln and set upon our mantelshelf to be loved. The figurine was not naked. No, a plain dress clung to sloping shoulders, and mostly it was enough to keep me hopeful that my own flesh would be covered up, to push away the hundred drawings of me naked in fourth position, to put my mind on the later drawings. Almost always I was dressed—a bodice, practice skirt, slippers, and stockings.

The wings extending from the back of the figurine made it clear Marie Taglioni wore the Sylph's costume, that the little base she hovered above was not the practice room floor but the woodland ground of *La Sylphide*. Would Monsieur Degas show me as a ballet girl upon the stage instead of as a petit rat, worn out and waiting her turn? His pictures told the story of a heart and a body, just like the gentleman at the Durand-Ruel gallery said, and I had felt Monsieur Degas's eyes burrowing beneath my skin. What story would he tell with the statuette? What had he seen? For a tiny instant, I worried about wanting so much, about greediness, but Maman drained her bottle of absinthe, and hopelessness was the reason why.

Sometimes my mind fell to the massive sculpture jutting from between the two most easterly of the Opéra's arched entrances. When I was ten, I stood before the stone carving with Antoinette. "It's called *The Dance*," she said.

I stared, wondering how it was that solid stone could heave and twist, and waited for Antoinette to tell me what my opinion should be. She was fourteen and newly dancing upon the Opéra stage.

"All of Paris got fired up when it was unveiled," she said, tilting her head, still making up her mind.

The women held hands, making a circle around a winged man with raised arms and a tambourine and hair floating up like he only just landed upon the earth. They were naked, fleshy, cavorting, wild. There was a plump baby at their feet.

"Don't know about all the complaining," she said. "They look brimming with happiness to me."

The women's heads were thrown back, laughing, like I had seen in the cafés, like Maman's was from time to time, before the bellowing and the bawling and Papa being sick.

I had passed by the carving a hundred times since. Usually I did not look. The thought of those naked breasts—chiseled, scoured smooth under a living hand without so much as a thread of cloth in between—it made me want with all my heart for Monsieur Degas to keep in place the bodice and practice skirt and slippers of the later drawings.

There is no street number and even with the jumble of exposition posters pasted to the door, I check the addresses of the buildings on either side twice. The building is new, not finished, with two masons upon scaffolding and four roofers upon the roof. The windows looking onto the street are streaked with ridges of dirt, the cleaning cloth too laden with grime to be of much use. "This is it?" says Charlotte, and I swing open the door, as if I am not disappointed in the least.

The clamor coming to my ears pushes me back a step. There is the shuffling, scraping, and hammering of roofers, the sawing of carpenters. Charlotte covers up her ears, and though I want to do the same, I only say, "Stop the fuss."

A man with dirty fingernails and a painter's shabby smock sits at a table made out of a wooden plank upon two crates. Not a bit sure —no one else has come in to show us about exhibition-going—I set upon the plank the pair of one franc coins owed for admission. Charlotte shifts closer. "The two of us are petits rats with the Opéra," she says, bolder than a rooster. "And my sister here is a model for Monsieur Degas. It's his art-works we came to see."

"I should have guessed it," says the man, eyes glinting with the same light Charlotte draws from the pork butcher, the watchmaker, the crock-ery dealer in the rue de Douai, and from Monsieur LeBlanc, who Antoi-nette says we will see no more of with her again earning a steady wage. The man slides the coins back to our side of the plank. "Third salon," he says.

The first salon is large with some twenty pictures hung upon the walls or perched upon the easels in the center of the room. A good half of the frames are purple, with yellow mats. It is what I see first, and this noticing of the trappings ahead of the artworks does not put my mind at ease. "So much filth," says Charlotte. At the far end of the room, two women clutch at their skirts, their attention less on the walls than on keeping their hems clear of dust. With each blow of a hammer, heads turn, noses wrinkle, shoulders flinch. A few of those gathered in the room study the pictures— a woman with a knit brow, a gentleman stroking his beard, another two in top hats, leaned in close, muttering into each other's ears.

In the third salon, right away I see the paintings upon the walls belong to Monsieur Degas. My eyes sweep the room, seeking the statuette—a fourteen-year-old dancer in fourth position, arms clasped behind her back, hands nestled in the tarlatan of her skirt. It is the way I have thought up the statuette a hundred times. But it is not here.

There is the girl in the blaring red shawl, hunched over upon a bench, and beside it another picture, new to me. Two dancers sit collapsed upon a bench, their bent knees parted, their tired legs turned out from the hips, even as they catch their breaths. In the next picture, a dancer bends forward at the hips to straighten her stockings; and another, with a shock of red hair and a face turned to the floor, looks like she is stretching out her toes, but it is impossible to know because a good half of her foot is chopped off, and this time, the top of her head, too. Behind the dancers, fluffing the tarlatan of her daughter's skirt is the mother, with the puffy face of an old concierge, and her friend, rough with her raw nose and plume of feathers bristling from her hat. These girls, Monsieur Degas is saying, do not be tricked by the grace of their backs. These girls are of common stock.

After that, portraits. I barely look. And last, a washbasin and a pitcher and a woman in black stockings and nothing more, pulling a dress over her head. Her backside is plump, soft, spread beneath the fleshy folds of her waist. She is no laundress or concierge, no milliner or wool carder.

The shadow of her stockings lurches the mind from decent work, and only a whore slips on a dress with her backside still bare. I have looked away from such pictures in Monsieur Degas's workshop. But today I stay and gawk, wondering. Why does he make such things? Why is it on display, when he has so many pictures, some even a little bit pretty if you ignore the cutoff feet, if you do not mind a girl sweaty upon a bench. Why a fleshy backside instead of me in fourth position, a ballet girl sprouting wings?

"It isn't here," Charlotte says, flippant, like nothing ever mattered less.

"No." I give her arm a little tug. "Let's go."

And then my eyes fall upon Monsieur Degas, coming through the doorway of the salon, and the man from the table, pointing a paint-stained finger in the direction of Charlotte and me.

Monsieur Degas's face is grey, tired. Still, the slightest crinkles come to the corners of his eyes. "Mademoiselle van Goethem," he says. The hammering of the roofers swells in our ears, and he raises his eyes to the ceiling. "It's not what I hoped. The building was to be finished. I was told—promised—yet we shudder in the din."

"You have visitors," I say and lift a hand to the salon.

"Some." His shoulders inch up.

"Oh."

"I sold the painting of you fanning yourself."

Never was I made to ask for my six francs. Always I felt the heaviness of coins in my pocket before I pushed my feet back into my boots. Even when Monsieur Degas's eyes could not bear the strain and he cut a modeling session short, never once did he dock me a single sou. My spirits should lift at the news of the sale. Still, without the statuette not so much as a flutter.

"Monsieur Lefebvre bought it," he says and rattles his weary head.

"They went to the sweet seller," Charlotte says. "I only got a sugar-plum."

"The statuette?" I hold myself down from floating on a tiny crest of hope, the gutter of afterward.

"I can stand very still," Charlotte says.

"A failure," he says and takes off the blue spectacles meant to protect his sight. With his other hand, he makes a tent covering his eyes and then rubs the troughs of his lids. I think about the world fading—orange becoming tan, blue disappearing to grey, red waning to nothing more than blush.

There is no statuette, nothing for the ladies and gentlemen to admire. There will be nothing in black ink upon pages of *Le Figaro*, *Le Temps*, even *L'Illustration*, nothing about a statuette, the captured story of a heart and body, a petit rat called Marie van Goethem destined for the Opéra stage. I will not tear, straight as straight, a square of print from the newspaper and find some clever way to leave it in Monsieur Mérante's path, Monsieur Pluque's. It is the lofty place my imagination had soared to, the high rim of a precipice.

There is only Monsieur Lefebvre, who has the ear of the ballet master, the ear of the director of dance, a picture showing me holding a fan.

Antoinette

A Monday morning and I pull open the door of the washhouse, same as every Monday morning for the three weeks since Monsieur Guiot took me on. Two weeks have passed since the ruined shirts, since the night of the dead dog. He never did know about the linens I plucked from those awaiting delivery, not when the Monday afterward, I was back at the washhouse early, all those linens tucked up under my skirt, seeking a chance to return them—the three shirts to the neat stack with threads the color of leeks knotted into the collars, the reeking camisole to the heap being sorted for the tubs.

Upon leaving the house of Madame Brossard, I did not go looking for Émile at the storage shed of the father of Pierre Gille or the Brasserie des Martyrs. I was wretched in the morning, vomiting into the bucket Madame Brossard put beside the spare bed in Colette's room after pulling the linens up under my chin. Midday, my head still throbbing, my belly still heaving but churning up nothing more than spoonfuls of gleaming yellow sludge, I got to my feet. Marie would be half out of her mind. I tottered back to the rue de Douai only to bear the flogging Maman delivered in the stairwell with the borrowed broom of Madame Legat. This, after Maman asked for payment toward a meat pie and I told her my week's pay was gone, spent in a cabaret. "Eighteen francs gone in a single night," she hollered, but her heart was not much in beating, and soon she was slumped upon a step.

"In truth I spoiled two shirts and got docked."

She looked up. "Such a liar I never before seen."

"Ask Guiot."

She tugged a flask from the folds of her skirt but did not take a drink. No, she held the flask high up, offering it to me. I thought of Émile taking the smoke, siding with Pierre Gille, of me siding with Maman and the absinthe and batted away the flask.

Maman had the broom of Madame Legat to put back, and I watched her take the stairs like an old woman—one foot reached down a single step, the other moved to beside it, all the while gripping the rail.

Wishing for nothing more than to collapse upon my mattress, I opened up the door of our lodging room onto Marie stroking the curls of Charlotte. "You're home," she said, the words coming out like a great sigh, but the worry never left her face. No, Charlotte was slumped in a chair, her eyes glassy, her face pale. "She isn't feeling herself," Marie said. I touched the warm forehead of Charlotte, and without a mother there to say "Into bed with you," I said it myself.

The fever broke in the early hours of the morning, and I was back at the washhouse on an hour's sleep, restoring filched linens and wondering about the way Madame Brossard scolded but bothered to send me home with a pork cutlet and two tangerines, only a bit overripe.

All day at the washhouse, I ached for Émile. I went so far as to imagine a shadow passing over the steamy glass of the window was his broad shoulders, his scrub-brushy hair. When the day's slaving was finally done, I fled across the street to our lodging house, thinking to change my blouse and check up on Charlotte before finding that boy off somewhere, tilting a glass.

Well, that girl was wearing her practice skirt and balancing with one foot held high up over her head in her hand. After missing a class, Marie would be worrying about her muscles growing tight. She would be limbering up, too, but Charlotte was only doing what her body craved and, of course, chose the spot where her pose was prettily framed in the looking glass. I took my spare blouse from the gaping hole of the sideboard, pulled it over my head, dreaming up mauve silk and the dropped jaw of Émile to see me gleaming before him with heaved-up breasts, a frame of curls. I took a minute, plopped down at the table, and felt a weight, like a zinc bucket so full with water it slopped onto the floor. Only forty winks, I told myself and made a little pillow of my arms. Forty winks and the searching would begin. But when I woke up, the streets were quiet, and I knew my chance to find Émile was gone.

On Tuesday when I got home from a long day of cranking the wringing machine, Marie and Charlotte were waiting in the doorway of our lodging room. Their faces gleamed. Charlotte was bouncing on her toes. Marie took my hand and said, "We forgot to say thank you about a hundred times but not tonight." She had the zinc bucket packed with three roasted chicken legs, two pears, a pork terrine, and a baguette. No chance would I make some excuse and go off looking for Émile. They took turns holding my hand and carrying the bucket, while we climbed Montmartre to a patch of trampled grass in front of the basilica being built on the top. The sun set while we stuffed ourselves, and it really was pretty, all the rooftops of Paris cast in a rosy glow and the sky beyond, the bands of dusty yellow and orange and red. After that we lay back and watched the nighttime sky get lit up with pinpricks of light, and Marie said she was going to list twenty nice things I'd done for her so I would know that she knew. She counted them off on her fingers: combing out her hair, arguing with Monsieur LeBlanc, remembering her name day, saving her the larger sugarplum, buying the salami she preferred, stroking her to sleep, collecting wages from Maman, showing her about buying pears, on and on. Then Charlotte did the same, except she listed twenty-one. I swallowed tears and put an arm around each of their necks and pulled them in tight to my chest, and I knew they could hear my thumping heart.

On Wednesday I left the washhouse, wanting nothing but to find

Émile, and there he was across the rue de Douai, leaning up against our lodging house, looking more sheepish than a sheep. I nudged the neckline of my blouse lower, folded my arms over my ribs, squeezing like that corset that made my flesh swell above the mauve silk. I crossed the street and passed by him, feeling smug that I did not go chasing and telling myself I've got to work on being a haughty girl.

"Antoinette," he called up the stairs.

I took two more steps before turning around. "Don't want a boy full of swagger and meanness, a boy who don't mind another slapping his girl."

"You and Colette were screaming, carrying on."

I lifted up my chin.

"It was Colette who struck the first blow," he said.

"Pierre Gille murdered a dog." Émile Abadie, you watch me turn away. You watch me on the stairs, hips swaying no different from Colette's.

"She was taunting, Colette was."

I climbed a further step, then another.

"Can't bear Pierre Gille saying I got the guts of a flea," he said, his voice hushed as dew, and when I looked back, his head was hanging low.

"Pierre Gille is full of bluster."

"Isn't just bluster." He sat himself down sideways on the lowest step, and leaning his head back against the crumbling plaster of the wall, I saw him look so much like that boy I knew from the early days at the Ambigu.

Before the week was done, I hatched a plan to sew into the corner of a fine handkerchief—no one would miss a single one—the letter *E*, something for him to keep in his pocket, to pull out and be reminded of me. I was getting along just fine at the washhouse, figuring out about whether a stain was wax or fruit or tree sap and knowing to use a warm iron or boiling water or turpentine. It turned out the bearded woman—Paulette—liked nothing better than telling a good joke, except maybe hearing us laundresses cackling; and sometimes there was singing, especially Justine, whose voice was strong and clear, like a tolling bell, and we scrubbed those linens counting out the beat. And Marie said three times already about appreciating the way I was slaving to keep Monsieur LeBlanc from our door. She did her best to make up for Maman, who only said it was a surprise every day I bothered to get up for the washhouse, and Charlotte, who saved her sweetness for the pork butcher, with his held-out scrap of crackling, and the fruiterer, with his pyramid of apples soon to turn soft. Oh, the days were long, tiresome, and Monsieur Guiot thought nothing of keeping us past seven o'clock. Any one of us was welcome to leave, to find work as a housemaid, bowing and curtseying and curling up with the rest of the servants at night and never again seeing a café; or as a textile worker, choking in dingy, cramped quarters and getting cooked by the heat and working alongside the snotty-nosed urchins who brought the wage down to two francs a day. A seamstress could do better, milliners, too. But any of us laundresses with a knowledge of needle and thread and hems and embroidery would've left the washhouse ages ago. We were fit only for the boredom of scrubbing, the brute strength of cranking the wringing machine. And so I was careful about the handkerchief, having the sense to jam it into my pocket before Monsieur Guiot even had it marked in his book.

Bent over my tub, feeling the heaviness of the beater gripped in my hand, I pound away at a tablecloth. I am taking a minute to wipe my brow, when who should come hurtling into the washhouse but Michel Knobloch, wild-eyed, looking right, looking left. Last time I laid eyes on him, it was at the Brasserie des Martyrs, the evening Émile called him a liar and he pushed himself up from the bench and stomped off.

Monsieur Guiot scrambles down from the perch of his overseer's booth and makes chase. Is it bare arms Michel Knobloch has come to see? Is he dodging laundresses, dashing along a row of zinc tubs on a dare? I look to the window but glimpse not a single face pressed up against the steamy glass, not a single pair of roving eyes. My attention goes back to Michel Knobloch, to his flitting gaze, bouncing from one laundress to the next, to his coiled-up legs, ready to spring. Monsieur Guiot reaches, aiming for the collar, and I open up my mouth to call out a warning, but I cannot. Monsieur Guiot has not yet forgot the burned shirt, the knocked-off button, the hole left behind. Michel Knobloch ducks, darts, tears deeper into the washhouse, his eyes no longer flitting, but steady, set upon me.

I let go my beater, wipe suds from my hands, ready to shove him away, to say "Leave me to my work," but a step from me, his silent mouth moves through the shape of a word: *Abadie*. I wait, arms hanging at my sides, to hear he is dead, but the hands of Michel Knobloch become a tunnel around his lips, and I shift my ear to the receiving end. "The constables took him to Mazas, Pierre Gille, too," he says. "They're accused of murdering that tavern owner over in Montreuil." No doubt Michel Knobloch is lying or proving once again how he always jumbles the facts. Still, my heart pounds in my chest.

I don't say a single thing, not until I step around Michel Knobloch to face Monsieur Guiot. Loud enough for the account to spread, I say, "My sister fainted at the Opéra, hit her head. She is asking for me."

Maman is there, crowding close, taking in my words. I think about sparing her the greater pain of the wounded daughter being Charlotte. But Marie don't have the sense to back up such a story, not without a hundred questions, and so I have no choice. "It's Charlotte."

Maman will be coaxed to sitting down, fussed over, offered a cup of strong tea. In my mind's eye, I see her pat her chest and dab at her eyes, dredging up the consternation of a waiting mother. "My cross to bear," she is saying. "Two daughters at the Opéra dance school. The effort they put in, enough to make a girl faint." She wrings the linen handkerchief Monsieur Guiot passes to her. "Those girls, like swans." She raises up her chin. "Mark my words. Each will dance upon the Opéra stage."

Monsieur Guiot looks from me to Michel Knobloch and back to me, a cloud upon his brow, and so I undo the strings of my laundress apron, making the decision to let me go on his behalf.

"You'll be docked," he says.

I hand my balled-up apron to Maman and flee the sweltering, smothering steam. I set out, running like the dickens, even if Mazas is in the eastern reaches of Paris. A sharp pain wells up beneath my ribs, but I keep at it, one foot flying in front of the other, panting and puffing and doubling over every couple of blocks.

After an hour of people staring and making way, I come upon the back of Mazas, the hefty, towering wall. There is little to see, only mortared stone reaching for the sky and higher up the roofs of six blocks of cells and the central watchtower.

I lope around to the front, take in the massive archway of the entrance, the four navy-cloaked jailers, each standing, leaning his weight onto a rifle fitted with a bayonet of cold steel. I step closer, close enough that one of those scowling jailers lifts up the butt of his rifle from a paving stone. "I come to speak to Émile Abadie," I say, setting my jaw to look fierce. "They brought him in today."

Another of those jailers bothers to look up from cleaning yellow fingernails. "You need an appointment for visiting," he says. "Come back in the morning to put in your request and then again the next day to see if the warden put down a time for you." He pats the pocket of his trousers. "Won't hurt none to sweeten the pot."

"Not above gorging yourself on the bread snatched from others?" I say, jutting my chin to the swell of his belly, fat like a woman's in her ninth month. Two other jailers look my way, mouths twisting to keep down their smiles.

"Might think better than to insult the fellow passing along the visiting requests."

"Might think better than to steal the sous of an honest working girl with a dead father and a drunken mother and two baby sisters aren't capable of feeding themselves."

He plumps his bottom lip, don't retreat in the least from my hard stare. The pork butcher, with his fondness for Charlotte, he will put up with waiting for his money a further week.

"Don't even know if he is truthfully here," I say. "It's only what I heard."

"Wouldn't know," he says, going back to his nails.

"He come in with a devil looks like an angel, all blond locks and milky skin."

Another of those jailers, one with the cherry nose of someone too often seeing the bottom of a glass, says, "Those boys that slit the throat of the tavern owner?"

"Can't speak for Pierre Gille," I say, "but Émile is gentle like a lamb."

He folds his arm, drawing the muzzle of his rifle tight against his cloak. "You his sweetheart?"

I feel my mouth twitch with the desire to say "Don't see it's any business of a drunkard," but already the one claiming to pass along the visiting requests is sneering, and who knows which of those guards might bring Émile his meals. And so until a count of three, I clamp the end of my tongue with the sharp edges of my teeth. "Kindhearted, he is," I say. "Gentle like a lamb."

"Me and the peach, here," says the drunkard, shoving a thumb toward the only jailer too green to not yet wear the girth of bribery, "we escorted the both of them to the sixth block, one to a single cell, number fourteen, and the other to shared quarters. Fine cellmates, we left him with. You know Vera and Billet?" He smirks, and I keep my mouth from gaping even the smallest bit.

If there is daylight or the stub of a candle left, Marie reads to Charlotte and me from the newspapers, and so I know Billet is a butcher from the rue Flandre, that he hacked his wife to death with the cleaver he used for dividing meat from bone, and Vera, an Italian, who pierced his brother full of holes, stabbing him with a kitchen knife twenty-one times. "Which of those two brought in is lodging with the murderers?" I say, holding my voice flat as paint.

"The dark one, the one with the face of a beast."

My lungs cease their billowing and my blood halts cold in my veins. The world goes black, collapsing from the outside in. And then there is light, dazzling and bright, like the glow of an angel. And I feel the passage of air over my skin, like the breath of a Goliath, like the whoosh of a giant wing cutting through the air. A picture—a vision—comes into my mind. There is blanched skin, a river of blood, a blade being wiped clean, a hand clutching the knife—hairless, pale, pretty, not like that of a man except in the square shape of the fingernails. The hand of Pierre Gille.

ARRESTS MADE IN THE
MONTREUIL MURDER

Two arrests have been made in the brutal slaying of Elisabeth Bazengeaud, the tavern owner stabbed to death three weeks ago in Montreuil. Nineteen-year-old Émile Abadie and sixteen-year-old Pierre Gille are being held at Mazas until their day in court.

Chief Inspector Monsieur Macé sought out Émile Abadie for questioning after patrons of the tavern indicated the youth was once the woman Bazengeaud's lover. He was discovered with Pierre Gille, his constant companion of recent months, in a storage shed belonging to Gille's father where the pair had established sleeping quarters.

Initially both youths vigorously denied being in the faubourg on the day of the murder. The claim proved to be their undoing when several witnesses were able to identify the youths as having entered the tavern. While Gille had thus far avoided trouble with the law, Abadie has a string of petty theft convictions. Monsieur Bazengeaud reported eighteen francs and a watch as stolen from the strongbox at the tavern.

The tender ages of the criminals will no doubt fuel the growing public anxiety over the moral gangrene that appears to have infected the youth of Paris since our defeat by the Prussians.

~ Marie ~

Like he does every morning, Alphonse puts two baguettes on the wooden counter and says, "The best for you." But today is Saturday, the day he counts out the twelve francs I am owed and puts them into my waiting hand, folding my fingers over the coins. And already, without paying my wages, he is back to arranging loaves on the cooling racks. Sometimes his gaze stays put, and more than once I have wondered if there is nothing he likes better than handing over to me two perfect baguettes. Today, though, his eyes were bashful, lowered to the baguettes on the counter. "The best for you," he said, his voice gone shy.

I gather them up. Golden. Even. Perfectly slashed. I clear my throat. "Alphonse?"

"Yes." He does not turn from the cooling racks.

"It's Saturday."

He moves to the counter, stands there, arms hanging at his sides. "The pork butcher wasn't paid what he was owed." His hands press against the wooden countertop. "He went to the washhouse to collect, but Monsieur Guiot said Antoinette cut short her hours all week. So Papa paid the pork butcher, on your behalf." His eyes lifted up, meeting my own. "It was two francs more than you were owed."

I am beaten down by a week such as I have lived. And now I will fall short the six francs owed to Madame Théodore for the private lesson she will give me in the afternoon. I do not know the reason for the unpaid pork butcher and Antoinette cutting her hours short, but now that Émile Abadie has been put in jail, she is home in the evenings, pacing and sighing and shaking her head. And there is no chance of me broaching, with a boy as good-hearted as Alphonse, my sister's attachment to an inmate of Mazas, one who was already sucking the joy from her even before he was locked up.

Often Émile Abadie would come by before Antoinette was home from the washhouse and say to tell that sister of mine she would find him at the Rat-Mort, or some days it was the Brasserie des Martyrs. And when I did, in a split second she went from tired and gloomy to brimming with hope. Always, the scurrying began, the washing of her underarms, the sniffing away at each of her two blouses, the arranging of her hair, the sorrowful huffing in front of the looking glass. Some days he did not come at all, and those days Antoinette would grumble that I had not gone to fetch water or that Charlotte had ripped the hem of her skirt. Other times he would show up in the middle of the night, and I would hear him on the landing, tapping on our door, calling out for Antoinette, starting with a whisper, abandoning quiet when no one stirred. Maman did not wake up. No, it was me, clenching my fists upon the mattress, thinking whether to nudge Antoinette or leave him suffering upon the stairs. But the racket did not let up, and what if Madame Legat heard and reported us to Monsieur LeBlanc? I started poking Antoinette as soon as I heard that boy in the night. It did not mean sleep though. That was when the arguing would start up, about a dead dog, about him taking a smoke, about where he was yesterday or the day before that. Other times there were low voices and soft laughter and then moaning and the creaking of the planks of the landing in a steady beat. Oh, how I hated that boy, the way he snatched the lightheartedness from

Antoinette, the way he left nothing more than a moping girl for Charlotte and me at home.

𝘑 open my palms to the rafters over our heads, and Alphonse says, "All of us in the rue de Douai are thankful it wasn't one of you girls killed instead."

I nod, and, weary as rain, I turn to the door. It is the same treatment Blanche got from me yesterday, climbing the stairs to the practice room. She came up from behind and swung an arm tight around my neck. "I'm growing again. Maman is sure as can be." I did not put my arm around her neck and squeeze back. I only made the slightest nod and kept climbing, one foot in front of the other. She unwrapped her arm from my neck and said, "Scowling isn't helping your monkey face," unlike Alphonse, who does not say a single word.

I cross the rue de Douai quickly, wishing to avoid the magnifying lens all the street is holding up to the van Goethem girls. But Madame Legat is waiting, gawking toward the bakery from the entrance of our lodging house. She puts herself in the doorway so that I cannot pass. "Antoinette was expected at the washhouse this morning," she says and crosses her arms. "She told Monsieur Guiot that come Saturday he could count on her for a full day, an early start. That's what I been told, and yet I seen head nor hide of that girl this morning, and already it is late."

All week I came in from the bakery to find Charlotte with her satchel slung over her shoulder, waiting to set out for the Opéra, and Antoinette already off to the washhouse, or so I thought. But now Madame Legat is telling me Antoinette is not at the washhouse this morning, and Alphonse said she cut her hours short all week. What is Antoinette keeping from me? What is this growing gulf where my own sister has a secret life? Why was the pork butcher not paid? With my wages gone and no money for Madame Théodore, Antoinette is putting in jeopardy my chance at the Opéra, my chance for grace upon the stage, and meat in all our bellies and cups that are not cracked and walls that are properly whitewashed instead of black with soot. A lump swells in my throat even as my fingers curl into tight fists. I choke out, "Antoinette is not my business," but Madame Legat does not budge.

She points, the claw of her fingernail almost touching my chin. "Someone needs to tell that girl mornings visiting with a boy about to meet the blade of a guillotine don't put nothing toward the rent."

In an instant I know what she said is true, that Antoinette is carrying on with Émile Abadie, even with him jailed.

"I got a right to speak," Madame Legat says, "considering the rent is due." She lifts her chin, showing her ropy neck. A neck ready to be wrung. But, no, it is not her throat I want my gripping fingers tightening around. A dozen times in recent days Antoinette said, "I know beyond a shadow of a doubt it wasn't Émile." What I know with the same firmness is that all week, mornings at the washhouse have been traded for mornings at Mazas. She pocketed the money meant for the pork butcher, money that was not hers. It is her fault I am made to stand here, forced to bear Madame Legat's beady eyes, her prying ways. A strength I have not felt all week comes to my limbs. I shove past Madame Legat and take the stairs two at a time.

I push open the door of our lodging room to a view of Antoinette, standing before the looking glass hung above Papa's sideboard. She fusses with a lock of hair, twisting it around her finger, tucking it up behind her ear, inclining her head as she takes in the effect. Her blouse is fresh, her lips tinted, her neck pink from the scrubbing that has taken place. Charlotte hops up from the table. "No waiting for me," she says. "Not once this week have you had to wait." And my heart flutters that she knows to tread lightly on the floor giving away beneath her feet.

"Monsieur Guiot is expecting you at the washhouse," I say to Antoinette.

"I got an errand to run first."

"You're off to Mazas. You've been going to Mazas all week."

Antoinette turns to me from the looking glass. She opens and closes her mouth, trying to decide, then opens it again. "Haven't," she says.

One hundred times I heard her lie to Maman, about money, about what time she came in the night before, about anything at all. One hundred times more I heard her lie to Monsieur LeBlanc: There was a rat in the stairwell. She saw the health inspector poking around. She washed the landing herself because Madame Legat's back was sore. She lied to the pork butcher, telling him Charlotte was meant to eat liver because she was low in iron. To the fruiterer she said Charlotte's hair was falling out, that she would be cured by an orange every week. She told Madame Gagnon that Monsieur Pluque was waiting for Charlotte and me upstairs with such certainty that for a flash I believed it was true. Most of the time Maman stayed ignorant, like Monsieur LeBlanc and the pork butcher and the fruiterer and Madame Gagnon. And even if I never caught her lying to me, plenty of times I wondered. But always, I remembered she loved me. The only lies she could say to me were of no account, trifles like calling me "pretty as a peach" before I went to see Monsieur Pluque that first time, when it was not true. But that was different from now. That lie was told for my benefit, and this new lie is not. "All week you cut short your hours," I say.

I see her wince that I know, watch her shrink at being caught. She puts her hands together, like a prayer, like she needs me to hear. And she says she went to Mazas first on Monday because she got the news and then on Tuesday because an appointment is needed for visiting and then on Wednesday and Thursday because it is how you find out when your appointment is, and again on Friday, when she was finally told she could visit Émile Abadie on Saturday.

"My wages from the bakery went to the pork butcher, who you never even bothered to pay."

"Those jailers at Mazas," she says, "they want a bit of grease upon their palms."

My voice grows louder even as I step closer, my chest puffed out, my muscles tense. "I have nothing for Madame Théodore. My exam is six weeks away."

"It's one lesson, Marie."

"You're stealing from me to visit a murderer."

Her hands drop from their prayer. She gives a look of such defiance that I know the thing she wanted to keep to herself—she passed the money owed the pork butcher to a guard at Mazas, and in that moment put Émile Abadie ahead of Charlotte and me. My hands reach for her shoulders and shove with all my might.

She stumbles, and I shove again. She shoves back, knocking me to the floor, and falls upon my chest, shrieking into my face, "He is no murderer. I know it for a fact." She shifts herself up, so that her spread knees pin my shoulders to the floor. "Don't you call him a murderer." She raises her arm in a threat.

"Murderer!" And there it is: the thousand pinpricks of a slap on my face.

Her hand flies up a second time, and then, Charlotte's arms wrap tight around Antoinette's elbow.

"He is going to the guillotine!"

Antoinette breaks loose her arm, and in a flash Charlotte falls to her knees and rounds over me, the armor of her small shoulder blades covering my face.

All is quiet, and then Charlotte sniffles. Her back heaves.

Antoinette gets up from my chest. "Émile is innocent," she says.

I wrap my arms around Charlotte, stroking and rubbing, easing her up from my face, wondering that she put herself between Antoinette and me.

Never before have the two of us screamed and shoved and come to blows. Never before has she told me such a lie. I push up onto an elbow, feeling alone and scared. Is this the end of Antoinette looking after Charlotte and me? And what is wrong with her that she is devoted to such a boy? Why is she undaunted, even with him put in jail for slitting a wom-an's throat? Maybe, mixed up with feeling afraid, I feel sorry, too. As bad a week as I have lived, her week was worse. I hold Charlotte's trembling body tight against my thumping chest and watch Antoinette wipe tears from her cheeks before she pulls open the door.

Antoinette

A jailer with breath like boiled onions clomps ahead of me, past a string of weighty doors opened up onto dingy cells the breadth of two arms spread wide. Each is bare plaster, except for the iron grate forming the far wall and the single chair just in front. "These cells are for those coming to visit?" I say, and his highness slows his clomping and bothers with a flicker of a nod. "Don't see why I been made to wait." For every cell with a caller sunk onto the chair, a dozen more are as empty as my week's been long.

The jailer halts, grunts, pointing the muzzle of his rifle, and I cross into the cell and hear the groan of the door closing behind my back. The cane seat of the chair has a gaping hole, a hole tearing wider when I plop down, not bothering to be light. I peer through the iron grate, across an intervening passageway, to a long row of cells, and guess Émile is to be put in the cell exactly facing my own. Another jailer, this one patrolling the length of the passageway, trudges by, his footsteps growing fainter as he retreats and then louder until he is again in front of my own cell. Three times more he passes by on his way to either end of the passageway, and I wait, feeling a breath away from my breakfast—fried potatoes nicked from a street vendor—rising up in my throat. It was Marie who started with the yelling, Marie who shoved first, Marie who screamed "murderer" when already my arm was raised. The hunched back of Charlotte, the bony rises of her ribs, were like the rolled-up shell of a pill bug awaiting a squashing fist. But I did not strike. I got up from Marie. Charlotte will forget. And Marie, she would have clobbered me worse than I did her if she had so much as a clue about how to fight. But still, the grease of the fried potatoes churns in my gut. I told a lie to Marie, a lie that was not white, and she knew it. I explained the rigmarole of getting an appointment, but already it was too late. Already I lied, saying I had not gone to Mazas. I only wanted to leave without a fuss, without Marie's lip trembling and her eyes welling with tears, to hang on to the scrap of hopefulness that morning, finally arrived, had brought. But Marie yelled and shoved. The shoving back was a mistake. The hitting, too. I scared those two girls, and already they have more than enough to be fearful of in their lives.

The patrolling jailer passes by yet again, and still the cell exactly facing my own stays empty of Émile. I swallow hard and curl my fingers around the iron bars and wonder about him getting delivered to the wrong cell. Such dopey jailers. Such callousness. I lean my face in close to the iron grate, but they have it rigged so a visitor's only view is into the cell straight across the passageway from his own. "Émile," I call out. I turn my face, calling out again, and then I call louder.

The patrolling jailer is back, the brass buttons of his navy jacket winking in the light of the lamps. He pokes the bayonet of his rifle through the iron grate of my cell. "Shut your trap," he says.

"Maybe if you brought the boy I come to see." How long have I been waiting? An hour? Twenty minutes? I cannot guess. The passage of time must be the same for each prisoner, for Émile, all locked up.

"Another word and I'll be arranging he don't come at all."

I lean back in that feeble, broken chair and watch him turn from the most brutish glare I can muster, taking his time, like there is pride in moving slow.

All the boys of Paris awaiting trial are jailed at Mazas, and I heard from more than one about the tedium of the place. They wake at six o'clock to the sound of a clanging bell, opening up their eyes to four white plaster walls and then rolling from the crammed hammocks where they spent the night. They wait for the door to creak open and the tray holding a paltry jug of bitter wine and a section of stale bread to be set down. The last of the drink sopped up, the last of the crumbs put into their mouths, there are six blank hours to fill with nothing more than folding up the hammocks and sweeping out the cells. At last the weariness is broken by the midday meal, the filling of the mess tins with soup swallowed so slow that always the last mouthful is cold. In the afternoon each prisoner goes to what they call the promenade but is really nothing more than a span of long, narrow walks open to the sky and cordoned off, one from the next, by towering walls. At Mazas there is no chance of a boy scheming with another about what is to be said before a judge, no chance of the comfort of an old friend while waiting out the hours. Émile suffers the same tedium but with the way they have him holed up with Vera and Billet, I imagine always he is watching his back, fear turning his blood sluggish and dragging out the hours even worse than for the rest.

I cling tighter to the iron grate, and next thing, there is the voice of Émile from beyond the cell facing mine. "No word of a lie," he says, "those eyes of hers." Passing into his cell now, he juts his chin in the direction of me, looks back to the escorting jailer. "Like I told you, chocolate pools."

On Monday, after getting the news and rushing from the washhouse to Mazas, I went to the Opéra and joined those knitting, gossiping mothers lining the back wall of the practice room where the youngest petits rats were taking class. Upon catching my eye, Charlotte wrinkled up her forehead. I waved away her bewilderment, blew a kiss, and after that her attention was back on the string of steps Madame Théodore was calling out, the music streaming from the violin. Other girls jumped higher. Two were lighter upon their feet. But I could see the music reaching deep inside her and for a minute, just watching, I was lifted up. It was not right that

Charlotte, with her air of boldness and courage and heart, and her dingy practice skirt and grimy cheeks and uncombed hair, like a rooster tail springing from her head, was the most bedraggled of those skinny girls.

Afterward I said, "You feel the music deeper than those other rats," and that snippy girl, she said, "You're supposed to be scrubbing linens with Maman."

I stroked her cheek, and she stood there, arms limp at her sides, eyes too weary for so young a face, and I felt a little pang that the child was taking on Marie's habit of worrying. "I was delivered a message at the washhouse, and I told Maman you fainted at the Opéra, that you were asking for me. I can't say more but just let on."

"You went off, shirking work for that boy." Her eyes shifted from weary to stone-cold. Already, even without the news of Mazas, she was poisoned against Émile, poisoned by Marie.

I took the hands of that small girl. I could not endure the questions of Marie, the brutality of Maman if I was forced to tell the true message of Michel Knobloch. Not tonight. Not after such a day. "Just this once."

"I want a new sash—scarlet," she said back; and later, in the evening, with her spinning a story of collapsing at the barre and getting a pastille to suck from Madame Théodore and then answering the queries of Maman without stumbling a single time, I felt not a bit proud about the lying of that small girl being an equal match to my own.

Émile sits with those burly thighs of his a little parted, those brawny hands clutching just above his knees. He leans in from the waist, forehead almost touching the iron grate, eyes peering out steadier than a flat rock. There is no twitching, scratching, swallowing. No glancing away. "I had no part in the butchering," he says.

The day after Michel Knobloch brought the news of Mazas, I opened up the door of our lodging room in the evening to Marie sitting at our small table, bent over a newspaper, and I knew that somewhere between the Opéra and the rue de Douai she came upon a news seller hollering the names of Émile Abadie and Pierre Gille. "Antoinette," she said, hopping up. "Sit down. A glass of water? Maman, pour a glass for Antoinette."

Maman said, "You're pale as bleached linen."

"Émile is in Mazas," Marie said, "arrested for robbing and murdering the tavern owner in Montreuil." She put a hand to her heart, and I saw the rawness where, worse than ever, the flesh of her thumb was picked away.

Maman fell onto a chair. I watched her hand twitch, longing for the flask in the pocket of her skirt.

"I already know," I said. Marie's hand dropped to her side and ease came to her face.

"That boy who keeps you out half the night?" Maman said.

"Wasn't Émile," I said.

Marie touched the newspaper, quiet as a mouse. "Witnesses saw him going into the tavern. Two of them."

"It was the other boy, Pierre Gille, slit the neck," I said.

"Émile Abadie told you that?" Marie said.

"It's what I know to be true." I lifted my chin, looked hard at Maman and then Marie. "I saw it in a vision. It was the hand of Pierre Gille upon the knife."

The mouth of Marie gapes open, then closed, like a fish.

"Spit it out, whatever it is you got to say."

Again she touches the newspaper. "It says right here Émile Abadie was the lover of the woman Bazengeaud," she said. Maman took the flask from her pocket, slugged good and long, licked the shine of the absinthe from her lips.

The face of Émile collapses into his cupped hands. He rattles his head. "I only wanted money," he says, and face still hanging, adds, "Not a single sou saved. Always spending what's in my pocket."

Better than anyone I know his generosity, but I say no such thing.

"I got to be such a disappointment." From beneath his eyebrows he looks between his fingers, waiting. Waiting for what? A choked no from me? A head shook? I feel a tiny tug, the slack of a leash taken up. But, no, he's got to say about the woman Bazengeaud, whether all those times on the chaise, in the stairwell, pushed up against a stone wall with me were not even real.

He drops his hands, and his eyes lock onto my own. "I found my pockets empty one night. My belly was aching and rumbling for food." He licks his lips. "Gille, he was going on about how he collected fifty francs from his mother's old housemaid, all for keeping quiet about her lowering her drawers for him."

He tells me how pretty soon he and Pierre Gille were galloping over to Montreuil, all feverish with the idea of threatening the woman Bazengeaud. One hundred francs she would pay him, that, or Émile would squawk to her husband about the whore she truly was.

"Always she was pulling up a chair beside me, groping at the buttons of my trousers, stroking, bringing me a cognac on the house," he says. "But, Antoinette, what you got to know is that every scrap of that toying was before you. Rest assured. A long time ago."

I breathe deep, slow, think about Marie as a tiny fly creeping along the wall. That fly, with its doubting mind and wary eyes, even it would see the way each detail meshes with those plucked from the newspaper. And didn't he say about carrying on with the woman Bazengeaud without a bit of prodding from me? That fly would see the way it points to the truth of his words. The gas lamps flare a moment, licking bright the dull plaster of the walls. "You're not a disappointment," I say.

"I got it in my head you were going to find another sweetheart, Antoinette. You are always saying about a lodging room of our own, and that little drawstring pouch you're keeping safe, I saw a chance to triple the weight."

He goes on to tell me it turned out the woman Bazengeaud only smirked and snapped her cleaning rag against his chest. "Wouldn't have bothered with a boy, now, would I, if I had a husband cared in the least?" she said. "You go ahead, Émile. Tell him whatever you please."

She topped up his cognac, told Pierre Gille to pay up if he wanted a drop more. She was off, wiping down the counter, when Pierre Gille pounded a fist against the tabletop and spat low words about not coming all the way to Montreuil for a thimbleful of swill, about the strongbox yawning open not five steps away.

"There wasn't a speck of fondness in me for the old hag," Émile says, "but I got more decency than to rob a woman just topped up my glass."

He drained the last of the cognac down, and left Pierre Gille railing and fuming and calling Émile skittish as a wet cat.

The clacking heels of the patrolling jailer grow close, and the two of us shift to sitting straight, away from the iron grate, until he is past. Then Émile rocks onto the hind legs of his chair. "Gille told me it'd be easy," he says, staring at the blankness of the ceiling above.

"The blackmailing?"

He tips back to upright. "Course the blackmailing. I wouldn't never have gone along if I knew he had a knife. I swear to you, Antoinette, it was Gille slit the throat."

I make a tiny nod, feel my elbows, drawn tight against my sides, turn slack. "I know it's true."

And then for the first time in all my days, I see the eyes of Émile Abadie grow damp. A noise—like the sash of a window getting unstuck—comes up from the back of his throat and then he is wiping at his eyes with the back of his hand. "You're all I got in the world, Antoinette."

I want to fix what is broke, to say about the court hearing both sides, those great minds all trained on learning the truth, but I remember him being put with the butcher from the rue Flandre, the Italian with the brother pierced full of holes, and even with the door behind me tight against the jamb, I feel a waft of cold breath upon the back of my neck.

He strokes the weighty ridge of his brow, wagging his head from side to side. "When we first come to Mazas," he says, "Gille was in front, with an inspector, and me following behind." He shuts his eyes. "The inspector, he said to Gille, loud enough to ensure I was hearing the words, 'Come on, Gille. You look honest enough. You couldn't have committed a murder. You were led by Abadie, in which case, you should tell us everything. We'll keep your honesty in mind. Be sure of that.' "

Behind me there is the sound of metal against metal, a key turning in the lock, and then the voice of the jailer who brought me to my cell saying, "Your thirty minutes are up."

"I just finished sitting down," Émile says from behind both my grate and his.

The jailer smirks, folds his arms across his puffed-up chest. "Shouldn't have finished that smoke." He takes my arm, hauls me to my feet.

"Tomorrow, Antoinette? You'll come?"

Tomorrow is Sunday and already I arranged it with the jailers Sunday would be my regular visiting day. I nod, looking over my shoulder as I get hauled from the cell. "Tomorrow."

We are a dozen steps away when the called-out words of Émile echo in the passageway: "All I got in the world."

My hand goes to my heart, and I think of that boy counting on me above everybody else, loving me the most.

The jailer loosens his grip on my arm, says, "It'll be the guillotine for him."

I suck the inside of my cheeks, land the gob of collected spit on his polished boot. I crumple with the blow that comes. On my knees, I grip my aching ribs, gulp dank air.

⊱⊶ Marie ⊷⊰

I feel the smallest creature in the world, leaning a shoulder into the massive door of the Foyer de la Danse, budging it open just enough, passing through into a place reserved for the abonnés and the senior-ranking ballet girls they come to admire. Always it is off-limits to the petits rats, nothing we are allowed to taste, always except today.

I stand there, neck craned, feet shuffling in a slow circle. No doubt each of the girls already limbering at the barre did the same on seeing the glory for the first time. Every bit of ceiling is painted or carved with cherubs and flowers and scrolls. The walls are gold and glittering, lined with velvet banquettes, lit with a chandelier dripping crystal, ringed at the highest reaches with a garland of medallions, each framing a portrait of an étoile. Will I ever be deserving of the glory of this place? It is a question we are meant to ask ourselves today, the reason we were told to gather here, awaiting our names, called one by one, our moment upon the stage, our moment of proving ourselves capable of flitting and fluttering and hovering over the earth, of otherworldliness and grace.

Around me mothers fluff perfect tarlatan, new skirts bought for fifteen francs, and tie bright sashes costing a further six, and pin into place silk flowers paid for with the last of the sous they scrimped to put aside. All of it is doubled by a looking glass taking up the space of an entire wall. I glimpse myself reflected there—my monkey face, the hair Antoinette did not put up—a worm among peaches, well, except for my new slippers and the scarlet sash Charlotte wrung from Antoinette. Charlotte had me begging to borrow it in the morning. How could she be so ungrateful, considering the bakery wages, the baguettes, the buckets of water I haul? I did not mind too much, though, not when it gave me a chance to say out loud about the importance of the day. "Oh, Christ," Antoinette said, fingers thumping her brow. "I meant to do your hair. I really did. And now it's too late."

It was true she had turned forgetful about little things like asking how was my day or was my allegro coming along or was Blanche being nice. Still, allowing something as momentous as my examination day to slip her mind was new.

She stepped between me and Charlotte, who was still gripping her sash behind her back. A hand on each of my shoulders, Antoinette said, "Let the music fill up your head. Let the music push away the fear. You're ready, Marie. Not a speck of doubt." She whirled around then and faced Charlotte. "You got one second to hand that sash over to Marie, or it won't take me but a further second to tear it in half."

I tell Lucille that her flowers are the prettiest of all, Ila that her sash is the pale pink of a cherry blossom, Perot that a skirt so white shows the creaminess of her skin. And they say they wish they had backs as supple as my own, that we are sure to be asked for fouettés en tournant, that mine are the steadiest of all. Blanche holds me tight, and I look firm into her eyes and say, "Together, soon enough, upon the stage," and we touch a post holding up the barre because maybe it is iron underneath the gilt. It is how we are today—golden, good.

Madame Dominique had gone over exactly what to expect, how each of us will stand, alone, front and center, upon the Opéra stage, awaiting the instructions called out by Monsieur Pluque. He will be seated in the first row of the orchestra stalls, she told us, alongside Monsieur Vaucorbeil, the director of all the Opéra, and Monsieur Mérante, the ballet master. She and Madame Théodore will be just behind them, in the second row.

A good way back from the examination board, in the boxes of the first balcony, will be any abonnés or senior-ranking dancers caring to watch, also the mothers—crossing fingers, pinching the crucifixes hanging from their necks, their knitting needles for once left quiet in their bags. Every mother will be there, except my own, which is what I prefer. I have worries enough without fearing her calling out to me upon the stage or deciding she might have a bit of sway with Monsieur Pluque or thinking she is whispering to the other mothers when she is cackling worse than a hen laying an egg.

Monsieur Pluque will call out a series of adagio steps, slow movements like taking sixteen bars of music to rise up onto the toes of one foot and make a grand rond de jambe en l'air. There will be a pianist in the orchestra pit, accompanying the movements, which means the tempo is up to someone who cannot even see whether a girl is teetering and wanting the adagio over and done with before she topples from her toes. It is not the part I fear most, though. Madame Dominique says I have the balance of clockwork and the suppleness of a green twig. It is the allegro combinations that fill me with dread. Feet flying, beating together in the air, slip-sliding across the floor, then up in the air again but this time toe to knee and remembering to land in fifth position, right foot behind. On and on and on. My mind races. My shoulders inch ever higher. It is what happens when I think too hard about my feet, that and Madame Dominique thwacking her cane upon the ground. "Two entrechats," she said just the other day, holding up two fingers, like it might help me count. "Then a single glissade—just one—before the saut de chat." She nodded to the violinist, starting up the music again, and turned away, her focus on another girl. And getting the steps right is not even enough. "Each step must be given a particular character, your hallmark as a dancer," Madame Dominique says. "That's what will earn you a position in the quadrille."

With the girls called in an order decided by the lengths of drawn straws, I will be the very last in front of the examination board. Like every other waiting girl, I labor to keep my muscles limber, making pliés deep and slow with feet wide apart in second position, laying my torso flat over the leg propped upon a barre. I join the others in calling out good luck when a girl leaves and searching her face for some sign when she comes back. Sometimes there are tears—the pianist did not keep an even tempo, Monsieur Vaucorbeil twisted around in his seat before even three bars of the adagio were done, she forgot to grind a bit of rosin beneath her slippers and slid on landing a grand jeté. We nod, lips tight and brows knit, cloaking any gladness at our own chances improved.

I stand stock-still upon the Opéra stage, feet in fifth position, arms en repos, waiting for Monsieur Mérante to look up from his notebook and give the tiny nod signaling Monsieur Pluque to call out the last of the steps. My gaze moves beyond the examination board, across the stalls of the main floor, to the four rows of balconies, all of it plush red velvet and elaborately carved gold and veiled in dusk with only three gas lamps lit, two upon the stage and the third casting a halo of light around the examination board and also Monsieur Degas, hunched over his drawing pad three rows behind.

I ache to hear the step, the piano cleaving the air and coaxing the place behind my heart, filling me from inside out. I want to dance again, to feel the music lifting my limbs, arching my back, streaming from my fingertips, my toes. Grace is with me today, also steadiness and lightness and speed. I have seen Madame Dominique's quiet smile, Monsieur Mérante's lifted eyebrows, Monsieur Pluque's bewildered gaze.

"Four fouettés en tournant," says Monsieur Pluque, pushing himself up in his seat. "Eight, if you can manage it."

I swallow the smile that appears with being asked for the turns that have come so easy to me ever since Antoinette told me the trick of an imagined string pulling me up from the crown of my head. It is the step I wished for when I stroked the horseshoe on the small table in front of the stage-door keeper's loge. I ready myself in fourth position, conjure up the string, fix my gaze upon Madame Théodore's orange head scarf, the spot where my focus will linger even as my body turns and then snap to again each time I return to facing downstage. Spotting adds sharpness to a turn, but more important, it stops the giddiness that comes from whirling like a top. I breathe in a single bar of music before rising onto the toes of my left foot and whipping around fast, not four times. Not eight. But sixteen. Sixteen fouettés en tournant. I land quietly, steadily, feet in a perfect fourth croisé, and I hold myself still, feeling the joy of a step perfectly done rolling through me like a wave.

Madame Dominique's smile is wide, so much so that until she leans her mouth against her fist, I think she will laugh. After a bit of whispering and head tilting and nodding among the examination board, Monsieur Pluque calls out, "If you please, Mademoiselle van Goethem, a révérence."

I make a révérence, arms reaching out in front to the examination board and then opening wide. My gaze, solemn as ever, moves from face to face—Monsieur Vaucorbeil, Monsieur Mérante, Monsieur Pluque, Madame Dominique, Madame Théodore. I spend the final seconds of the révérence honoring Monsieur Degas.

Yesterday I climbed the stairs to Madame Dominique's practice room—one last class before facing the examination board. I went to the very spot where every day I began the chore of loosening my back. But there, dangling from the barre by the ribbons, I found a pair of ballet slippers without a single scuff. A small tag was attached: *Mademoiselle van Goethem, so your feet will shine.* Monsieur Degas knew my spot at the barre. Only his burning gaze could be as accurate as a ruler in measuring my feet.

Outside the Opéra there is a moment of pure joy, bliss, and I bound across the courtyard to the back gate, hanging on to that moment, but hanging on so hard I give shape to the thought I wanted to keep away: With the quadrille comes the stage in the evenings and late nights, an end to my early morning laboring at the bakery, the wages I need, no different than I need air. I slow to walking, and when I look up it is to see Monsieur Lefebvre's carriage glinting in the sunshine of the day. The plumed horses whinny and bluster and stamp, their tails whisking away the flies gathering with the warmth. "Mademoiselle van Goethem," Monsieur Lefebvre calls out, leaning from the carriage, beckoning for me to come.

"You were splendid today," he says, stepping clear of the doorway, waving his hand in a way that makes me think he means for me to go inside. I inch closer to the carriage, not so boldly that he will think me brazen if his waving meant something else. "Yes, yes," he says, "out of the hot sun."

Inside he points for me to sit, takes the spot beside me, crowding a little close, considering the bench is wide enough for four and that across from ours a second runs the width of the carriage. "Your turns at the end," he says. "Even Vaucorbeil pulled himself up at little straighter in his seat."

"You were in the house?" Monsieur Vaucorbeil sat straighter on account of me? But does Monsieur Lefebvre know the seriousness of such a claim?

"My little gift? The size was right? Of course I was in there."

"The slippers?"

"Come now, Mademoiselle van Goethem. There's hardly a girl in all the corps buying her own."

"It's only that I thought they were from someone else." I feel a dunce, now, for assuming the slippers were from Monsieur Degas. With three months come and gone since he asked me to model and the statuette being a failure, it was a stupid thing to think.

He puts his face close to mine, and his voice snaps from light to stern. "I told you I would put in a good word with Monsieurs Pluque and Mérante. I kept my promise. Now, who did you think the slippers were from?"

Almost, it is like I am back in Sister Evangeline's classroom, fearing the answer I am about to give is wrong and wanting so badly to get it right. With the slippers, was Monsieur Lefebvre showing a desire to help? Now more than ever I need his charity. "Monsieur Degas."

He waves away Monsieur Degas with the flick of his wrist, like men with rumpled waistcoats and sloppy beards are no more than vapor in his mind. He opens the velvet-lined box sitting at his feet and takes out a glass etched with garlands and wreaths and hands it to me. Then he lifts the cloth draping a silver bucket of ice and twists the cork from a dark bottle sweating the heat of the day. "I've been assured of your elevation to the quadrille," he says.

He does not seem like the sort of man to say what is not true, not like Maman getting weepy and calling me her dearest dear when we all know it is Marie the First, or if we are only counting those who are not angels, then tiny Charlotte. To hear such a thing and then not find my name upon the list posted outside Monsieur Pluque's office in the morning will break my heart a thousand times worse than if he never opened his mouth. "Please, Monsieur Lefebvre, I can only hear what is cast in stone."

He fills my glass. "I understand the seriousness of what I said." He puts a hand on my thigh, gives a gentle squeeze, like Papa, and it is all I can do to keep myself from dancing my happiness. His hand lifts to my glass and tips it to my mouth. "Now, my dear, be a good girl and drink your champagne."

Should I ask about Blanche? She came into the Foyer de la Danse after her turn, and I saw right away her hands clutched together, holding in her glee. She would not leap and carry on, fueling bitterness, not today. She gave me the little smile that said the examination board had seen her very best. And I have no reason to turn Monsieur Lefebvre's mind to her dove arms. It is not a thought I am proud of thinking, not when she is my only true friend at the dance school, but the truth is, if he has more to give than slippers, my need matches that of Blanche.

I wet my tongue, swallow a mouthful. Champagne, which I never before sipped, is like drinking air. I feel tiny bubbles breaking open in my throat, taste the tang of a metal knife slicing a tart apple. "In the rue de Douai we are used to tasting the cask in our wine."

He laughs, fills his own glass, slides open a little window across from our bench and tells the driver we will pass along the Seine. Once we are under way, he says, "A celebratory drive, mademoiselle?" and I nod and wonder about him opening the closed drapes blocking out the lapping Seine.

He leans his head up against the back of the carriage, looking not a bit like he desires to talk, and we ride in quiet for a bit, me sipping away. In this moment I should be thinking of nothing more than the tiny bubbles at the back of my throat, but never have I showed a talent for dwelling on what is good; and in my mind's eye appears Antoinette, last Sunday, coming in from visiting at Mazas and burying her head in her arms folded on the table. I sucked in a deep breath and reminded myself about the hundred times she was patient with me. "Well?" I said.

"They found the knife. The inspector told Émile."

"Oh," I said, feeling a glimmer of hope rising up. Was Émile Abadie's guilt finally slithering into her mind?

"Can't you see? Pierre Gille wouldn't give up the place where he got rid of it unless he knew not an ounce of blame was aimed at him."

She looked up, skinny and tired, her eyes rimmed in red, and it made my heart ache. Stirring hope in a girl crumpled on a chair was not right, not when it was only putting off the further heartache just around the bend. But her anguish was such that in that moment I forgot about the promise I made myself to show her Émile Abadie through the clear lens of my own eyes, and I said, "Maybe the inspector was bluffing."

"He showed Émile the knife."

She would have to give up her fantasy of Émile Abadie's innocence, and I put my palm upon her shoulder, as tender as I could. But I felt her bristle, irritated by my touch, like it was traitorous of me to think the news might tip her over to seeing his guilt. Was it possible she was not swayed in the least? "There is no doubt, then, that those boys slit the throat." I stated it like a fact.

"Don't prove a thing," she said and shrugged off my hand.

Monsieur Lefebvre blinks his head straight from resting against the back of the carriage, and I remember I have not said a word of thanks for the slippers. Such a gap. "Well," I say, feeling the boldness of the champagne on nothing but a crust of bread, "if my feet shone even the smallest bit today, it was on account of your gift. You sent me to the stage with my spirits soaring high."

And then his hand is upon my thigh again, but there is no squeeze like Papa's. No, the hand stays put. I remember Josephine's claims of abonnés dreaming up the unnatural, forcing it upon a girl, of fingers creeping where they do not belong. My back grows rigid, my shoulder blades pushing hard against the back of the bench, and the hand lifts. Perot said the abonnés only helped out so a girl could keep her mind on her work. "Madame Dominique tells me you're up before the roosters, kneading dough at a bakery."

"It's true," I say, and then I cannot really remember what made me so skittish about a hand upon my leg. It seems like nothing, now, with even the memory of that hand's weight gone.

"It can't continue," he says. "You'll have performances in the evening. You should be sleeping late. How much do they pay you?"

Is he right now thinking about altering my situation? For a bit of luck, I slip my hand into my pocket and touch the black iron of the key waiting there. "At the bakery? Twelve francs each week and two baguettes a day."

He reaches inside his jacket, pulls out a wallet, and hands me a twenty-franc note. "Quit," he says, and it appears Perot has a truer view of the abonnés than Josephine. I think of the dust-licking curtsey of a coryphée Monsieur Mérante had switched from the lesser role of a maenad to a nymph in *Polyeucte* and get up from the bench, wanting to copy it, but am only jostled back into my spot. Instead, with Monsieur Lefebvre's laughter spurring me on, I bring Charlotte's easy smile to my lips and find the voice she uses with the pork butcher. "Such generosity," I say. "I am in your debt."

"Nothing pleases me more."

He tilts the champagne bottle to my empty glass, and I hold it out to him. I lap at the froth filling my glass, laugh when it tickles my nose, which keeps the smile upon his face. It is then, with my glass again drained and filled back up, that he opens the sliding window and says to the driver, "The Bois de Boulogne," which I have never before seen but know to be thickly wooded and far away on the western outskirts of Paris.

I swallow the bubbles of air at the back of my throat.

LE FIGARO

3 AUGUST 1880

THE MONTREUIL MURDER

Next month Émile Abadie and Pierre Gille go to
the Court of Assizes to answer for the murder of
the tavern owner Bazengeaud, that brave woman
of Montreuil who was massacred with the knife
these young scoundrels were able to locate for the
chief inspector. While both have confessed to
going to the tavern with the intention of blackmail,
Gille claims Abadie slit the woman Bazengeaud's
throat in a moment of panic. Abadie denies anything beyond enjoying a cognac at the tavern
after the blackmail attempt failed and leaving in
advance of Gille.

I saw the two of them up close last week when
they were taken to the Montreuil tavern by the
chief inspector for questioning. One could not help
but be immediately struck by Abadie's bestial look.
He is barely nineteen years old and yet is shaped
like a herculean man—stocky, wide shouldered,
arms of steel. His head is solidly planted on a short,
thick neck, and a large and powerful jaw gives it a
brutish air. His coloring is yellowish—the skin

color of prison. This young thug oozes crime from top to bottom. Meeting him in a dark place would send one's hand flying to the hilt of one's sword.

Gille, on the other hand, is fresh faced, all smiles. He looks like a bright young man, who, on first glance, elicits sympathy. At sixteen years of age, he is tall, slim, narrow waisted. His coloring, despite his long detention at Mazas, is still of an elegant paleness. With his blond, abundant hair over a large, well-proportioned forehead, his look is exceptionally gentle; I will say more—it is distinguished. If he were dressed by a fashionable tailor, all the girls of Paris would yearn for him. On the night of a premiere, with his lovely adolescent head seen in the front rows, he would be taken for the son of an English lord.

Antoinette

Today, the final day of the trial, I stand for the first time in the crammed gallery of the Court of Assizes, awaiting the judges, the prisoners. Just yesterday, a day of recess, I sat across the iron grates from Émile, and when I asked a string of questions about the trial, he snapped I should bother showing up if I was so concerned. But once when he was fuming, he called all those court-goers gawkers and degenerates—both the society ladies, who petitioned for a spot on the witness benches up front, and the hordes, who lined up for hours to get a place in the gallery. "I didn't want to gawk," I said, which did nothing to alter the hard look on his face, and so I made the promise I keep today: "Tomorrow I will be in the court."

For weeks the nose of Marie has been glued to the newspapers, and since the trial got under way, she spends every waking moment worrying and planning and licking her lips, getting herself ready to prove to me the guilt of Émile. Just last week, she tapped the newspaper spread open on our little table where I was digging the last of the marrow from a bone. "They found a pair of trousers and a shirt flecked with blood in the storage shed belonging to Pierre Gille's father," she said. "The trousers are the right size for Pierre Gille, not the shirt though. The shirt is more the size of Émile Abadie."

Such news was not good. I had intelligence enough to know that. Yet seeing hopefulness on her face that finally my mind was turned against Émile, I pouted my lips and gave a saucy shrug. "Proves Pierre Gille slit the throat, don't it?"

"Proves he was close enough to get splattered, which isn't different from what he's been saying all along."

I stood up from the table.

She tapped another spot, lower down the column of print. "The missing watch has yet to turn up. Émile ever show you a fancy lady's watch, Antoinette?"

A week ago an inspector came waltzing into the washhouse, asking if I was the sweetheart of Émile. He pulled open a portfolio and shoved underneath my nose a drawing of a watch with the face behind a heart-shaped opening. "Missing from the strongbox at the tavern," he said, poking the drawing. "Your darling make a habit of giving you gifts?" I never laid eyes on such a watch and said, "Don't know a thing about it," which turned out to be the exact words Émile used when I next sat across the iron grates from him and asked about the watch.

I gave my harshest glare to Marie, standing there, chin pushed forward, hands on her hips. "He gave me a dozen watches," I said, "all of which I pawned."

"Yes or no, Antoinette?"

"What makes you think I'd tell you if he did?" It got my back up, her harping, her going on and on. I felt like she wanted him proved guilty more than she wanted happiness for me, and it made me wonder if at the heart of all her fussing was some dream of not sharing me with Émile.

The next evening, she was at it again, this time following me about our lodging room with a newspaper like I could not hear her blathering unless she was breathing down my neck. "Émile Abadie's stepfather—a Monsieur Picard—was in court today," she said. "He called Abadie . . ." She finds the spot in the newspaper. " 'A no-good boy who always had money for women and drink, even without a day of honest work in his life.' "

I snapped around to face her. "He hates Émile."

"Antoinette, listen. Just listen with your mind open to the possibility that maybe Émile Abadie isn't what he seems." She cleared her throat and, reading from the newspaper, said, " 'Under oath Monsieur Picard said, "That boy, he pulled a knife on the missus once, threatened her life, all because she refused to pour him a glass of wine when he was already soused." Madame Picard corroborated the story.' "

My face must have blanched because next thing I knew Marie was reaching out, tenderly laying a hand upon my arm. I steadied my voice and said, "She is lying for her husband, just showing a bit of loyalty, which is more than I can say for you."

Her hand fell away. She bit her lip. And maybe I felt a tiny bit remorseful for rebuking the girl. But still, it worked to shut her up.

It is a stinking, sweltering day, and the heat is even worse in the courtroom than it is outside. I feel my skin growing damp, smell the tobacco and garlic and sweat of those crowding close in the gallery. My stomach flip-flops, and I wonder how I will endure the day, even as I shove an elbow into a toothless fellow taking advantage of the tight quarters to press himself against my hip.

The court is long and narrow, with the seats of the judges at the end farthest from the gallery. Beneath the tall windows running the length of a side wall, the men of the jury wait, stroking mustaches, brushing lint from their jackets, straining to look full of thought. I shift my gaze from one to the next and see, just like Émile said, each is the kind who admires Baron Haussmann for flattening the lodging houses of the poor to open up the boulevards, the kind who believes it is nothing but dance halls and cafés keeping the lowly from eating meat every night. Across from the

jury are the defending attorneys, those heroes of the court according to
Émile, and behind them, perched high up and awash in the harsh light
spilling through the windows, the prisoners' box where Émile and Pierre
Gille will be held.

The din of the crowd grows, and then the ladies, sitting in their finery
on the twelve benches up front, shift to their feet. In the gallery, the gawkers rise up on tiptoe, straining to see. More than one points. Émile and
Pierre Gille, blinking into blinding glare, shuffle to the prisoners' box, a
jailer each gripping their arms. A moment later the attention shifts over to
the three judges filing into the court. Any other day, I would howl at the
ridiculousness of those men, each wearing a little hat, like six inches of
stovepipe propped upon his head, and a heavy red robe trimmed at the
front opening with a wide band of white fur spotted with black. Even
before the presiding judge takes his seat underneath a carving of Jesus suffering upon the cross, sweat is creeping down his face. I glance to the windows, the still curtains hanging there, the laden sky beyond, and wish for
a clap of thunder, a breath of cool air upon the neck of that roasting judge.

After I said I would come, Émile told me what to expect—first, the
final plea of Monsieur Albert Danet, the attorney defending him, and that
of the attorney lying through his teeth on behalf of Pierre Gille, and then
the summary of the judge and last the verdict of the jury and the sentencing. Émile said more than once about Monsieur Danet slaving like an ant
on his behalf, and the scrawny, black-robed gentleman with the bruised-
looking eyes has got to be him.

He approaches the jury, and with his gaze locked upon the face of one
or another of those stern men, he says, "The prosecutor asked you to con-
sider why Émile denied being in Montreuil the day of Elisabeth Bazengeaud's death. The answer he supplied—that Émile knew his guilt—is in
fact true. The part, esteemed jurors, where you were misled was the prosecutor's suggestion that the boy knew himself to be guilty of murder,
when in truth, he knew himself to be guilty of nothing more than an

attempt at blackmail. To accept any other conclusion is to shirk your responsibilities to this court."

He goes on about the blood-speckled trousers, saying they were no doubt worn by the scoundrel who held the knife to the throat of the good woman Elisabeth Bazengeaud. "Much ink has been spilled describing Émile's herculean physique," he says, "and I can assure you of this: Even with the pulling and yanking of the inspector, the blood-speckled trousers—the very pair that fit Pierre Gille like a glove—never made it more than halfway up the thighs of Émile Abadie." Then Monsieur Danet slips off his robe and holds it by the collar, out from his side, and turns in a slow circle. Back to facing the jury, he explains about being more or less of the same build as Pierre Gille and how he himself is wearing a shirt that is a replica of the blood-speckled one that turned up in the storage shed. "Not the best fit, to be sure," he says, "but good enough, particularly for a youth—estranged from his family, without employment—such as Pierre Gille."

He moves on to recounting the stories of three witnesses, each showing the stepfather of Émile to be a known liar, a brute to his wife, her son. I lean in and lean in farther, and Monsieur Danet, he goes on for two hours, showing the worthlessness of every scrap of evidence against Émile.

To finish Monsieur Danet pulls a handkerchief from his pocket, takes his time wiping his brow, then says, "Is Émile Abadie one of the murderers of the good woman Bazengeaud? The prosecutor instructs you not to hesitate even one minute before declaring him thus. I can still hear his words asking you to hand down a verdict without pity. But is it right to pretend the details of this case are as clear as day? Wouldn't it be truer to say that never before has a case left spirits more uneasy and consciences less reassured? Émile Abadie, at nineteen years of age, with his life before him, has not been proven guilty, and I remind you, esteemed jurors, of the vow you have taken, the duty you have to fulfill."

I search the face of Émile, looking for some sign he is just as hopeful as I am after the brilliance of Monsieur Danet, but he is looking to his feet, his lips pressed to a line. Did he not hear? Has fear made him deaf as mud? No. He is only taking the broken posture of a boy deserving of the mercy of the court.

The attorney of Pierre Gille walks to the same spot where Monsieur Danet stood and opens his hands to the jury. "Why," he says, "would young Pierre Gille divulge the location of a knife that could prove the guilt of a murderer? There is only one answer. The murderer is other than Pierre Gille." Three times more he asks the same question and answers using different words, but always the meaning is the same. The chins of four men of the jury bob down, then up, and the attorney replies to those timid nods with a forceful one of his own. "Elisabeth Bazengeaud was not a small woman," he says, "nor was she meek, not with the long hours she kept, laboring in a tavern. My colleague Monsieur Danet asserts that she was murdered single-handedly." He points behind him to the prisoners' box. "It is impossible that such a scrawny boy as Pierre possesses the strength required."

In the prisoners' box Pierre Gille sits with his head bowed, his shoulders falling forward, his hands in his lap. He has grown skinnier at Mazas, and slouching like he is, he looks to have no more power than a newborn bird. Across the room, the men of the jury shift their attention back and forth between the waifish frame of Pierre Gille and the hulking one of Émile. Pierre Gille looks up, giving those jurors full view of his face. He wipes at the corner of his eye with the back of his hand before going back to bowing his head, and I hate that boy a thousand times more than in that moment when he slapped my face.

I lace my fingers together, knock my knuckles against my chin. Those men, what they need to be told is Pierre Gille is no weakling. They need to hear about the shove throwing Colette onto her rump, the slap sending my head jerking to the side, the kick snapping the neck of a dog. I want to scream it out. Never mind about the rules of the court, and the presiding judge in the robe of an emperor and the attorney with his gazing and pausing and velvet, practiced tongue. But with those final words between me and Émile yesterday, I know better than to open up my trap.

Both his hands were clutching the iron bars of the grate. His face was hanging low and his voice no louder than a whisper, when he said, "Monsieur Danet told me to prepare for a verdict of guilty, for a sentence of death by guillotine."

I felt a creeping coldness, like Death breathing alongside me in the cell. My limbs lost their vigor, my heart ceased thudding in my chest. Those words, they hung between us, beyond my strength to grasp.

Then Émile was speaking again, his lips moving, but I could not hear. I mustered the strength to wag my head the smallest amount, and he repeated himself. "Wait," he was saying. "All is not lost."

I bent forward from the waist until my forehead was resting against the iron bars of the grate.

"Monsieur Danet, he told me to prepare because, in the court, I need to show only remorse. He said the president of the Republic has got the power to lighten a sentence. No hoisting fists, he said. No hurling threats. Not unless I want to spoil any chance of clemency."

After the jury comes back into the courtroom from the deliberating, each of the men stares at his shoes instead of straight ahead into the faces of Émile and Pierre Gille. Sweat trickles down my back, even with the bit of breathing room I been granted by the others in the gallery grown nervous of me. Already, during those thirty minutes the jury was away, I glared at an old nanny goat, swearing she could see the mark of the devil upon Émile, and batted the coins from the hand of a man collecting wagers on the outcome of the trial, and spat, "Stupid enough to eat hay, the both of you," into the faces of a pair of girls giggling about the prettiness of Pierre Gille.

I wait alone in the courtroom for the only judgment I ever cared about in my life. Alone and afraid. There is a part of me wishes Marie was here. To have her fingers laced with my own would be a comfort. To have her wanting what I want would be enough to make me a little brave. But she would not be waiting beside me, wishing with all her might for the court to declare the innocence of Émile, and I could not bear it any other way. And so I wait, trembling in the courtroom. Alone.

The head juror gets to his feet, and with the court-goers holding their breaths, he says, in a low voice, "We, the jury, find defendants Émile Abadie and Pierre Gille guilty as charged in Elisabeth Bazengeaud's murder."

Émile closes his eyes, puts a hand upon his heart, and the presiding judge says, "First I ask Émile Abadie, have you anything to say?"

Émile lifts his eyes, higher than the bench where the judges sit, to that carving of Jesus upon the cross. "I only ask for my good mother to find it in her heart to forgive me." He sits, still as a stone, through the judge asking the same of Pierre Gille and Pierre Gille making a little speech about the dishonor he has brought his family, about how his father and brother are upright and hardworking and should not be persecuted because of their association with him.

Émile don't scratch or shift in his seat or move his eyes from the carving as the judges leave the courtroom to decide the sentencing, as the noise of the gallery rises up, as it quiets with those sweating, red-faced judges filing back into the court. The only sign of life is the ripple of a swallow in his throat when the presiding judge says, "The court condemns Émile Abadie and Pierre Gille to death by guillotine."

Yesterday, with Émile saying, "All is not lost," I waited for a bit of brightness, and when it did not come, I said, "What is it I should be hoping for, Émile?"

"Forced labor," he said. "Forced labor in New Caledonia."

The first thought leapt into my mind was that knowing him to be alive and well in a place called New Caledonia would be worse to bear than a separation enforced by the guillotine, and it made me ashamed. I only wanted him here, with me, those moments of happiness—his smile coming when I appeared; his hands so gentle upon my cheeks; his body wrapping my own, hanging on with a fierceness that said he was never letting go. Those other moments, too, when, hands buried in suds, my mind drifted to the evening, to him, the possibilities. "New Caledonia?"

He tilted his chair back onto its hind legs, making wider the gap between me and him. "Monsieur Danet is writing something to stir up public sympathy. I don't know what, but he wanted every detail of my sorry life."

I looked up from my hands. The idea of President Grévy showing clemency did nothing to lighten the air, nothing to bestow the ease that was upon the face of Émile.

LE FIGARO

29 SEPTEMBER 1880

ABADIE'S MEMOIRS

Émile Abadie, condemned to death for murdering the Montreuil tavern owner, has written his memoirs while awaiting the guillotine. Here, without further delay, is the moving preface of his "The Story of a Man Condemned to Death":

This story was written by a poor prisoner, who begs the reader not to judge his style too harshly. It was written as well as I could manage with my meager skills and in the hope that it would serve to prevent others from taking the wrong path.

He continues, telling us that at the age of twelve, shortly after his first Communion, he left the hearth of his mother's home with the shadow of his stepfather's boot imprinted upon his skin. He found work as an apprentice engraver but never stayed more than a few months with any one employer. An urchin kicked about the streets of Paris, he found shelter wherever he could.

From age sixteen, girls took over his life and became his undoing:

Girls, love, nights of decadence made me forget the healthier parts of life. I needed money to enjoy myself,

to live the high life. If, all of a sudden, work dried up
for one reason or another, I didn't want to abandon
pleasure. I feared losing the sweetheart who counted on
gifts of barley sugar and meals of mussels in parsley
sauce.

He had relations with many women and names
a half dozen. One of the sweethearts was the
woman Bazengeaud.

He met Pierre Gille at the Ambigu Theater,
where each was an extra in Zola's naturalist play
L'Assommoir. Gille invited Abadie to share his clandestine living quarters in his father's storage shed.
Fed and lodged, Abadie was, in his own words, the
happiest of men. But then, after a run of more than
a year, *L'Assommoir* closed, and the pair found
themselves out of work.

They committed petty thefts to survive and
plotted out the crimes that would keep them in clo-
ver. One of these was blackmailing the woman
Bazengeaud. The memoir continues, with Abadie
laying out the details of the blackmailing going
awry, but the story he tells ends differently from
the one he told in the Court of Assizes. Here, he
does not leave the Montreuil tavern after enjoying
a cognac, but rather he and Pierre Gille rob the
tavern and in a moment of panic, slit the throat of
the woman.

The poor woman was in my arms and I had my
hand over her mouth. Gille stabbed her in the stomach
and again in the chest. I let her go, grabbed the knife
and went after her, cutting her throat. In the end she
lay on the ground, looking up, in a pool of her own

blood, and I was overcome by the horror of what we had done.

After the recounting, Abadie pays tribute to his mother, waxing eloquent in his regret of his savagery toward her.

One day, hungover and drunk on absinthe, I wielded a knife on my poor and good mother. I didn't strike, it is true, but I raised my hand against what is most sacred to me in the world. Poor mother, who so loved me, who did everything for me, who denied herself to feed me. Believe it, I repent and ask that she forgive me.

In the bitter setting of a prison, Abadie concludes his memoir, soothing himself, daring to hope.

I await the day I am awoken to be walked to the guillotine or to be told that my stay of execution has been granted. All I hope for is life, a chance to show my jury that it is more important to judge the heart of a man than a moment of panic. It has reformed me, as hard as I may have been, when at night in my prison cell, I see the good woman Bazengeaud rise before me.

The guillotine. Is that where this story will close? Will it be the end of me, one who so deeply regrets having led a criminal life, a horrible life?

I have quoted Abadie as much as I can and, in the analysis, used his own words and expressions. In cases like these, no rhetoric from a journalist can replace a cry from the heart.

Marie

Monsieur Lefebvre is very rich and sometimes he is mean but usually he is kind. Always, he is generous. And every now and then, he is a man I do not know.

"You'll undress," he says.

And I say "All right," because it is what I have said twenty times in the past months.

I put down my satchel and step toward the screen in the corner of the apartment that he calls his artist's workshop, even if draperies with tassels block the light and three sofas and nine chairs, all tufted and ornate, one with gilded arms shaped like swans, take up the space where Monsieur Degas would have placed a sturdy table holding a jumble of brushes and palette knives.

I stand naked and waiting while he pours water from a kettle into a zinc tub, like an oversize pie plate. "You'll bathe today," he says.

I place one arm across my breast and the other around my waist.

"Come now, Marie. Surely you've seen Monsieur Degas's bathers?"

Last week, as I turned toward the screen, he said, "I'll watch you undress," and when I paused he said, "You attended the exposition of the independent artists? You told me you did?"

"Yes."

"You saw it, then, Monsieur Degas's monotype, a woman slipping a dress over her head? *Toilette* he calls it."

I nodded, and he waited, and then I began loosening the drawstring of my blouse. He smiled and took up the spot behind the single easel in the apartment. In less than an hour I was leaving, and same as each Tuesday, he put a twenty-franc note upon my palm, almost twice the amount I was once paid for a week's labor at the bakery, more than three times what Monsieur Degas counted out for four hours of modeling.

It was my fault, more or less, what happened that day back in June when I passed the examination elevating me to the quadrille, vomiting as I had onto the floor of Monsieur Lefebvre's carriage, the cuff of his pressed pants, his polished shoes. It is what I remember but only in scraps—flashes of spattered black leather, spattered black wool, foul black floor. I vomited, and Monsieur Lefebvre hollered to the driver, snatched away my pretty glass with its pattern of garland and wreaths and hollered again. The carriage stopped, the door opened, and I was sent flying, Monsieur Lefebvre's foot on my backside—I am pretty sure—into the brightness of the day outside. Then I was on my hands and knees, spewing onto packed dirt. He called me a wretch—I know that—and told the driver, Louis, to leave me there, at the side of the road. "But, Monsieur Lefebvre, we are just arrived at the Bois de Boulogne," said Louis, "and she is in no state to find her way home?"

"Now."

After Monsieur Lefebvre was settled on the groom's seat at the back of the carriage—he would not suffer the stink of traveling inside—Louis, on the way to his bench up front, said in a low voice, "Now, you stay put. I'm coming back."

Once they were off, I crawled from packed dirt to struggling grass to the shadow of the woods bordering the road. Would Monsieur Lefebvre tell Monsieur Vaucorbeil? Monsieur Mérante? Monsieur Pluque? Would my name be posted with the others joining the quadrille in the morning? Gut heaving, I hardly cared.

I rolled onto my back and looked up into the heaving, spinning, cloudless sky; the heaving, spinning canopy of green. I remember being struck by the beauty of the leaves, the sun shining through, turning them to a pale yellow green. Stretching my neck, I looked deep into the woods, to the black places where there were—I was sure—wild boars snorting and pawing the dirt. The newspapers made a habit of saying how dangers lurked in every corner of a Paris gone to pot in the ten years since the Emperor Napoleon III got our country beat. The rot was spreading, they said, turning the youth of Paris into thieves and murderers. They pointed to Émile Abadie and Pierre Gille as proof. I did walk quickly on the pavements, particularly in the evening, glancing over my shoulder from time to time. But the fear was nothing compared to the terror that put my eyes skittering about the woods with each rustle, each snap. My heart stopped at the noise of a leaping red squirrel kicking up leaves. Never before had I seen a woods, a place so full of shadows and shifting darkness, blackness in the broad light of day.

My head ached. My tongue was thick. I would have licked a dewy leaf, lapped up a puddle, but there were none. At one point, I started wondering whether the memory of Louis saying he would come back was even real. With evening coming on, it would be easy to change his mind. I got up and walked a hundred feet down the road, following the direction of the retreating carriage. But a way off, the road forked and so I sat down, thinking of nightfall and crying into my skirt.

Then Monsieur Lefebvre's carriage was back, and Louis said for me to climb up front. Once my backside was upon the bench beside him, he swatted the rumps of the horses, and we set off but heading away from Paris. "There is a fountain up ahead," he said, and then after a pause, "I've got two daughters of my own, and you needn't be afraid."

At the fountain, instead of collecting water in my hands, I pressed my cheek flat against the stone, allowing the water from the spigot to wash over my face and into my mouth. I stayed like that a long time, getting cleansed, even when my thirst and the dried-up vomit on my chin were gone.

Then Louis said we were heading to the lake so the horses could have a drink. "This heat," he said, wiping a handkerchief across the back of his neck. Many times I looked out over the Seine and saw the silver moon twinkling on the lapping river, but I never before saw a lake. Still, I only wanted to go home, to put my cheek upon my mattress, to gather the wrinkled linens and bury my head underneath. It is something I regret, now, the way I hardly looked—the tiny islands, the rowboats, the mossy rocks with greenery clinging to the crevices in between. There was a waterfall connecting the upper and lower parts of the lake, falling like a veil, the prettiest sight in all my life, and yet I shut my eyes and held my throbbing head in my hands.

On the way home he asked about the Opéra, and I told him about the examination, about sixteen fouettés en tournant at the end. "Monsieur Lefebvre told me I was moving up to the quadrille," I said. "Don't know about that anymore."

"He isn't one for holding grudges." He gave a crooked smile. "He has me driving like the dickens to get to the Opéra gate in time."

I saw a scene, then, with Monsieur Lefebvre leaning forward, sliding open the little window in the carriage wall, and calling out, "Faster! Onward! We'll miss her!" and Louis rolling his eyes that once again Monsieur Lefebvre told himself he was not going to the Opéra gate, not today, not at all, and put off leaving until it was close to too late.

I knew, then, always he would see his way to giving me a second chance. Same as before the retching onto pressed trousers, with the sixteen fouettés en tournant came spread-open wings, a lowly scuttling rat raised up to a swan. It was in that moment, half a year ago, when I knew already I was his protégé.

. . .

Once Monsieur Lefebvre finishes emptying the kettle into the zinc tub, he moves to behind the easel, and I step ankle-deep into water hot enough to sting.

"Wet yourself," he says.

I crouch, pick up the sponge he put beside the tub with a cake of soap and a pitcher of water with steam rising above. I pass the sponge through the water, squeeze it over my shoulder and feel warm rivulets running down my back. Monsieur Lefebvre lifts his arm, preparing to draw. With the smallest of glances, I see the concentration on his face, and the ache between my shoulder blades lets up. Daylight, like always, chases away the blackness of night, the wide-awake hours of knowing Monsieur Lefebvre and I are playing at something that is not drawing, something that an easel and charcoal lets the both of us pretend is nothing at all.

I come to the apartment on Tuesdays before heading to the Opéra for the quadrille's afternoon class and the rehearsing that comes afterward. There is never a maid nor a wife nor the son he once told me showed a scientist's mind with his fondness for dissecting frogs and mice. I asked once where everyone was, and Monsieur Lefebvre said, "I gave the maid the day off and Madame Lefebvre prefers our other apartment, in the Avenue des Ternes, and Antoine attends the Lycée Louis-le-Grand."

Still crouched with my belly tight against my thighs, I again squeeze the sponge over my shoulder. "Shall I warm up the water, Marie?"

There are two fireplaces, one at each end of the room. Flames fill the mouth of the closest, and in the other a large kettle, with steam spilling from its spout, dangles from a hook above a bed of glowing coals. "Might just be the warmest bath I ever had." Even Monsieur Degas, who has nowhere near the same wealth, would never stoop to hauling a kettle himself. He would call Sabine to warm up the tub.

"Perhaps you might stand a little straighter? You're all knees, crouching like that."

I had grown used to modeling naked for Monsieur Degas, but now with Monsieur Lefebvre's strange ways and my own body altering by the week, there is a new wariness. The hair that was gauzy between my legs, beneath my arms, has thickened to a mat. Bones no longer jut from my hips, not with the meat the modeling for Monsieur Lefebvre allows. The small mounds of my breast have swelled, like an apricot cut in half one day and then a yellow plum the next. It meant the fastening hooks of my practice bodice pulled too tight and tore three little holes where before there were none. I said to Monsieur Lefebvre how with the bodice I felt I could hardly open up my ribs to breathe, and a day later, I was being measured by a seamstress after class, and a week after that, I was wearing a new one with a layer of ruched tarlatan adding to my new fullness across the front and a neckline trimmed with lace. Such prettiness, for practicing! In my satchel were two more bodices, one with a low, scooping back and the smallest of pink rosebuds upon each shoulder, and the other with such ruffles that I feared Monsieur Pluque scolding me. I wore it anyway and saw him eyeing me once. He said not a word, though, and I figured out that he knew such a bodice could only be a gift from an abonné, from Monsieur Lefebvre.

𝓘 straighten my knees to standing, arms hanging at my sides, dripping sponge clenched in one hand.

"Wash yourself," he says. "You're bathing. I'm not even here."

I pass the sponge over each arm, both legs. I keep up the bending and straightening, the soaking of the sponge, the washing of my shoulders, my neck, until the water grows cool and my skin is like gooseflesh. "Enough," he finally says.

I have not held a single pose, which proves he does not know the first thing about how to draw. He takes a towel from the top of the sideboard and whirls his finger through the air, telling me to turn. "I'll dry your back," he says, and because he expects it, I shuffle my feet in a slow circle, stopping only when I face away from him. He is gentle, taking his time, and I can tell he is very close by the heat rolling off him, by the sound of his breath heavy in my ear. Then he moves low, upon one knee, and the towel passes over half of my backside, travels down one leg. Its roughness is upon the other cheek and then still and there is what feels like two fingers, prodding, through the towel, at the softest of spots between my legs. I snap to rigid, faster than a thought, just like the other time Marie the First had me flinching from his finger on my spine, and he pulls away.

He nudges the towel against my hanging hand, and, taking it, I scuttle from the tub, slopping water onto the carpet with its pattern of laurels and vines. It is the kind of mistake that in a wink switches him from kindly to mean, but today he only flops down into the swan-armed chair and puts his face in his hands.

Behind the screen, I drop the towel, tug on my drawers; my stockings, not bothering to pull them up past my knees; my skirt; my blouse. My boots, I leave undone.

"Take your money from the middle drawer in the sideboard," he says. "Take thirty francs."

Without truly glancing toward him, though I can see, from the corner of my eye, the black outline of him still slumped in the chair, I open the middle drawer to find it heaped with coins, some bronze, mostly gold. There are stacks of notes—tens, twenties, fifties, hundreds. I put my hand upon the tens, peel back three notes, but I let one settle back onto the pile. "I'm taking twenty," I say, and he looks up, an old man. "All right," he says. "All right."

What I know is I have to tell Antoinette. But how to get to two prodding fingers when I have not said about never holding a pose or the maid who is not there or the draperies blocking the light. All of it seems like the whining of a child. And already she is gloomy and grumpy and pacing the plank floor of our lodging room, wringing her hands on account of that boy. With two ten-franc notes inside my pocket, I open the door and close it quietly behind my back and then stand in the vestibule, a steadying hand on the cool marble of the wall.

~ Antoinette ~

I am rushing in the dark, dodging the ridges of ugly, yellow slush masking the pavements. My boots are filthy and soaked, no different from the hem of my skirt. How I hate the month of December, the sun that don't show itself until after eight o'clock in the morning and then has the nerve to disappear before five o'clock in the afternoon. And this at a time when bones are aching with damp, shivering with cold, craving a needle of sunshine hot enough to breach the wool of our winter cocoons.

I intended to leave our lodging room early and, by eight o'clock, to pass under the great archway of La Roquette, the prison where Émile and Pierre Gille been sent to count the hours. They wait, like all the others there—most for transport to New Caledonia; some for the dawn they greet the guillotine; Émile and Pierre Gille for word from the president, news of their fates.

It was Marie kept me from leaving on time. "Can you spare a minute?" she said, pushing herself up from the table, traipsing after me to the door. Same as always, when preparing to open her trap against Émile, she wore a particular look—nervous as a whore in church.

Her heart was cold and black, rigid like a rock when it came to Émile, and there was no way to think of it except that she did not love me all the way through. I was a good sister and a decent laundress, but also a failed ballet girl and a walker-on who had let down Monsieur Leroy, and all of that was just fine with Marie. Such was not the case, though, for the part of me that was the lover of Émile. That part she would feed to the dogs. And it stung, her hateful talk, the way she did not love me enough to shut tight her trap.

Tugging my shawl up over the back of my head, I said, "Tonight." She would be out, at the Opéra, rehearsing for her debut in *La Korrigane*, and I was done with her poking a finger at the newspaper, all those stories cropping up about whether Émile was deserving of clemency. Never once did she think to keep from my ears the arguments favoring the guillotine. In all the long months since he first got hauled off to Mazas, her yammering has not let up, not a bit, not even with his "Story of a Man Condemned." No, after that, all she bothered to spit out was "He says, 'It's more important to judge the heart of a man than a moment of panic.' A moment of panic! He confessed to slitting a woman's throat." It was the beginning of the hundred times I would say to her, "He was only showing remorse, Marie, saving his own neck. Monsieur Danet decided what to write."

This morning, just like always, there was no dodging the girl. She put herself between me and our lodging room door and touched my arm. "A minute? A single minute, Antoinette?"

"Émile didn't have a papa like our own," I said, cutting her short. "There wasn't a papa putting sprigs of lavender upon his mattress or bringing home a figurine of Taglioni hovering above the earth. Émile didn't get none of that."

Her bottom lip quivered. She sucked it into her mouth, and I felt sorry for stirring up the memory of Papa. I let my face go gentle, and it was enough to bring about her cheek against the matted wool of my shawl.

I counted to ten, before I said, "I need to go, Marie. I really do."

She looked up, like a starved dog snuck into a café. "Please."

"Not a word against Émile," I said.

She rattled her head, like all her harsh words were only something I dreamt up. "It's about modeling." She bit her lip.

"Don't got all day."

"Monsieur Lefebvre, he doesn't have a proper workshop."

"Those artists up in Montmartre, half of them paint in the same rabbit hutches where they sleep." Her lip was again between her teeth. "If you're worrying, don't see why you wouldn't ask to be paid up front."

"It's not that." She looked as earnest as a cat after a bird. "He isn't much of an artist at all."

"Christ, Marie." Always she was complaining about Monsieur Degas cutting off feet.

"He does more looking than drawing."

I shrugged.

"He had me standing in a tub the other day. Bathing."

Was she going to ask me to accompany her, like that first time she went to Monsieur Degas? I missed a day's wages from the Ambigu and was sent home within five minutes of arriving at his workshop. "The water was warm?" My voice was like the edge of a knife.

She nodded.

"Sounds rosy, getting paid to take a bath." I pulled my shawl tighter, and she cleared out of my path. The skin below her lips was pink with the rawness of being grazed by her teeth, and a rotten feeling came into my gut, but already the street outside our window was waking up. Already I would be running and panting half the way to La Roquette.

Close to the prison the streets grow congested with carriages and carts. The cobblestones are crawling with street hawkers, as if all the flower sellers and coal peddlers suddenly got word the rue de la Roquette was the best place in all of Paris for selling their wares.

A boy, no more than ten, grabs at the sleeve of a shorter one. "Hurry up," he says. "Dawn is nearing." And it comes to me that this morning, set up on the five smooth stones not twenty paces outside the arched doorway of La Roquette, the guillotine looms. Already those boys watching the shed in the rue de la Folie-Regnault, from where it was brought, ran the boulevards, hollering the news. I lurch, clutch the lapels of the taller boy, tug him close. "Who?" I say. "Who is facing the guillotine?"

"Billet." The boy struggles, and his lapel tears. "The butcher who hacked his wife to death."

I let go, run my hands over my skirt while the boys scramble away, each looking over his shoulder from a distance before slowing down.

I sit on the sill of a low window, put a hand over my heart, racing more wildly than when I was hurtling along the pavements. And in that moment I feel myself shifting, believing in the realness of Émile's bare neck upon the lunette of the guillotine. The tale I was clinging to, the one with him free on the streets of Paris, his fingers on my back, steering me around corners, like that first time we met, I see with an icy, new clearness it is a memory, something past, nothing that is yet to come. Never again will that tale be coaxed into my dreams at the end of the day, drawn there by longing and hope. For Émile there are only two options—New Caledonia and the guillotine. And knowing it is a blow to the gut.

Eventually I push myself up from the sill and put one foot in front of the other, following the crowd. Not once before did I join the horde gawking at the misery of another; and maybe it was a mistake, the blunder that allowed the tale I went to sleep with at night. I conjure up what Billet has already this morning endured: a flash of lantern light in his sleepy eyes, a jailer calling him from his cell, the prayers of the chaplain, the promise of forgiveness, the disbelief crippling his knees, the cold steel of shears touching his flesh, the hair clipped from the back of his neck.

I shoulder my way through the crowd, until the scaffolding of the guillotine comes into view—the two straight posts supporting the lintel, the struts of the base. In the darkness of early morning, only the light of the blazing faggots glints from the blade. Between the two posts, it hangs from the wheel of a pulley, like savagery forged into a shape.

A man all Paris knows by name—Monsieur Roch, the custodian of the guillotine—walks in a broad circle around the machine, the eyes of the gathered tinsmiths and bankers and fishmongers following him. Without touching the cigar hanging from his lips, he puffs smoke from his nose. Three times, he hauls on a rope, causing the blade of the guillotine to slide up and down. Then he strokes the lever, testing. The blade falls with a thud upon the wood below, and a contented look comes to his face.

The gates of La Roquette swing open, and there, between the two aides of Monsieur Roch, is Billet. The moment he is brought into open air, he surely sees the rosy tints of morning appearing in the east and knows with daylight his time has come. Pale, he faces the gawking, hushed crowd. He takes a few steps, stumbles but is pushed forward, his feet lagging, his eyes moving up and down the guillotine at the end of his path. Once there, his waistcoat and shirt are removed, leaving him in trousers and a knitted undershirt. His hands are tied, and he turns toward another man all Paris knows—the Abbot Crozes, chaplain to the condemned. Billet kisses him upon the lips. "Good-bye, my father," he says, in a trembling voice. Monsieur Roch draws the straps and fastens Billet to the plank of the guillotine. The plank turns over on its pivot, laying his neck upon the lunette, and the yoke with its slit for the passage of the blade comes down.

Quick as quick, Monsieur Roch puts a hand upon the lever, and there is a dull thud and the severed head of Billet falling upon the mound of sawdust piled in a large basket. I stagger backward at the quickness of life snuffed out, and Monsieur Roch and his two aides send the rest of Billet rolling into the basket after the head. A cover is put into place.

I want to erase the memory of that severed neck—the glistening white bone, the pale flesh, a second later turning dark with seeped blood, and a further second after that, awash in the brightest of reds. I lift my eyes to the sky turning from grey to blue, strain to hear a bird warbling its morning carol even if there is no chance with wintertime all around. I want New Caledonia for Émile.

If I could feel the glow of hope instead of the knife's edge of dread, I might imagine myself to be back in a visitor's cell at Mazas rather than at La Roquette. The bare plaster walls, the brickwork floor, the two sets of iron grates, the intervening passageway—the stench of it all is exactly the same.

The door of the cell opposite my own opens up a crack, and the low voice of Émile reaches my ears: "When the Abbot Crozes gets back, you'll let him know I want him to come to me?"

A jailer answers back, saying, "You sure it isn't the warden you want me to tell?" And then with his tone changing to that of a child, he adds, "Monsieur Warden, that Émile Abadie, he is consumed with remorse. Be sure to let the president know."

The door opens fully and there is Émile, sunken hollows under his eyes and lines etched upon his brow. "Just tell the abbot," he says.

He slumps onto the chair waiting in his own cell, and the door closing behind him, his shoulders heave. "Old Billet went to the guillotine this morning," he says.

"Yes."

He slumps further, eyes closed, arms now wrapping his waist. "I can't take the waiting."

"It's a good sign. You said so yourself."

"Old Billet was hoping for clemency." Émile looks up.

"Never mind about him."

"I'd hang myself if I had so much as a belt. I could braid strips of sheet. Make a noose."

"New Caledonia," I say. "You got to keep your mind on that."

He waits, staring hard, his chest rising and falling. "You'll follow me?"

A promise to follow him to New Caledonia don't seem like much, only words to bring comfort to a boy. But what if it turns out the promise is more than just words? With all the ink spilled daily in the newspapers about youth and remorse and reform isn't there a chance? Even Marie is not against hard labor and New Caledonia for Émile and the rest so long as not a single one ever comes back to France. I think of Maman, her sodden snoring, her reeking breath, her life of widowhood and soiled linens and a tipped bottle of absinthe. I remember the old chaise in the storage room, about being adored, how I felt so awake, like nothing in the world was dusty and grey, not the colors or the creaks of the chaise or the feel of his breath, the smell of the smoke in his hair. He chose me above the rest, and my world was shifted to dazzling and sharp.

I nod. Marie and Charlotte have each other. They have the Opéra.

"Say it. Say you'll follow me."

"I'll follow you."

There is a tiny crack of the smile I have not seen in a hundred years. "Since that first day, outside the Opéra, you been my one and only, Antoinette. Always will be, too."

I swallow his promise, the warmth of it swelling in my throat.

He runs his hands over his thighs. "You'll need money. Not just for passage. The guards in New Caledonia, you got to bribe them to get assigned the better jobs."

I nod for a second time.

"More than you make at the washhouse."

I understand what he is not saying—that riches do not come to the poor girls of Paris by way of honest laboring. "I know it." I inch up my chin.

"Tell me," he says. "Tell me how it is going to be."

And so, my feet numb with cold in soggy boots, my skirt soaked through to my knees with grit and filth and wintertime, I spin a tale. A small house by the sea. A roof of thatch. A garden. Sunshine spilling down. Him, his freedom won, with a hoe. Or maybe a fishing net. Yes, a fishing net. And me, a settler's wife, cooking up those fish all but jumping into his tiny boat.

Begin, you darlings, without the futile help
Of beauty—leap despite your common face,
Leap, soar! You priestesses of grace.

For in you the Dance is embodied now,
Heroic and remote. From you we learn,
Queens are made of distance and greasepaint.

—EDGAR DEGAS

～ Marie ～

In the long, narrow loge of the second set of the quadrille, I close my eyes, blocking out the scuttling, limbering, nail-chewing girls, the greenest of the corps de ballet, all of us awaiting our debuts upon the Opéra stage. My mind flits to the theatergoers I know to be lurking in the darkness beyond the reaches of the gas lamps lighting up the stage. Antoinette and Charlotte are not in the house. Antoinette has turned stingy in a way that is new, and with opening night seats, even in the fourth balcony, going for eight francs, she said she would have to wait. Charlotte would come later, too, once the house was no longer selling out and Madame Théodore arranged for her class to attend a matinée, and I hardly cared. She had called me chickenhearted for saying how I feared my debut, and I wanted to say how she should keep her mouth shut since she would someday be trembling in the wings, but it was not true. She would be licking her chops at the chance to get out there and shine. It was something in her I envied, more in this moment than ever before.

I put my hands on my belly, suck in a breath counting to four, let it out counting again, just like Madame Dominique said for calming the nerves. Oh, how I want to get through the night, to make Madame Dominique proud, to be admired. What I need is quiet, to shush the shuffling feet, the nervous giggles, the words spoken low. More deep breaths, I tell myself, more counting to four.

Tonight is the opening of Monsieur Mérante's new ballet, *La Korrigane*, and in the first act I appear as a Breton peasant, wearing a costume more fine—I am sure—than any worn in all the countryside of Brittany. Two gold bands mark the hem of my skirt and the cuffs of my blouse, and the prettiest of laces edges my apron, collar, and cap, all of it far too white for any girl who ever tugged the teat of a cow or snatched an egg out from underneath a hen.

The first time I set foot upon the decorated stage, I gaped, eyes growing wide. A massive church with carved stone doorways and colored glass windows and spires of fantastic height towered over the square where the dancing took place. Off to one side were cottages and on the other, shops bedecked with garlands and flags and beyond all that, soaring trees, so real-looking I stroked a leaf to decide if it was truly silk. I could not believe such a thing of beauty existed in the world, but now with the costumes, I have the idea that no public square in Brittany matches what is built upon the Opéra stage. A single glance around the quadrilles' loge, and I know I am right. We are the daughters of sewing maids and fruit peddlers, charwomen and laundresses, dressed up and painted to look like something we are not. All the years of practicing, the sweat and toil, the muscles aching at the end of the day, it comes down to learning trickery—to leap with the lightness that lets the theatergoers think of us as queens of the Opéra stage instead of scamps with cracking knees and heaving ribs and ever-bleeding toes. Sometimes I wonder, though, if for the very best ballet girls, the trickery is not a little bit real, if a girl born into squalor cannot find true grace in the ballet.

When finally we were rehearsing on the stage—the full orchestra coaxing the place behind my heart, the floorboards beneath Rosita Mauri's and Marie Sanlaville's feet the same as were beneath my own—the joy of it lasted more than a week. But in truth, for the peasants of the second set of the quadrille, rehearsal amounts to a lot of standing around and being fully ignored. The Breton dance takes place at the beginning of act one and is no more than six minutes in length; and when we rehearse, the coryphées and the sujets are straightening their skirts and kneading their calves and the première danseuses and the étoiles are in the wings, posing and lifting up their legs for the lurking abonnés. The rest of the time we are props, a backdrop of color, nothing more. Still, when it is time, I dance my heart out, never leaping lower than my best, never forgetting to hold my neck long, always remembering to keep my teeth out of sight.

La Korrigane tells the story of Yvonette, a poor tavern maid all of a sudden furnished with the silks and jewels that win the heart of handsome Lilèz, the role Monsieur Mérante gave to himself, never mind his thinning hair. The Korrigane—the wicked fairies of Brittany—steal Yvonette away, until Lilèz overcomes their treachery and claims her as his prize. Blanche had me laughing at one rehearsal, saying how it was the best part of choreographing a ballet, casting yourself in a role where you are fine-looking and young and allowed to paw at the girl of your choice.

I do not mind being a prop so much when Rosita Mauri is dancing upon the stage as Yvonette. No, I watch her feet, the way they beat in the air, flying this way and that, neat, quick. She dances one section in wooden clogs. No one else could manage the steps. It was something I made the mistake of saying to Monsieur Lefebvre, and the next time I went to his apartment he handed me a pair. "Now dance," he said. One of the sofas had been pushed back and the carpet rolled up, leaving an area of bare floor.

"What dance?" I said, gripping the clogs.

He stared, and it felt like he was daring me not to do as I was told. "Rosita Mauri's dance, of course."

I knew the steps from watching at the rehearsals, and alone in the practice room I had tried to copy them, dreaming all the while of someday having the same lightness and speed as Rosita Mauri. But even with my feet in canvas slippers instead of wooden clogs, I was nowhere near capable of what she was.

I said the truth to Monsieur Lefebvre, and he took me by the arm, walked me over to the pushed-aside sofa and pointed, telling me to sit. "Do you know about Emma Livry?" he said, lowering himself to the spot beside me.

Everyone knew. Ever since Marie Taglioni, the people of France had been waiting for an étoile of the same skill, talent enough to capture the hearts of all those seeing her upon the stage. Emma Livry was to be such a sensation. At the age of sixteen she appeared before the public for the first time—the role of the Sylph in *La Sylphide*. *Le Figaro* called her a second Taglioni, and by nineteen she had reached the rank of étoile. But two years later she was bedridden, suffering. While she awaited the moment of her entrance in the wings, her skirt shifted into the sphere of a gas lamp and in an instant she was aflame. Even with Marie Taglioni herself rubbing greasepaint into Emma Livry's charred skin, even with the straw that was placed on the cobblestones before her apartment to deaden the clacking of the wheels, she drew her last breath at the age of twenty-one. All that took place before I was even born, but still every ballet girl knows to look right and left in the wings, checking the locations of the gas lamps, before giving a final fluffing to her skirt.

I told Monsieur Lefebvre all I knew about Emma Livry, and he nodded, staying quiet, until I ran out of words and said, "I can't think of anything else."

"Have you never wondered why a child was cast in the role of the Sylph? The house was full the night of her debut and the press eager to report her success." He said Emma Livry was the daughter of a sujet called Célestine Emarot and her protector—a baron—that when the arrangement between the two of them ended, Célestine found herself a new protector. "This time, a viscount."

It was through the viscount's influence, he said, that it was decided Emma Livry would make her debut in a major role. With him footing the bill, no expense was spared. She was prepared for four months. Three weeks in advance of her debut, he arranged for publicity in the newspapers, with the end result that she appeared as the Sylph before a full house. He lifted up his eyebrows. "You know about the claque?" I had heard of the famous Auguste, of the money he was paid by the director of the Opéra for stirring his colleagues in the orchestra stalls into a fervor of clapping, the fury of which had everything to do with the weight of the coins put into his hands. "All that was a long time ago," I said.

He gave me a pat, a pat for a girl green as the first shoots in the spring. "The viscount spent a fortune, making sure no one in the house was left making up his own mind about the greatness of Emma Livry."

"I don't see why you're telling me all this," I said.

"After the debut the viscount embraced Emma Livry, and he told her, 'You were only a caterpillar, but I made you into a butterfly.' " He smiled.

I swallowed, dipped my chin the tiniest bit. Tuesday mornings with Monsieur Lefebvre I was earning the twenty francs that allowed me to go on making the meager wages the Opéra paid to the girls in the second set of the quadrille. But it was more than that, too. He had clout with Monsieurs Pluque and Mérante, maybe Monsieur Vaucorbeil, too. He had the money to line their pockets, if that is what it took. He made a habit of getting his way. And even a girl with the talent of Emma Livry had an abonné greasing the wheels.

Monsieur Lefebvre knelt before me, unlacing my boots and slipping them from my feet. He held each of my ankles, pressing one foot and then the other into the wooden clogs. Standing up, backing away, he said, "Now, do as you are told."

I made a mess of it. I told him I would. Me standing there, disgraced, my lip sucked between my teeth, he said, "Again." I tried. I failed. He said, "Again." Repeat. Repeat. Repeat, until my feet bleed in the clogs and his voice was like vinegar in a cut.

"Undress," he said.

I did.

"On the sofa."

I sat down and he went to his easel, on the far side of the cleared space. From behind it, he called out for me to lie back, to open my legs. And then more instructions—lower my knee, close my eyes, part my lips.

There were other times, when I almost knew. There were his knees, below the bottom edge of the canvas, shifting slightly, back and forth. There was his trembling breath, the final stifled grunt, and afterward the quick handing over of the twenty francs I was owed. But he pretended, and so did I. I thought about the steps of *La Korrigane* or listened to the sounds coming in through the shutters—the hollering groomsmen, the boats on the Seine, the chatter of the ladies passing by in dresses fine enough that they would be let into the Jardin des Tuileries at the bottom of the street. That day, with legs spread open on the sofa, I told myself to put my mind on Antoinette, the scent of soap clinging to her skin and hair, the tavern where she says she now works, her new stinginess. But I could not send my mind beyond his apartment.

Sister Evangeline's catechism laid out the rules about sin, the two different kinds. It said smaller sins—venial sins—were easier for God to forgive, even without confessing to a priest, especially if the sinner was forced or did not fully understand the breach. Mortal sins were deliberate, and without confession and God's mercy, they meant everlasting damnation of the soul. The difference was important. I did not own a skirt fine enough to climb the steps of the église de la Sainte-Trinité to the confessional booth, and even if I did, even if I managed to work up the nerve, I did not want to hear how I should seek virtue, the hundred ways a ballet girl's life was not pleasing to God. That day, lying back on the sofa, my mind stayed put and Monsieur Lefebvre's panting and grunting, the final swelling moan filled up my ears, and there was no more clinging to the idea that the sinning going on would pass as the lesser kind.

Afterward when Monsieur Lefebrve put thirty francs in my hand— your new allowance is what he said—I did not refuse the extra ten francs. Sister Evangeline's catechism was a long time ago. Was I even correctly remembering what it said? Antoinette would say it was only drivel, written up by the priests because they were in love with rules, not that she wasted a minute thinking about some old catechism. No, Antoinette was too bold in speaking her mind to end up with her legs spread open for a slumming gentleman.

From the stage the theater is a black, gaping hole, but you can feel the breathing coming from the seats, the thousand pairs of eyes. My heart beats wildly, and my feet move, only because they know the steps of the Breton dance like I know to write my name. My mind skitters—elbows soft, shoulders down, mouth shut. I grip Perot's and Aimée's hands for the portion of the dance we make in a line. A hundred times I took their two hands and never before was there the slipperiness, the gripping of today. Never mind the earlier grinning, the whispers of "Long last, the stage!" in the wings. We are all afraid. It is the moment when I know I will not trip or collapse or make a mess of a single step, and the chatter inside my head stops.

Like sometimes happens in the practice room, when I am at my very best, the music goes inside me, then comes from inside, spilling out. There is the sheer pleasure of dancing, a knee extending, a foot striking the wooden planks of the stage, of breath. There is something words cannot explain, a moment of rapture, a moment of crystal clearness. I know the miracle of life, the sorrow of death, the joy of love, and I know none of it is any different for a single soul in the world. Oh, how I want the moment to last. But then Rosita Mauri is whirling across the stage, and the second set of the quadrille is retreating to our waiting spot amid the cottages and shrubbery. And, oh, I want that moment back. I want that moment again.

Did Antoinette ever snatch such a moment? No. She would have kept her mouth shut in front of Monsieur Pluque to get the moment again. And Charlotte? Sometimes that small girl was coming down from the practice rooms when I was going up, even though her class was over and done two hours before mine began. Every chance she had she sat with her legs spread wide and lowered her chest to the floor. She wanted to know the allegro combinations Madame Dominique called out to my class, wanted to know was her cabriole high enough, landed soft enough. Would I say the beating together of her calves was good and neat? She badgered until I showed her the steps of the Breton dance, kept it up until she knew every one. Charlotte had tasted that moment, the one I wanted again.

The debut of *La Korrigane* goes off without a hitch, and afterward the applause is like thunder. While Monsieur Mérante hops around, clapping the backs of set painters and étoiles and Madame Dominique and even Perot, the entire corps de ballet lines up in the wings for our final bows. "The curtain. The curtain," the stage manager yells. "Your place, Monsieur Mérante, if you please."

The curtains part, and starting with the lowliest of the production, which means the second set of the quadrille, the bowing begins. We flit to center stage and curtsey deeply, arms held in low à la seconde, one foot sliding out to the rear. We were told to be quick, that it is Rosita Mauri and Marie Sanlaville the abonnés want to applaud. I glance at Blanche, awaiting the left tilt of her head, the signal for the Breton peasants to turn and dart to our curtain call spot. But my ankle is hit with a soft thud and, daring to peek, I see a bouquet of roses lying at my feet. Another appears, then two more. From the wing, Madame Dominique calls out, "Pick them up. Pick them up." But are the flowers, the hollered instructions meant for me? I cannot decide and next thing I know, Monsieur Mérante is there, on one knee, back to the audience, scooping up the bouquets. With a little flourish he offers the flowers to me.

I take the heaped-up roses, only because it is what I always do when a loaf or a sausage or a newspaper is held out to me. I catch Blanche's eye, her flushed, glowing cheeks, her falling-open mouth. She tilts her head left. We were told to move to our curtain call spot, silently, gracefully, our eyes glued to the cap of the peasant ahead of us in line, but I cannot, not the part about the eyes. I glance toward the house, lit up by the chandelier now blazing overhead, searching. My eyes land upon the wildly applauding Monsieur Lefebvre, standing amid a group of black-suited abonnés in the stalls just beyond the orchestra. Half embarrassed, half choked with pride, I nod, a quiet nod, only for him.

He grins wider, holds his booming hands higher, a sylph reflected in the shine of his face.

1881

LE FIGARO

4 JANUARY 1881

THE POOR MURDERERS

BY ALBERT WOLFF

His pen put to paper, the deplorable Émile Abadie has saved his skin as well as that of the sweet Pierre Gille. These two charming sorts touched the president of the Republic, and he has spared them the guillotine.

I watched this human carnival without publishing even the smallest argument against the rising groundswell of dangerous pity for a pair of convicted murderers. But now President Grévy's clemency has roused the pen of this writer, who will take this opportunity to say what he thinks of the case of these villains for whom so many tears have been shed.

Little by little, the murderers were raised to the rank of martyr. Abadie's fictitious memoirs awoke a perilous sentimentality in readers and stirred the pens of the most credulous of my colleagues. They painted Abadie as someone led astray, who now spends his days repenting and his nights in prayer. They played on the filial piety of this monster, who was not thinking of his mother the moment he slit the woman Bazengeaud's neck. The storytellers transformed Gille into a good lamb of the Lord, shamed by the dishonor brought upon his worthy family.

Not once in the trial did Abadie shed a tear over his mother or Gille offer a rueful glance to the bench where his dismayed family sat. The two arrived cold and hardened before the court, and until the verdict, nothing touched them. Only once they found themselves condemned to die did terror rise, and these murderers, who felt no pity for the woman Bazengeaud, made others pity them.

President Grévy has been accused of heartlessness for not putting matters of state aside to more quickly take care of these most fascinating prison guests. They savage a woman and kill her for eighteen francs so that they might go and enjoy a drink. How dare we not handle them expeditiously! Far from feeling sorry about what has been called "moral torture," I console myself with thoughts of Abadie and Gille trembling in the face of death for four months.

I save my pity for worthier folk and will not permit these two cruel villains to leave for New Caledonia with crowns of laurels on their august foreheads.

~∞~ Antoinette ~∞~

The cherub—Jean Luc Simard—likes to be told he is a magnificent lover. He likes to hear that for the two days since I last spread open my legs for him, I been pining, longing for his cock, a rough word, one he likes me to use. Even in the company of others, I whisper it quietly into his ear. "I long for your cock," I say, by way of greeting, when he appears in the alcove at the top of the stairs of the house of Madame Brossard. From behind the sofa where he sits, I reach around, cupping his ear. "The sight of you," I say, "and I feel my slit growing hot." I pour his wine, lean in close. "I ache for your meat."

He is not a magnificent lover. He is a boy who cannot last, no more than two minutes, and plenty of times, I don't allow him even that. Feeling mean or selfish or tired, I take his sex in my hands, giving him the pleasure of a few gentle strokes before working him hard. Those occasions he bucks, writhes, collapses, my mauve silk still fully in place. Other evenings, lying naked on my back and growing fed up, there is a place I can reach around to, the softest of skin just beyond the taut, ropy flesh bearing the weight of his sac. When I caress, even the tiniest bit, he is gripped by bliss. "Wait," he says, gulping air. "Stop." But I want out from beneath his pale, near-hairless body, those shoulders, so frail compared to Émile's. Like a woman's.

"Can't help myself," I whisper moan. "Honestly, I can't."

Of course there are times when, on all fours, with him thrusting inside me from behind and calling out, "A hound riding his bitch," I let him continue. His neck arches with pleasure, and I swallow the laughter rising up in my throat.

A month ago I gave my word to Émile and that same day submitted to the speculum, the medical examination that meant a stamped card. I went to Madame Brossard, showed the proof I was an approved, uncontaminated coquette. She took me on, and in the days since, I collected two hundred and twenty francs and saved every sou except the eighteen weekly francs Maman and Marie and Charlotte were used to me contributing. I kept the stash and those fifty francs handed over to me by Émile out of sight, tucked into the little drawstring pouch hanging from a nail behind the sideboard. I did not want them to know my plan for New Caledonia—firm, now, with the president sparing Émile—not yet, and worse, I did not want Marie with her forever-churning mind considering how I was earning passage.

My savings, so far, amount to one hundred and ninety-eight francs. Such a tremendous sum. But no one I asked, not even Émile, knew the cost of getting to New Caledonia. In a moment of clear thinking, I struck up a conversation with Monsieur Mignot and Monsieur Fortin, seeing how they owned a fish-packing house in Le Havre. "Any boats come into port from New Caledonia?" I said.

"From New Caledonia? The whalers, you mean? You'd be more likely to catch sight of one in Marseille."

"Marseille?"

"Down south. On the Mediterranean."

"Of course," I said, thinking I would ask Marie to draw an outline of France and point out the location of this Marseille. "I'm only asking because a cousin of mine wants to be a settler in New Caledonia. Whaling would suit him just fine. It's Marseille, then, where he'd find a boat heading that way?"

Monsieur Mignot lifted up his shoulders, gave Monsieur Fortin a quizzical look.

"I suppose," Monsieur Fortin said.

"His sister might accompany him," I said. "What would it cost? How long would it take?"

More lifted shoulders. A bit of chatter back and forth. And then, Monsieur Fortin said, "A thousand francs for steerage, maybe more, but it is nothing a lady should endure, not for the six weeks such a journey would take."

"Oh." Another six months of putting up with Jean Luc Simard, and even then, nothing extra for bribing the guards like Émile said. I held my face from slipping. "She's a hardy girl, a country girl, used to hard work. Maybe the captain would take her on as a cook?"

"Best to pay the extra for a cabin and keep herself locked up," Monsieur Mignot said. "Those sailors, all that time without the comfort of a woman." He shook his head.

A week ago I ran my fingers through the blond curls of Jean Luc Simard and asked what he pays to Madame Brossard for the pleasure of my company. "Now?" he said. "Twenty francs."

"Now?"

"I used to pay fifteen."

And so I told Madame Brossard it was not fair, him paying more, her handing the same old ten francs over to me. "I want a cut of fifteen francs," I said to her. "Monsieur Simard is dedicated to me."

"Twelve and you can take the spare bed in Colette's room."

"Thirteen," I said. "You know there are young ones counting on me at home."

I had spun a story about the death of Papa and the debts left behind, and the drinking of Maman, and Marie with her crippled leg, and Charlotte always wanting candles and chrysanthemums for the graves of the three babies we put in the ground. She'd listened with her hand over her heart.

"All right, then," she said. "Thirteen."

Jean Luc Simard is lounging on his back, his fingers laced together behind the nape of his neck. His elbows, sharp like the edge of chiseled stone, point out to the sides. I lie turned toward him, head propped by one arm, going rigid with his words. He is saying how he will be married in a week, to a girl—Patrice—with blue eyes and white skin, like freshly fallen snow. "Her papa has a forty percent stake in Papa's bank," he says.

Already he got what he comes to the house of Madame Brossard to get. He talks, breathes with the laziness of a satisfied man. Still, instead of the usual rushing off to wash what remains of him from between my legs, I put a hand on his measly chest, the dozen fine hairs a boy so soft has managed to sprout. "This girl," I say, "your fiancée, she knows her good luck in finding a lover so magnificent as you?" I lick his nipple, the one closest to me, tell myself that a girl with skin like fresh snow don't take even the pleasure of an afternoon in the sun.

"Can't say."

"But when you kiss her?" I want to know does she dodge away or kiss back. I slide my hand lower, to the blaring whiteness of his belly.

"You're worried," he says. He cackles, the only word to describe laughter so womanly as his, and how I want to smack his cherub face. "Needn't be. I tried putting my tongue in her mouth once, and she jerked away like it was a snake."

A cold fish, then. I roll away from him, onto my back, breath coming easier.

"After the wedding, we're visiting Patrice's brother in New Orleans. We'll be gone five months."

"Five months?"

"You're jealous," he says. Laughed-out words.

I pick myself up from the bed, plop back down on top of him, and feel his sex stir. Such a puppet. Putting on my sulkiest face, I say, "Once more. On the house. No need to tell Madame Brossard."

Then I paw and nip and writhe and moan, all the while racking my brain.

Afterward he falls asleep, facedown, the featherweight of his scrawny arm across my belly. I leave him, still asleep, while I think, staring at the ceiling, at the chandelier I know so well, the six crystals hanging down, the shape of teardrops, the color of blood.

Do I find this Patrice? Would she break with Jean Luc Simard, son of a banker, apprentice banker to her own father, if I told her about the evenings at the house of Madame Brossard? Would he turn from me, hate crushing lust? One thing for sure, Madame Brossard would put me out, a blight upon her house.

Was there some other patron of the house who could take his place? Monsieur Arnaud prefers Colette; Monsieur Picot, Petite. Monsieur Mignot and Monsieur Fortin only want company. A dozen of the others are too old, desiring the flesh of a woman no more than once a week. Monsieur LaRoche is always patting my rump, pawing at my skirt, but with the way he sips his wine, Colette says he don't have a sou to spare.

The walls, the ceiling, the blood-dripping chandelier grow close, and I shift the weight of the arm of Jean Luc Simard, move like a snail, bit by bit, until my feet reach the floor. I pour water from a pitcher dotted with tiny blue roses into a basin ringed with the same, make a cup with my hands and drink. I run wet palms over my face. In the looking glass beyond the basin, my wet lashes are clumped together, appearing like the points of a star. I blink those eyes Émile Abadie called chocolate pools, think they are more like the brown glass of an elixir bottle—brittle, hard.

As I turn away, the bulging breast pocket of the frock coat of Jean Luc Simard snags my eye. I step closer to the fine wool coat, draped over the back of a chair, and place a hand upon the square lump, the wallet underneath. Glancing over my shoulder, I listen for the deep breathing of that sleeping boy. Then I reach inside the pocket, open up the wallet, and count out more than seven hundred francs in twenty- and fifty-franc notes.

I wonder about my eyes landing upon the bulge, about it happening now, about the wallet being crammed to such an extent. What was it that caused the coat of Jean Luc Simard to be draped with the bulging breast pocket calling out to me?

New Caledonia is my destiny. The crammed wallet is the parting gift of Jean Luc Simard, of Providence. And a girl would be a fool not to take what is held out on a silver plate. Calmness comes. Sureness. A feeling of strength.

I put on my stockings, my rushing fingers clumsy in attaching the silk to my garters. I pull closed the front opening of my corset, fumble with the long row of hooks. I lift the mauve silk over my head, squirm, helping it fall into place. And that wad of notes, I roll it into a thick cylinder and push it into the hollow place between the two mounds of my breast.

In the corridor, I look left and right, wanting to spy Colette or Petite, someone to button up the dress clutched to my ribs. And more Providence, there is Ginny—a housemaid—making the rounds with fresh linens.

"Ginny," I say. "Would you mind?" I point to my back.

She puts down the linens, gets to work on the buttons. "Such a dress," she says.

When she finishes, I put my hands on her shoulder and kiss both her cheeks, making her laugh. And then, using the back staircase and without seeing a single soul, I leave the house of Madame Brossard.

In our lodging room, Maman is quiet upon her mattress and Marie is tucked around Charlotte on our own. I hover over my sisters, hearing only breathing, low sighs. And then there is a snort from Maman—soused and remembering to breathe. She turns onto her side.

I fish behind the sideboard until I touch the drawstring pouch. I lift it from the nail, add to the stash the roll of notes. From the dresser I gather my belongings—two blouses; two pairs of wool stockings, both with the heels worn through; three pairs of dingy drawers; two skirts, one not fit for wearing but useful, now, as a carrying sling and someday as a source for the patches I will sew onto the trousers of Émile. I leave behind my calendar, the black leather covers and in between, the pictures of robins and strawberries, all those tiny *x*s marking out the happy days on the chaise, my old life.

In the larder I find a length of salami and a round of hard cheese. I cut away a large chunk of each, wrap them in cheesecloth and tuck the parcel into the sling of my skirt.

With my plan of gathering my things and scrounging in the larder done, I sit on my haunches in the corner of the room, knees under my chin, arms wrapped tight around my shins. I count and breathe, an old trick Madame Dominique told to the girls turning pale with fright in the wings of the Opéra stage. Back then I never once felt the need, and I remember Madame Dominique folding her arms and saying to me that any ballet girl worth her salt should feel her senses heightened, her flesh prickling, her heart racing with the desire to be admired, even loved, before setting foot upon the Opéra stage. "Don't know that I much care about arousing the old pisspots in the crowd" is what I said back, and she slapped my face.

The breathing works, and I coax the thousand thoughts rattling in my head into a line, starting at our lodging house, ending, for now, in Marseille. I will walk southeast in the rues Fontaine and Notre-Dame de Lorette and du Faubourg Montmartre, east on the boulevards Poissonnière and de Bonne Nouvelle and Saint-Martin and south on the boulevards du Temple and Beaumarchais and rue de Lyon, all leading me to the Gare de Lyon, where I will get onto the first train headed for Marseille, somewhere in the south, on the Mediterranean, or so said Monsieurs Mignot and Fortin.

At the edge of the mattress of Charlotte and Marie, I lower onto my knees. I memorize the sight of Marie's arms draped over Charlotte, Charlotte's fingers laced with Marie's, and know that without me, Marie will step up to mothering Charlotte, that without me, Charlotte will figure out the fragileness of Marie. In the grey light, I see the imprint of creased linen on the cheek of Charlotte, pink even in sleep. I bow lower, my lips floating over her ear, and then I whisper to her about conjuring up the desire to be loved before stepping onto the Opéra stage. For Marie, I whisper not to worry, not to suck her lip, not to scrape her thumb raw. I tell her she is pretty, and it is almost true, now, with a bit of meat on her bones. I say there is nothing to the nonsense about protruding jaws and bestial sides. And for a moment my mind shifts from her to me, to my own pushed-forward jaw, to the stolen seven hundred francs and my pleasure in the suffering of Jean Luc Simard. It is for both our sakes when I whisper about Pierre Gille having the face of an angel, yet the heart of a fiend. It is risky, but I put my lips on the soft skin of her cheek and kiss her with a tenderness that makes me want to cry. "I love you, Marie van Goethem, best friend of mine in all the world."

I unfold my knees, linger, looking at Maman. Did she ever stand with her life before her, trembling but sure? Did she ever make a choice? Did she ever love Papa enough to follow him to the end of the earth? "Goodbye, Maman," I say.

I take the steps of our lodging house two at a time, push open the narrow door leading to the rue de Douai. I breathe in the cold morning not yet arrived and turn to the east. Immediately I see the carriage of Madame Brossard, the curtain shifting. And there she is in her grey hat with the tall feathers, striped yellow and black. She looks at me with no trace of the pity that comes so easy to her face. She gives a short nod, and I hear quick footsteps behind me and snap around to take in the two gendarmes grabbing at my arms.

Marie. Already I did not accompany her to the exposition of Monsieur Degas and snatched the money she was planning to pay to Madame

Théodore and shoved her to the ground and slapped her face and forgot about her examination and accused her of not showing loyalty. Already she did not love me all the way through. And now this. Such a blow. I want a chance to explain, before she frets and fusses and decides she don't love her sister in the least. I want to go backward in time and be there for comfort when there is no statuette and remember her examination and fix her hair and say she showed me loyalty a hundred times. She don't know I whispered in her ear about being my best friend.

LE FIGARO

19 JANUARY 1881

ABADIE IMPLICATED IN MURDER OF WIDOW JOUBERT

Michel Knobloch has confessed to the murder of the widow Joubert, the rue Fontaine news seller bludgeoned to death the eleventh of March 1880. As accomplice, he named Émile Abadie, who was granted a stay of execution by President Grévy late last year and is currently slated for the sunny shores of New Caledonia.

For a moment it appeared Knobloch's confession was false. The widow Joubert was murdered on a March evening when both he and Abadie were marked present at one of the final performances of *L'Assommoir* at the Ambigu Theater. In the third tableau, which took place between eight thirty and nine o'clock, both appeared among the procession of workmen heading to their labors. They next appeared shortly after ten o'clock, in the seventh tableau, drinking in a pub. On Monday, though, Chief Inspector Monsieur Macé walked the distance between the Ambigu and the rue Fontaine, ascertaining for himself that there was in fact ample time between nine and ten o'clock for Abadie and Knobloch to commit the crime.

Surely Monsieur President will think twice about saving the hide of a scoundrel such as Émile Abadie a second time.

⁓ Marie ⁓

I go to see my sister at the Saint-Lazare, a prison for women. The tribunal ordered her locked up for three months for stealing seven hundred francs from a gentleman as he slept. It happened at the house of Madame Brossard. A brothel, not a tavern. I asked the girl Colette, who came to our lodging room after Antoinette did not come home for three days. I stood in the doorway, not sure, until I said, "My sister Antoinette, she worked at this house as a servant or a coquette?" and Colette looked away to the wooden threshold at our feet.

She looked up after a while, set her eyes on my own. "A respectable house," she said. "We are registered. No *fille clandestine* at the house of Madame Brossard."

I stood there, across the threshold from Colette—her low, overflowing neckline; her pouty, glistening mouth—grasping that Antoinette was not dead. And there was some amount of joy bubbling up, but the bubbles were bursting faster than they were being made. Antoinette was a coquette, jailed for robbing a gentleman. The truth of it was like the sharp point of a pin.

But still, even now, walking to Saint-Lazare, I say to myself, "Wake up, Marie. Wake up from this ugly dream." But I do not wake up. No, I put one foot ahead of the other, taking a step, peering into the fog cloaking the lampposts, the carriages, the shops not a half block away. Again, I step, swallowed up in a blanket of murk.

The visitors' parlor at Saint-Lazare is a square room split in two by a partition of iron bars, with chairs on either side, an ugly place I never hoped to see. Three jailers, all leaning up against the walls, keep watch of the six visitors, sitting, waiting, like me, or already talking in low voices to the prisoners on the other side of the bars.

What should I have done to stop her slide, her fall away from the girl who told me not to linger in stairwells, to walk quickly on the way home from the Opéra? She blamed quitting the washhouse on raw knuckles and chapped skin, and maybe they were enough to push a girl from laundress to tavern maid, but rough hands were not the cause of Antoinette giving up on a life of honest work. What was? Did she mind the four bouquets that brightened our lodging room for a week, the flash of happiness every time I remembered the soft thud of my ankle being hit?

When she finally came to see *La Korrigane*, she sat in the fourth balcony, squinting to see the gold bands of my Breton peasant skirt, the fine lace of my apron, collar, and cap. And afterward she said I ranked in the top five of the second set of the quadrille and that my dancing was superior to that of a half dozen girls in the first. She kissed me on the brow, and I lay my head on her shoulder. We stood like that a long while, and I felt the calm of a caterpillar inside his cocoon. But was her mouth, the mouth I could not see, sneering bitterness?

The Opéra, it is what I have that she does not. And, yes, it is something—all the moments when I am lifted above the grind of climbing the stairs and the strain of laboring at the barre and the boredom of holding still upon the stage. "To seek grace," Madame Dominique says. "To dance is to seek grace." Is it what I have found? For upon the stage, sometimes in the practice room, I close my mind to the worry of Antoi-nette, the coolness of Maman. Sometimes a shimmering moment of crystal clearness comes.

I am not happier than I was in Sister Evangeline's classroom, back when Papa would get me laughing without bothering to cover up my teeth. But no point in thinking about all that. It is what came afterward—Monsieur LeBlanc rattling our door, demanding what was owed—I need to remember when tabulating how I am getting along. As things are, with the arrangement I have with Monsieur Lefebvre, we have pastry for break-fast, thick soup at the end of the day, sometimes a few sous left over for a sweet. Monsieur LeBlanc does not come, or did not come, not with Antoi-nette contributing, too.

Still, the flesh alongside my thumbnail is picked raw, more raw, I think, than it was before I was elevated to the second set of the quadrille, and Monday nights, I find myself begging for sleep to come or waking up to blackness and filling with dread that with the first light arrives a Tues-day and then a morning at Monsieur Lefebvre's apartment. Twice Maman barked for me to stop thrashing and put her hand upon my brow. "No fever," she said, and in the blue light of the moon, I watched her pull a small bottle from beneath her mattress. Rim upon my lip, she tilted the bottle and I swallowed licorice so bitter that my tongue grew hard as a knot. But afterward sleep came, and three times since I have spread my hand flat, seeking Maman's bottle for myself.

I caught Antoinette watching me once, a Tuesday morning, while I combed out my hair. She just stared, her head tilted to one side. "Every-thing all right, Marie?"

I almost said about the wooden clogs, the opened up knees of after-ward, but her eyes were red rimmed and puffy underneath. She had her own sorrows and I was not sure I should add to her load a second heavy heart, not when already I was fifteen. "I'm tired," I said.

"You called out in the night. You called out two times."

"I didn't mean to wake you up."

She shrugged.

"That Charlotte sure knows how to sleep," I said, putting brightness in my voice.

"A gift of innocence." Our eyes met, clung, and for a flash, it was like she already knew about the wooden clogs, like I already knew about the house of Madame Brossard.

"The way it should be for a girl of ten."

"Yes," she said. And we nodded, so grave, and a feeling came over me, like our nodding had sealed the most solemn of pacts.

Sometimes I think how I could make a change.

In the rue de Douai, on my way home from Madame Dominique's class, it is not unusual to see Alphonse in his baker's apron and cap, smoking on the stoop of his father's shop. Always he bothers to dip his chin. Sometimes I stop, and he says, "Ah, the ballet girl," and I smile. A week ago, he said, "One moment," and disappeared into the shop. Quickly he was back, holding out in one hand a vanilla sable and in the other an orange Madeleine. "Which do you prefer?" I picked, and we stood there, me nibbling at the orange Madeleine, him brushing sable crumbs from his lips. It gave me the courage to ask if his father was happy with the girl he had taken on to knead the dough for the eighty baguettes.

He gave a little laugh. "Twice a week I listen to him complain about that girl not having half the strength of you. She doesn't hum, neither," he said.

"Hum?"

"You always hummed. Sweetly." His eyes fell.

I felt my cheeks growing rosy. He gave my arm a little punch with the side of his fist, and even if I did not work up the nerve to ask about his father giving me work again—maybe I could train myself to rise early, even after a late night—I knew there was a chance.

That evening I thumped Monsieur Degas's heavy door. He had not called me to the workshop in nine months. Sabine answered and, wiping her hands on her apron, said, "Well, look at you, Mademoiselle van Goethem. Almost a lady, now."

The workshop was dim, lit by a handful of lamps, but still Monsieur Degas stood in his painter's smock, one arm across his ribs and the other propped on top, holding up his chin, as if, after a moment of considering, even with the late hour, he would get back to his work.

"I've come about modeling," I said. If Alphonse's father would give me a few hours, if Monsieur Degas wanted me steady again, if I went around to the pork butcher, the watchmaker, the crockery dealer and any one of them saw his way to a few hours more, I could get by without Monsieur Lefebvre's thirty francs. The trick would be finding the hours to sleep.

Monsieur Degas looked up, his eyes meeting mine.

I lifted my arms from my side. "I'm not so skinny anymore, no longer a petit rat."

I saw him every few weeks at the Opéra—in the wings, in the orchestra stalls, in the practice room. Usually he greeted me by name, and once he said, "Your allegro is improved." Always he wore his blue spectacles, and always his gaze was steady, burrowing. But that evening in his workshop, without hardly bothering to look, he said, "The statuette, it troubles me."

He waved a hand, and I followed with my eyes to his statuette, two-thirds the size of me in real life, and my breath quickened that he had not given up. I walked closer, taking in the canvas ballet slippers, the tarlatan skirt, the leek-green ribbon tied in a bow around the thick plait of what looked to be a wig of real hair. The skin was smooth or rough, uneven in color—deep honey on the face, reddish brown on the legs—all of it formed from a substance neither polished nor dull, opaque nor clear, soft nor hard.

Wax, I decided, thinking of the way it bled down the sides of candles, hardening as it cooled, always changing shape, even, on a hot day, without the heat of a lit wick. There was a thin film of the same covering the hair; tinted yellow, covering the bodice; tinted red, covering the slippers.

No stone. No bronze. No porcelain. Only wax. Temporary. Second-rate.

And what was Monsieur Degas meaning, dressing up the statuette in real clothes and, worse, a wig of real hair? Was it woven together from the sold tresses of a starving girl? The clipped locks of the dead?

That freakish doll's body—the skinny limbs, the too-large elbows and knees, the ridges of muscle sticking out from the thighs and the collarbones jutting below the neck—was no longer like my own. But in the face— the low forehead, the apish jaw, the broad cheekbones, the small half-closed eyes—the statuette was the mirror of me. The only mercy—Monsieur Degas hid my teeth behind closed lips.

What was the story, the story of a heart and body, Monsieur Degas was trying to tell? What was I thinking as I stood those long hours in fourth position? I was craving the stage, a position in the second set of the quadrille, a kind word from Madame Dominique. Muscles aching, stomach rumbling, I wanted the four hours to end, to find a scrap of sausage left for me at home. But I held still, dreaming up glory—a real ballet girl, captured in pastel and chalk, even oils, and then after he said, "A statuette," my desire swelled. I dreamt of Marie Taglioni, wings spread, hovering above the earth.

I looked into the statuette's face, and I saw longing, ambition, pride. Her chin was tilted up, and it seemed a mistake, too hopeful, on such a face. Such an ugly, monkey face. I turned away, still feeling small half-closed eyes upon my back.

Monsieur Degas was not looking my way, awaiting some comment from me. No, he was lost inside his own head, and so I stood there, quiet, wishing I had not come.

Eventually he turned to me, saying, "Perhaps. Perhaps." He took up the pose I had held for so long, the pose of the statuette—feet in fourth position, fingers laced together behind my back. "Would you mind?"

I slipped off my shawl and, knowing his impatience, let it fall to the floor. I arranged myself, easily. Memory, Madame Dominique said, was not only the domain of the mind.

For a moment he was gleeful, almost clapping his hands, but then he paused. "No," he said. "You're not teetering between rat and sylph anymore." He touched me on the shoulder lightly, and in the touch I felt sadness that girls grow into women; that men crumple, hobbling over walking sticks; that flowers wither; that trees drop their leaves. The graceful, childish back Monsieur Lefebvre, more than a year ago, felt driven to touch was gone and with it Monsieur Degas's interest in me modeling for him. He wanted only the heart and body of a little dancer, aged fourteen.

"All those sketches," I said. "They won't change."

He straightened his glasses, turned away from me to a notebook, one I knew to hold drawings of me.

I wrap my fingers around the iron bars, give a little tug, but the grate is firmly lodged, and there is no more chance of rattling it than the brick floor beneath my feet. Monsieur Lefebvre is my protector, and there is no other way, especially not now, not without Antoinette.

I want to put my face in my hands, to howl, for me, for Antoinette, for all the women of Paris, for the burden of having what men desire, for the heaviness of knowing it is ours to give, that with our flesh we make our way in the world. For there is a cost. But would Antoinette agree, or would she say there was no cost other than what a girl decides to believe in her own head? I look from one jailer—bored—to the next, idly fingering a brass button on his coat. Would they say there is no cost, not so long as a girl takes no more than what a man decides her flesh is worth? Could I put my mind over to that way of thinking? Would it mean I could stop wishing for Antoinette to be different than she is? Could I sleep Monday nights?

I look from the long face of one visitor to the wringing hands of the next. Are any of them saying why? Why take up the life of a coquette? Why steal seven hundred francs, especially when it meant hiding, running away from all she knows? From Charlotte. From Maman. From me. And now, before the iron bars, my face falls to my cupped hands. She was leaving behind nothing, only Charlotte, who is selfish; Maman, who drinks; me, who calls the boy she loves a murderer, a coldhearted slitter of throats.

But, oh, it is true. I swallow hard, a trick I learned in the company of Monsieur Lefebvre for clearing tears, for switching my mind to some detail—the laurel wreaths of the carpet, the pinkness of his scalp. And eyes still dry, I put my hands in my lap. On Wednesday, the same day Antoinette went to Saint-Lazare, the newspaper said a boy confessed to the widow Joubert's murder and swore under oath Émile Abadie took part in the bludgeoning.

I am grateful for the grey silk dress I am wearing today, even if before I opened the beribboned box Monsieur Lefebvre put in my lap, I hoped for a dress not as lavish as those worn by the ladies at the Opéra but maybe with a neckline opening across the shoulders, maybe with a bit of lace, even a single rosette. But, no, my dress is high-collared, grey, stern, something a banker's daughter wears to Mass, something a coquette's prideful sister puts on to visit her in jail. On opening up the box, I know my face fell. The air took on a chill, and Monsieur Lefebvre said, "You are only a girl."

"I'm fifteen."

"And an ungrateful one at that."

I bit my lip, like I should have my tongue. Always, the minute an abonné was in sight, Perot put on a sultry pout. When I started to tell about modeling and Monsieur Lefebvre not being an artist at all, Blanche rolled her eyes and snapped, "The price of roses at your feet. Tell him I won't be nearly such a prude."

I stroked the smooth coolness of the silk. "So beautiful," I said. I kept my chin tucked in but dared to lift my eyes. "I never dreamt of such softness against my skin."

"The way you parade around—buttons missing, neckline gaping, underclothes threadbare or not there at all—it isn't decent." He said it all curt, hateful, like I sat there in the evenings, plucking off buttons and fiddling with the drawstring of my blouse until it was worn too thin to hold anything in place, all of it with a mind to luring him into blundering the next day.

Antoinette sits down across the iron bars, and I want to close my eyes to the prison gown of brown coarse wool, the faded cape of dusty blue, the tatty cap of threadbare cloth, the half-moons the color of dusk underneath her eyes. A shyness comes over me, a feeling I do not hardly know Antoinette. "I was afraid you wouldn't come," she says.

She reaches through the bars, and I take her hand. "Oh, Antoinette."

Her shoulders fall. She shakes her head, but she does not explain about taking up the life of a coquette, about stealing seven hundred francs. No, her eyes fall to my dress, and she tightens her grip. "That dress you're wearing, where'd you get such a dress?"

"A gift." She eyes me, her gaze sorrowful, her brow lined, but she says nothing more. I had imagined urgent whispers, our heads leaned in close, and sobbing and wiping away each other's tears. I take a breath and, wanting to erase the gaping quiet, I leap into explaining how Colette—your friend from the house of Madame Brossard is what I say—came to the door. I wait for her face to change, for her to speak, but there is nothing to show her grasping that I know it was not a tavern she headed off to all those evenings. "She said you took seven hundred francs. But why, Antoinette?" I sound like Charlotte, whining for a piece of barley sugar, a second egg when we only have four.

"That dress?" she says.

"It's me who should be interrogating you." I say it quiet but hold my gaze firm.

"All right," she says. "You're right. First though, I got a favor to ask." I nod.

"I need you to let Émile know I'm here, at Saint-Lazare."

Like always, I bristle at the mention of that boy, but I do not let go of her hand. If we fight, if she stands up and leaves, the iron bars would hold me back from following her. I lean in. "Tell me," I say. "Tell me why you worked in such a place." When she only presses her mouth into a tight line, I go on, "There was enough for meat twice a week."

She rubs a thumb over the back of my hand. "You don't want the answer."

"I do." Again, Charlotte's whimpering voice.

She blinks, and even with her face toward me, her gaze upon me, she is staring clear through me to the wall at my back. "I need money for passage to New Caledonia," she says.

"Antoinette?"

Her eyes drop to the brick floor at her feet but only for a flicker. Then they are back upon my own.

My vision blurs, and there is nothing to be done about the tears rolling onto my cheeks. "You can't." I tug my hand free.

She drops her face into her palms. Her shoulders quake. She is sobbing, without making noise. I lift up a bit from my chair, but the iron bars, they keep me from putting in my arms a girl who does not make a habit of tears.

What to say? Do I explain about the equator, about one hundred and eighty degrees reaching the other side of the earth? She cannot know. "A tunnel drilled through the center of the earth will end in New Caledonia,"

I say. "But there is no drilling of such a hole, no such thing as a tunnel stretching that long."

Her head bobs slightly, and she takes her hands from her face. "Six weeks, maybe more, on a ship, sailing from Marseille." I see in her steady gaze the willfulness that led her to the house of Madame Brossard, that allowed her to lift her skirt, the pigheadedness that says she will one day set foot in that faraway place.

I wipe at my eyes, lick my lips, lace my fingers in my lap. "You love Émile Abadie. I know it. I've seen you happy. I've seen you on his arm in the rue de Douai. But sometimes you despair." She opens her mouth to speak, and I hold up my hands, soft though, a gentle hush. "I've heard you sorrowful. More than once I heard you argue with that boy about a dead dog, about letting another boy slap your face, about the money he wasn't saving up. You have a darkness under your eyes, and that boy, he put it there."

She touches a dusky half-moon.

"Again, he is in trouble," I say. "This time for the beating death of the widow Joubert."

She puts her arms over her ribs, clamps her jaw tight, closing herself to me. Still, maybe because of habit, words lurch from my mouth, a cart loose on a hill. "A boy confessed and said Émile Abadie took part in the bludgeoning." The flesh of her face falls. She forgets to breathe. Her arms wrap tighter, fingertips digging into her ribs. And my words come faster. "The inspector says the widow Joubert was murdered the eleventh of March, in the gap when Abadie and the other boy were absent from the stage at the Ambigu."

Her lips part. "What gap?" she says.

"Between the third tableau and the seventh."

Antoinette claps a hand against her thigh, and the half-moons beneath her eyes fade. "I never told you about the storeroom and getting adored," she says. And then before I say a thing she is telling how the gap was the exact hour she spent with Émile Abadie in a storeroom most every day, about the calendar where she marked it all down. "Nine days out of ten, printed on that calendar you'll find the tiny x, proving his innocence."

She keeps up her rosy, rushed blathering, asking when the trial will take place, and once I say, "It's two months away," telling me to find the calendar, wedged into the opening between the chimneypiece and the wall, and to take it to Monsieur Albert Danet, Émile's attorney. She says I am to explain the meaning of the tiny x I am sure to find marking the eleventh of March. "I won't be out in time," she says. "You got to do this one thing for me, this one important thing." And there is such hope in her glowing, pleading face, such trust, that I nod.

"Now tell me," she says. "Was the boy did the confessing Michel Knobloch?"

"Yes." Again she claps her thigh, her face alive with happiness.

"He's the biggest liar Paris has ever seen. People will line up to say so in court."

"No one lies about murder," I say, fingernail digging into the raw patch of my thumb. "Why would anyone lie?"

"He only wants to get to New Caledonia," she says. "The land of milk and honey."

Such joy. From a girl leaving me behind. How my heart aches.

I lay my cheek flat against the wall of our lodging room and peer into the gap behind the chimneypiece and sure enough, there are two small brass rings holding together what has to be Antoinette's calendar. I fish a knife into the gap, catch one of the rings and lift the black leather covers and the pages sandwiched in between from their hiding place.

I put the calendar on the table, and stand there, hands on my hips, just staring and wondering where Antoinette found such a pretty thing. I step backward, take in from the side the scalloped edges of the stacked pages.

Quickly, with a single finger, like it is hot, I tip open the top cover and come upon a bookplate reading *Property of William Busnach*. Without a minute of wondering why Antoinette has the calendar of *L'Assommoir*'s playwright, I flip to the month marked March, see two birds, green with yellow breasts, their red beaks tipped together in a kiss. A single glance tells me there is an *x* in every box but three, that each of the empty boxes falls in the final week of the month.

Antoinette called Charlotte's easy sleep a gift of innocence. We made grave nods, and I remember the feeling of a solemn pact to keep our sister from the harshness of the world. Not for a flash did I think Antoinette meant for me to work out just how all on my own. I could not. Would not. It was not something I knew how to do. Even putting Charlotte aside, if it was just me, I could not get along without Antoinette, could not work out the living and breathing, the haggling with Monsieur LeBlanc, the hollering for Maman to get up.

She lifted her skirt on behalf of Émile Abadie, a boy who was rude and ugly, a boy who let another slap her face, a boy who would never provide a roof over her head, a boy who slit a woman's throat. Such a boy, she would follow to the ends of the earth. The hold he had on her, it was like a sickness. And the blade of the guillotine upon his neck was the cure, a gift to Antoinette. And if I was truthful, a gift to Charlotte and me.

I find a match, pull pages from the book, twist them into crumpled bows and toss them to the stone floor of the fireplace. Match struck, a blaze flares. Red hot along the edges, paper turns black, and then it disappears, nothing more than soot, ash, air.

Antoinette

Through the puny window in the oaken door of my cell, I catch sight of the wimple and pimpled, ruddy cheek of a sister. I hear the sliding shut of the iron bolt locking me in until daybreak, a sluggish twelve hours away. The bell of the Angelus in the courtyard rings out seven times. Then there are the cries of a sister calling out gibberish—Latin words about the angel of the Lord speaking to Mary—and after that, all the prisoners answering back. More Latin, this time about the child inside of Mary being put there by God. At least it is what the Superioress said yesterday when I was sitting before her on a hard bench, repeating and repeating until I knew the opening lines of the Angelus by heart. Fallen girls is what they call those of us holed up in section two of Saint-Lazare—all coquettes without the good sense to follow the rules. It gets tedious, those dreary sisters announcing the virtue of Mary three times a day. "Maybe this old prison should have took its name from Mary," I said to the Superioress once she was satisfied with my reciting of the Angelus. "I expect she was fallen herself."

"Hold your tongue, Mademoiselle van Goethem." I been spared knowing a single Superioress in my life, but this one, she looked exactly like she should—jowly, droopy neck, eyes like a wolf.

"Can't help but wonder what you sisters were meaning, naming this place after Saint Lazarus. Wasn't he a lowly beggar with the open sores of a leper upon his skin?"

Oh, how she clenched her lips, the Superioress.

The walls have ears, and so behind my oaken door, I stoop to my knees, to the stubbly brickwork of the floor. Fingers laced, knuckles lining up, I move my hands to under my chin. But after mumbling the first chorus, my mind drifts to thinking that, doomed to an evening of prayer, I should at least be asking for Marie to take my calendar to Monsieur Danet like she said. Of course some snitching sister has an ear pressed up against my door, and there comes the sound of chalk scraping over oak. In the morning I will find a blaring white slash marking the outside of my door, the sign instructing me to report to the Superioress for more lessons upon her hard bench. This, instead of a free hour, walking the pathways of the courtyard with the rest of the fallen girls.

It is not so bad here, even if I miss combing out the locks of Marie and sharing a bit of custard from the pastry cook with Charlotte. I have a bed, an entire cell to myself, also a little table and chair. The problem is I need to count on Marie to get my calendar to Monsieur Danet, and I cannot go to Émile and put his mind at ease or get back to saving for New Caledonia. Every day I wake up hopeful of being called to the parlor, of Marie coming with some news, but doubt is creeping into my mind. Marie, she nodded yes to taking my calendar to Monsieur Danet. But with a month come and gone, my mind slips to thinking that pigeon-hearted girl does not come because her dipped chin was a lie. Oh, but she won't let me down, not Marie, who bothers to notice when I give her the better shawl, the larger piece of mutton, who said thank you about a hundred times for a pair of stockings I bought from the pawnbroker for a good price, who put her hands on my cheeks once, after I combed out her hair and said, "I love you, Antoinette van Goethem, best friend of mine in all the world."

．　．　．

At half past seven in the morning, we fallen girls of section two rise and make our beds, tucking in the linens just so, pulling tight the brown woolen coverlet, the single bit of housework we are expected to accomplish in a day. A maid comes later, sweeping up after me, and another after that, to take away for scrubbing the brown earthen porringer I use to collect my meals. I wait on my tidy bed, listening for the sound of metal on metal, a bolt scraped open. Then we are off to the sewing workshop to sing a hymn and say the stinking Angelus before we get down to our prison work of stitching underclothes. Every day my stitches get neater, faster, and not once did a sister work up the nerve to stand over my shoulder, clicking her tongue, telling me to pick undone the stitches of my work. At the break-fast hour we walk single file to the refectory, a large room with tall windows spilling light onto the flagstones of the floor, to collect our day's ration of brown bread—a full loaf—and get our porringers filled with a soup of vegetables, unless it is Thursday or Sunday, when they add meat to the broth. We pray, then eat—our soup, a portion of our loaves—at long, gleaming tables or in the courtyard adjoining the refectory when the weather is fine. Girls with chalk slashes upon their doors are told to gulp their soup and hurry off to the Superioress. Myself, I blow on each spoonful, leave the bowl of the spoon lingering in my mouth, wait for the tapping of the presiding sister's foot to begin.

At five o'clock we put down our needles only to pick up rosaries and begin more reciting, stopping only at the end of each decade for a hymn about getting freed from the tyranny of Satan or dispersing the gloomy clouds of night. Plenty of the singing girls have their glowing faces lifted up, their lashes lightly resting upon their cheeks.

After the singing comes the evening meal and a second period of recreation. Some of the girls make a habit of complaining about the sameness of the fare—Sunday, beef and dried peas; Monday, red beans; Tuesday, rice; Wednesday, potatoes; Thursday, beef and pulse; Friday, white beans; Saturday, potatoes. And once I was close to blurting out to those sniveling girls about the vegetables being cooked in fat and there being less gristle than lean in the meat, but the Superioress was loitering close enough to hear. They are not stingy with the portions neither, and I have a layer was not there before, filling up the troughs between my ribs.

Bellies full we head back to the workshop for the part of the day when sometimes my mind is coaxed away from worrying about Marie and the calendar, Émile and his suffering at La Roquette. While we stitch— drawers, camisoles, petticoats—one of the sisters reads from a book. Each of the stories has some lesson we are meant to learn, and usually it is easy to figure out. The girl, who sat by the cinders after slaving, was humble and good. Her stepsisters were haughty, and in the end those haughty sisters were begging for the mercy of the sister who was not. There was another one, about a girl with a red cap making the mistake of telling a wolf where she was headed one day. At the end of the story, that wolf, he ate the girl up whole. It took a while to work out why we were read such a tale but finally I knew. It was a warning, about speaking to men we did not know, about finding ourselves tricked into their beds, about getting too close to their sharp teeth. Those sisters, they are blinkered like those mares pulling the hacks. If it was not for another day passing, another day without hearing from Marie, I would have snorted good and loud about such a tale.

The Superioress, she says to me, sitting on the hard bench, "Now, Antoinette, you know the opening of the Angelus, and yet you are not joining in."

"My heart is heavy, Mother."

She nods, almost smiles. "On Sunday, Father Renault will hear confessions."

Imagine the job of listening to all that the girls of section two have to tell. The confessional booth here at Saint-Lazare must be the most interesting place Father Renault ever sat doling out Hail Marys in his life. Those girls spilling their guts to him, the same ones singing with rapture upon their brows, I can guess how they are going to make out once they are again feeding themselves. "The thing is, Mother, I saw a sister picking her nose and right when she was handed the body of Christ, too."

"Willfulness, such as yours, is exactly what a girl needs to raise herself up, to do something useful with her life."

"I got that chalk slash for thinking about the herd of little ones holding their empty bellies at home, now that I been stopped from doing something so useful as filling those bellies up."

Slow as a snail, she turns the pages of the large black book spread open upon her writing desk. "You have two sisters," she says, tapping midway down a page, "both on the payroll of the Opéra, a mother employed as a laundress." She puts folded-together hands on top of the book, her knobby knuckles bulging but not in the least showing the white of strain. "We make exceptions from time to time and release a girl's earnings to a family in need."

I know about the earnings, the share of the profits from the sewed underclothes that are doled out to the fallen girls. It was explained my first morning upon the hard bench. So long as we work, we are given a weekly eight francs to spend on wine or candles or white bread here at Saint-Lazare or to put aside, a nest egg, the Superioress called it, for when a girl is finished her time. I listened to the little speech, arms crossed in front. I would not fall for trickery meant to keep us working day and night. But then, my first time in the refectory for the evening meal, I saw glasses of wine and those maids handing them out marking strips of paper with ticks.

"Shall I make arrangements for your earnings to go to your sisters in the rue de Douai?" the Superioress says.

Émile needs me saving, even if it is a measly eight francs a week, and not saving feels like giving up on the court declaring his innocence in the murder of the widow Joubert. But I think of Charlotte, despairing over a limp skirt, the frayed tails of a ribbon, also Marie, boiling the bones of a chicken a second time, fretting about a pinch of salt. I don't have my mind quite made up when the Superioress, she has the nerve to pick up a fountain pen and get herself poised to write a note about wages going to the rue de Douai. "Don't you send them a single sou," I say.

She clutches the pen tighter, her knuckles turning white.

But afterward in the sewing workshop my mind is on Marie, the grey silk, how she acquired such a dress. In the visitors' parlor after I called New Caledonia the land of milk and honey, her sobbing was such that I could not bring myself to ask about the dress again. I still my needle and call over Sister Amélie—a nervous mole with beady eyes and hairs sprouting on her chin—and she scuttles off to the Superioress with the changed instruction of my earnings going to the rue de Douai.

Two days later Sister Amélie, or Mole as I like to call her, crosses the workshop and says to me, "Your sister is waiting in the parlor." It gets me hoping and holding my breath that Marie is here with good news. But in the parlor, Marie is looking jumpy, fidgeting and sucking on her lip. "Well?" I say, feeling the slithering coldness of that dipped chin—her promise to take the calendar to Monsieur Danet—meaning nothing at all.

She shrugs, opening up her hands like she don't understand.

"The calendar?" I say. "The calendar that is going to save the neck of Émile?"

"I brought you some barley sugar." Her eyes dart. She scrapes away at the flesh of her thumb.

"Marie." I move to my knees, put my locked-together fingers beneath my chin. "Please. I beg you." It is not possible that I should be betrayed by my own flesh and blood, by Marie. It is not possible in the least. She is fretting so only because her shins have started aching when she leaps, because Maman did not get up for the washhouse, because Charlotte lost her scarlet sash.

"The sisters took it, the barley sugar. To inspect." Her bottom lip quivers. She clamps it still with her ugly teeth, and I know.

"You got to get that calendar to Monsieur Danet."

"It wasn't there, behind the chimneypiece," she says in the meekest little voice.

"Don't believe you. I know you saw an x on the eleventh of March."

"I told you." Her eyes flit to mine, flit away. "It wasn't there."

"Look at me. On my knees. On my knees, Marie." Never before have I begged. Never before have I begged on my knees.

She tilts her chin up, the faintest little bit, and, voice dropping to a whisper, she says, "Like I said, it wasn't there."

Sure enough she saw that x. Otherwise she has no reason to lie. I hop to my feet, leaning forward, onto my toes, putting out my chest. "Liar." I huff it out good and loud, and then a jailer grabs at my shoulder, pushing me back down into my chair.

Marie shifts her arms to tightly wrapping her ribs. Her eyes take on a gloss. The cords of her neck grow taut, then, with swallowing, slack. I want despair spilling onto her cheeks and again hop to my feet. I spit hateful words: "Upon your hands, the blood of an innocent."

She wags her ugly jaw slow, and the dampness welled at her lower lashes disappears.

A jailer nudges his chin toward Marie. "Best be going," he says.

She stands, eyes dry, jaw set, and appearing a harder girl than ever I saw her look in her life, she turns away.

She comes again in three days, but I have no wish to see a sister with a heart so cold as hers. I tell Mole, sent to fetch me, that if I went to the parlor now, I would miss the singing, that without the singing my mind slips to devilish thoughts. Marie comes again in a week. I look up from a camisole, from the straight line of slip stitches holding the ribbon of the neckline in place, and say to Mole, "That girl, the one with the habit of sucking on her lip, she is not my sister but a girl sent from the house of Madame Brossard, one I no longer wish to see." I think of Émile, the guillotine, his thick neck held to the lunette by the hands of Marie.

Maman comes after that and is aflutter with the happy news of Monsieur Mérante singling out Charlotte and another petit rat called Jocelyn, telling them that on Wednesdays they are to take class with Marie and the others of the second set of the quadrille. "Imagine," Maman says. "Some of those girls are a full head taller than our Charlotte."

"You got to tell her no showing off." Marie would be the better one to say about no one, including Madame Dominique, thinking much of a petit rat without the good sense to take a spot at the back of the barre, but I will not give Maman a message to deliver to Marie.

After that Maman gets all quiet and thoughtful-looking, and I wait for her to scold me about stealing or the house of Madame Brossard. But she puts her hands in her lap, draws in a breath and says, "Marie's been bawling like the world is coming to an end. She said you two had a squabble, that you'd be leaving Paris, your heart all full of hatred, and I said to her, 'Now, Marie, enough with the blubbering. Your sister isn't going anywhere. She isn't so tarnished as that. There are other houses for Antoinette,' but she just stared, those puffy, swollen eyes of hers as hard as glass, and then she pulled the linens up over her head."

Marie deserves to bawl, and I won't allow sorrow for the girl holding in place the neck of Émile. What I feel instead is the burn of bitterness about being born to a mother who don't appear disappointed with her jailed daughter, a thieving coquette, one she assumes will go back to the same line of work, a mother who is not promising to speak to Monsieur Guiot about the possibility of him taking her daughter back. I should not care, not in the least. There is no chance of me again breathing the soapy, steamy air of the washhouse. Already, in recreation hour, I prod the other girls. What houses do they know? Which madams take too large a cut for nothing more than owning a velvet sofa and a polished-up chandelier? Which beat a girl? Which know the trick of bringing a stingy gentleman to opening his wallet? The girls are careful, dropping few crumbs about this house or that, almost never giving away much about the places she will call on once she is free of Saint-Lazare. But I gather up those crumbs, and already I've got myself the names of three houses.

"Now, Antoinette, you got to be nice to your sister," Maman says. "She isn't cut from the same cloth as you and Charlotte."

"And what cloth is that?"

She pulls her lips into a tight ring, focuses her eyes on a high corner of the room. "I would've said silk; it don't tear, but it scorches even if the iron isn't hardly hot. Cotton is too soft. Linen's got strength. Course it wrinkles, but it's nothing to iron it out flat."

"You're thinking, I got myself cut from linen?"

Brightness comes to her face. "No, Antoinette." She shakes her head. "You are cut from jute. Strong enough for hauling potatoes and making rope, and no chance of finding it in the washhouse, no matter how hard you look."

My mind flits away from the lying finger of Michel Knobloch, the betrayal of Marie, the looming trial of Émile. And for a second I wonder about the usefulness of jute in keeping the starlings from pecking the ripening fruit of the cherry trees—if there are such things in New Caledonia as starlings and cherry trees.

Maman yammers on, so-and-so lifting her skirt for Monsieur Guiot behind the washhouse and always getting assigned the easy work of ironing, so-and-so complaining and Monsieur Guiot assigning her to the wringing machine, and then after that so-and-so drawing a heart with *Guiot* written inside on the steamy glass and him flying into a rage. I pass the time thinking about Marie, about whether she is more like flannel—soft, worn through easier than most. Or knit wool—eaten up by moths, unraveling when a single strand is broke. I been harsh. Too harsh? Maybe. Probably. Stop.

Once every bit of washhouse gossip is spilled from her mouth, Maman says, "Well, got to get back. Monsieur Guiot said any more than two hours and he was docking me a full day."

She puts a hand deep into the pocket of her skirt and pulls out a tatty scrap of newspaper. She is reaching through the iron bars, holding it out to me and saying, "It's for you. From Marie," when one of the jailers snatches it away.

"It's nothing," Maman says to him.

He looks it over, front and back, before handing it to me. "Once caught a madam passing the answers a girl was to give in the court," he says. "Stuffed them inside a walnut shell."

The newspaper is creased and soft with handling, like it was carried around in the pocket of Marie, even brought to Saint-Lazare those two times I said no to visiting with her. I make out *Émile* spelled in bold lettering across the top, but not the word that comes first, long and starting with a *J*. Still, I know what all those words say, why Marie sent it with Maman. That hateful girl, she is still working to turn me against Émile. "Don't want it," I say, crumpling the paper, flicking the wad through the bars to the feet of Maman. "Tell Marie I don't want nothing from her. None of her arguments. Nothing. Never again."

"No need to raise your voice," Maman says, eyes racing about the parlor, from prying ear to gawking eyes.

And in that moment it is clear to me she came for a lark, a laugh, a bit of gossip, a morning away from her arms up to her elbows in suds. Me heading off to New Caledonia, it might bring on tears, but only a few and wiped away easily with the back of her hand.

LE FIGARO

23 FEBRUARY 1881

JURISPRUDENCE AND
ÉMILE ABADIE

In a few short weeks the court will decide the guilt
of Émile Abadie and Michel Knobloch in the beating death of the widow Joubert eleven months ago.
Knobloch has confessed to the crime and named
Abadie as his accomplice.

Knobloch, if found guilty, could be condemned
to death. The same, however, cannot be said for
Abadie. By virtue of jurisprudence, any individual
sentenced to the maximum penalty cannot be pur-
sued for a crime committed before the offense that
brought about the sentence. And for Abadie that
means the verdict of the court in the Montreuil tavern owner murder has whitewashed his whole past.
The widow Joubert was slain before the Montreuil
tavern owner, and Abadie's sentence of forced
labor in New Caledonia will stand no matter the
findings of the court.

Is not jurisprudence lovely?

⤌⤍ Marie ⤌⤍

Three weeks ago I read the story about Émile Abadie not going to the guillotine no matter what, and then I read it again. He was heading off to New Caledonia, and there was no more dreaming up a fairy tale of Antoinette rid of him and staying put with us in Paris, her heart full of loathing, but after a while growing rosy toward me again. But there never was comfort in dreaming a dream of the old Antoinette curled around me on our mattress, her fingers in my hair, not from the start, not when the dream was not a sliver true. I turned my back on Antoinette, who never once groveled in her life, except to ask her sister to deliver a calendar to Monsieur Danet. But by the time she was pleading on her knees, it was too late. The calendar was burned. And whether Antoinette went to New Caledonia or stayed in Paris, the ending was the same: She was lost to me, a sister who did not love her sister anymore. Such a stupid thing, striking that match.

Antoinette combed out my hair, like she had all the time in the world. She raised her voice against Monsieur LeBlanc, with Charlotte and me shuddering as far from the doorway as we could get. She was not paying interest, she spat, not when the stink of the courtyard was so strong, not when the health inspector should be issuing a fine. She walked in a slow

circle, studying the attitude I held, the same one Madame Dominique earlier said made me look like a pissing dog. "Gorgeous," Antoinette said.
"Her bellyaching don't mean nothing more than it's her time of the month."

It is like a broken rib, the way I miss Antoinette.

How puffed up I was in the moment the match and then the calendar
caught, flickering ablaze. In my mind I was altering Émile Abadie's fate,
saving Antoinette from him, saving her for me. But, oh, how I duped
myself. Imagine the trickery, the weak-mindedness in thinking a lowly
ballet girl of the second set of the quadrille could switch the court's verdict
from innocent over to guilty and in doing so, wrench a murderer from
boarding a ship to New Caledonia. That kind of magic was for presidents
and abonnés and the high-minded men of the court, not a girl spending
hours each day as a prop, a girl with filth clinging to her skirt. My true and
only feat in striking the match was never anything more than filling Antoinette's heart with loathing for me.

But with a newspaper picked out of the gutter, where it waited like a
gift, there was new hope, printed in *Le Figaro*. The men of the court said it
was not Émile Abadie's fate to fall upon the guillotine. He would go to
New Caledonia, and that meant Antoinette would, too. I waited for swelling panic, rising dread, but it did not come. I sighed the greatest of sighs,
bigger than meat in the belly, a door closed against a bitter wind, Monsieur
Mérante announcing the end of rehearsal when already the twelve peals of
midnight had rung. With the words in *Le Figaro*, proving Émile Abadie's
life was never in my hands, might Antoinette forgive my lie, my treachery? Might I get my sister back, maybe only for a bit, snuggling close
under the linens? It was better than a sister forever lost.

Twice I tried, and twice Antoinette said no to seeing me. For two
weeks after that I badgered Maman. "She'll want her mother," I said.
"You should go." Then, just this morning, Maman rolled over on her mattress and, staring up at the ceiling, said, "Old Guiot's got me on the wringing machine today. How I hate that wringing machine."

"Take the morning for calling at Saint-Lazare," I said. "A nice little break."

She pushed herself onto an elbow. "I just might."

"I have something for you to give to Antoinette." I held out the folded-up story of "Jurisprudence and Émile Abadie" in one hand and in the other fare for the omnibus. Any one of the sisters would be able to tell Antoinette what the words said. Quick as lightning, Maman snatched.

𝓘 stand at the barre, bending and arching and thinking I was ridiculous to have taken to bawling and lolling upon my mattress, getting up so late it meant running to reach the Opéra before the practice room door was shut and twice, shrinking under the harshest glare from Madame Dominique when, even with the rushing, I brushed past her, already pulling closed the door. Three times, too, I had stood at the barre with the booming headache I deserved after taking more absinthe than I should. Today, though, the routine of the exercises, the way ronds de jambe always follow battements tendus, is like liniment upon my frayed nerves and the narrowing of my thoughts to just the exercise called out, like salve upon my jumpy mind. In center, the allegro is full of grand jetés en tournant, and I feel myself lifted up, landing with a lightness that dodged me for weeks. Afterward Madame Dominique calls me to the front of the practice room. Once the girls are gone, she says, "A better effort today."

I nod, wait, one arm across my ribs, fingers gripping the elbow of the other. Always she says *dismissed* when a girl is free to go.

"The Opéra," she says, "it's your chance."

I put a hand upon my heart and mean it when I say, "I want to dance. I'll do better. No more being late."

She gives me a hard look—her lips pulled in tight, her head tilted to one side—intending to show me she is not a bit sure. I tell myself not to glance away or lick my lips or shuffle my feet, nothing a liar would do.

After a while she sucks in a breath, puffs it out through her nose, and says, "Monsieur Lefebvre was in the other day."

Seven Tuesdays have come and gone since Monsieur Lefebvre gave me the grey silk and snapped that I paraded around, indecent, luring him into blundering. I wore the dress each visit, but still, each week meant more of the usual from him—the stepping behind the easel, the swaying knees—except that he started letting his trousers drop to the floor instead of holding them up so we could pretend that behind the easel he was doing nothing more than drawing. Last week the panting and moaning jerked to quiet, and like rotten meat spit from his mouth, he called out, "You're flushed again, all steamy." He shoved the easel, as if he had no taste for drawing such a lustful girl. Still, like a beekeeper hardened to getting stung, there was far less quaking from me than seven Tuesdays earlier.

Madame Dominique rubs her thumb hard over the palm of her other hand. "He asked me to teach you the slave dance," she says. "Monsieur Mérante needs six more girls, and they have agreed you are to be one of them."

Le Tribut de Zamora was opening the first of the month and the nerves of half the opera were ready to snap. Nearly thirty years ago Monsieur Gounod gave the world the pretty song "Ave Maria" and then he went and followed it up with an opera called Faust that Madame Dominique says is the finest to ever grace the Opéra stage. And now we have Monsieur Vaucorbeil saying every chance he gets that Le Tribut de Zamora will bring glory to the Opéra once again. But we all know the opera was to open at the beginning of the year, that it was pushed back on account of Monsieur Gounod's desire to perfect the score. All of us heard the rumblings about him having the nerve to beg Monsieur Vaucorbeil, a second time, for another three months. "Enough fussing" is what I heard he said back. "Le Tribut de Zamora will open the first of April."

The opera tells the story of Xaïma, a maiden stolen from her fiancé as one of the hundred virgins owed by the Spaniards to the Moors after Zamora was sacked. I have been doing nothing more in the rehearsals than posing as one of the virgins, which means crossing the stage twice in a series of glissades and filling out the scenery in act two when the virgins get auctioned off. At first I used up the time by marveling at the set, which they say was copied from a place in Spain called the Alhambra, but mostly the rehearsing was boring and dull, and my mind wandered to Antoinette, working herself into a lather of hatred in her cell, forgetting about the feast atop Montmartre, the Savoy cake on her name day, the orange Madeleines that Alphonse sometimes gave me but said he did not mind me saving for her. I told myself I did not care about getting such a measly part. It was an opera, not a ballet. Only ten girls from the quadrille—not a single one from the second set, not even Blanche—were picked for the dancing, a divertissement, put into act three. And all of the ballet—the slave dance; the Georgian, Tunisian, Kabylian and Moorish dances—even if the story tells us it is performed for the purpose of the maiden's new owner winning over her heart, everyone knows the whole divertissement was only put into the opera for the sake of the abonnés.

Monsieur Mérante had taken to saying the absence of so many ballet girls would leave the abonnés sulking in their seats and Madame Dominique to thwacking her cane and holding her head like it might come off and raising her voice to shriek that all of us should be watching the rehearsals more closely and learning the steps, just in case. After a while there were whispers among the quadrille about how Monsieur Mérante always got his way, and pretty soon ballet girls pressed into the wings during rehearsal, trying to see, and afterward, swapped the steps they picked up. "I've got the Tunisian dance figured out."

"I'll show you the Moorish dance. I know all the steps." Then the two would go off to some nook where the others could not too easily spy.

Not me though. I slouched against a pillar of iron scaffolding, wondering if we might be dismissed early enough for me to get to Saint-Lazare, if today would be the day Antoinette would come to the parlor.

But now with Maman delivering "Jurisprudence and Émile Abadie" to Antoinette, I pull myself up tall and say to Madame Dominique, "I won't let you down."

"Monsieur Mérante doesn't tolerate tardiness. He dismisses girls for tardiness."

I bob my head.

"There are a dozen girls more deserving, even in the second set of the quadrille. Blanche has most of the slave dance worked out for herself."

My eyes fall from her unblinking gaze and, oh, how I regret all the moments slouching against the scaffolding. There would be huffs, lifted eyebrows, talk, more than if I was deserving or at least among the girls struggling to learn the steps. How will I look Blanche in the face?

"Tomorrow, then," she says. "You'll come to class an hour early." There is more of me staring at the floor and her waiting, holding off on saying *dismissed*. Finally she says, "It's good of Monsieur Lefebvre to take an interest."

Was it a chance to say about the zinc tub and the opened-up legs and the trousers pooled at his feet? I lifted my eyes to a face not soft but hard, her mouth set, daring me to gripe. Madame Dominique, what she really wants is me in her practice room, upon the stage, like a nymph, a sylph. No tatty slippers. No hollow flesh. No mark of the gutter to spoil the trickery. "I do a bit of modeling for him."

"Good." She brushes her hands, one against the other, like she is getting rid of dirt.

Crouched at the hearth, I stir into bubbling broth two carrots and a potato and scraps of roasted chicken plucked from the bone. Maman comes in, all cheery with the news of visiting at Saint-Lazare. "Our Antoinette, she's enjoying her little rest." She sniffs at the air. "Is that a bit of chicken boiling up?"

"You gave her the story from the newspaper?" I say.

She squats down beside me, holding her hands up to the warmth. "I did, Marie. I gave it to her, just like you asked." Then her hand is upon my cheek, all tender like. "Now, you promised, no more bawling."

I stir the soup, wonder if I should add a bit of salt. "No more sleeping late," I say and give her a little smile back.

She takes a picked-clean thigh bone from the small mound collected on the hearth and snaps it in half. "Don't want yourself chucked out of the quadrille." She puts a splintered end in her mouth and sucks hard. She reaches for a second, then a third, and I know she will clean out the lot, that I should have, earlier, put aside a few bones for Charlotte. "Nothing wrong with being able to buy ourselves a little meat."

She did not ask me to tell her what the newspaper said or why I wanted it brought to Antoinette. Plenty of times she had nipped across the street from the washhouse midmorning to cuff my ear, to pluck at my linens, to holler "Get up" into my face, but she did not want to know what kept me from facing the day. Why clutter her head? Why cloud the picture when all she really wishes for is me to stay put at the Opéra, earning wages enough to keep the richness of marrow in her mouth.

"Now, Marie, just smell that cooking up nice." She moves her face closer to the steam rising over the pot.

Antoinette

Maybe refusing to see Marie was a mistake. The trial of Émile started early in the week, and still I have no word. I asked Yvette, then Simone, both prisoners of section two, who sometimes got picked to read the stories we listen to in the evening time. But Yvette shrugged and then thought to ask if it was true, what the girls said about me being the lover of Émile Abadie, to which I answered, "He is my half brother and the favorite of my maman." Simone only said, "You know we aren't allowed newspapers inside," and gave me a look like I had two noses upon my face.

Not knowing is eating me up, inside to out. Still, I put on an ugly snarl and slouch low upon the hard bench, all the while getting lectured to death by the Superioress: The woolen coverlet of my bed is not pulled tight. I do not join in the singing. She will not tolerate me calling Sister Amélie by the name of Mole.

What the Superioress don't know is how my fingers gone shaky, how I prick myself when I sew. Yesterday I had to bend my head low over my work, teary eyed as I was over a speck of red upon a length of lace. I pace the floor in the pure blackness of my cell and snap at the Superioress in the morning when I sit before her—a loafer—for sleeping late. "No workshop for you," she says. "You'll stay in your cell."

I look down my nose, cross my arms. "Dock me the few sous I get for slaving all day. I don't care, not in the least."

"When, Mademoiselle van Goethem, will you learn to bite your tongue and put that quick mind of yours to better use?"

I jut my chin, stick out my tongue, clamp down with my teeth, and the Superioress, she pretends interest in some item written in the ledger on her desk.

I use up another day of banishment from the workshop laying on my bed, wondering and chewing on my lip, a new habit, like that of Marie. Was truth spoke in that court I have no faith in, not since that verdict in the woman Bazengeaud trial? Is nothing changed, even with the betrayal of Marie? Is Émile still dreaming of New Caledonia? Or is he back to fearing daybreak, a cell door opened up to the solemn faces of the Abbot Crozes and Monsieur Roch? Just thinking the thought, my tongue goes dry, a hand goes to my heart.

I get onto my knees to pray because, well, why not? I spend the twelve hours of each nighttime behind the bolted oaken door, pacing or flat upon my bed. A good part of that time I spend wishing for justice in the court. And isn't that what praying is? Wishing hard, asking for something for someone other than yourself?

After begging for truth for Émile, I pray for him to be warm and nourished and feeling hope. "Let him know there is something keeping me from visiting him at La Roquette," I whisper into my lonely cell. "Put it in his head that it is jail or sickness, anything but my heart gone hard against his own." For Charlotte, I ask for her to dazzle in her Wednesday class, for her to have the good sense to let the older girls take their spots at the barre before grabbing her own. For Maman, I request a bit of peace, a bit of cackling among the hens ironing wrinkles flat, scrubbing away at other people's dirt. I skip Marie, because what I really want is the hole in my heart filled up, that place where she used to be. What I asked was easy: Take my calendar to the office of Monsieur Danet. Explain the meaning of the tiny *x* marking the eleventh of March. She said there was no calendar behind the chimneypiece, a betrayal no different from twisting an auger into my heart. There is no point praying for the hole left behind to disappear, because it is not possible to turn back time, to undo what already is done.

I hear the bolt of my door scraping open, and thinking better than to be caught on my knees, doing as the sisters would have me do, I scramble to my feet from the brickwork of the floor. They gloat, chins tucked, mouths hidden behind their wimples. I know they do. Another lost sheep herded into the flock. But, no need to trouble myself. It is only Mole in the doorway, and she is far too caught up in twitching her nose to waste a moment speculating about me shaking out the creases of my prison gown. "You have a visitor in the parlor," she says.

"My sister, is it, Mole?" I keep hope out of my voice but make a small lurch in the direction of the door.

She shakes her head.

"My mother, who was here two weeks ago?"

"A girl calling herself Colette." I gallop through the doorway, the coarse wool of my gown brushing past the fine black serge of her own, and she follows me into the corridor on tiny, scuttling feet. Finally, news of the trial.

The sight of Colette is a shock after months of the sisters in black, the girls in drab brown and faded blue. Her dress is velvet, orange red, like the breast of a robin, and edged with black lace. The bodice is tight and a ridge of her flesh is bursting from the neckline, low and wide and square. The jailers gawk, and Colette makes her mouth pouty. She leans forward, touches fingertips to her heaving flesh, strokes the silver chain of the watch hanging from her neck.

"Antoinette," she says, when she sees me looking. "A sight for sore eyes."

I drop myself onto the chair waiting across the iron bars from her own. My gown is shapeless, dull. My face is unwashed. Locks of hair hang loose of the plait I bothered making yesterday. "A sight, all right."

"Never mind," she says, waving. "You were just as scruffy the night we hauled the dead dog." She smiles, pretty teeth shining, even if what I remember of the night is a whole lot of tears.

She never was more than lukewarm on Émile, and so instead of jumping straight into asking about the trial, I give her a little smile back and say, "You look a queen in that dress."

She makes a tiny, tilting shrug. "When you getting out?"

"Twenty-eight days. Not a single one more."

She huffs a short laugh, leans in close to the iron bars. "You planning on another house?"

"Seems so." And then I have Jean Luc Simard nipping into my head— his probing, choking tongue; his tugging, prying fingers; the taste of him that no amount of gargling can take away.

"When you're out, I'll take you around," she says, and pinpricks of sweat collect to beads at the back of my neck. "Go to the tavern downstairs at Madame Brossard's and tell Maurice—you remember Maurice— tell him a place and a time. We can meet up any afternoon."

The first of those beads slips down my back in a straight line between my shoulder blades.

"A girl gets used to it," she says.

"Don't mind in the least." There was singing in the washhouse, a glint of pleasure the first time I poured boiling water through a stain and saw it disappear, another when Monsieur Guiot put his hand upon my shoulder a month after those two spoiled shirts and said I was doing just fine. And for a tiny second I see myself scrubbing and joking and singing along. But breathing in the steamy heat of the washhouse would mean I gave up on Émile and New Caledonia, that or he never got to go. "You tell old Maurice to be expecting me."

"Maybe I'll find a house for the both of us." She says it quiet, like she is not so sure what I think of tying myself closer to her, and a little knot rises up in my chest.

At the house of Madame Brossard, Petite and Odette and Constance shared a single room, with Colette getting one to herself. She was the prize of the house, and always I thought that room of her own was the doing of Madame Brossard. But now I think maybe it was the scheming of the other three. Sometimes I walked into the kitchen and found Petite and Odette slapping down cards in a game of bezique. Sometimes Odette was whispering, head tilted close to that of Constance. Sometimes Constance was teaching Petite about crocheting a tiny drawstring purse or a flower for pinning on a hat. Once the three of them hired a carriage and went to the Bois de Boulogne on a Sunday afternoon. I knew because in the evening each was scorched red across her nose. But not Colette. "You didn't go?" I asked. "A headache," she said.

That knot in my chest swells, and I gulp it down. She don't need to know about New Caledonia, that I won't be staying in Paris long. Me and Colette, her arm linking mine before a string of madams in doorways, all admiring her pouty lips. It is just what I need.

Then she says, "Never had a sister before."

And out of my trap comes, "I got to tell you, Colette, once I save enough, I'll be going off to New Caledonia."

"You're following Émile Abadie?"

It is my chance to find out what she knows about the trial. "Assuming he don't get the guillotine first." I say it almost like a joke, even as I grow rigid, fearful of what her next words might say about his fate.

"No, Antoinette." She waves her head slow. "Don't. Just, no." She presses her mouth against a knuckle of her lifted up hand. She shuts her eyes tight, like someone with an aching head, and there is dampness when she opens them back up. "He isn't going to the guillotine. You never heard?" And then, twisting the lace of her cuffs, she tells about Émile getting spared his head no matter what.

"You're sure?" I clutch my hands together.

"Isn't a soul in Paris don't have an opinion about it all," she says.

Those gripped-together hands, they go to just under my chin.

"Once already the court proved his guilt," she says. "You got to think of that."

"The court!" I arch my neck, laugh, stamping my feet. I leap up, cover my face and shake my head until I feel a jailer hovering close, getting ready to shove me back down into my chair. "All right, all right," I say, holding up a hand to within a fingerbreadth of his fleshy nose and dancing a tiny jig, which don't end even when I have my rump plopped back down upon the chair.

Colette watches, pouty lips clamped to a skinny line, fingers continuing to work the lace. "Antoinette," she says, "you've got to listen," but she is talking all quiet, like she don't want me to hear.

"You'll take me around, still?"

"Émile Abadie, he isn't good." Again, that quiet voice.

I laugh. "I love that boy, that boy who is not setting foot near the guillotine."

She licks her lips, locks her eyes onto my own. "He poked fun when you weren't there."

Of me? Is that what she is meaning? "Those boys from the Ambigu, they talk nonsense half the time."

"He called you *my old mattress*. Pierre Gille said it to your face that night you were sniffling outside the Brasserie des Martyrs."

I keep my eyes still, my mouth from twitching hurt, while I remember, while I wonder, while I decide it is true. But New Caledonia is far-off from the bluster of raised beers, and Émile called my eyes chocolate pools, too. I've got to remember that. He said about adoring me every single day. "Don't believe it," I say. "You want a friend. You want me staying put."

"He isn't deserving, Antoinette."

"Being a sow about him isn't going to change my mind."

"He don't love you."

She looks close to bawling. But there are all those times in the salon at the house of Madame Brossard—her catching her breath and patting her chest even when a joke was flat; her flattering and flirting even when a gentleman was foul; her looking gripped even when the company was dull, the hour late. That girl, Colette, she is the champion of putting on a face. "I heard enough." I get up from my chair.

"Don't." Something in her voice—a whimper like a prayer—stops me. She fiddles with the watch hanging from her neck. "I took more than two hundred francs from him."

She don't breathe a good long while, until I say, "How?"

"Like you think." She is shrinking in her chair. "Don't follow him, Antoinette."

"You'll say anything." I whisper it through my teeth. I spit, aiming for her feet, hitting the hem of her skirt when she don't lurch away.

Her fingers grip the watch. She tugs, snapping the chain. "Here," she says, shifting, like she is intending to lob the watch through the iron bars. But I don't put my hands up to catch. No, I leave them at my sides. Then she is stooping, putting the watch on the ground, and sliding it across the floor and between two bars. It hits me in the toe, but I keep my eyes upon her still.

The jailers snap back awake. "You're done with visiting," one says and grabs me roughly by the arm. Another is picking up the watch, turning it over in his hands, wiping a thumb over its face.

"Payment from him," Colette says, her face shriveling, tears spilling. "I told him no, always, once you were my friend, after the dead dog."

"Where'd you get this?" The jailer holding the watch jerks his chin toward Colette.

She wipes at her eyes with the back of her hand. "Émile Abadie."

"It's the watch," he says, with all the wonder of a blind man seeing for the first time. "The woman Bazengeaud's watch."

The jailer wrenching my arm lets go, shifts his attention to the watch, a pretty thing with an enamel dial laying underneath an opening shaped like a heart. In that moment I remember the inspector at the washhouse, the portfolio he opened up, the drawing of the watch. I remember Émile saying about the failed blackmailing, the drained cognac and then leaving straight after that, a story that is not true, and my breath is gone.

EXCERPTS OF COURT TRANSCRIPTS
PUBLIC PROSECUTOR VERSUS ÉMILE
ABADIE AND MICHEL KNOBLOCH

23 March 1881

PROSECUTOR: Do you admit that on the eleventh day of March in the year of 1880, you, with the help of Émile Abadie, murdered the widow Joubert?

KNOBLOCH: Monsieur Prosecutor, I lied. I never touched the widow Joubert.

PROSECUTOR: What? Is this your new claim?

KNOBLOCH: Yes, I lied. Everything I said is untrue.

PROSECUTOR: It was not you who conceived the crime and then discussed it with Émile Abadie? It was not you who forced the widow Joubert to reenter her shop as she closed the shutters and then, with Émile Abadie, beat her to death?

KNOBLOCH: I lied, I tell you! I confessed only because I wanted to go to New Caledonia. *(sensation in the crowd)*

PROSECUTOR: For the last time, do you deny your guilt?

KNOBLOCH: Yes, Monsieur Prosecutor. I am not guilty, and I lied when I pointed a finger at Abadie. *(sensation in the crowd)*

~

PROSECUTOR: According to the confession of Michel Knobloch, you beat the widow Joubert with a hammer while he held her arms behind her back.

ABADIE: I am innocent. I'd put my hand in a fire to prove Knobloch is a liar.

PROSECUTOR: So you persist in asserting that you did not participate in the crime?

ABADIE: Monsieur Prosecutor, I am a changed man. I would like to serve justice. If I had anything to say about the unfortunate death of the widow Joubert, I would have said it.

24 March 1881

From the plea of Monsieur Crochard, attorney for Michel Knobloch: In his alleged confession, Michel Knobloch never ceased lying. His description of the widow Joubert, the snow on the ground, the stolen hundred-franc note changed at a money lender, the hammer discarded behind the newspaper shop—in each of these points, he is proved to be out and out lying. He changed his confession over fifty times and has been caught daily grossly misleading or lying. The truth is he is a liar and braggart. Everyone who knows him describes him as such. His obvious and stated goal in the alleged confession was to get to New Caledonia.

~

From the plea of Monsieur Danet, attorney for Émile Abadie: Why would Michel Knobloch implicate Émile Abadie in the widow Joubert's death? The answer is simple: At the precinct where Michel Knobloch made his alleged confession, his outlandish claims were at first dismissed as untrue. But the moment he said he knew Émile Abadie, he was listened to and lavished with attention. When he went so far as to claim the assistance of Émile Abadie in committing the crime, he was offered breakfast, brought a carafe of wine, spoiled. In short, his lying was encouraged.

∼ Marie ∼

I fly down the hundred stairs leading from the practice room to the bright day outside the Opéra. I am supposed to be rehearsing my tricky role as a stage prop in act two of *Le Tribut de Zamora*. But Madame Daram, who plays the maiden snatched out from under her fiancé, shrieked about more time upon the stage to practice the duet she sings with him in act four, and Monsieur Vaucorbeil sent all but the two of them away.

What a week I have lived. I learned the slave dance faster than I would have believed I could, running through the steps a thousand times—in the practice room, the wings, on the stage, in my dreams. I saw Blanche watching, just once, and asked in the meekest voice if she wanted me to show her any of the footwork, but she only glared and said "slut" loud enough for three stagehands and a dozen of the quadrille to hear. I swallowed and got back to work, because still my shoulders crept up and it meant the slave dance was not yet easily enough remembered by my feet. And then there was the disaster of my Wednesday class. I did not much like that Charlotte was put up with the older girls one day a week. She thought nothing of edging over to me and asking for help with a combination I was still sorting out for myself. And once she muttered "easy" when Madame Dominique asked for sixteen entrechats in a row, which made her huff and ask for thirty-two instead. Always Charlotte stepped in front of me in line, and it was no different two days ago when I was awaiting my turn to make a string of piqué pirouettes. Madame Dominique thwacked the floor good and hard with her cane. "Enough, Mademoiselle Charlotte," she hollered. "Over there." She pointed to a corner at the back of the practice room. "Not so much as a twitch, a peep from you, or you won't be coming back."

I made my pirouettes, and after that an allegro combination including assemblés and glissades. Awaiting my turn to make a chain of grands jetés en tournant, I glanced over to Charlotte, to the strange look of dread twisting her face, and that was when I saw it—the puddle at her feet, the shadow of wet on her stockinged legs. Madame Dominique nodded, and I began leaping diagonally across the room. Once finished we were expected to run gracefully, arms in low à la seconde, back to the corner where we began. But that day, as I ran, I knocked into the watering can, toppling it onto its side with a thud. Water poured from the mouth, swamping the puddle at Charlotte's feet. Madame Dominique's cane skittered across the floor, and she yelled, "Dismissed, the lot of you," without even asking for a révérence. Afterward Charlotte bawled, shuddering and gasping like never before. "But no one saw," I said. "No one noticed a thing."

"It isn't that," she said. "I just wish I was as kind as you."

The last two days Monsieur Mérante has not shouted, calling me "you" or "you with the teeth," and Madame Dominique has not said how a dozen girls know what I do not. And now, with Madame Daram's fit, I am free to go to the Court of Assizes, to squeeze myself into the gallery and watch the last moments of the trial of Émile Abadie and Michel Knobloch for the murder of the widow Joubert.

And this is what I think: Madame Daram's shrieking, it was no accident. Her nerves were plucked taut by the hand of Fate, laying at my feet the chance to make things right with Antoinette. Before the boys are on the pavements calling out the news, I will arrive at Saint-Lazare and tell the greeting sisters I have come straight from the court with word of the trial. With the worn-out scrap of newspaper brought by Maman, my treachery was already shrunk. And soon, a verdict of innocent will shrink it even more. Antoinette will nod yes to sitting across the iron bars from me.

I blink away, getting used to the lesser light inside the court, when who should come into view but Monsieur Degas, sitting in the first row of the benches on the jury side. I am stumped for a second, until my eyes fall upon the notebook opened up on his knees, no different from when he is in the practice room or the stage wings. Beside him, a woman with a plumed hat is making a show of brushing charcoal dust from her skirt. But his attention is on the prisoners' box, on the watchful faces of Émile Abadie and Michel Knobloch. Monsieur Degas leans forward, and even if my view is of the back of his head, I know behind his blue spectacles his eyes pull tight, seeking the story he is putting down in charcoal lines.

After a while of standing in the gallery of the court, struggling to follow a story already mostly told, I suck in my bottom lip. In summing up the trial, the presiding judge started with the findings showing the innocence of Émile Abadie and Michel Knobloch, including listing the many ways the details of his confession do not mesh with the known facts, and it seems he has shifted over to saying he made the whole business up, just like Antoinette said. The men of the jury nodded along. But they keep up the nodding now, as the presiding judge reminds them about the sack of hammers found in the storage shed that once served as the lair of Émile Abadie and how Chief Inspector Monsieur Macé proved there was ample time for the murder between the third and seventh tableaux of *L'Assommoir*. The jurors, their chins bob up and down, even as he finishes up his long speech, saying, "Members of the jury, you will have to choose between two Knoblochs; the one who confessed and the one in court, who denies. I need to remind you that he confessed in front of the widow

Joubert's sons, even his own sobbing mother as she begged him to tell the truth, that always, he answered, 'Alas, Maman, alas, I am guilty.' "

The men of the jury leave, and suddenly, like a clap of thunder, the courtroom boils with the views of the one-eyed butcher behind me, the hacking mason beside him, the plump matron next in line. I strain, gathering snatches, keeping a count.

"An acquittal."
"No doubt."

"Take his head. It isn't worth the expense to get him to New Caledonia."
"Stupid as they come. But I say he's going to get his dream."

"Knobloch opens up his trap and every time a new lie."
"He isn't going to get the guillotine for lying."
"They'll have his head just for tying up the court."

"Those boys, they did the bludgeoning, all right."
"Brutes, the both of them. The jury only has to look."

The jurors return, take up their seats, arms grimly folded, faces stern. The head juror gets to his feet, looks at the paper gripped in his hands, clears his throat. "We, the jury," he says, "find defendants Émile Abadie and Michel Knobloch guilty as charged in the widow Joubert murder."

I clamp down hard on my lip and grip my hands together, as the judges file from the court to deliberate the sentencing. My knuckles turn white, ache, and I grip harder, fearing those judges coming back, the news they will bring. Antoinette said Michel Knobloch is a known liar, and I saw the tiny *x*, the proof that he lied in naming Émile Abadie as his accomplice. The odds are stacked that his entire confession was a tale made up with a dream of New Caledonia on his mind. Yes, I have cast further shame on Émile Abadie, but a thousand times worse, on account of me that lying boy could get the guillotine.

Upon their return the presiding judge stands up, an emperor in his great red robe. With a scowl that looks like he has been sucking a lemon wedge, he says how Émile Abadie was sentenced to the harshest extent of the law in the Elisabeth Bazengeaud murder and so is prevented from suffering further chastisement for his previously committed murder of the widow Joubert. "As such," he says, "the court, as penalty, can only order Émile Abadie to pay court costs." The gallery breaks into hissing and stamping feet. Not me. I stand quiet and still as a scared cat. The presiding judge, he just watches, his thumb stroking the fur trim of his robe. When finally the court falls to quiet, he opens his mouth. "The court condemns Michel Knobloch to death by guillotine."

Michel Knobloch lied when he pointed a finger at Émile Abadie. Add this one last bit of proof to all those lies already listed by the presiding judge, and the only possibility is that the entire confession was made up. Michel Knobloch is just as innocent in the murder of the widow Joubert as Émile Abadie. My hand goes to my throat, and I make the two or three steps to the closest wall. I slide down the wainscot, end up curled in a hard knot with a ridge of molding digging into my back. The opinions, said earlier in the gallery, there were as many calling for an acquittal as the guillotine. A tiny x? A lowly ballet girl of the second set of the quadrille? A grain of rice? Was any of it enough to tip the scales? I put my face in my hands, feel the clamminess of the palms on my cheeks.

Around me there are the sounds of the courtroom emptying out, first the rustling skirts and clacking walking sticks of the ladies and gentlemen ranking a bench up front, afterward the flapping shoe soles and shuffling feet of those standing in the gallery, knowing it is their place to wait. Then a hand touches my shoulder, and I look up to see Monsieur Degas's blue spectacles, the muddle of his beard. "Mademoiselle van Goethem," he says, shifting his hand from my shoulder to his frock coat pocket. "The statuette, I'll be showing it at our sixth exposition in a week's time."

I dip my chin, wipe at my eyes. There were broadsheets pasted up all over Paris again this year. I stopped dead on seeing the first, wondering, scolding myself for sniffing around a trap I already knew; but still, I had hoped, just a little, the tiniest bit. If Monsieur Degas put the statuette out for everyone to see—Monsieur Lefebvre and Monsieur Pluque and Monsieur Mérante and Monsieur Vaucorbeil—was there a chance they would overlook the wax, the hair, the skirt, the slippers on my feet? Wouldn't they think nicely about a girl singled out?

"You're not crying, not over those ruffians?" Monsieur Degas says, now that I am looking him in the face. "I bought my newspapers from the widow Joubert."

I want to tell how the men of the jury with their scrunched-up brows and stroked beards and the others with their red robes, how they see a stone in the gutter same as he does, no different from me. No one can make out the flecks of dark, the quartz vein, not from standing tall, not without knowing to look. It was wrong to think the high-mindedness of a man gave him a special lens, one to make clear a little scratch he does not even know is there. I should say about the tiny x, about Émile Abadie having an alibi in Antoinette, about Michel Knobloch's confession being a lie, about the court's mistake. But I do not, not even with a boy sentenced to the guillotine. No. Proving my wickedness, I only say, "Michel Knobloch said he made everything up."

"Both are beasts. Their physiognomies tell us."

I nudge up a shoulder because what is *physiognomies*?

"The facial features spelling out the character of a man," he says.

He means the features on Cesare Lombroso's list, the ones his born criminals have in common with the savages that turned into the human race.

"Those two murderers are marked," he says.

"By looking like apes." My fingers go to my own brow, drop to my jaw. I have peered into the looking glass above Papa's sideboard and seen the beast staring back. I have seen it in the lowness of the forehead no amount of cut bangs can hide, in my protruding jaw, its sturdiness matching the muzzle of those brawny dogs with the pushed-in noses and wrinkled-up mugs. A match struck, flame caught the edge of a calendar page, and I made true the prophecy told by my face the day I was born.

Monsieur Degas's lips press tight, and then his eyebrows pull together, the ends closest to his nose lifting up. He holds a finger up to his lips, taps, lets his hand drop to his side. "Sabine will be expecting me," he says, but he stays put, his pulled-close eyebrows holding still.

At first tenderness is what I see. But tenderness comes with the shadow of a smile and there is none. No, it is pity upon his face. My forehead drops back onto my knees, and I listen to his retreating footsteps, growing quiet, then quieter still. Gone.

After a while there are more footsteps, uneven and approaching this time. I look up to see a charwoman with a kerchief upon her head and a mop in one hand, a bucket set down by my feet. "You got to go," she says, and then when I stay crouched, "I got the cleaning up to do."

"When will the boy go to the guillotine?"

"What boy?" She scratches at her kerchief, using the hand holding the mop, which means water dripping onto the floor.

"Knobloch. The one who made the confession up?"

"Don't know about that." She bumps the wooden stick of the mop against my knee and makes a little upward nudge with her chin, and so I get onto my feet.

Outside I find a stoop, dark, out of the way. I sit my backside down on the cut stone, grip my shawl, pulling it tight around my shoulders. After a while of peering into daylight fading from brash to soft, I switch to looking at my hands, and in the low light I see it there, red dried to black, lodged in the wrinkles of my fingers, the beds of my nails.

Antoinette's spit words come: "Upon your hands, the blood of an innocent."

I push myself up from the cut stone, point myself in the direction of the Pont Neuf, leading to the rue de Douai, instead of the Pont au Change, leading to Antoinette. Still, there is Maman's small bottle, waiting, beneath her mattress.

What I want is the sleep of the dead.

～ Antoinette ～

The last day of March, I wait for the Superioress on the same old hard bench I sat on a dozen times before. The bones of my rump dig in, bearing the weight of slumped shoulders, the tired head propped up by my hand. I been tossing and turning and staring into blackness through the night ever since Colette showed up with the watch of the woman Bazengeaud strung from her neck. For six days my eyes were red and swollen and weeping misery, and the skin of my nose was glistening raw from being blown a thousand times. But since yesterday not a single tear more. The bawling is done.

Even before Colette fled from the visitors' parlor, I put my hands over my ears, scrunched closed my eyes, tucked my chin tight against my chest. But it did not stop the ambush, not in the least. The money Émile was not saving up was going to Colette. He gave her the watch. The promise of being his one and only was nothing but a lie. It don't make me proud, these being the first of my thoughts, knowing there passed at least a full minute before my mind went to the woman Bazengeaud. A lady's watch was not something she gave her lover as a gift. It was not a blackmail payment made to Émile. No, he told me the threat failed. It was something he snatched, along with the eighteen francs that went missing upon her death. He took part in slitting the throat of the tavern owner and then in the thieving. My arms wrapped my gut. I leaned forward, folding myself in half. "Stop," I said. "Just stop."

I remember rocking, clenching, every muscle pulling in tight. I wanted to grow smaller, to become a tiny crumb—a fading, shrinking speck. I craved blackness, like I never craved anything before, and I wondered if it was the kind of praying reached the ears of God. But, no, God does not care. What He put into my mind was the small house by the sea, the roof of thatch, the garden, the sunshine raining down, and it was what I clung to for six days, a dream I could make true. I lay there facedown on my little bed, not bothered in the least that Mole was standing over me.

"I'll tell the Superioress if you don't get up."

The Superioress came five days in a row.

"Get up."

"Get up now, or no recreation hour for a week."

"No evening meal for you unless you go to the refectory."

"You're due in the sewing workshop. The girls miss you there." She put her hand on my shoulder, and I shrugged it away.

"On your knees. I've had enough."

I did not go to the refectory, and at first I was hungry. Always the evening meal was brought to me, but never once did I pick up a spoon, and after four days the hunger went away. I got up to use the chamber pot and felt my legs shaking and shaking more the next day. I took a glass of water twice, because the Superioress said Father Renault was coming if I did not, and, I suppose, I did not really want to die and she knew to give me an excuse for taking a glass.

I bashed my wrists against the iron frame of that bed until they were swollen purple and red. All the while I racked my brain, sifting through scheme upon scheme that could make the dream of a small house by the sea true: Pierre Gille put the watch into the hands of Colette. The watch only resembled that of the woman Bazengeaud. I dreamt the visit, the words *payment from him.*

But yesterday I found myself parched of tears. I blinked my lids open over dry, stinging eyes, and I knew never was I anything other than a mattress to that boy. And no amount of wishing, no amount of telling myself a different story of Émile and Antoinette, changed a single fact. The house by the sea was a dream, a dream I spun myself. It was nothing more. Same for getting adored. And having eyes like chocolate pools. And enchanting a boy putting mussels with parsley sauce into my mouth.

I thought about Marie. That first time Émile came to our lodging room, she saw what he was. "There goes a beast," she said after he was gone, and the next morning she was clutching a package wrapped in brown paper behind her back. It took a lot of nerve, a lot of love, knocking on the door of Madame Lambert, coming away with the advice about the vinegar, especially for a girl so skittish as Marie. She was firm in what she knew, in what I refused to believe. I pushed her onto the floor and screamed, "Don't you call him a murderer," and she screamed, "Murderer!" and I slapped her face. She tried reasoning after that, saying how Émile was the lover of the woman Bazengeaud, how the found knife was proof, how the blood-spattered shirt fit only him, how his stepfather said he was no good, how he held a knife up to his own mother for refusing a soused boy a glass of wine. But I stuffed my ears with woolen batting and covered them with my hands. "The missing watch has yet to turn up," she said. "Émile ever show you a fancy lady's watch?" I have come to think now that I saw that watch another time, long ago, catching the flickering light of a lamp, hanging from the neck of Colette. But I let myself forget. Marie heard me sorrowful in the stairwell, she said, those rows about a dead dog, about standing idle when Pierre Gille slapped my face, about the money he was not saving up. She said he put a darkness under my eyes. I pretended it was not true.

And then she said there was no calendar in the gap behind the chimneypiece, the only lie I ever knew the girl to tell. I was on my knees begging, and in that black moment, I turned my sister into the liar she never was before. She would not bring the calendar to Monsieur Danet, not when I filled my ears with woolen batting, forgot, pretended the truth was not true. It was like asking her to open up a door so I could step through to the ruined life she knew to be lurking on the other side. But in refusing me, did she step through the door herself? It is what I fear, what I don't know, what I fear worse than ever since Charlotte turned up in the visitors' parlor, twisting the fringe of her shawl.

"I know I should've come before," she said. "I don't have an excuse except that I'm only ten and just figuring out about being nice."

"It's a good excuse, pet."

She looked up, her eyes wide as saucers, taking in the iron grate, the jailers, my dull gown. "You're coming home soon?" Her pretty brow was crimped with lines.

"Three weeks." She let out a happy sigh, and a little river of relief swelled through me that I would not ever be saying to her about New Caledonia.

"Marie said you were never coming back, and I said it wasn't true and it made her bawl." Small shoulders drift up. "I don't know about Marie."

"What is it you don't know?"

She leaned in close to the iron grate, like whispering would make the telling not so bad. "She got picked for the dancing in the *Le Tribut de Zamora*, and she doesn't even care."

The Superioress is slow settling into her chair, fingering her crucifix, fiddling with the wimple already hanging perfectly straight. It is what she does, giving herself time for eyes to scuttle, for words to find her mouth. "My dear," she says, leaning forward, reaching out across the desk to my hands gripped together atop the oak. "Such sorrow on a young face?"

My head tilts forward a further inch, and the Superioress, her jowly cheek is almost upon the desktop as she peers up into my red eyes, their haloes of blue grey. "Antoinette," she says, petting the knot of my fingers, "tell me why you have come."

I lift up my face, keep my voice meek. "I want news of the trial of Émile Abadie and Michel Knobloch."

"Ah." She pulls back to sitting straight.

Never have I begged, except that one time with Marie, a black moment. Still I drop onto the floor, bow my head. "Mother, I beg you."

"Antoinette," she says, flicking her wrist in a way that commands me up off the floor and back onto the bench. "This Émile Abadie, it is true what the girls say—he was your lover?"

I nod, a tiny, sheepish nod.

Voice like a tack, she says, "The devil lives inside that boy," and then she is back to fingering her crucifix, head rocking side to side. Eventually she clears her throat, making way for a flood. "I've seen you staring down the brutish girls in defense of those too timid to do it for themselves. I was told about you sharing your evening meal with Estelle when she missed lining up. And Sister Amélie says you are diligent and quick in the sewing workshop, always assisting the others not so adept with needle and thread." She holds her palms out like an opened book. "You're a good girl, Antoinette."

I lick dry lips. "I need the outcome of that trial."

"You've seen the painting of Prud'hon, hanging in the chapel here, no?"

The picture is dark, black except for the light on the stretched-wide ribs of Jesus, the nails in his feet, the shoulder of the lone girl huddling beneath.

"The mourner is Mary Magdalene," she says, "a prostitute cleansed by our Savior, the first He showed Himself to once He was risen from the dead."

The fallen girls sit shoulder to shoulder in the chapel Sunday mornings with Father Renault filling up our ears, the message always the same—a promise of a great reward awaiting beyond a pearly gate. Eyes lingering on that picture strung high above our heads, our minds are meant to dwell on following in the footsteps of that girl with her shoulder all aglow and purging ourselves of the boys with the devil lurking inside. I know what the Superioress is thinking: She will not hand over the bit of news I seek. She will not add to the rot keeping that pearly gate from opening up for me. But what she don't have figured out is already I scrubbed myself clean of Émile Abadie, washed away the filth of him in a river of tears.

"Antoinette," she says, her face soft. "He murdered two women, one a paramour."

Two. Two women is what she said. I breathe in her blundered words, the verdict of guilty for Émile Abadie. For him it don't change a single thing, but sure as sure, Michel Knobloch got the same verdict and for that lying, brainless boy, it means a sentence of either New Caledonia or the guillotine. But which? It is what I need to know in order to answer the question of whether Marie put her own foot across a threshold, stepping over to the blackness awaiting on the other side. It is why I sit before the Superioress, breathing in her blunder, forgetting to let the air back out. Marie is grave and solemn, and her mind gets stuck on nonsense about an apish face, the truthfulness of *L'Assommoir.* I fear it is stuck again, on the tiny x she did not show Monsieur Danet, the way the x showed Michel Knobloch was lying, guilty of nothing more than bluster and a dream of New Caledonia. What I know to be true is only one of those two sentences—New Caledonia or the guillotine—is an ending Marie can bear. My heart flutters, and I see the Superioress see it, that tiny movement no greater than the flicked wings of a butterfly. "And Michel Knobloch?" I say. "Is it New Caledonia or the guillotine for him?"

Her lips shrink to a thin line, and her fingers leave her crucifix, fall to her desk. Twice she strums the oak, the sound of patience stretched thin.

"My worry isn't for Émile Abadie," I say. "Michel Knobloch, neither." I rattle my head. "It's for my sister Marie. You got to understand."

The band of her wimple creeps lower on her wrinkled brow. "You had better start at the beginning then, Antoinette, because I don't understand."

I take in a deep breath, and the Superioress, she strokes open my gripped-together hands. She holds one in both of hers, a little cocoon of warmth. I say first about Marie, the way she was awaiting the moment she showed herself to be a beast. I tell about *L'Assommoir* and the sorry life of Gervaise and how Marie's got herself believing it meant a miserable end for her own self. "She is smart," I say, "smart as a whip, always reading *Le Figaro*, knowing the meaning of every word, tallying faster than even the fruiterer in the rue de Douai. But none of that intelligence ever done her a speck of good. The mind of that girl is a churning, brewing storm."

After that I halt, and the Superioress makes a little, coaxing nod. I scratch my ear, a spot where it don't itch. I don't want to say no more. In the rest of the story I slip up. Blunder. Fail.

"You have more to tell," she says.

I keep up the scratching.

"I wasn't always a sister," she says.

I shrug.

"I was born in the place Bréda, raised in the rue Pigalle and then the boulevard de Clichy and after that the rue Lamartine." I know the streets, none far-off from the rue de Douai, and with so much hopping around, I know her father—if there was a father—was not always paying the rent owed.

I start up again, spill my guts about the old chaise, about getting adored in between tableaux, except I call it *suffering the needs of a boy*. I tell about the calendar, about the tiny x, about Marie seeing that x and refusing to show Monsieur Danet, all because I stuffed my ears with woolen batting the hundred times she tried to tell me Émile Abadie was as rotten as a long-dead rat. "Marie knows going to Monsieur Danet was something she could've done," I say. "She knows it was a choice. What's got me filled up with dread is Michel Knobloch getting the guillotine and Marie figuring it was her cost him his head."

The Superioress sighs, shoulders lifting, slipping down. She shakes her head. "The verdict of the court was guilty and the sentence, death by guillotine."

The blood of Michel Knobloch is set to spill; the spirit of Marie is broke. Even here at Saint-Lazare, I know it to be true. Sleepless. Not going to class. Not caring about *Le Tribut de Zamora*, like Charlotte said. She is wretched, staggering, wracked with guilt. Her thumb picked to a bloody pulp, she sucks her lip raw. And for comfort only Maman, who takes her own from a bottle of absinthe, and Charlotte, who is only just starting to bother about anyone other than herself. I remember the dress Marie was wearing at Saint-Lazare, a fine grey silk she said was a gift. Tears run down my cheeks, even if there is not supposed to be a single drop left. Snot, thin as water, seeps from my nose. My face drops, and the Superioress clutches my hand more tightly, and I confess to spitting, hateful words: "On your hands, the blood of an innocent."

"Antoinette, sweet child." Her grip is like a vise. "You've got a heart big enough to cure what ails Marie."

The lines of her brow are erased, her cheeks lifted up the tiniest little bit, her lips pulled into the most tender of smiles.

LE FIGARO

12 APRIL 1881

DEGAS AND THE SIXTH EXPOSITION OF THE INDEPENDENT ARTISTS

Although the catalogue lists only eight entries for Degas, the artist shows additional works, brought in yet again at the last minute. The statuette he first promised last year is again listed in this year's catalogue but has not arrived. The glass case meant to shelter the statuette stands empty, waiting. This vitrine, Monsieur Degas, is not enough for me!

He offers exposition-goers portraits, scenes of the stage, laundresses, nudes, and a study of criminal man. In this remarkable study, employing only the meager tool of pastel, Degas captures Émile Abadie and Michel Knobloch—their wan and troubling faces, taken in the dull light of the criminal court. Only a keen observer could portray with such singular physiological sureness the animal foreheads and jaws, kindle the flickering glimmers in the dead eyes, render the yellow-green flesh on which is imprinted all the bruises, all the stains of vice. In titling the piece *Criminal*

Physiognomies, Monsieur Degas makes clear his intent. A masterwork of observation, the study is informed by the findings of science in regard to innate criminality. Émile Zola, with his argument for a scientific literature, one where the inescapable forces of heredity and environment determine human character, has met his match among the painters.

~ Marie ~

I walk the pavements I have walked a hundred times before: the rue Blanche to the rue de la Chaussée d'Antin, where I make a habit of turning to see the église de la Sainte-Trinité. Sometimes I bother walking to the far side of the church and looking up at the statue called *Temperance*. Everyone says the main figure, who is lifting a fruit out of the reach of the babies at her feet, was chiseled to appear just like the Empress Eugénie. And those times when I have looked at the fat thighs of the babies, their rounded bellies, their grabbing hands, I have seen the empress as a mother, teaching her little ones about gluttony. But today, rather than seeking that lesson being taught, I turn away. Today I would find only a stingy mother protecting the bit of fruit she wants for herself.

Usually I pass through the Opéra's back gate, but today I continue past. Out front I look up at the writhing, naked flesh of the stone dancers on the eastern side. Antoinette saw pleasure, bliss. Not me, though, not now. The dancers' faces radiate wickedness, call out to passersby in the street, "Look, here. Glimpse what is to be found inside."

From the boulevard des Capucines, I will turn into the rue Cambon, a quiet street linking the grand boulevards to the Jardin des Tuileries, a street with little balconies held up by the fanciest of stone scrolls and not a single shutter with peeling paint or hanging lopsided from a hinge. In the rue Cambon, outside the grand door of Monsieur Lefebvre's apartment house, I will suck in my lip and ring the bell, calling the concierge, like I have so many Tuesdays before heading to Madame Dominique's class. Just thinking about it, I feel a flutter in my belly, bats opening up wings. I was told to stay away. But this morning I opened up our lodging room door to Monsieur LeBlanc's great belly. I thought about the small bottle of absinthe, bought with my earnings, how already it was gone, but there was no remorse about eight sous spent, not when Monsieur LeBlanc is owed for a full month.

Maman was already off to the washhouse and so it was just me and Charlotte, left there trembling when he was gone. "It's going to be all right," she said. "Tomorrow Antoinette gets home."

"Like I said, she isn't coming back."

"Well, she is."

On such a morning I did not have the strength to explain. Instead I thought about lying down, the emptiness of sleep, but already I spread my fingers wide under Maman's mattress and her bottle was not there. Charlotte slipped her hand into my own, and when I looked, she smiled up at me, the put-on smile of a ballet girl patting another's back in a wing. It does not help, this small girl's efforts to keep me from wallowing upon our mattress. Yesterday she left the small stub of a candle on my satchel as a gift. And last week when she came home from her morning class at the Opéra to find me still lying there, staring at the ceiling—the water stains, the lath where the plaster had fallen away—she crawled under the linens. My head was aching and cobwebby, and she put her fingers in my hair, like Antoinette used to do. "Don't," I said, and she took her hand away.

"Do you want to hear how Madame Théodore's petticoat fell onto the floor?"

"No."

"Are you sick, Marie?"

I felt I could heave into a bucket, like my tongue was made of paste. "No."

"Maman feels better after taking a bit of water." She got up, dipped a cup into the zinc bucket and held the water out to me.

I took the water because there was pleading in her eyes and wondered when it was Charlotte turned kind. I put the cup to my lips, but for me there was no comfort in water slipping down into my throat. Still it was clear as glass, even in my cobwebby head, about allowing a boy to go to the guillotine for nothing more than telling a lie. I was the one who set loose the blade, and only absinthe took the clearness away. Only absinthe let me forget.

Standing there in the doorway, listening to Monsieur LeBlanc huffing and puffing his way down the narrow stairs, Charlotte gave my hand a little squeeze. "I was saving it for a surprise," she said, "with Antoinette coming home tomorrow and everything." Her face grew hopeful.

"Saving what?"

"Yesterday Monsieur Mérante came into the practice room in the middle of the barre and called out a chain of leaps and pirouettes. He made us line up, and I waited like everyone else." She gave a smile like an imp's. "We showed him one at a time. Then he said, 'A cartwheel' and pointed to me, and I made one, and he pointed again. 'Our new acrobat,' is what he said."

She bounced on her toes, and her hands were knotted tight together in front of her chest. I knew what was coming, that she got a part in *Le Tribut de Zamora*. But I did not muster the will to put my arms around her shoulders and pull her in tight.

She made a little jig. "Jocelyn, another petit rat, she was the acrobat, but she got the white pox. Her fever broke, but she's spotted worse than a Dalmatian dog."

I took her face in my hands and in a hard voice said, "Stroke of luck," which was not nice or even true, not when she was always pushing our little dining table to the corner of the room to clear a path for a string of piqué pirouettes.

"Tomorrow I debut." She made a little curtsey. "Antoinette can come, and I get three francs for leaping across the stage." She left her arms opened up wide, embracing all the goodness she found in the world. I would go to Monsieur Lefebvre, collect my thirty francs. A chain of steps repeated a hundred times grows to be as easy as breathing air.

My last time calling at his apartment, even in the doorway I knew the visit would be different from the rest. He stood there, crossing and uncrossing his arms, looking me up and down, instead of moving aside to let me in. "A glass of wine?" he said after a while and stepped out of the way. "Or have you already had enough?" He did not say it nicely, like there was a chance of him pouring me a drop, but I was not fearful, no. Absinthe made me a little brave.

I walked toward the screen, careful to keep down whatever drunkenness he had seen, but before I was even halfway there, he grabbed my arm and pulled me the couple of steps to the sofa. He shoved me onto it, and then he was on top of me, grinding his hardness into my thigh and digging his chin into my shoulder and kneading whatever flesh he could clutch through my blouse. The whole time he was saying "whore" and "drunken whore" and "Jezebel" through clamped-shut teeth.

I did not open up my mouth to say, "Stop, Monsieur Lefebvre. Stop," or knot my legs together or wedge my hands over my breast. I swallowed the promise of everlasting damnation of the soul and thought about the day Marie the First made me flinch from his finger on my naked spine in Monsieur Degas's workshop. Was it the trick of a wicked angel lying in wait, working to gain my trust? I had not said the Act of Contrition in a hundred years, but still a line about the perfection we were to seek swam up into my head: "This day I shall try to imitate Thee; to be mild, chaste,

devoted, patient, and charitable." But I was none of those things. I knew it
in my heart, and Marie the First knew it, too. By his moaning I could tell
that with a slow count to twenty he would be done, and it came into my
mind that this was easier than posing and waiting and wondering how it
was that time was so slow to pass. When I got to eight, his head lifted
away from my shoulder, and his face twisted into ugliness, and then he
went limp, his whole body. I pushed him to the side and wriggled out from
underneath.

Right away he stood up and turned his back, shoving into his trousers
the shirttails that had come loose. Then he took my allowance from the
drawer. "Enough of you, your scheming," he said, pitching three ten-franc
notes to my feet. "Just stay away." His voice broke, and it was at that
moment the harsh tang of fear, like the skin of a walnut, came into my
mouth.

Close to the corner where I will turn onto Monsieur Lefebvre's fancy
street, my feet grow sluggish. So what if I collect enough to pay the rent
owed? I put off by a week or a month or a year the misery steamrolling my
way. Cesare Lombroso and the rest measuring the heads of the criminals
in the jails and the skulls of the ones that already visited the guillotine,
they would say, "Go ahead. Get your thirty francs. Keep yourself warm
another few nights. But it won't change a single thing. Still you have the
face of an ape." Of course I struck the match. Of course I have blood on
my hands, absinthe on my tongue, Monsieur Lefebvre's pawing hands on
my skin. But is it the same for Charlotte? Was wretchedness coming to
her, same as it came to Gervaise, no matter that she scrubbed linens like a
slave, no matter that she saved close to every sou, tried to become what she
was not. Charlotte was born of the same stock as me, as Antoinette, with
her own apish looks, her fate of becoming a thieving coquette already
jailed for stealing seven hundred francs. Charlotte knows the same reeking

courtyard, the same foul gutters, the same slummy corner of Montmartre where we put down our heads at night. The same selfish mother, who does not bother with me, does not bother with her. Monsieur Zola would say Charlotte does not have a lick of a chance. But he would not have taken into account her face like a cherub's, her rosebud lips, her dainty chin. There is no mark of a beast, and Cesare Lombroso would agree. He would say there was no feature hinting at a criminal life for Charlotte. I push a leaden foot out in front.

Ahead of me a gentleman, escorting a lady with a lavish bustle of indigo silk, drops her arm. He opens the door of a plain building with windows running across the front. She dips her tiny, perfect chin as she passes inside. The door falls closed, and the six posters covering it up, all exactly the same, catch my eye. The gentleman, his lady in her indigo silk, are visiting the sixth exposition of the independent artists, the show where Monsieur Degas said he would put on display his statuette of me.

It was Monsieur Lefebvre I was thinking of this morning when I put on my grey silk and only the smallest smear of tinted pomade. But now a tiny sliver of me latches on to the idea that, dressed up like a lady, I was meant to come upon the exposition in the boulevard des Capucines. I follow the pair down a corridor leading to a series of small rooms with low ceilings and walls crammed with pictures, some hung so low even a child would have to stoop to get a look. In the corner, a gentleman with hair bristling from his ears looks up from a small notepad, letting me know I am interrupting his peace. The light is poor and with my eyes still adjusting from the day outside, it takes a minute to figure out the exposition is no different from the one I already saw. Absinthe drinkers in a café—tattered clothes, unkempt beards, sunken eyes. A naked woman sewing on a bed—rumpled linens, sagging breasts, hands red with work. One signed by Raffaëlli, the other by Gauguin.

The woman in the indigo silk steps back from the wall to get a better look, and with the room so cramped, her bustle brushes up against the wall behind. The gentleman with the ear hair clicks his tongue. She looks across the room, doubtful, to her gentleman, and he makes the face of a boy bewildered about tying up his shoes.

Upon entering the fourth, a room with yellow walls, I see the statuette, like before, in Monsieur Degas's workshop, except that the girl, who is me, is inside a vitrine. My immediate thought is that the vitrine is not right, not with the way it makes the statuette look like a specimen, something for scientists. There are three other people in the room: an old man with a woman, who has to be his daughter or his nurse, and a man with a cravat knotted with one tail long and the other short and paint staining the beds of his fingernails. With him studying the statuette and rubbing the scruff of his chin, I turn to the wall at his back, hiding my face. Hanging there are a dozen pictures belonging to Monsieur Degas. A singer at a café concert, one with a vulgar face, leaning over, her open mouth and plunging neckline taunting the men crowding the stage. A woman, bent over a hot iron. Another woman, this time, lumpy and naked, scratching at her backside in what has to be the salon of a brothel. Each is caught being who she is in everyday life. I look hard at the woman scratching away. She is exactly herself in the picture, not some other woman, one made up by the men usually visiting her.

I look over my shoulder. The man with dirty fingernails is still transfixed, still stroking his bit of scruff. He moves in a slow circle, taking in the statuette from in front and behind. Between his eyebrows is the crevice that comes with concentrating hard, but nothing says what he thinks of the wax girl. His back toward me, he folds his arms, spreads his feet, settling in. I take the chance to look past him to the wax face, the face that is mine. I see a girl, who is not pretty, looking forward, a girl a little bold.

The transfixed man goes back to circling, and I turn back to the wall, this time to a pastel. I let out a little gasp to see Émile Abadie alongside Michel Knobloch, each caught in profile in the prisoners' box at the court. The boys in the picture, by their looks, anyone would say they are beasts. No one would guess a mistake was made. But I know.

It was not easy walking home the day of the trial. A lady dropped her gentleman's arm and twisted around, gawking at my face as she passed. The eyes of a maître d' out front of a café landed upon my muzzle and, too quick, glanced away. Same for an old woman, sweeping the street. A boy stuck out his tongue on catching sight of me. I walked with my face tilted toward the ground after that, turned my head away from anyone coming toward me in the street. I told myself I would go to Abadie's attorney, explain about the calendar, do what I should have done before. Then I told myself it would not do a speck of good, because I knew I would not go, and how else was I to continue on, knowing I did not have the bravery, the heart, the goodness to seek out Monsieur Danet? I stopped on the Pont Neuf, leaned out over the stone wall of a little balcony jutting from the bridge. The light was soft and yellow, and the Seine was like a ribbon of golden green. I leaned out further, hips against the stone wall. I let my feet come up from the sidewalk beneath, balancing, until a gentleman put his hand on my shoulder and said, "It's colder than it looks." I sprung to standing straight. "Go get yourself a cup of chocolate." He held out a one-franc coin, and I snatched. Up ahead, on the right bank of the river, I could see a café. With its view of the Seine, it would not be cheap. Still, a full franc was more than enough for a glass of absinthe.

It was awful turning into the rue de Douai and seeing Alphonse in his baker's apron and cap on the stoop of his father's shop. "Ah, the ballet girl," he called out, even if my head hung, my back slumped. I waved, low, halfhearted. It might have looked like I brushed my skirt. "An orange Madeleine for you," he called out, holding up the sweet. I kept my line to our lodging house straight as I could, and his hand fell, like the orange Madeleine was heavier than lead. Behind the closed door of our lodging house, I thought about the way his voice went meek and not so sure anymore before he even finished calling out, and I leaned my forehead against the wall.

It was not easier two weeks later, coming into our lodging room, beaten down from six evening performances of *Le Tribut de Zamora*, from not a single decent sleep. In the grey light I saw an overturned chair,

Maman's shawl on the floor, our little table cluttered with a candlestick, two cups, the greasy wrappings of the evening meal. Maman pushed herself up from her mattress, and next thing she was upon me, slapping my face and raising her arm to slap again. "More than half a bottle," she yelled. "You took more than half a bottle from me." I crossed my arms in front of my face, and she snatched up the candlestick and bashed the side of my head. I dropped onto my knees, and she bashed me again. "You don't take what isn't yours." I was crying and then Charlotte, too, and then Maman, because there was a lot of blood and she was used to a girl fighting back. She bandaged me up with an old stocking, and I thought how I would have to haul a bucket of water up the stairs in the morning, how the wood bin was empty, how wearying rinsing away the blood would be. I bawled even more when Charlotte said she was going out to collect the wood, the water needed to get me cleaned up. Maman tipped a bottle of absinthe against my bottom lip, and finally I stopped. "Take as much as you want," she said.

Worst of all was the loge of the second set of the quadrille, the quick silence when I came into the room. Each evening I pinned the beaded head scarf of a slave into place. My attention on the looking glass, I saw beneath the greasepaint and rice powder to what was really there, to what the girls all knew. Blanche glared. Perot whispered, covering up her mouth. A tiny swallow at the Opéra's back gate, not so much that I would stumble, kept me from crumpling under the weight of that head scarf I never did earn.

I knock a single hard knock at Monsieur Lefebvre's door. It is our usual time, but I did not call the last two weeks and am only guessing he still makes a habit of visiting his apartment Tuesday mornings. After a long wait I hear footsteps approaching and then he opens up the door a crack and leaves it ajar while his eyes take in the length of me. He will not send me away. No. He is like Monsieur Degas, who continues to draw when his head aches, when the sunshine is gone, like Monsieur Mérante, who pleads with Monsieur Vaucorbeil for another hour with the orchestra when already we have been rehearsing eight hours, like Monsieur LeBlanc, who licks the greasy paper when the sausage is done and his belly stuffed full. "Marie van Goethem," Monsieur Lefebvre says, like I am someone come to collect the rent. "Are you drunk today?"

I look to his shoes, gleaming black without even the beginnings of a crease across the toe. "No," I say. "I am not drunk."

"I didn't send for you."

I lower my lashes, a timid girl. I make a tiny smile, careful not to show my teeth.

"You were told to stay away."

"Still," I say, combing loose a strand of hair, twirling it through my fingers. "With the expense of the extra lessons for the slave dance, it wouldn't be right not to call." It comes to me that I hate Monsieur Lefebvre, his fleshless face, his smell like a room closed up too long, the tiny flicker of his tongue as I fiddle with my hair.

He opens up the door the tiniest bit, and I slip through the gap, pushing the door shut behind my back. His fingers fold into his palms, and so I put a hand upon his chest, upon his starched shirt, at the spot over his heart. It is not even difficult, which maybe is the way things get to be when you are not striving, when your sole ambition is collecting thirty francs. Was it the same for Gervaise when she called out to the men in the streets, when she wanted nothing more than a glass of wine tilted to her lips? Or maybe it is only that Marie the First has taken over, knowing what is best, how to beguile, lifting my arm, placing my palm. He looks down, up. Then he bats my hand away. "A bit of modeling," I say, treading quick to the screen. I undress, holding my breath, hearing the noise of shoes clapping hardwood, drawers opening, slamming shut. Then I make out the shuffling of paper. Drawing paper? It has to be. The habit of all the old visits is coming back to him.

I find him standing over the sideboard with the drawer holding my thirty francs. His arms are spread wide, his fingers open, the tips pressing against the gleaming wood of the top and bearing his weight. His face tilts forward, his eyes on the heap of folded newspapers lying between his hands. But he does not see the pages before him, the blocks of words singled out, boxed in heavy ink. No, his attention is inside his mind.

He clears his throat, and without looking up, he picks up the first newspaper from the stack, says, "From *Le Figaro*," and begins to read:

The realism of Degas's statuette makes the public distinctly uneasy. All their notions about sculpture —its cold, lifeless whiteness; its methods copied again and again for centuries—are here overturned. The fact is that with this, his first blow, Degas has knocked over the traditions of sculpture, in the same way that he some time ago shook up the traditions of painting. This statuette is the only truly modern attempt I know in sculpture.

He looks up, and I make a half smile. "Modern" is good. Something new instead of "cold and lifeless" is all right. He holds up a hand, says, "Let me finish," and picks up the next newspaper from the stack. "From *Le Courrier du soir*."

With her vulgarly upturned nose, her protruding mouth, her little half-closed eyes, the child is ugly. But let the artist be reassured. In the presence of this statuette, I have experienced the most violent artistic impression of my life. The work will one day be in a museum, looked upon with respect as the first formulation of a new art.

"I know I'm not pretty," I say, almost a whisper. "I knew it before." I put an arm across my bare breast. I want my shawl. It is like an ache, the way I want my shawl.

He fishes among the newspapers, until he finds what he wants. His lip curls. His nose shrivels with the stink of reading to me.

Her chin upturned, her complexion sallow, sickly, lined and faded before its time, her hands clasped behind her back, her flat chest crammed into a wax-clogged singlet, her legs set for struggle, her fine thighs which exercise has made nervous and sinewy surmounted by a tarlatan skirt, her neck stiff, her hair real, this dancer comes alive and seems about to step down from her pedestal.

Monsieur Degas must be rejoicing, unfolding the same newspapers, lapping up the words—"modern," "new," "alive." Has he wondered about me, about the same words that build him up beating me down? Has it stopped him fiddling with his pastels and brushes long enough to tap a curled finger against his lips? Does a man such as he think nothing of plucking from the depths of the Opéra a girl capable of baring a boy's neck to a falling blade and putting her on display for all the world to judge?

He paid up. He paid his six francs.

Monsieur Lefebvre's attention is back on the newspapers, and I use the chance to take a tiny step backward, in the direction of the screen and my shawl hanging there. "Modest, all of a sudden?" he says.

I bite my lip, blink, fluttery blinks meant to clear my eyes.

He snatches up another of the newspapers, reads:

The vicious muzzle of this young, scarcely adolescent girl, this little flower of the gutter, imprints her face with the detestable promise of every vice.

"Your humility is a sham," he says. "The way you taunt. No one knows better than I."

I saw the promise of every vice in the pastel of Émile Abadie and

Michel Knobloch. It was there in the brutal muzzles, the dead eyes, the cruel flesh. I had seen the viciousness before, in my own face reflected back to me. "My shawl." Like a chirped plea. Tears now, hot on my cheeks, stinging my eyes.

"Brazen," he says, his chin jutting up as he chucks the word from his throat. "Brazen enough to stand on my doorstep, pouting and twirling your hair, after I told you to stay away."

My fingernail finds a frayed edge of skin. I dig, hard. Skin lifts, tears, a comfort. My flesh weeps. Sticky, wet. Blood on my hands.

"It isn't just the one that saw it," he says. "From *Le Temps*."

With bestial impudence she thrusts her face forward. Why is her forehead, half hidden by her bangs, already bearing the signs, like her mouth, of a profoundly heinous nature? Perhaps Degas knows of the dancer's future things we do not. He has picked, from the hothouse of the theater, a sapling of precocious depravity, and he shows her to us withered before her time.

He brushes past me, clipping my arm. Then he snatches my shawl from the screen, hurls it at my feet.

The quiet tears of before are gone. My shoulders heave, my stomach lurching between slack and taut. I bawl, gasping, whimpering, wiping at my eyes, smearing across my face a stew of tears and snot and blood. Against the trembling shin of one leg is the heaviness of the shawl balled at my feet. But I leave it untouched.

"My thirty francs." The words come out in Maman's pleading voice, the one she uses to ask can I spare a few sous when she has drained a bottle to empty the evening before. I step over the shawl, grab the front of Monsieur Lefebvre's shirt. With one hand I pull him tight against my naked skin. The other, I move to the front of his trousers, to the buttons of his fly, the waking up beneath. "Come on, Monsieur Lefebvre," I say. "A bit of fun." But it is not me at all. It is a different voice. It is not the sound of

Charlotte whining or Maman begging. It is pretty and tinkling, the voice of a wicked angel no more lying in wait.

There is a moment with his hand hovering over the small of my back, the small hairs growing there feeling the weight of it, before he shoves me away.

He straightens his collar, yells for me to get out.

Little Dancer

Dance, winged scamp, dance upon the wooden lawn,
Love that alone—let dancing be your life.
Your skinny arm in its chosen place
Balancing, holding your weight in flight.

Taglioni, come, princess of Arcady!
Nymphs, Graces, come you souls of yore,
Ennoble and endow, approving my choice,
This new little being with impudent face.

May she for my pleasure know her worth
And keep, in the golden hall, the gutter's breed.

—EDGAR DEGAS

Antoinette

The Superioress glances at the watch strung from her hip, peers through the gate to the pavement out front of Saint-Lazare, looking left, looking right.

"No one's coming," I say.

She turns back to me, strokes my arm, meaning to console that I am going to be set loose without so much as a mother at the gate.

"Maman sent a message she was expected at the washhouse," I say, but the minute the words leave my mouth, I know my mistake and swallow hard, which is what I have to do with all those lies marching to my lips, except earlier, before the lie gets out. It is harder than I thought, this telling no more lies. I blundered a handful of times in the weeks since blubbering before the Superioress, nothing of importance, only claptrap like claiming to the mistress doling out the red beans that I did not get my share or saying to one or another of the fallen girls that I reached the rank of coryphée or that the story of being the sweetheart of Émile was not true. Still, it is what I've got to do, quit the lying, all except the single lie I have left to tell. I've got to do it for Marie.

I shrink a little smaller, like a bellows with the air squeezed out. "Maman didn't send word," I say. "She isn't the kind of mother to think of that."

The Superioress gives my arm a little squeeze, like we are friends, and I make a bobbing little nod, awkward as a hen.

She hands me a drawstring pouch, the same one I brought to Saint-Lazare three months ago. What I want is to open it up. I know the money I robbed from the wallet of Jean Luc Simard to be long gone, but what about the payments handed over of his own free will? I roll the worn-out leather of the drawstring between my fingers, thinking how I once would've blurted something about expecting the sisters helped themselves. I tuck the pouch into the pocket of my mauve silk, a frock I would not choose for going back out into the world but I did not have a say, not when Mole scurried into my cell early morning with it hanging over her arm and then back out again with my homespun prison gown.

"One hundred ninety-eight francs," says the Superioress. "The money you came to us with."

I will get something nice for Marie and Charlotte, trinkets, maybe combs, strung with blossoms of silk. Maman, I will send off to the Nouvelle Athènes up in the place Pigalle for a meal, maybe with Paulette from the washhouse. It might mean a few words on my behalf when I show up, tail tucked between my legs and promising Monsieur Guiot I grew handy with a needle and thread at Saint-Lazare. He sends the mending at the washhouse out, and what I have to do is convince him to send it to me.

Mole arrives, scuttling, carrying the same bundle I brought with me to Saint-Lazare—an old skirt as carrying sling for two blouses, two pairs of stockings, three pairs of drawers, a second skirt—my belongings in the world. I take the bundle, touching the wool of the old skirt, faded to a weary yellow grey. I remember streaming sunshine, lapping blue, a needle and thread, a pair of trousers patched on the knee with a square cut from the skirt. A mind playing tricks.

"Stay for soup, vegetable today," the Superioress says. "We'll send word, a reminder of your release." She turns, mouth half-open with instructions for Mole to get a message to the rue de Douai.

"Got to go. Got to see about Marie." I been waiting and waiting, itching to get out, to find Marie, to pull her tight against my heart.

The Superioress spreads her arms wide, her sleeves falling open like wings, and wraps me in a thicket of black wool. Girls leave bawling, stroking their rosaries, wondering how with their new devoutness, they are to get themselves sent back. For a moment I want to linger, warm, held tight. But I have a plan for nudging Marie back through the door, over to the side where she belongs. I've got to go before it is too late. If already it isn't too late. I send a little wish up to the clouds, which is maybe a prayer, and pull away, soft enough not to insult the Superioress with her beaming, jowly face, her wolf-sharp eyes. She reaches for the great ring of keys hung on a ribbon from her neck and slips the largest into the lock of the gate. Click.

"God bless," she calls out. "Say your prayers."

Her voice and Saint-Lazare fade as I run.

～ Marie ～

The carving knife has a long ivory handle, cracked in two places, enough so that I have to squeeze it tight to keep the blade from coming loose. The handle of the sharpening steel vanished so long ago that I cannot say if the pair was ever a matching set. I run the blade over the roughness of the steel, one side and then the next, just like Papa taught me when I was a girl. Scissors would work better, but like everything else not broken, they went to the pawnbroker a long time ago.

I grip the high collar of my grey silk, but in the looking glass everything is reversed, and I make a mess of cutting into the silk. I wonder about pulling the dress up over my head and laying it flat to finish up, but I am weary after staying out all through the night —wandering, shivering, glaring hard. So many gawkers staring at my red nose, my swollen eyes, my beastly face.

I finish the cut. Only absinthe takes the clearness away. I will get my absinthe.

~ Antoinette ~

Bursting into our lodging room, I call out, "Marie," and then, "pet, Maman," but no one remembered and only a yawn of silence answers me back. I stand there panting, gripping the handle of the door, knowing feeling sorry for myself is a waste of time. Still, my shoulders slump.

Stooped before the fireplace, I fish from the cold ash a piece of grey silk. That scrap laid flat on the sooty hearth, I trace around the edge—a shape like an oval sliced in half, the size of my two hands put side by side. A narrow band, properly sewed, runs the length of one edge, but the curved part looks like it was cut by a child just getting familiar with the workings of scissors. I study the scrap spread flat on the hearth, wondering. Then I fling that bit of silk cut from the neckline of the dress Marie wore to Saint-Lazare back into the fireplace and snap to standing straight.

～ Marie ～

I stroke the red plush cushion of the bench bounding the café and rest my aching head against the wall. The partition between the room up front and the one where I sit is oak to the height of a man's shoulder and glass on top of that. It allows the proprietress, knitting on a high stool, to overlook both rooms. Without breaking the click, click of the knitting needles, she glances out from under her brow, eyes lingering on the ragged neckline of my grey silk. I fiddle with the porcelain match holder, shifting it a little to the right, a little to the left on the stained marble slab of the tabletop.

Already I ordered the glass of absinthe that means I cannot change my mind. My pockets empty, I need some boy to pay—maybe him, a table over, in the trousers of a mason, already moved on from drinking bitters to drinking cassis.

I sit a good hour, watching the mason, waiting for him to look up from his cassis. But never once do I get the chance to make the little smile that might get a boy who drank two glasses of bitters and three of cassis to desire a bit of flesh. I order another absinthe, watch the departing tavern maid glance in the direction of the proprietress, see the tiny nod that says I will get a second glass. Two boys play dominoes. Another shuffles *Le Temps*. The mason stares into his glass. An old man yawns, his eyes weeping rheum, his mouth gaping wide enough to see black teeth.

Antoinette

Alphonse lopes across the rue de Douai from the bakery, calling out, "Antoinette. Antoinette."

"What?" I say when he is close.

"It's about Marie." He opens his mouth, presses it closed, keeping whatever he wants to say locked up inside.

"You seen my sister?" I say, coaxing that bashful boy.

"I was watching for her yesterday." He knocks the toe of his boot against a cobblestone. I keep my face blank, still as stone, not so much as a blink to deter shuffling Alphonse. "I thought maybe she was rehearsing, but even very late, she didn't come home." He pushes the knuckles of one hand against the heel of the other. "On Wednesdays she goes to the Opéra at noon," he says. "Always. But not today." And then he is called away by a tavern maid, standing on the stoop of the bakery with a dozen baguettes tucked up under her arm.

Should I head up to the place Pigalle, stopping in at the Nouvelle Athènes and Rat-Mort? Or should I go first to the rue des Martyrs, the lowliest of the cafés and brasseries there? My face falls to my hands. There are a hundred places to search for a broken girl.

Marie

There is still the clack, clack of dominoes, one game finished, another one begun; the click, click of the knitting needles, a wide band of pea green lengthening to a square; the shuffle, shuffle of newspapers, picked up, read, folded and put back, growing worn with each handling, sticky with cassis, bitters and absinthe.

The old man blows a kiss, lifts his glass, drinks. I lift my own in return. But the old man, he does not come, and so I order myself another glass. I take a long swallow, wipe away the bit of absinthe slopped onto grey silk.

The mason has gone home.

~ Antoinette ~

In one tavern a boy smokes, another nods off. In the next a coquette straightens stockings already straight. "You seen a girl," I say to her, "grey dress, fine, but with the neck cut away?" Hats are on or off, sometimes silk. Shoes are varnished, collars starched. Shoes are scuffed, collars frayed. Always smoke, dominoes, newspapers fixed on sticks, glasses getting drained. Never Marie.

~⚘~ Marie ~⚘~

I grip the marble of the old man's tabletop with both hands, steadying myself. I lean close enough to breathe in the stink of rotten teeth. "Hello, darling," I say.

His eyes move down, then up. "You sixteen?"

"Course," I lie.

"Don't want no trouble."

"Marie the First," I say, sitting down, but he does not give a name back.

He takes a long sip of his bitters, slides the heel of his hand along the top of his thigh. "Your dress?" He juts his chin. "What happened to the neck?"

"Was getting choked to death the way it was before."

"Another?"

"So kind," I say, nudging my glass to him.

Antoinette

I open up the door of the practice room partway. Beyond the back of Madame Dominique there is no Marie, only Charlotte, and I remember about her getting put up with the older girls of the quadrille Wednesday afternoons. She draws her one foot up the leg of the other and unfolds that lifted leg in front of her, a développé, high as any other in the room, even if she is a sprite among the girls at the barre. She floats that lifted leg to the side, opening up her arm, turning her face. She catches sight of me, and then she is skittering across the hardwood between us, crushing the breath out of me, and saying, "I knew you would come."

Madame Dominique thwacks the floor with her cane. "Charlotte!"

"Tonight," she says, grabbing my hand, making a bridge out of our arms as she steps away. "I debut tonight. *Le Tribut de Zamora*, act one." Then her face falls. "I don't know where Marie is. You have to find Marie."

Madame Dominique holds up a finger, telling me to wait. To the violinist she says, "Slow the tempo," and to the girls, "Left side."

On the landing outside the practice room, she grips the handle of the door pulled shut behind her back. "Where is that sister of yours?" she says.

"I come looking for her here."

"A class missed yesterday and now a second."

"Maybe tonight? She is dancing tonight?"

"Tell her not to bother." She pushes the door open, says over her shoulder, "Blanche had the good sense to learn the part."

~∞~ Marie ~∞~

The old man says, "You sit so ramrod straight."

I slide lower in my chair and say, "Ballet girl." But it is not true, not anymore, not with missing Madame Dominique's class yesterday and then again this afternoon. Definitely not, when even if tonight I managed to dodge the watchful eyes of the concierge and costume mistress, both on the lookout for girls not able to walk a straight line, there is no chance I could hold the opening arabesque of the slave dance to the slow count of four.

"Don't think so," he says, drumming yellow fingernails.

But I hardly hear. I am with Charlotte. I see her brushing rice powder onto her nose, rubbing greasepaint into her cheeks, painting tinted pomade onto her lips, touching the horseshoe on the small table outside the stage-door keeper's loge. In the wings, she dabs white onto her arms, grinds rosin beneath her slippers. But where is Marie? she wonders. Watching from somewhere, maybe from the wings on the other side. Yes. That's it. And Antoinette? She is high up in the balconies, leaning close as she can.

It is the only possibility Charlotte knows.

I jerk up from my chair, stumble quick enough to dodge the old man's reaching hand.

Antoinette

Marie and I were in the visitors' parlor of Saint-Lazare, a partition of iron bars in between. I said, "On your hands, the blood of an innocent," and the words glided through the gaps. I wanted her to despair, and I said it. I spat the words into her face.

~∾~ Marie ~∾~

Monsieur Degas stands beneath one of the archways out front, watching the operagoers filing past. The crowd is thick. Still, a sight so familiar, I snag his roving gaze. I see him look, take in my weariness, my unsteady step, the cut silk. I watch him know. I stumble and pick myself up. Even with me out of sight, approaching the rear entrance, the labyrinth of corridors leading to the balconies, I expect he is still stroking his beard, contemplating the heart and body, the story of a little dancer, aged fourteen.

Antoinette

In the first row of the fourth balcony I sit, stand, sit back down again. There is nothing I could tell Charlotte that would explain me missing her debut. I search the orchestra pit for a lifted bow, the conductor, some signal the curtains are going to be pulled open soon.

Beside me a woman with a velvet ribbon circling her flabby neck leans close. "Your flowers," she says, holding out a brooch with two yellow roses attached. "The clasp must've come loose."

I reach for the pretty brooch, thinking it could fetch a few sous, but I pull my hand away in time. "Not mine."

Only a single lie left.

~ Marie ~

Antoinette is there in the first row, wearing mauve silk, strumming her thigh and bouncing her heel, more jittery than a squirrel. But even in such a dress she does not appear a bit cleaned up, the way she used to when she went off to the house of Madame Brossard. She looks like she came from running a race, like she has been running one for the nineteen years of her life.

"Antoinette," I say in the tiniest voice. She can pretend she does not hear, if she wants. But right away her face snaps to mine, and it is like a breath of air on smoldering embers, the way her eyes light up. And then she plows past the two ladies sitting in the seats between her and me. The one with a patchy bit of fur dangling around her neck says, "Might try excusing yourself," and Antoinette, she does not say, "Might try getting out of my way." No, she puts a hand on the shoulder of the lady and gives it a tiny squeeze. And then she puts both her palms on my own two cheeks and looks at me with the fierceness of a lioness guarding her cubs.

Antoinette

When did Marie get so old? When did her cheeks grow hollow, her eyes sunken? She smells of absinthe, tobacco. My mouth wants to twitch. Instead I press my lips into a smile. "I come to my senses," I say. "It was Abadie who told me to mark the x on the day he and Knobloch bludgeoned the widow Joubert."

A hundred, a thousand times before Marie heard me lie. A thousand times I gave her reason to doubt my word. But no more. After a thousand truths, the stain of doubt will wash away.

I keep my chin up, my eyes steady on her own. One last lie, the only one that counts.

Marie

Her eyes are so steady. She does not look away or touch her mouth, her nose. Her feet stay still, stuck to the ground. Still, it could be a lie.

"I knew it," I say, putting the shadow of a sneer into my voice. "I knew it all along."

Her hands stay tender upon my cheeks. Tilting our faces close, our foreheads touch.

A lie said as a gift?

And then a gift given back.

I cannot say for sure.

Antoinette

A few bars from the orchestra swell, and then those tasseled curtains of rich velvet open onto archways and towers and turrets, a passageway leading off a square and snaking up a hill. From the wings, a petit rat with the face of an angel enters the stage of the grandest opera house in all the world. I lean closer to the stage, Marie clutching my hand. The audience gasps, bursts into applause. Like magic, that rat, she bedazzles, queen of the wooden lawn, graceful as the moon, lighter than air.

1895

∽ Marie ∽

I put my hand on Matilde's brow, and her eyes blink open. "Maman," she says, her lashes drifting closed. I blow a tiny puff of air into her face, and then she is awake. "It's my name day tomorrow," she says. "You remember about my slippers?" And so she has not forgotten, this child of eight, what I agreed to a month ago, that for her name day I would darn the toes of her ballet slippers, adding the stiffness that aids a girl in rising onto the tips of her toes. Madame Théodore had explained the trick to Matilde's class, and Matilde said a dozen times afterward how it was the only gift that would do.

Geneviève, her older sister by eleven months, pushes herself up to sitting in their shared bed. Wiping sleep from her eyes, she says, "Don't do it, Maman. Rats are meant to scuttle flat-footed." And then those two sisters roll in the linens and pinch and laugh, nightdresses hiked to their thighs. "Up with the both of you," I say. "Wash your faces and go downstairs for your chocolate."

In the stairwell I breathe the odor of hot bread wafting up from the bakery and wonder how it is those two girls are not babies anymore. How did it happen so quick? Just the other day Geneviève said her mind was made up, that she would be a milliner. It was Antoinette who put the idea

in her head, going on as she does about Geneviève's talent for putting vio-
let with yellow, this bit of ribbon with that bit of cord. Her comfort with
needle and thread was Antoinette's doing, too. Always when Geneviève
goes missing, she can be found amid the frayed buttonholes and split-open
seams Antoinette takes in for mending, also the scraps of lace and trim she
snips from the heap piled in the ragman's cart. It is an exchange. He gets a
pair of trousers or a waistcoat from his collection stitched up well enough
to pawn. Antoinette gets the adornments, and Geneviève, hour upon hour
of twisting ribbon into bows, lace into rosettes. Matilde used to follow
Geneviève across the rue de Douai and up the stairs to the lodging room
where I passed my childhood, where Antoinette and Charlotte still live,
now with a larder always stocked and the walls freshly whitewashed and
proper beds behind a partition of heavy brocade. But Matilde did not like
the finicky work, those bits of cord lost in her fingers, those bits of ribbon
nudged and coaxed and slipped from her grip. No, she will dance, she
says, like Tante Charlotte.

So many times we have watched from the fourth balcony, Matilde
gripped, Geneviève growing restless, me never knowing when that lost
life of dancing might sneak up, when I might find myself swallowing hard
in the dark. It is not regret, exactly, more a lament for the dancing, those
moments when I knew the world in all its joy and sorrow and love. And
maybe, too, I miss the dream that once spurred me from bed to bakery to
practice room, the dream that filled me to the brim with desire, that has
been replaced by the quieter ambition of raising Matilde and Geneviève.

Charlotte has climbed the ranks of the ballet, from second quadrille to
first and then on to coryphée and after that sujet. She is a favorite of the
abonnés, with two love affairs put behind her, her heart broken twice. But
now there is a set decorator, who does not give her a yellow bird in a gilt
cage or send a seamstress around to measure her for a silk dress. He has
honest, sorrowful eyes, though, and at Eastertime he blew the insides
from an egg and painted it up with tiny chicks and Charlotte made a fuss

and now there is a collection of painted eggs upon the mantelshelf. When Matilde goes across the street it is to stand at Papa's sideboard making pliés and stretching her legs, to hear Charlotte say, "That's it. Hold your neck long, like Taglioni, Matilde," to appear no different from a child Monsieur Degas would take up his charcoal to sketch.

He moved from the rue Fontaine workshop to I do not know where, and I do not ask. I see him at the Opéra from time to time, and I duck around a pillar or put my attention on the knitting in my lap. Once, though, when Charlotte was appearing in the *Faust* divertissement and Matilde and Geneviève and I attended the debut, I saw him see me and then watched his eyes shift to the girls. I put them behind my back and waited for his gaze to return to me. "Monsieur Degas," I said, but he did not say my name, and I wondered if he had forgotten it. "Fine girls," he said, and I did not loosen the grip that kept them from his sight. Whether it was that rudeness or something he saw in my face, I do not know, but he knew that still I could feel the sting of the words printed in *Le Figaro*, *Le Temps*, *Le Courrier du soir*, and what he said next was, "I keep the statuette in my workshop. It seems I always will. My dealer suggests casting it in bronze. But it's too much responsibility to leave behind anything in bronze."

"Yes," I said. "That substance is for eternity."

Maman does not know of Antoinette's endeavors with needle and thread or of Charlotte's triumph at the Opéra. She never met Matilde or Geneviève. She set out for the washhouse one morning but never did arrive according to Monsieur Guiot. "Was she assigned to the wringing machine?" Antoinette said, and he nodded, loosening his cravat. She had up and left us, disappearing in those dark days when Antoinette was mending for Monsieur Guiot without getting paid a single sou. She was, she said, fulfilling a pledge—to mend to perfection all she was asked, to allow him to inspect every stitch for three months. If she succeeded, only then would he waste a minute deciding whether to give her the work for good. I was not working, not at all. No. I was resting up—Antoinette's words— even if every day the sun was out she made me climb the height of Montmartre and then back down. We had only Charlotte's regular wage from the Opéra and the three francs extra she earned each night she danced upon the stage. Already Antoinette had given Monsieur LeBlanc the pouch of coins she brought with her from Saint-Lazare, this after extracting from him a steep discount for paying three months' rent in advance. For meals we ate the broken orange Madeleines and scorched loaves Alphonse sent up to our door. Licking crumbs from her fingers, Antoinette would put on a cheery voice and say, "How many trays can a boy drop? That boy, his papa is going to wring his neck if he burns another loaf."

The two of them—Antoinette and Alphonse—argued once. They were on the pavement, and I was setting out to climb Montmartre but still behind the door of our lodging house, listening to what I was not meant to hear. "Not yet," Antoinette said. "She still isn't herself."

"I don't know how long Papa will wait," he said. "That girl we have doing the kneading rubs her back, stalling, the minute he turns away."

"Well, you got to do this thing for Marie. You got to make your papa wait." I put my shoulder against the door, but I did not push.

"And how do you suggest I accomplish that, Antoinette?"

"Pat that slothful girl on the rump from time to time. It'd make a girl work harder, thinking she stood a chance with the son of the owner. A few months of slaving and she saves herself a lifetime of drudgery."

"I wasn't patting Marie."

"Marie don't need patting. She was born working harder than an ox."

I pushed the door open, and Alphonse took off his baker's cap and wrung it in his hands. I felt my color rising, same as his, and I did not mention the kindness of the ruined loaves. I dipped my chin and spun away, striding off quicker than a rabbit escaping the stewing pot.

I am pretty sure I know the exact moment when Antoinette changed her mind about Alphonse telling me his father wanted me back at the bakery. She was mending at our little table, and I came in from climbing Montmartre and said how I had seen colors—oil leaked from the battered old lantern lying there—floating on the wet pavement. "I dipped my boot into the puddle and gave a little swirl. Those colors, how they were shining and drifting." Antoinette set down her mending and put her hand on my cheek, and I saw joy well in her eyes.

𝓘 knead at a little table pushed to the front window of the bakery, a spot where I can keep an eye on Matilde and Geneviève in the street. Alphonse, as he sometimes does, lingers, stroking my arm. His brawny baker's hands are soft as velvet with their dusting of flour. I say to him, over my shoulder, that such silky hands feel like a trick, and he says back how he could never devote himself to a woman with fleshy arms. "All those hours in the practice room gone to waste," I say, "all those hours learning to make my arms appear soft." I feel him watching, wondering if this morning will turn into one where I miss the Opéra, those moments of being lifted up. But today I think of Matilde catching such a moment and basking in the golden glow. I push the heels of my hands into the dough, turning the ridge of muscle beneath his fingers to hard, so he will know I am not dwelling, lost.

Antoinette comes in for the croissants she collects each morning, one for herself and one for the girl she has taken on as apprentice. "And how is Agnès?" I say. Every day there is a story: How she claimed to be sixteen when that age was still more than two years away. How she stole a sewn-up bonnet that turned up in the window of a pawnbroker in the rue Fontaine. How she called Antoinette a cow for making her rework a sloppy hem and then hurled a spool of thread when Antoinette said back, "If you're saying I keep you in milk and cheese, then it's absolutely true." In Agnès,

Antoinette gained exactly what she asked for when she took on a second washhouse and the mending piled up. "I need an apprentice" is what she said to the Superioress at Saint-Lazare. "A girl who isn't quite thundering through those pearly gates."

Antoinette gives her head a little shake. "Yesterday she told me an account of being robbed on Saturday evening and asked me could I advance her a few sous."

It is not a reason for a pair of eyes to gleam hopefulness, but just now it is what I see in Antoinette's.

"Well," she goes on, "I put my hands on her shoulders and said, 'Now, Agnès, was the robbing before or after applying the scent clinging to your hair, before or after putting the new laces in your boots, before or after enjoying the red caramel still streaking your teeth?' By the time I finished, her hands were in her lap and she was looking mournful as a wilted rose. I gathered up the ham from the larder, the onions and potatoes from the root bin and set them at her feet. 'Don't know why you're lying,' I said, 'but I can see you are in need.' And then she was bawling and saying about being a dunce and going out to the Chat Noir and waking up with nothing more than a thick tongue and a blaring head and a whole lot of sorrow about wasting what she worked so hard to earn."

"There is such goodness in you, Antoinette," I say. "In no time, you'll have Agnès ripened up to an honest working girl." A girl like herself, industrious as a bee, honest as a looking glass.

Antoinette sticks to the truth, always, now, even when it means saying to Charlotte that, no, her set decorator does not have a regal look or to Alphonse that she would not agree his meringues are the best she ever tried or to me that, yes, it is true Matilde does not match Geneviève in humility and then, after I sucked in my lip, "Christ, Marie. You know lying isn't for me." Sometimes there is a gap, before she says her wounding words, like she is arguing with herself about the supremacy of truth, and what I figured out is always when such a gap blooms, the asking was a mistake.

She swallows, laughs, and I do the same, because no one coming in for his morning loaf wants the awkwardness of finding the baker's wife and her sister misty-eyed at the front of the shop. We take a moment— Antoinette and I—standing side by side, shoulders touching, and peering through the window into the rue de Douai. Matilde holds a feather, rose-colored and magnificent with long strands of the vane wafting in the breeze. She draws the feather over her cheek, along her neck, taking pleasure in the tickling. "One of yours?" I say to Antoinette.

"From an ostrich. Must've fell from a lady's hat."

Matilde tilts her head, the way she tends to when she is making up her mind. And then she is off, running like a dog is nipping at her heels. She stops, abrupt, a few steps short of Geneviève and holds out her find. She gives it the little nudge that makes Geneviève understand, and she reaches for the feather, those wispy tendrils of love offered by her sister as a gift.

Author's Note

The Painted Girls is largely in keeping with the known facts of the van Goethem sisters' early lives. In 1878 Marie and Charlotte were accepted into the dance school of the Paris Opéra, where their older sister, Antoinette, was employed as an extra. Their father, a tailor, was dead, and their mother was a laundress. They lived in the ninth arrondissement, settling in 1880 in the rue de Douai on the lower slopes of Montmartre, a few blocks from Degas's rue Fontaine studio. That year Marie passed the examination admitting her to the corps de ballet and made her debut on the Opéra stage.

Between 1878 and 1881, Edgar Degas drew, painted, and sculpted Marie in numerous artworks, most famously in *Little Dancer Aged Fourteen*, which appeared at the sixth exposition of independent artists in 1881 alongside Degas's pastel of convicted criminals Émile Abadie and Michel Knobloch, *Criminal Physiognomies*. Critics lauded *Little Dancer* as "the only truly modern attempt at sculpture," and saw a street urchin, her face clearly "imprinted with the promise of every vice."

A half dozen years ago I happened upon the BBC documentary *The Private Life of a Masterpiece: Little Dancer Aged Fourteen*. It questioned Degas's intention in exhibiting *Little Dancer* alongside his portraits of convicted criminals. Was he hinting at the future criminality of the girl in the vitrine? I was inspired to investigate the notion that—not unlike Émile Zola, who was simultaneously putting forth arguments for a scientific literature, one that presented a deterministic view of human life— Degas bought into the idea that certain facial features hinted at a person's innate criminality and sought to incorporate it into his artwork. How might such perceptions have affected the life of his teenage model?

At the same time, I delved into the stories of Émile Abadie and Michel Knobloch. According to the historical record, Abadie was implicated in three murders. The woman Bazengeaud was murdered in Montreuil when her throat was slit by Abadie and Pierre Gille. Each was sentenced to death, sentences that were commuted to forced labor for life in New Caledonia after Abadie published "The Story of a Man Condemned to Death." The widow Joubert, a news seller in the van Goethem's neighborhood, was beaten to death, prompting further investigation of Abadie and Gille. Though neither was convicted, the proceedings went far enough to determine the pair had ample opportunity to carry out the murder between scenes when they were absent from the stage of the Ambigu Theater, where they were extras in an adaptation of Émile Zola's *L'Assommoir*. A grocer's boy was murdered in Saint-Mandé, and Knobloch confessed and named Abadie as accomplice. Both were convicted, though the evidence was scant and Knobloch repeatedly claimed in court to have made up his confession as a means of getting to New Caledonia. For the sake of this story, I collapsed the three murders into two and took liberties with dates. The newspaper articles, court transcripts, and critiques of *Little Dancer* throughout the story are faithful to the tone and, in many instances, the content of the original documents.

In the year that followed the exhibition, Antoinette served a three-month sentence for stealing seven hundred francs, and Marie was dismissed from the Opéra after a string of fines for being late or absent. Charlotte, however, prevailed, becoming a dancer of some distinction and teacher at the dance school during her fifty-three-year career with the Opéra.

There is no evidence the van Goethem sisters knew Abadie, Gille, and Knobloch. The intertwining of the sisters' story with theirs, that fateful day when Antoinette met Abadie behind the Paris Opéra and later swallowed the mussels with parsley sauce he fed into her mouth, is nothing more than imagination and ink.

Little Dancer Aged Fourteen remained in Degas's studio all his life. Despite his reluctance "to leave anything behind in bronze," in the years following his death, his heirs arranged to cast the twenty-eight bronze repetitions that appear around the world. The original wax sculpture is in the collection of the National Gallery of Art in Washington, DC.

Acknowledgments

I am deeply indebted to my agent, the brilliant Dorian Karchmar. I count the day she offered representation as the day I was hauled from the murk of the woods onto the lit path. I am immensely grateful to my editors—Sarah McGrath and Iris Tupholme—for their tremendous intelligence and diligence in shaping this book and finding its readership. A writer could not ask for more capable, dedicated allies.

A heartfelt thank-you to the following: Ania Szado, my first reader, for encouragement and thoughtful criticism; Sarah Cobb, for patience and skill in translating primary source material; Jack and Janine Cobb, for expertise in proofreading; my parents, Ruth Buchanan and Al Buchanan, for being guiding lights; Nancy Buchanan, for being my best friend in all the world; my boys, Jack, Charlie, and William Cobb, for making me laugh (and yes, cry) and love being a mother; my husband, Larry Cobb, for the gift of time to write and most of all, for love.

I am grateful for the generous assistance provided by David Baguley, author of *Émile Zola: L'Assommoir*; Douglas W. Druick, president and director of the Art Institute of Chicago and author of "Framing *The Little Dancer Aged Fourteen*" (*Degas and the Little Dancer,* Yale University Press, 1998, 77–96), his groundbreaking essay detailing the link between

Little Dancer Aged Fourteen and Degas's criminal portraits; Martine Kahane, author of "Little Dancer, Aged Fourteen—The Model" (*Degas Sculptures: Catalogue Raisonné of the Bronzes*, International Arts, 2002, 101–7), her seminal essay on the circumstances of the van Goethem sisters' lives; Sylvie Jacq Mioche, History of Dance teacher at the Paris Opéra Ballet School; Pierre Vidal, director of the Bibliothèque-Musée de l'Opéra.

Many books were important in researching this novel, particularly David Baguley, *Emile Zola: L'Assommoir*, Cambridge University Press, 1992; Jill DeVonyar and Richard Kendall, *Degas and the Dance*, Harry N. Abrams, 2002; Robert Gordon and Andrew Forge, *Degas*, Abradale, 1988; Ludovic Halévy, *The Cardinal Family*, George Barrie & Sons, 1897; Richard Kendall, Douglas W. Druick, and Arthur Beale, *Degas and the Little Dancer*, Yale University Press, 1998; Leo Kersley and Janet Sinclair, *A Dictionary of Ballet Terms*, Da Capo, 1979; Charles S. Moffett, Ruth Berson, Barbara Lee Williams, and Fronia E. Wissman, *The New Painting: Impressionism, 1874–1886*, Richard Burton, 1986; Spire Pitou, *The Paris Opéra: An Encyclopedia of Operas, Ballets, Composers, and Performers*, Greenwood, 1990; Émile Zola, *L'Assommoir*, Orion Group, 1995.

The newspaper account "Criminal Man" that appears in this novel draws on a translation of the article "Fous ou Criminels?" *La Nature* (August 23, 1879), 186–87. The newspaper account "Concerning the New Painting Exhibited at the Gallery of Durand-Ruel" draws on the translation of Louis Emile Edmond Duranty's 1876 essay "The New Painting," which appears in *The New Painting, Impressionism, 1874–1886*, 38–47. The newspaper account "Degas and the Sixth Exposition of the Independent Artists" draws on Fronia E. Wissman's essay "Realists Among the Impressionists," which appears in *The New Painting, Impressionism, 1874–1886*, 337–50. The critiques of *Little Dancer Aged Fourteen* draw on critiques presented in the aforementioned essay; *Degas*, pages 206–7; George Shackelford, *Degas: The Dancers*, W. W. Norton & Company, 1984, 69;

and Charles W. Millard, *The Sculpture of Edgar Degas*, Princeton University Press, 1976, 28. The remaining newspaper accounts and excerpts of court transcripts draw on translations of articles that appeared in *Le Figaro* between March 1879 and August 1880. Text by Edgar Degas is from *Huit Sonnets d'Edgar Degas* and is used courtesy of Wittenborn Art Books, San Francisco, www.art-books.com. The translation is largely from *Degas* and is used with the permission of the estate of Andrew Forge.